Gregory Day is a writer, poet  novel, *The Patron Saint of Eels*, v
Literature Society Gold Meda
The Black Tower: Songs from th
was hailed by the Yeats Society of Ireland as the most musical interpretations of Yeats ever made, and *The Flash Road:
Scenes from the Building of the Great Ocean Road*. His second
novel, *Ron McCoy's Sea of Diamonds*, was shortlisted for the
2008 NSW Premier's Prize for Fiction. He lives on the
southwest coast of Victoria.

The Grand Hotel

A NOVEL

Gregory Day

VINTAGE BOOKS
Australia

A Vintage book
Published by Random House Australia Pty Ltd
Level 3, 100 Pacific Highway, North Sydney NSW 2060
www.randomhouse.com.au

First published by Vintage in 2010

Australian Government | **Australia Council** for the Arts

This project has been assisted by the Australian Government through the Australia Council,
its arts funding and advisory body.

The author would like to acknowledge and thank the Boyd family and the Bundanon Trust
for the time he spent as writer in residence at Bundanon.

Cataloguing-in-publication information available on request
Cover and internal brolga image from the collection of the Australian Museum Library
Internal design and typesetting in Caslon by Xou, Australia
Printed in Australia by Griffin Press, an accredited ISO/NZS 14001:2004 Environmental
Management System printer

10 9 8 7 6 5 4 3 2 1

FSC

Mixed Sources
Product group from well-managed
forests and other controlled sources

Cert no. SGS-COC-005088
www.fsc.org
© 1996 Forest Stewardship Council

For Jamesie in the future, and Dazza in the past

I

⤮ II ⤭

'I was born very young in a very old world'

Erik Satie

$$\frac{\text{I}}{\text{II}}$$

A Brolga in the Clearing

I REALISED EARLY, EVEN AS A KID TRAIPSING ABOUT THE coves and clifftops and bush tracks here in Mangowak, that you can see pictures in fallen gumleaves on the ground, just like you can see pictures in the clouds of the sky. You can, in fact, if you're that way inclined, create pictures out of pure blue air.

Another thing I learnt early on, though a little after my revelations with the gumleaves, is that time is music. In all the long hours I've spent doing part-time jobs over the years, digging ditches for my brother in sticky pink clay, counting roadkill for the council on the verges of the Great Ocean Road, clambering up ladders to clean the spouting of seldom-used beach-houses, I've always reminded myself that it isn't drudgery I'm enduring, boring and demoralising, but rather a slow and difficult section of a natural symphony, a necessary movement that will soon be resolved with a sweet high note, a bright blast of brass, or a long and stately return of life's most luscious strings.

I've rested on that notion over the years and it's funny really because I'm quite unmusical, in the sense that I can't hold a note or play a tune. Of course like nearly everyone else on earth I do love music – I hardly know whether I could live without it – but the fact remains that I've stuck to working part-time jobs not because I enjoy those hardcore symphonic movements they provide but because they allow me the time I need to make pictures in my barn on the days off. Yes, my thing is vision. And there's no paint like the air. It's what I see that gets me moving. That's when the singing starts for me. That's when the planet hums.

Ironically it was that very singing, that visual music I live for, which seemed to have disappeared, along with time itself, at the moment when my greatest vision of all, The Grand Hotel, was about to be born.

I'd come back into town on the roads without names, the ones with just numbers from when the country round here hadn't even been settled yet. The fire blokes built them, and the council, and the coal plant, and I swung a wide arc along them for a day and a half without seeing a soul, until I was out the northeastern side of Mangowak and could make my approach.

I'd been gone nearly ten weeks. I'd been drenched and washed out, savaged by mosquitoes and bitten by ants, I'd gone hungry, and I'd hovered like a third-rate criminal under willows by the creeks at the edge of towns, with blank eyes, never daring to step onto a bridge. Time and again I retreated, walking back over the old dairies and the hobby farms, slowly back up the slopes to the hills above the coast, seeking shelter in the forest on the ocean side, in the clefts and overhangs I knew, from where I could gaze down on my home ground and try to come up with a way to continue, or even just a feeling, any feeling, anything but the terrible wooden sensation that had taken over my heart and mind.

To myself I called it the Reverse Pinocchio, that wooden feeling, because Pinocchio was a boy made of wood whose heart had come alive and I was the other way around – a man of flesh and blood whose heart felt like dead wood. I wasn't upset as such – there'd been no tears, I certainly had no particularly dark thoughts – it was more the case that I had no thoughts at all, and certainly no inspiration. Or that's how I saw it. Looking back, though, I suppose my getting up and going in the middle of the night was exactly that, an *inspiration*. It just didn't feel like it at the time.

Fact was I simply didn't know what else to do. So I decided to go. I went to bed as normal that night but after midnight I got up, came down the ladder from my loft in the barn, arranged a small swag, a few clothes, a knife and plate and spoon, a ball of string, my billy, my sketchbook and ink, and a couple of cigarette lighters. I grabbed the shotgun my friend Darren Traherne had lent me, half filled a bag with apples from the tree on the way out, and headed off along the Dray Road. Out of town. Presumably for good.

That first night I simply walked, like a bit of a zombie I suppose. I walked up out of the riverflat and into the hills, thinking nothing, hardly even noticing the features of the bush about me, just putting one foot in front of the other. By the time the sun started coming up, I was on high ground, out past the Birdsong Quarry. I cut down through a swale of tall manna gums on a track there to the duck ponds, without even a hint of tiredness. I was the Reverse Pinocchio you see, incapable of feeling, even the most obvious things. I sat down on the lichened rocks by the ponds, took a drink from the river and watched the light rising. Eventually, when I could feel what little warmth there was of the day to come, I spied a stony cleft under a big blackwood canopy, crept in with my swag, and fell fast asleep.

That's basically how I lived during my time out there. I'd catch yabbies, fish, shoot a duck or a rabbit, then find a sheltered spot in the late afternoon to cook and sleep. Tragedy hadn't struck, I hadn't been betrayed in love or missed some great opportunity. It was something far more inexplicable than that, something that took a few weeks alone in the wind and sun and rain to understand.

The only other time I'd left Mangowak was when I went away as a teenager to art school. Back then, and against the wishes of my father, I'd left with relish and loved what I'd found: the charismatic people, the fantastic studios and expensive equipment, the new methods and techniques I was made aware of. It was an exciting life and I'd stayed on in the city for a year and a half after the course was finished, to save enough money to go to Europe.

But this was different. There was no creative purpose in this, and certainly no romantic stories of the different ways the artists of history had seen and represented the world. Instead I roamed in a kind of coma, from east to west along the ocean-facing ridge, and occasionally south to north when I felt the need to hover like a runaway near those little inland towns. In the bush I sought out the stone overhangs, because on the warmer days they were cool and when it rained they gave me shelter. Gumtrees, even big ones, are next to useless in the rain. Blackwoods are alright but they still drip, and sometimes the drips that gather and fall off tree leaves are heavier and wetter than the clear rain itself.

Of course I saw things in those hills, things you don't normally come across, things you never see in town. I saw a litter of fox cubs supping from their mother in a patch of cushion bush, a wedge-tailed eagle chick attempting to fly for the first time. I saw magpies soaring high up in the thermals, as if in admiring imitation of the eagles, and echidnas sipping daintily at the edge of creeks. I came across unexpected human things too, like the perfectly preserved shell-heaped haunts of the Wathaurong people, whose country this had been for so long until they were rounded up, or murdered, or had to flee to save their lives.

Nothing seemed particularly easy; even though it was winter, most of the available water I could find was brackish, I had to keep a lookout for spiders and ants, and at night it was genuinely freezing. But not once did I ever consider heading back into the comfort of town. Until of course I met the brolga.

I had found my way into a large patch of level ground above the course of the river. It was open to the warmth of the northern sky yet was protected from the southern and western winds by the river's dog-leg meander, and to the east by a high crop of ironstone. It also had an almost pre-prepared shelter between the solid boughs of two old mountain ash trees and a blackwood. I had arranged my swag under the shelter, made my camp, and before long started noticing odd things lying about: a rusted old hammer with the broadest, most oversized head; broken sections of what once would have been iron barrel hoops; bits of hardwood planking pronged with handmade metal ties; and in a recess behind the biggest of the two mountain ash trees a pile of ancient looking bright-green copper pipes. Later on in the day, when I was sitting up on the crop of ironstone, I found a sheaf of nineteenth-century girlie pictures wrapped in calico and leather and twine and stuffed into a small dry cleft between the slabs. Looking down on the camp, I realised this had obviously been somebody's private spot a long time ago. It was good timing. The bush had been drenched with rain, there was no dry kindling to be found, so the carefully stashed pornos started the fire. In the state I was in, I certainly had no inclination to put them to any other use.

Looking back, the brolga seems like a punchline to a joke, a joke at my own expense. There I was, a wooden heart among wooden trees, staring humourlessly from this camp on an upper reach of the Mangowak Creek, when it simply loped into the clearing, as if to say hello.

I was sitting by the fire, in my usual hunched state but just beginning to feel the benefits perhaps of the ghosty old dell I'd found. I remember noticing the homely warmth of winter sun on the side of my cheek and then a curious sense of something crimson away to my right.

On long stilt-like legs it preened in the stubble, the sinuous neck leaning down, before it stood abruptly upright and picked its way along. I had to double take. For a start it was so tall. As tall as a man it seemed. With its light-grey scalloped feathers, its long jointy black legs and the furry blaze of crimson on its head just the sight of it came as a real shock. It was an unbelievable looking creature and the last thing I was expecting to see.

Then suddenly it skipped, playfully it skittered, briefly spreading its wings into a fluttering cape before seeming to high-kick the air right in front of it. My jaw dropped. Unlike any of the other creatures I'd come across, this bird seemed not only at home in the bush but completely incongruous at the same time. Nevertheless I instinctively knew what it was, and slowly my lips began forming the word. Brolga.

The clearing beside the river stretched for sixty-odd metres towards the northern light and I sat entranced as the brolga moved about between me and the trees. Alternately it loped along looking straight ahead, browsed the grass, or scissor-kicked playfully in the air. At one point it picked up a twig in its beak, threw it high towards the sky, made a rough barking sound as the twig hovered, before catching it again as it fell. It was like watching a performance, a jovial play-act, a piece of whimsy, as if a bright spirit had entered the bush. Its attitude seemed neither predatory nor cunning. It simply pranced through the clearing, without a care in the world, and suddenly I felt a smile rising within me, for the first time in weeks.

It was then I remembered someone telling me about a brolga breeding program that had been mooted for our district. The bird had been a fixture in the landscape in times gone by, and now from what I could see it was about to be again. I couldn't believe my luck. Along with my smile, a deep affection was awakened within me for the bird. I raised my hand, as if to beckon it towards me, and for a minute I thought it was going to respond. It stopped still, seemed to look my way, but I soon realised it was not looking but listening to something. Something I couldn't hear. Perhaps its mate was not far off, I thought. I had a dim recollection that brolgas often travelled in pairs. And then it jumped again, made another guttural sound, flung its magnificent wings out briefly, before turning around and walking off the way it came.

Soon it was at the perimeter of the clearing, sniffing casually at the ground as it went. Briefly it hovered under a clutch of black wattles near the creek, pawed at something in the dirt, then drifted off into the larger trees further along the creek-bank. I began leaning my head this way and that but could only catch sight of it occasionally, through gaps in the foliage. A little while later it was gone for good.

I sat in a stillness, a deep fuzzy trance. Something must have been gradually loosening since I'd arrived in the old camp because now, with the visit of the brolga, I had quite suddenly come back to life. The bird had been so calm and so lighthearted among the difficult bush that I was left almost hypnotised. I didn't get up to follow it or see where it went. I just sat by my swag with an enchanted feeling, and an overwhelming sense of relief.

The night fell. My fire took centre stage. And yes, an endless procession of images danced once again before my eyes. Finally, after weeks of sodden solitude, and with the first clear thoughts of a new attitude appearing, I looked up at the stars, opened my mouth, and I laughed.

I laughed at the joke. The great joke that is life. I laughed at the Reverse Pinocchio, and at all the mad things back in town that had made me switch off, batten down, give up what I loved. The disappointments I couldn't face, that I was tired of facing, that had turned me away from home. All in a flash and by dint of one innocent creature, a revitalised brolga whose enchanted manner seemed to defy all contemporary odds, my little world had cracked open again. Like a seed. My wooden heart was split. Its sap was flowing again. The music had returned. And so I laughed, wild and long, and moist and easy too, and afterwards ate a feed of blackfish by the fire with a relish I hadn't felt for months.

Over the next few days I kept a lookout but never saw the brolga again. I began to draw in my sketchbook, and to think. I realised that back in town I had been wrongfooted, duped; I'd been naive, deluded. I had let myself be besieged by tawdry disappointments, one after the other and seemingly unstoppable, until I'd tricked myself into believing I couldn't bear it anymore.

In those last days out among the clefts and overhangs I began drawing the brolga from memory, with a few quick, fluent and easily repeatable lines. First I showed it emerging out of the bush, like a vibrant light out of the nondescript. I drew it sitting beside me at night, as a miracle companion by the fire. I drew it wide awake with a comical glint in its eye, and then asleep, with its beak and long neck tucked under its wing. That last image I keep as some kind of talisman in my wallet to this day. Simply put, it makes me happy. After all the uproarious flights and fancies of The Grand Hotel it seems the closest thing to the dreaming at its source. The world is sad, yes, tragic in fact, but out there in that little clearing by the creek I discovered how not to go under, how to survive as a stranger in an ancient land under siege.

The laughter came easily and with much relief. In the end I laughed so hard that I cried a comic's tears into the river below the little camp I'd found. And finally, with the searing taste of salt on my lips, I decided I could go back. Back to Mangowak.

With my new and unexpected lightness also came a surprising bonus. According to the geologists the land in our home valley had been inundated once, to the extent that migrating whales had swum right over the roof of my house. But thousands of years ago the waters had drawn back, leaving the two ridges and the riverflat etched in their current arrangement, like a three-dimensional print with the fluent inky line of the remnant river running seaward through the flat to the rivermouth. With the vision of the brolga in my heart and my swag hoisted high on the overhangs I now felt I could see this landform like never before. From my lookouts I understood the contours of the thing. The place where we lived was just like any dwelling: there were spaces, big and small, geological walls and balconies, wooded passageways, rocky verandahs, an entrance and exit. It was somewhere to be, a home, and of course it always had been, long before any of our houses were built.

Now I'd decided to go back, I realised I couldn't ignore this vision – that struck me right then as the worst kind of bad taste, to just walk in via the Dray Road, for instance, as I had walked out like a zombie on that earlier night. No, this time

I would enter the right way, take a deeper route, and I could see as clear as day what that deeper route would be.

On the western side of our rivermouth a straight white line of beach runs away for three or so kilometres until it ends at the imposing hills that formed such a barrier between us and the town of Minapre back before the Ocean Road was carved among them. On the eastern side of our rivermouth, however, there is no such obstacle or epic sweep, only a series of coves with high cliffs that dance away, one after the other, like the shore's own cursive script. These coves eventually end at a large reddish bluff, where they simply straighten out into low dunes and another stretch of beach. But just before the coves end at the bluff is a blowhole. As I stood looking down on the world from high on a mossy bush overhang, it came to me clear that I should enter from that side, from the side where each new day begins, where every morning the universe hauls its light up above the thin rim of the sea. I would re-enter my home through the front door, not as a prodigal son as such but with new knowledge nevertheless, and new respect. I would re-enter the town through the blowhole.

The Plinths

I CAME SCRABBLING DOWN THROUGH THE ROCKS AND TREES and hit the beach at Bowman's Bluff, its big ochre brow and nose jutting out above the sea. I crossed the Ocean Road warily and with a sudden rush to the other side, looking just like some shy marsupial no doubt. Then I stepped onto the sand with bare feet, stared at the waves like a twit, resisted the temptation to splash my face, and headed across the flat rocks under the bluff.

Once around the bluff it's only half a mile or so to the blowhole: just the two last smallish coves that resist the southwesterlies and are consequently good for garfishing, a flat stretch with a big ocean pool at the end, and then up onto a raw limestone moonscape and down again to the entrance all purple with mussels.

It was good to see the keyhole of the rock again, the blowhole, one of nature's true prosceniums, a golden arch of an altogether ancient order, a marine talisman, a natural front door to the house of the town.

Its orientation is east-south-east and the ocean pounds into its long wide gutter at high tides, sundering into the limestone and basalt with a satisfying woof and whack and then a subterranean *boom*. It slaps and shapes this little spot of the earth and creates the rhythmic turquoise upwellings my brothers and I dared so often to float on as children.

Looking down from the hills, I'd timed my entrance for an outgoing tide and stepped into the thigh-deep water of the ocean gutter with my swag held above my head. As the gentle waves approached and reached for my navel, I winced for the tickling cold. But with only a few slow wading steps I was directly under the arch, in the echoey acoustic of the blowhole. Then with a shiver and a pause I passed up and through to the quiet pool on the other side.

I'd arrived. I stepped carefully along the slickened flatstones of the pool while above me the sky had cleared. On the small strip of sand beyond the pool I felt like a broken wave. A broken wave made to sigh everlasting, to flow on, to ripple without end. I laid my swag down, coated in weeks of bushdust, and stretched. Then I got down on wet cotton knees and splashed my face.

It felt right. By returning this way, I already felt a tuning in me, a note struck well, a lightness, like the humour of the brolga. I felt a sudden rush of the power of the ground I knew best, and everything in a proportional relation to it.

Looking up with a salty face at the arch of the blowhole and then down onto the golden rocks on either side, I saw the letters and names, the dates, the proud claims and lovers' gestures too, that had been carved in the stone over countless summers.

I sat down smiling at those carvings, remembering some, noticing others for the first time, waiting till I was rested. I picked up the swag then and headed for home, along the broad beach of the Heatherbrae Cove.

Of course I hadn't expected to find balloons but as I came around the corner of the blowhole the beach stretching out in front of me was dotted with them. First a dot of lemon, then a dot of orange, then of black, then silver, then royal blue and pale blue, white, green and finally purple. I laughed – it was becoming a habit – my mouth opening skywards, and I walked along Heatherbrae gathering up the balloons.

By the time I got to the western end of the beach, where the steps lead up through the hook and the elbow to the clifftop car park, I held a bunch of balloons all tied together with their strings. I felt like I was headed to a party and, looking back, I suppose I was.

A man was coming down the steps. He must have thought I was quite a sight. The only mirror I'd seen in ten weeks was in the still upper reaches of the river, I must have been filthy, and now I had a bunch of balloons in tow as well.

On the narrow beach path we stopped to exchange pleasantries and he told me he'd seen the balloons strewn over the sand from his beach-house up on the headland. 'Where do you think they've come from?' he asked. 'Do you think they've been blown in off a boat?'

Having had the vision to re-enter the town through the

arch of the blowhole and then broken like a little wave on the beach, I simply smiled at him from deep within with my new attitude and said, 'You know what? I think they've come from somewhere a little while ago, sometime back in the past.'

Suddenly then he had scribble on his brow, his frown full of nonplussed consternation, and immediately he began to look at me suspiciously, scanning me up and down with a landlordish air. Well, okay, I thought, if that's the limit of your conversation . . . so I did the same to him: white hair the colour of the shore-break, polo shirt yellow as tinned counter-lunch corn, blue shorts for Rhode Island kudos on the sunny winter beach, stringy calves of an elderly golfer, black sandals smeared with silver trackdust.

Finally I pointed out to him that one of the balloons, the magenta one in the middle, had stars and spirals printed all over it, along with the words 'HAPPY NEW YEAR!'.

Given that it was July, his mottled jaw sprang open and he shook his head in a baffled way. I laughed again, this time a bit louder, said toorah and stepped on past him, off through the spinning cocoons that always seem to dangle over the hand-made Heatherbrae steps, no matter the season.

I decided, given my state of dress and the bright handful of balloons, that I'd skip the roads and the smalltown gaze, and make my way home along the relative privacy of the clifftop track.

I made my way along the high part of the track, then down through Tupong Gully and up again until I was approaching Horseshoe Cove. It felt great to be back – even greater with eyes that shone anew and flesh that had its feeling restored.

I virtually pranced around the lighthouse sitting out on the point in front of the meteorological station, excited now by the proximity of home. And then, as I descended through the bearded heath from the shoulder above the rivermouth, I saw them: the Plinths.

There were three of them, towering white above the water in the middle of the estuary. They were carved from the white local limestone, tapered, wedge shaped, in the manner of Romanesque piles. The front Plinth stood right in the mouth of the river, with sea and land water mingling uneasily on either side of it, and the two others stood side by side, about thirty metres apart and statuesque, further back in the stiller inlet water behind the dune hummock. And on the top of each one was a giant bronze bell, at least two metres tall. I could see each bell swinging ever so slightly in the breeze, and then gradually a little more strongly as it freshened, until finally they began to toll loudly in the wind.

I stood on the track digesting the scene. Three white stone Plinths in the grey-black river, with bells going clackety-ding-dong-clang. God knows how loud those bells would be if the wind really picked up, I thought. God knows what a racket they'd make in a storm!

Slowly I walked down the track towards the water, snorting through my nose, before laughing outright at the thought that I, little me, could ever think myself conspicuous merely by being covered in riversilt and bushdust, and holding a bunch of coloured balloons.

'Come on, Noely,' I said to myself out loud. 'How could you ever compete with this?'

Stepping onto the sand by the rivermouth, I found our world-champion local earbasher Givva Way, standing patiently in his white house-painter's overalls, his fawn terrier pissing by the sea wrack on the water's edge.

'G'day, Noel,' he said, in a friendly way. 'What's with the balloons?'

I snorted, happily. 'Never mind the balloons, Givva. What's with the bells?'

He looked over to the Plinths, their giant bronze bells slowly oscillating and ringing intermittently in the salty mid-morning air. He ran a hand through his black mop of paint-flecked hair and said with a lopsided grin, 'The Plinths? Bloody amazing aren't they?'

His dog finished pissing and Givva uncharacteristically left it at that. 'Good to see you back, Noel. We've all been waiting for you to arrive,' he said, before wandering off up the beach towards the road.

I stood still, swag on my back, fit but lean after my time away. With my left hand on a bony hip and my right hand clutching the string of the bobbling balloons, I stared in astonishment again at the Plinths. They were indeed 'bloody amazing', just as Givva had said, but more than that they were the first proof that although my exile in the clefts and overhangs was over, nothing in my life would ever be quite the same again. All ties were cut, all bets off, all melancholy and woodenness set free on a piteous chuckle.

Local Job for a Local Boy

I WALKED INTO THE DRIVEWAY OF MY HOUSE UNDER THE two towering pines and slung off my swag, wondering momentarily about Givva's comment that everyone had been waiting for me to return. Why on earth would they be waiting for me? Before I'd left, I lived so quietly – labouring part-time with my brother, rustling up pictures in my barn on the other days, seeing my close group of friends from time to time but consciously going out of my way to keep my head down. Most people would have had to be paying real attention to know I'd even gone at all.

I tied the balloons to the old tugboat rope that has hung from one of the pines since my exhibition of knot paintings in '96. The balloons looked good there, they brightened up the entrance, and below them on the ground two or three white polystyrene buoys sitting buff on the pine needles looked like part of the new arrangement.

I looked around. Nothing much seemed to have changed since I'd been gone. The only difference I could see was that the grass in the yard between my house and my barn was a foot taller, the house spouting was spiky with pine needles, and the two doors of the shed on the outside kitchen wall had come open. I walked over and closed the shed doors and was about to enter the house when my nephew Oscar drove into the driveway. In a white station wagon. Before I'd left, he didn't even have a licence.

Oscar was so proud of his new wheels he didn't get out of the car; he just wound down the window, beamed and gave me the thumbs up. A gust of breeze creaked in the pines and I heard the faint toll of the Plinth bells ringing back down at the rivermouth.

'Well hello, Ossie,' I said fondly. 'Your car?'

'Yep, Uncle Noely. My car.'

'How is it?'

'It's *good*,' he said, with great enthusiasm. He beamed at me, with a bright flash of his big teeth. 'Where you been, Uncle Noel? It's been months.'

'Oh, here and there,' I said lightly. 'Camping mainly.'

'I see your swag's taken a hammering,' he said, glancing over to where the tattered bundle of canvas sat on the ground.

'Yep,' I replied. 'It's been through a bit, that's for sure.'

We went inside for a cup of tea. Luckily we both have it black, as the only milk in the fridge smelt like expensive French cheese. I chucked it out for the magpies through the front doors of the living room and dug out some shortbread from the end cupboard. We went first things first then and talked about the Plinths.

'They're public sculptures,' Oscar told me. 'Commissioned by the shire.'

'I kind of figured that might be the case. But do the bells ring all night long?'

Oscar laughed. 'They did at first. They're designed to ring in the slightest breath of wind. And boy did they ring! But then after a week or so everyone kicked up a fuss. You know how the sound travels in this valley. In the end they had to do something about it.'

'So, what did they do?'

He laughed again. 'Well, Uncle Noely, they pay me eighty dollars a day to row out and tie the bells down at dusk, then go out again first thing and untie.'

I nearly spilt my tea. Then I made a few quick calculations. 'Let me get this right, Ossie. You're saying the shire pays you over five hundred bucks a week to tie and untie those bells every morning and night?'

'Yep. I just row out in the canoe. Or swim if it's warm. It's for something called "The Year of the Maritime". The Plinths are there to express a shipping feel. Well, that's what it says in my job description. They're gonna take them down again after twelve months, though there's a lot of people round town who seem to like them and want them to stay.'

'Like who, the cormorants?'

'Yeah,' laughed Oscar. 'Anyway, did you hear about the pub, Uncle Noel?'

'I did, Ossie,' I said, smiling. 'Just before I left town.'

It was actually the very day before I'd left town. I was walking down the hill from the general store with my dog, Pippy, when I saw the white planning permit flapping in the breeze outside the pub. With trepidation I walked over to read it. Our town's one and only pub was to be knocked down and replaced with a cluster of eco-apartments called Wathaurong Heights.

In my wildest dreams I'd never imagined that with one stroke of a pen our town's sole watering hole and communal meeting place could be obliterated. Nor had I imagined the proud and sorrowful history of the Wathaurong ever being used as a lifestyle lure, in cahoots with a famous English romantic novel, to appeal to the cashed-up classes. The whole thing was like a sick joke.

But this was the latest in a long line of rude shocks in the town. A few months previous, when our local shire had decided to roof in a section of our creek, so that young mothers and their children could sit on the bank and enjoy the river when it rains, we were simply flummoxed. Then, when it was announced in our local paper that roosters had been outlawed in the shire for reasons of acoustic pollution, we began to get pissed off. And finally, when we had all received a letter in the post informing us that Mangowak was officially no longer to be called a town but rather a 'village', my head began to brood. And then this. A piece of flapping white paper nailed to the treated pine pole below the 'LIVE CRAYS' sign. As I read what it had to say, some previously wholehearted thing inside me seemed to vanish forever.

I didn't lash out or fire into an indignant rage. Instead I

simply put one foot in front of the other, cut through the spare paddock down the hill to my home in the riverflat, dropped Pippy and my canary, Frankie, off with friends, and later that night walked out of town.

'Yeah, it's terrible isn't it?' Oscar was saying now, sitting opposite me at the table. 'They stand to make a lot more money with those apartments than they ever have out of the pub. But where are we all gonna hang out? There's plans afoot, you know, Uncle Noel. They're funny plans too, I reckon. I suppose you haven't heard, though, given you've just got back.'

'No, I daresay I haven't. What plans are they?'

'Well, it started off as a joke and that . . . but then . . . well, I dunno. Maybe I shouldn't be the one to tell you. Old Kooka's the one. He's got all the goss. Go and see him. He'll fill you in.'

Oscar started giggling, presumably thinking about these 'funny plans' to do with the hotel. Quickly he slurped down what was left of his tea and excused himself, saying he'd really only pulled in to the old house to pick up his wetsuit from the line.

I took his cup, clapped him on the back and said it was good to see him. He said, 'Vice versa, Uncle Noel.' At the back door I congratulated him again on finally getting his wheels.

Kooka's Bright Idea

KOOKA LIVED JUST A FEW DOORS DOWN FROM ME, IN THE house he'd built for himself and his wife, Mary, on the block where the original freshwater well was in the valley. The house still stands today but of course Kooka's huge historical archive of photos, documents and sound recordings is now gone. Unlike a lot of those worthy collector types Kooka was no wowser. Oh no, Kooka loved his grog with a champion thirst. Traditionally he would begin his drinking day with a heartstarter every morning at 6 am. He did this all through his working life as a builder and had never worked a day drunk. Of course he continued the habit after his retirement too, and when he purchased the old Grundig recorder and took to building his local history archive with such thoroughness after Mary died, he said the heartstarter – which usually consisted of a 7 oz glass of beer, or on holidays a flute of Mary's old favourite, Bodega champagne – became more essential than ever, to 'lubricate the mind and motivate the senses'. This was a phrase Kooka loved to roll off the tongue, having discovered it in a letter written by a labourer during the Depression who, when writing home to his brother in Beechworth about his search for work in the wintry southwest, had reserved all favourable comment for this eloquent praise of the effects of the coastal home brew. The phrase had stuck with Kooka and became a kind of mantra, not only of his pleasure in drinking but in his history-work as well. In both capers, he said, as long as the mind is lubricated and the senses are motivated, everything is well worth pursuing. But once you go beyond that point, he warned, once the mind starts to rust up or become sloppy, and the senses dulled or disorientated, it's time to give it away, to pack up the archive, put down the pen, or simply turn your glass upside-down on the bar.

I found Kooka that day washing up in the kitchen after his lunch, his big bull kookaburra's head bent over the sink with a typical look of intense concentration, as if he was perched on a gum branch watching for a worm. He yelled, 'Hooray, Noel!' as he saw me through the louvres around the side of the house, and welcomed me enthusiastically at the verandah's sliding door, with a tea towel over his shoulder, shaking my hand with his undiminished tradesman's grip.

From a moulting bit of lambswool behind him emerged Pippy, whom I'd left in Kooka's safe hands while I'd been away, thinking they could both do with the company. The dog was happy enough to see me, but by the look of her swollen midriff it seemed I'd got there in the nick of time. She'd been surviving on Kooka's famous cashew incentive scheme for sure.

After greeting the dog, and admonishing her dietician, I took the tea towel, dried as Kooka washed, and he told me I was just the man he'd been wanting to see. 'Been looking for you everywhere. Where the bloody hell have you been?' he said incredulously.

I told him a little of my exploits among the clefts and overhangs, though nothing of the reasons why I'd left to go out there in the first place, nor the reasons I'd come back in the end. He listened with his head aslant over the sink, his eyes fixed straight out the sink window, as if the worm he'd been watching had just turned into a tasty bush mouse. Then he asked me straight out if I'd seen the planning permit for the Wathaurong Heights development before I left. He said he'd been holding up the bar at the pub on the afternoon the permit was put up. Said he'd whipped straight out to photograph it.

I told him I had seen it and asked what he thought of the name. Kooka looked at me out the corner of his eye with a half washed china cup in his hands. Then without a word he opened his fingers and let the cup smash onto the tiled floor. It was an eloquent moment.

We finished the dishes and as he cleaned up the shattered cup with a brush and shovel he told me he'd had an idea about the Wathaurong Heights thing while I was away, an inspired idea, and he needed to run it by me. He said he was just about to head into his archive when I arrived, and that if I liked I could join him and we could talk the whole thing over.

When Mary died, Kooka had moved out of the conjugal bed in favour of sleeping on a narrow divan in the room that now housed the archive. Since her death the manilla folders, the cardboard concertina files, the metal filing cabinets, brown paper bags, yellow A4 envelopes, old fruit boxes and bookcases had accumulated around him like a new skin. We stepped off the floral lino of Mary's kitchen and entered the brown-carpeted archive to find stuff everywhere: papers, books, tape reels, photographs, all stacked high to the ceiling. Blu-tacked to the walls, between the piles of shelves, were unframed prints of some of the photographic archive: old shots of the stockbitten riverflat and old shots of the stockbitten cliff; a picture of the supply boat that used to anchor offshore at Tupong Gully, with the kerosene and other essentials that kept the meteorological station going; comparative shots of the burnt slopes after both the 1939 and the 1983 bushfires; shots of the rivermouth at various stages of opening and closing. There was also a glass cabinet against the wall near the divan with his cherished collections inside. As a young boy from the city billeted out with his cousins the Conebushes, Kooka had collected souvenir tea-spoons, tobacco pouches and beer coasters. He always said that in those collections could be found the seeds of his historical work that came later on.

Pride of place among the pictures on display in the archive was a framed photograph of Mary, which hung on the wall under the window near his massive red cedar desk. Kooka's interest in *collecting time*, as he sometimes called it, his history-work, had actually begun just before Mary got sick in the early 1980s, but it wasn't till after she'd taken her leave that it really picked up pace. Her death had rendered him speechless. They'd been a great couple, thick as thieves, a much admired dancing pair, always publicly affectionate, and there was no doubt the history-work was a way of coping with the grief. When our old council was incorporated into the Brinbeal shire and the draconian new building regs came in, Kooka took an early retirement, hung up his tool belt, and started scouting around, photographing, interviewing and documenting the history of Mangowak pretty much full-time. Since then the sight of his maroon Brumby ute choofing along in pursuit of living history, with its distinctive high timber canopy rigged up on the back to protect his photographic gear and the old Grundig recorder, had become a regular and reassuring sight around the place.

As we sat down at his desk, he pulled the cane blind up an inch or two to let a bit of light in. He also flicked on the orange standard lamp next to the desk and instantly a glowing pattern of swinging tassel reflections covered his chaos of documents and papers. Kooka casually picked up a black and white postcard from among the piles on the desk and handed it to me. It was a shot of the wooden bridge at Breheny Creek, just a couple of kilometres further along the coast.

'Rose Postcard Series number 362,' he said as I looked at it. 'You know old George Rose was an artist for life, Noel. Travelled round the country in his truck, darkroom in the back, taking snaps, cataloguing the vistas. He published thousands of official Rose Series postcards before he was finished. And had a fair time doing it.'

Kooka dug further among his papers until he found a white paper bag. He pulled out a ten-by-eight glossy photo with a white border and handed it to me. It was a picture of a smiling man camped under bluegums by the Minapre River. He was sitting on a director's chair beside a campfire, with a truck in the background. On the side of the truck were the words 'GEORGE ROSE PHOTOGRAPHIC ARTIST'.

'Looks happy dun' he?' Kooka said. 'That was 1951, as far as I can ascertain. He'd been on the road for years by then. Knew the country like a muso knows a score.'

'Did you ever meet him?' I asked, staring at the charismatic photo.

'Well, no, not as such. But I remember him up at the pub here when I was a young tacker. He'd always stop in for a drink when passin' through. His nickname was Beauty Spot. Used to get a lot of stick for havin' such a great life. "Shouldn't be allowed," everyone'd say laughing. But he was well liked I'd say.'

Kooka leant over now and dug out another photo from among the chaos on his desk. This one wasn't an old glossy, it was just an ordinary inkjet print on a piece of plain white paper. He handed it to me, smiling. It was his photo of the Wathaurong Heights planning permit.

'I dunno where to begin really, Noel,' Kooka began. 'I suppose the problem is that the old town's gonna need a pub. And, with my rates going up to billy-o coz of the value of the house, I'm already living well beyond my means.'

I looked at him quizzically, not quite sure where he was headed.

'I talked it over with your brother Jim and he thought it was a great joke.'

'Thought what was a great joke?' I asked.

'You running a pub.'

'Me running a . . . *what*?'

'Yep, that's right, son.'

I started laughing, out of pure confusion.

'See?' Kooka said.

'See what?' I replied.

'Jim was right. It's a funny idea. You running a pub. But, Noel, I'm deadly serious about it.'

'You are?'

'Yep, deadly.'

Kooka stood up in his singlet and jeans and began to fossick in one of the big filing cabinets on the opposite wall. I sat, staring straight ahead through the small gap of window I could see under the blinds. Before long he came back and spread a waxen old shire map of the valley across the desk. He pointed with his flattened carpenter's finger at my family property. He began to tell me how because our land was on the site of the original hotel of the town, The Grand Hotel, as it was known, it still held a much sought-after commercial zoning. He described with his finger how the grounds of the old Grand Hotel had pretty much sprawled along the riverbank, from my place to his, until it closed for business in the late 1890s.

I'd always been told the old Grand had been flooded out along with the rest of the valley buildings and that's why the town centre had been moved back up onto the higher ground of the ridge, but Kooka now corrected that misapprehension and assured me that although the butchery and the store and the other public buildings of the time had been flooded, The Grand Hotel itself had burnt down. *In a welcome conflagration*, the Methodist minister from Minapre had said, in his sermon of the following week. Kooka said there was 'some kind of shenanigans' involved in why the hotel had burnt down, and despite his research it seemed no one had ever told the story straight. That's why it had come down to me via folklore that The Grand had been washed away with the rest of the original town.

'It was a wild ol' joint by all accounts,' Kooka now told me, 'and I believe the conditions are cherry ripe for it to be so again. You've got the premises, I've got the financials, and the town's pretty soon gonna have its tongue literally hanging out for it.'

Perhaps it's the destiny of the vocational artist in a small town not to be taken seriously, for people to think of him as an idler or a soak, and therefore as someone perpetually only half looking for, or otherwise outright shunning, serious work. That fact, combined with my well-cemented position in the family as the youngest child (and therefore as someone incapable of ever maturing to full adulthood), perhaps explains why Kooka, in cahoots with my elder brothers, had thought it possible that with one bright swoop of enthusiasm they could change the whole tone and calibre of my life by installing me as a novice publican in my own house. And that I would agree to this without so much as a harrumph or an objection.

Slowly but steadily as we sat there, Kooka began to outline his scheme, how he would sell his house, which was now a millstone around his neck because of its exaggerated worth on the coastal market, and with the money raised by the sale help me fit out my house to become the town's hotel. He himself would happily become a permanent lodger in a room upstairs, from where he could continue his history-work and quite contentedly see out his autumn years in good company. I would gain much needed full employment as the licensee of the reawakened Grand Hotel, we would both make a few quid and perform a valuable community duty by doing so. Together we could ensure that the town still had a pub, and that the pub remained authentic, not tricked up with watered beer, inflated prices and shoddy gimmicks for the tourists, so that the good folk of Mangowak could continue to relax and drink in a manner they were accustomed to.

And so then, Kooka enquired, what did I think of the plan?

My first impulse of course was to laugh. But as my mouth opened, Kooka held up his hand and assured me again that it was no lark, that he was fair dinkum, absolutely serious. This only made me want to laugh even harder and in the chequered gloom of his fibro archive I proceeded to do so. I chuckled and guffawed, waxed sarcastic about the ease with which I could fill a publican's shoes, joked about how seamless the transformation of my ramshackle rabbit warren of an eighty-year-old home into a modern hotel would be, and how I'd always secretly hankered to live under the same roof as Kooka and his archive. I spoofed how I was at a loose end anyway, having just strolled back into town, and how good it was of my brothers to be on the lookout for my welfare and how perceptive they'd been to intuit my true 'mine host' vocation. I spoke of my innate talents for pouring a drink, the relish with which I would toss giant bikies off the premises and how, above all, I would enjoy the night-after-night tranquillity, the slow easy pace and gentle inconsequential quiet of not only living in, but also running, a hotel.

Kooka listened to all this without batting an eyelid. He simply stared at me and waited for me to finish, almost as if I was having some kind of regular fit. When I finally stopped speaking and my chuckling dwindled away, he was still staring at me. His big brow was lowered and his eyes were doleful.

'Jim said he thought you might get your back up a bit,' he offered at last.

I gave him an exasperated look, which he straightaway returned with an irrepressibly broad kookaburra smile. Three hours later, due mostly to the fuel of home-made shandies and fistfuls of peanuts, we were still in there, discussing the idea.

The Freedom Virus

THAT FIRST NIGHT BACK IN TOWN I WENT TO SLEEP IN
the barn thinking of the brolga, but when I woke to
Pippy's familiar yapyap the next morning all I could think
about was The Grand Hotel. Kooka had painted such a picture
the day before in the archive that by the time I'd left his house
just before midnight, I was almost considering his proposition
plausible.

He'd told me all about The Grand Hotel of yore, how the
bullock drays'd come down from Corrievale and Winchelsea,
do their business on the old coast and range track, and then
what? Have a few snorts of course. And then a few more.
Kooka had concluded that his block must have been the site of
the hotel bottle dump, due to all the nineteenth-century glass
he'd found lying around over the years. In a tartan shortbread
tin on his desk he kept his favourite shards of that curious

time-smoothed glass, which he himself said was the catalyst for the hotel becoming his number one obsession among the larger interest he had in the town's history in general.

He'd told me about Joan Sweeney, who was the last publican at the old Grand, and what a formidable person she was. As Kooka had said, to head out on your own to these parts as a young woman back in those days was a gutsy enough choice, but to take on the running of a salty frontier pub chocked with hard-hearted bullock drivers, lawless loggers and craymen, lonely-eyed swagmen and runaway saunterers was another thing entirely. Most of those men had blood of some kind or another on their hands, some of them native blood, but by all accounts Joan Sweeney ran a tight ship and was much respected, on both sides of the ledger.

Kooka had nothing but good words to say about her; in fact, on the strength of his research, he described her as nothing less than 'a woman of grace'. When the hotel had burnt down and the colonial police had tried to get to the bottom of exactly why, she'd walked out from among the debris and refused to cooperate. She hadn't even bothered to wind up the licence, which explained the strange fact of its still being current for the absurd option of my use. She'd taken a ship to America and settled briefly in Chicago, before returning to Victoria in 1906. Years later, in the heat of the anti-conscription debates during the First World War, she had been a well-known and outspoken participant for the case against. Kooka spoke of her with great animation and reverence, and the way he saw it the idea of being Joan Sweeney's belated successor as publican of The Grand Hotel, Mangowak, was far from a mediocre prospect. He said I'd have to have my wits about me even just to measure up.

After lying in my loft that morning musing about all this, I climbed down the ironbark ladder and made my way across the yard and into the house for my first indoor breakfast in weeks. I found four eggs in the door of the fridge and broke three of them into a skillet. Miraculously the eggs hadn't gone off, so I tossed in some herbs from the garden, a sprinkle of local forest pepper, and was just sitting down with great anticipation to the omelette and a pot of tea when Veronica Khouri appeared through the louvres at the sunroom door with my canary, Frankie.

She let herself in with Frankie in the bamboo cage. Veronica had cut off her usual long black ringlets and dyed what was left of them a vivid cinnamon colour. Her big brown eyes were shining. Frankie was dancing happily about on his perch and she was full of assurances about how comfortable and happy he'd been during his stay with her in the studio up on the cliff.

'He didn't mind the winds?' I asked, gesturing for her to sit down for a cup of tea with me at the table.

'No, not at all,' she declared. 'I put him on the shelf in the window on the southeast side and he'd just sing away every morning. Wouldn't you, Frankie? And then in the afternoons I'd let him out for a while and he'd fly around a bit and shit on my work. I had to have a special Frankie-rag always at hand, just in case the cack dried and left a stain. Apart from that he was perfect company, Noel.'

I looked at Frankie in the cage where Veronica had placed

it on the table and he did look a picture of health. His orange feathers had a real lustre. In a burst of self-pity I thought that both he and Pippy had perhaps been happier without me while I was away.

Veronica Khouri and I had originally met years before at art school in Melbourne. She was half Lebanese and half Argentinian, an exotic, precocious and heavily politicised star of that art school scene, whereas I was a little more inconspicuous, though I did have my moments. We didn't set eyes on each other for years afterwards, until her wealthy father bought Ron McCoy's land up on the Mangowak cliff opposite the Two Pointer Rocks. After that I'd bump into her every now and again when she was around but one day, a couple of years after old Ron died, she told me she was moving into town permanently. Well, this was quite a surprise. I'd followed her career over the years since we'd graduated – she had become a sculptor of some note internationally – but then, as we had stood chatting in the general store, she said she'd had enough of the travel and especially the art industry bullshit and just wanted somewhere quiet to live and work. Her father, Dom, who worshipped the ground his only daughter walked on, had agreed to build her a studio among the vegetable gardens and fruit trees he'd planted on the site of the McCoys' old house.

At the time this was a piece of news I found disconcerting, because it required me to knit together two disparate, and up until then entirely separate, threads of my life. On the one hand there was my artistic self, and my own private imaginings, which on a day-to-day level I kept pretty much contained within the confines of my barn, where I worked. On the other hand there was the quiet, almost nondescript life I led in my home town, where I preferred to shelter that artistic self behind a more homely persona. The news that Veronica, who'd been a provocative and even intimidating presence in those earlier days at art school, and with whom back then I'd shared a passionate love of Dada and the Surrealists, was moving into my provincial little realm, and setting up creative camp on the McCoys' old cliff, would require an interesting series of readjustments.

As I poured the tea, Veronica said her mother had seen me pass in front of their house the previous day on my way back into town along the clifftop track. She'd said I was carrying a bunch of coloured balloons. Briefly we talked about where I'd been in my time away but I kept the details hazy. I told her that I'd found the balloons on the beach but said nothing of the Reverse Pinocchio and even less about the brolga.

Then I changed the subject and we talked about how her work was progressing. She had constructed a transparent life-sized human body out of Perspex, which she was painstakingly filling with a collection of what she called 'three-dimensional techno-biographical influences'. To me it sounded like a twenty-first-century version of Giuseppe Arcimboldo's paintings, but in 3D. I was interested. I pressed her on it but got the feeling she wanted to keep her own details hazy as well. Fair enough. But then she surprised me by coming straight out and asking if I had agreed to open my house to the public as The Grand Hotel.

It seemed that Kooka's bright idea had already been floated widely in the town while I was away. It also appeared that everyone was in favour of it. Veronica said that at first when she was told she couldn't quite imagine me taking it on, but she was so outraged by the Wathaurong Heights development that she decided to offer any help she could.

And so, she wondered, what did I think about it all? Was I keen?

I answered with a diverting giggle and assured her that it could never happen. She must have picked up some other layer in my voice, however, because typically, in her hot-blooded way, she pounced. She demanded to know my specific objections and then, one by one, started dismissing them. To my protests that I was a hopeless businessman she assured me that Gene Sutherland's wife, Jen, had agreed to look after the books. To my confident objection that the house was not fit to be resuscitated to occupational-health-and-safety standards she said that my brother Jim had already had a shire building inspector suss it out and that, providing certain considerations were taken care of, the house had been deemed fundamentally solid and given the potential thumbs up.

'Phew,' I said. 'It seems a committee has already been set up without me. I feel ambushed.'

All the reservations I'd expressed so far, both to Kooka and now to Veronica, were of a practical nature, but it was to my more overriding objections, such as how my quiet life would be ruined and how the beloved house my grandfather had built would be plastered with huge signs advertising beer and skittles, my block mangled for car parking, etc. – in short how the whole hard-won atmosphere of my life would be ruined – that Veronica countered with her most convincing argument. Kooka had wooed me pretty well in his archive, with tales of continuing the independent traditions of his beloved old Grand Hotel, but it was only when Veronica reminded me of the freedom virus that I began to see the whole thing as perhaps being already written in the stars.

Becoming increasingly annoyed with my deflections and objections, Veronica said, 'You don't have to be a meathead about it, Noel. No one's looking for a pub like any other! Remember Kurt Schwitters, remember Hugo Ball, remember Dada and the freedom virus? Well that's it. Let's get infected. Isn't it possible to please the likes of Kooka and Givva Way and the other drunkards, and do something that's interesting as well? No one can be pissed off with you about it coz without you there'd be no pub in the town. C'mon, Noel, just see it as one big work of art.'

I said nothing. I just tucked into my omelette and jokingly rolled my eyes. A hotel as a work of art in little ol' Mangowak? It was about as unlikely as an indoor creek. But Veronica's mention of the Dada freedom virus had actually struck a chord. It was coincidentally just after the era of the original Grand Hotel in Mangowak when the Dada artists on the other side of the world had responded to the hellish capitalist machinery of the First World War by setting their own selves free. Free from the so-called rationalism that had produced such an in-your-face nightmare, and free from adding to the plush pile of comfortable art that seemed to serve no other purpose than to amuse the upper-class technicians of the disaster. Rather than picking up the usual instruments and singing some harmoniously predictable dirge of despair, the Dadaists had broken open European culture with an axe blow. They had declared their own war on meaning itself, and had taken the piss out of absolutely everything, particularly art. They had turned their backs on 'quality' and 'tradition' in favour of nonsense and relentless liberation. They called this burst springtime pod Dada, anti-art, the freedom virus. It was vivid, absurd, profoundly meaningless. No one had ever seen anything like it. And nothing in the art world had ever been the same since.

My own slow transformation out in the clefts and overhangs seemed suddenly to have been heading all the while to this point. A hundred years after the original festivities of Dada were unleashed, I'd been completely floored, not only by our human savaging of the planet on a global scale but also by the surreal appropriations that were happening in the tiny little realm of my home town. I'd stumbled off into the bush like a zombie until, with the vision of the brolga, I realised I could return, but only with a light step and a heart reconfigured for laughter. I had come back not knowing where this new attitude would lead, and not needing to know either, only to find that, lo and behold, my friends and loved ones had somehow already divined an unlikely solution on my behalf: The Grand Hotel.

From down at the rivermouth I could hear the Plinth bells beginning to chime in the sea breeze. I sipped my tea. It would be my pub after all, on the site of the old Grand Hotel and in my grandfather's house. I could do what I liked. There were no rules about what beer you had to serve, what pictures you had to have on the walls, and surely it wasn't compulsory that every publican turn into a pot-bellied Sky-channel addict!

As I chewed on my omelette, a spicy burst of Vietnamese mint exploded in my mouth. My brain started to buzz with excitement. My skin began to tingle. Two definite symptoms of the freedom virus. But I said nothing. Across the table Veronica was peering at me ferociously, in a vain attempt to read my mind.

Eventually I looked across at her and winked. I put down my knife and fork, leant across the table and unhitched Frankie's birdcage door. He flew straight out and joyfully began to circle the golden cypress ceiling of what would shortly become the main bar of The Grand Hotel.

The Fire Still Burns

AFTER VERONICA LEFT, I SPENT THE REST OF THE DAY moving about the house, in quite a welter of excitement as I tried to imagine the details of its transformation. The house had many rooms, both upstairs and down, small pokey rooms for the most part, built by my grandfather back in the days when northern hemisphere architecture still ruled Australian houses. Upstairs, though, my mum's old sewing room was the major exception, with its high pitched ceiling and large windows facing both north and south.

Originally the room was intended as a study for my papa when he retired from the meteorological station, but as he never did retire the room was never finished. Its floor was never polished, its walls never plastered, the pitched ceiling remained unlined and it still had that lovely astringent smell of open raw timber. Eventually, when we were kids, Mum took it over as a place to sew at night. Climbing the stairs and entering the room in the middle of the afternoon, listening to the familiar warpy music of my feet on its timbers, in my mind I'd already assigned that one cavernous and unfinished space to Kooka and his archive.

By nightfall I found myself still sitting on the wicker chair by the single bed in The Sewing Room, quite dumbstruck by the realisation that Kooka's idea of continuing in the tradition of the original Grand Hotel and Veronica's notion of reviving the Dada freedom virus were not entirely incompatible. This wasn't so much a case of opposites attracting as the desire for freedom to unify all things. As a result my brain started flooding with ideas for the new establishment, ideas which I would only realise later were completely and unwittingly at the service of that freedom. Duchamp the Talking Urinal, which turned out to be the first great hit of The Grand Hotel, was among the initial deluge of inspirations I had while sitting up there in The Sewing Room, but as the ideas kept coming I quickly realised that the logistics of everything would have to be discussed, that I would need a lot of canny practical help to bring it all to fruition. By the time I went back down the stairs and out to the barn after dark, I'd decided to call the first of a series of meetings to get the ball rolling.

I was plain exhausted from all the excitement but as soon as my head hit the pillow the bells on the Plinths down at the rivermouth began clanging away in the southerly and I couldn't sleep. Oscar had obviously gone out on the tear and forgotten to tie them down. The ding-dong-clackety-clang travelled across the sedge and tea tree and right on up the riverflat. Were the bells ringing for the end of the world? I wasn't sure. But I did know there was no way anyone could sleep with the racket.

Eventually I put on some clothes, climbed out of my loft and walked to the rivermouth with a surfboard, rope, and occy straps, intending to tie the bells down myself. When I got to the water, however, Givva Way was already halfway across to the bells in his canoe. I stood watching in the moonlight as Givva climbed up onto each of the three Plinths and manhandled the bells. When finally he'd paddled from Plinth to Plinth and the last bell had fallen silent, the whole riverflat seemed to let out one huge sigh of relief.

I couldn't help but giggle as curly-headed Givva, with paint flakes in his hair from the long days swabbing house-sides, cursed and swore and plashed his paddle back towards the shore. When he finally got to the bank, I could see he was still in his pyjamas. He noticed me standing there with the surfboard under my arm and grunted. I said g'day and he let out a kind of 'Bah!' sound. Then, as he dragged his black canoe up out of the riversludge towards its hiding place in the bearded heath, he looked at me and said, 'Fuckin' world's gone mad, Noel. Fuckin' cunts.' Then he stormed off the beach, stumbled across the road and disappeared into his front garden.

It was too good an opportunity to miss. First thing the next morning I grabbed some charcoal from the open fire and made a sketch of Givva grappling with the bells on the inlet in his pyjamas. Around the base of the glowing Plinths I added piranhas snapping and agitating the water. In the sky great vultures loomed and swooped below the moon. I photocopied it eight times at the post office and sent them out as invitations to a meeting regarding 'THE REAWAKENING OF THE GRAND HOTEL (THE FIRE STILL BURNS!)'. I sent them to my brother Jim and Oscar, Veronica Khouri, Nan Burns, Darren Traherne, Ash Bowen, Kooka, and my old mate from the banks of the Barroworn, Gene Sutherland.

A Village Atmosphere

ON THE DAY OF THAT FIRST MEETING THE WEATHER WAS fine and it soon became apparent that everyone's real concern was to welcome me back and to ply me with questions and taunt me with absurd speculations about what I'd been up to while I'd been away. Ash Bowen, who when he's not tiptoeing around his bush block in an apiarist's suit is quite the cultural connoisseur, reckoned I'd taken some cushy flat in Melbourne and hung out with the art crowd. And that I was too embarrassed to admit it. Nan Burns, my oldest friend going way back, who to this day likes to think of me as innocent, wide-eyed and idealistic, reckoned I might have gone away to work in one of Steve Waugh's orphanages in India. My brother Jim and Oscar were prepared to believe just about anything when it came to my flights of fancy, and Darren Traherne only wanted to know how the shotgun I'd borrowed from him before I went stood up to the rigours of my exile.

'Bloody well,' I told Darren. 'I spent many a night on a cleft or under an overhang oiling that gun, wiping it, kissing it and bowing to it, terrified that you'd shoot me with it if I brought it back in bad nick.'

Big Gene Sutherland was the only one present who was certain he knew what I'd been up to. He let out a huge dairyman's laugh as each person uttered his or her speculation, slapped his big thighs as I tried to explain where I'd actually been, and then asked me for the name of the child.

'C'mon, Noel,' he said, as I looked at him nonplussed. 'You've always been a dark horse. Where're you hiding the bird and what're you calling the kid?'

Nan scoffed. 'What are you on about, Gene? You reckon he's been sheltered by the Sisters of Mercy or something? What a load of old fashioned crap. We all know Noel can't get a root.'

Gene burst into loud laughter again, his big Otway dewlaps shaking. And so it went, for the next half hour, with everyone seated on the pews around the living-room table and me pouring wine and handing around stubbies of beer while providing plenty of clownish fodder for the jokes. Finally I had to draw their attention to the purpose of the meeting. I cleared my throat loudly, like a councillor, and began with a grin.

'In my time away with the art crowd,' I said, 'reflecting on the possibilities for creative expression in the new century, and in the months I spent working with the sick, the homeless, the poor and unloved in India, and, of course, through the invaluable insights and maturity I have gathered since conceiving and then having my first child, I have come to the conclusion, which you may have all already realised a long time ago, that God's a comedian. I used to think he was airbrushed and perfect, then I thought he was drunk and negligent, then of course I considered the possibility that he didn't exist at all – but you know in my time away I just couldn't come to terms with any of those ideas. Eventually, with the wise counsel of some very accepting and good-humoured animal friends, I decided he could very well exist, but only if he was a jokester. Because how else can we explain the goings on around us? The indoor creek, Wathaurong Heights, and now of course the Plinths and the bells, eh?'

'What about the meteorological station?' interrupted Darren Traherne. 'That's pretty sick.'

'What about it?' I said.

'What, are you fuckin' blind or something, Noel? They painted the chimneys red.'

I went straight to the double doors leading onto the verandah, stepped out and had a look. Sure enough, up there on the cliff the old white limestone chimneys of the meteorological station were painted a bright Noddy-from-Enid-Blyton red.

I returned inside. 'Well that's pretty cheery,' I said.

'Yeah, you can't have white chimneys, mate. They get dirty,' said big Gene, with another hearty laugh.

Kooka piped up. 'Funny how they used the local stone to put the Plinths in, to give the place a maritime feel in the year of the bloomin' ship, but when it comes to the met station it isn't good enough for 'em. They reckoned the red lent much more of a village atmosphere.'

'A village atmosphere,' repeated my brother Jim.

'Yeah, a village atmosphere,' said Kooka.

As I began to outline my ideas for the hotel, everyone except Veronica was raising their eyebrows and shaking their heads in disbelief. I made it clear from the outset, however, that absolutely everyone would be welcome at The Grand and that the Dada-style shenanigans would never interfere with the genuine hospitality. I told them also that although I was ready to give over the house as The Grand Hotel, I didn't want to renovate it, that it had to stay as close as possible to how it presently was, how my papa built it. Sure we'd need to put in a coolroom, a bigger dunny, and turn the kitchen into a bar, but it wouldn't be tarted up, not in the least. In fact I suggested we go the other way: keep it unfashionably dark, like some nineteenth-century hole in the wall, with its ocean-facing windows boarded up, and that we keep the same furniture, right down to the daggy cane chairs and the laminated brown timber tabletops that had always been in the house. I kept reminding them that as we were running the only hotel in town, we could pretty much do as we liked. I also announced that there was a sweet logic to the idea that for once the economic principle of demand and supply was gonna unleash a crazed originality.

'But who's gonna work it?' asked Nan, rolling a smoke with a sceptical look on her weatherbeaten face. 'It's all very well to have all these crazy things going on but who's gonna pour the beer? Who's gonna do the hard yards? You're not a publican, Noel.'

I smiled. 'Well, technically I'm about to become one. But I was thinking we could all help out. Like in a co-op. And for a wage of course. And remember, we don't have to open till three in the afternoon if we don't want to.'

'Well that'll piss people off,' said Darren Traherne. 'What about counter lunches?'

'Look,' I began, 'I'm not doin' this to become head of the Hoteliers Association. Kooka's told me some stories over the last few days about the original Grand Hotel. I think we should follow that spirit. We mightn't have spotted quoll on the menu and we won't be amputating fingers on the bar, hey, Kooka, and there won't be goats kipping beside exhausted prostitutes by the fire, or crayfish races on the verandah, but we'll do it our own way nevertheless. How does live-streaming Vatican Radio in Happy Hour sound?'

Outside the window a cockatoo screeched. The group all looked at each other, confused. Eventually Gene Sutherland started laughing again and said, 'Well, no weirder than an indoor creek.' His humour was farmy and infectious, and pretty soon he was gasping for air, with tears running down his cheeks, as we discussed my idea of the talking urinal. Kooka kept nodding and said that was all very well but that Nan was right, we'd have to know what we were doing with the grog, that someone'd have to take a real interest.

Big Gene thought this was stupendously funny. 'Don't think we'll have any trouble finding someone with a "real interest" in the grog, Kooka. There'd be more volunteers for that than ants on a lolly.'

'Well, actually, Gene,' I said, 'I was thinking that you'd make a pretty fine head barman. You could go on a full-time wage and keep the whole grog side ticking over.'

Gene Sutherland's family had run a dairy farm on the

slopes of the Barroworn River for five generations. It was only recently that he'd given up the ghost and leased the place out to a bloke who wanted to try olives. He had come over to the coast to live in Mangowak with his wife, Jen, and their two boys, with a hint of despair in those friendly eyes of his. There just hadn't been enough rain, and the big milk consortiums weren't looking after the small suppliers. I knew he'd been scratching around for work since he came to town. I also knew his expansive good cheer would be perfect behind the bar. He'd been a bit like a bull in a china shop in Mangowak so far – a lot of the new suburban blood just couldn't handle the sheer volume of him – but the freedom of The Grand Hotel would suit him just fine. It'd be like hand in glove.

For the first time that day Gene's features went blank. I think he was more shocked by the job offer than by any of the other ideas I'd presented during the meeting. His broad wind-bitten face settled still. Then he gradually started nodding his head, pushing his bottom lip up against his top lip in affirmation, until Nan Burns confirmed it. 'That's a great idea, Noel,' she said. 'You'd make a purler barman, Gene.'

'I agree,' said Kooka, solemnly. 'Gene'd be a natural mine host.'

'You'd have to watch your tipple, though,' Jim said with a wink.

A smile broke back out on Gene's face and he nodded in agreement at Jim. Then he said, 'Yeah. Why not, Noel? I'll give it a go. Never worked in a pub before. Especially not one with a talking pissoir.'

I was rapt. I might have been the publican but with Gene

Sutherland's agreement The Grand Hotel had found its lynch-pin and anchor, and there'd be no going back.

Fourteen Good Luck Spoons

KOOKA CAME GOOD WITH THE MONEY. HIS BEAUTIFUL OLD
shack, which he'd built with his own hands, sold within
two weeks of going on the market. He packed it all up, cup by
cup, sock by sock, and went through the heartbreaking task of
finally taking Mary's mothballed dresses and cardigans, slacks
and shoes, to the Minapre op shop. Big Gene, Darren Traherne
and I helped him move on a Tuesday, and despite the distance
between his place and mine being no more than a couple of
hundred metres we didn't finish hauling the boxes containing
the historical archive up to The Sewing Room until lunchtime
on the Wednesday. Completely buggered by then the three of
us and Kooka agreed that we should leave everything in the
boxes until he could muster enough energy to sort it out and set
it all back up.

Downstairs we hired friends to fit out the bar in the

kitchen and the toilets in the bathroom, all to health-and-safety-inspector guidelines. The old kitchen was just big enough to work with as the bar; we could squeeze enough of us in there to cook the meals and pour the drinks once the taps and drains had been installed in the hardwood benches. And our old L-shaped living room, which the benches gave onto, and which had been quite a modern feature when Papa had built it all those years ago, could fit enough of a crowd to warrant the moniker and mythical status of 'the public bar'.

Gene Sutherland was keen, happy to be employed again, and worked with the chippies, the refrigerator mechanics, the electricians and the plumbers on all the jobs. After each day's work he would sit with me and Kooka, Darren and Nan, among the tools and construction, where we would drink through a range of beers all micro-brewed in Australia to work out which one was gonna become our Grand Hotel Recommended Loosener – in other words, the beer on tap.

It was a strange form of connoisseurship we were developing, from hearsay, from internet notes, from our untrained local palates, and from our enjoyment of each other's company. We were sitting right in the lap of the riverflat of our home town, where the winds had blown the spring pollens about for thousands of years, constantly renewing the landscape, and with our new project we had a sense of something similarly fresh.

By the end of August the bulldozers had made short work of the gutted shell of the Mangowak Hotel back up on the hill above the valley, clearing the path for the eco-cluster that was to be Wathaurong Heights. Watching our old town living room being wiped from the landscape in a fury of mustard-coloured machinery and shrill reverse beeping was surreal. Meanwhile, down on the riverflat, my new found appreciation for the chief staple of the publican's trade, i.e. beer, was already blossoming. On many a night with big Gene and the others I sang old-timey drinking songs I had never up until then properly understood. Now, of course, after my weeks out in the clefts and overhangs, I knew that the famous old attitude 'Tonight we drink for tomorrow we may die' was just another way of acknowledging the power of a cackling deity.

Both Jim and Ash Bowen had worked in hotels when they were young, and before Nan had moved out to the farm with her kids and her ex-husband, Miles, she had worked part-time in restaurants in Minapre. They all now offered valuable advice. We decided, for instance, that there'd be no dinner menu but rather a different set dish every night that we'd serve as ballast against the booze. That way we'd be able to get by with just the small kitchen, as well as quashing any expectations the clientele might otherwise have had that they were gonna get some stylised epicurean/lifestyle experience.

The beers we tried were both good and bad, but because the general store still ran a small liquor section we felt free of any responsibility to provide the mainstream alcoholic necessities of the town and could keep our range small. All we wanted to supply was the meeting place. We cast a wide net around the new wave of micro-brewers. We drank paw-paw and coconut beer from Queensland, chocolate and cardamom stout from Western Australia, something called 'Crocodile Juice' from Borroloola in the Top End, Cloudy Sky Coriander Cider from Tasmania, Billy Tea Beer from the Flinders Ranges (which you drank hot with milk and which tasted so medicinal that Kooka ended up bathing his sun-cracked feet in it), and lots more. We had a couple of local contenders too: Darren Traherne's home brew, which was pretty much straight out of a Coopers Pale Ale kit but for some added boobialla currants, and another one that an intimidating fella by the name of Rennie Vigata, a retired bodyguard for one of Melbourne's underground figures, brewed out on the Poorool saddles and that seemed to benefit from the quality of the mountain water out there.

It was a great delight to me to learn that Rennie had called his beer 'The Dancing Brolga Ale', and as we tasted it I began to tell everyone about the performance I'd witnessed in the old camp out in the bush. To my surprise Nan assured me that the local brolga breeding program I'd presumed the bird was a product of had been called off. 'It couldn't have been,' I protested. 'I saw the bird with my own eyes.'

But Nan was adamant. 'Come off it, Noely,' she said. 'I was talkin' to a fella from the DSE just last week about it. He reckons they weren't ready in time for this season but might get their shit together next year. I dunno what you saw out there but it wasn't what you thought it was.'

I shook my head slowly and went silent. There was nothing I could say in reply. What I'd seen while sitting beside that campfire in the bush, real or imagined, was deep inside me now. It had reanimated me, perhaps even saved my life, and as I brought the glass of Rennie Vigata's beer to my lips I was for the time being too grateful to question it further. Plus, The Dancing Brolga Ale had an unmistakably lovely crispness and tang. It was no surprise to me, therefore, when it eventually became the unanimous choice as our Grand Hotel Recommended Loosener. For a while there in the ensuing months it was so popular in the hotel that Rennie Vigata joked with Gene that his life would be more relaxing if he was back working for the Mob.

In an unbelievable show of confidence at the final meeting before our opening day, Kooka brought fourteen of his souvenir teaspoons downstairs as good luck donations for the life of The Grand Hotel. I'd like to record here the full list of the teaspoons Kooka laid out that day on the bar, as a tribute to his friendship and also, I suppose, to boast that up until the fateful last night of the hotel's shenanigans not a single spoon of Kooka's was stolen, lost, or bent for the purposes of a seance. I'd also like to reiterate his logic as to why, even though he was the financial mainstay of the whole affair, he specifically donated the teaspoons rather than part of his locally famous beer-coaster collection. Simply enough it was because the spoons could be used without ruination. And as Kooka sagely said, 'People don't mind a tea or coffee in a pub these days.'

The fourteen spoons were as follows:

PLATYPUS SPOON – silver spoon with double-struck shell pattern engraved in bowl. The badge depicts a platypus swimming over a white wooden bridge under flood. Purchased at Gellibrand General Store, 1966.

WATERTANK SPOON – silver/nickel spoon, wattle embossed. Badge depicts a watertank standing alone in the middle of a sheep station at Wilcannia. Purchased by Kooka's brother-in-law Vin, at Hay, where he briefly settled after leaving the priesthood.

BIGGEST BABY IN VICTORIA SPOON – pewter and nickel-plated spoon depicting baby Willy Cooper, born weighing fourteen pounds on 13 April 1927 at St George's Hospital, Kew. Donated to Kooka's collection by the publican of the Inverleigh Hotel, who unwittingly offered Kooka the spoon to stir his tea after a very pleasant meal with Mary in the autumn of '61.

NED KELLY GOLD SPOON – gold-plated spoon purchased from Euroa Newsagency in 1994. The badge depicts a wistful Ned on the train journey south to the Melbourne Gaol, in the full beard of his captivity.

SYDNEY HARBOUR BRIDGE SPOON – electroplated nickel and silver spoon. Badge commemorates the opening of the bridge in 1932 with a picture taken on that momentous day. Purchased at Manly Beach in 1960 after a weekend with Mary visiting her brother Vin in the Catholic seminary there.

DES FOTHERGILL & HERBIE MATTHEWS 1940 BROWNLOW MEDAL SPOON – gold-plated spoon with elaborate scrolling and ornamentation around the badge. Depicts the only tied Victorian Football League Brownlow Medallists unable to be separated on a countback. Purchased by Kooka's father, Gil, at the Cathedral College fete in 1942. According to

Kooka this spoon was one of the few mementos of his dead father in his mother's possession when Kooka was growing up, and was the spoon that first sparked his interest.

OLD PIECE OF CLOTH SPOON – silver spoon depicting a 'very old piece of cloth', a historical exhibit from Kryal Castle, Ballarat, where it was purchased on a school excursion by Horny Conebush's grandson Joe in 1976.

GUNSYND THE GOONDIWINDI GREY SPOON – gold-plated spoon struck in Goondiwindi, Queensland, to celebrate the champion racehorse. Picture on the spoon depicts the local marble monument to Gunsynd. Purchased in Kuarka Dorla op shop, 1988.

PYRAMID HILL SPOON – blue-tinted silver-plated spoon depicting the Pyramid Hill west of Echuca. Delicate embossing of rock wallabies in the bowl. Purchased at Grassy, on King Island, 4 January 1968.

CEDAR OF LEBANON SPOON – brass-plated spoon featuring the trident shape of a lone cedar at the end of a half length filigreed handle. Purchased at the Queen Victoria Market, 1955. One of the first international spoons in Kooka's collection.

SEAGULL MONUMENT SPOON – silver/white opal spoon depicting the Seagull Monument on Temple Square in Salt Lake City, erected as a memorial to the seagulls that saved the Mormon crops from locusts during the swarms of 1848. Purchased by Mary at the Apollo Bay op shop in 1972.

YEHUDI AND HEPHZIBAH SPOON – electroplated nickel and silver spoon commemorating the Australian concert tour of Yehudi and Hephzibah Menuhin in 1940, Kooka's tenth year and his third with the Conebushes in Mangowak. Purchased in a second-hand shop in Rainbow, Southern Mallee, 1997.

TALLEST TREE IN GIPPSLAND SPOON – a metal spoon depicting a memorial pole erected after the tallest mountain ash in Gippsland was felled. Bartered for a cocker spaniel pup in Lang Lang, 1979.

'TRUCK ON' SPOON – silver spoon featuring an exhibition road rig on the badge. Kooka has no recollection of how he came by this very colourful spoon.

Our patron explained in his usual fastidious fashion that he'd given exactly fourteen spoons because the original Grand Hotel had burnt down after thirteen years' trading and he hoped that this time we would at least go one better. I had my doubts about the longevity of the kind of hotel I had planned but said nothing, of course, so touched was I by Kooka's gift from one of his most cherished collections.

Duchamp the Talking Urinal

ONCE THE BAR WAS FITTED OUT AND A COOLROOM ADDED in the loamy old space between the side wall of the house and the Dray Road hedge, it was time for Veronica and me to instigate our first creative flourish: Duchamp the Talking Urinal.

All those years ago when we were studying in Melbourne, Marcel Duchamp and the rest of the Dada gang had represented a creative spark that could defy the fads and fashions and never fade. Their attitude to making art had been so free and radical, so anti-everything and yet at the same time so inspired and full of life, that it remained fresh nearly a hundred years later. Despite their signature air of abundance and colour their great trick was actually one of renunciation and as such had something in common with the sages and hermits of old. By renouncing not only the world of capitalism but also the world of 'Art', the Dadaists had refreshed all the channels by which creative inspiration could come to them. They had made their spirits receptive again by casting all outmoded categories to the wind. In the end, rather than dusting off the furniture in the galleries and parlours of Europe they actually set fire to it and kept themselves warm by the blaze.

Relishing our time in the college studios as much as we did, like a lot of art students Veronica and I shared a particular dread of the written component of our course. Apart from anything else it seemed like such a waste of time to be writing cold sentences when we could be getting down to tin tacks with our own tactile inspirations in the studio itself.

So one day, near the end of our second year, when a deadline was looming for an essay concerning twentieth-century art movements, we had the brainwave to combine the writing of a piece on Dada with the creation of an actual readymade work of art. On an old chest of drawers we found abandoned in the back lane behind a Collingwood terrace house, we applied a thick layer of cadmium-red paint and then proceeded to write a joint essay all over it, about the different ways Dada had evolved in the various cities of Europe, and New York, during the years of the First World War and immediately afterwards. We covered the top, back, sides, and even the underneath of this chest of drawers with our colourful script, inserting tiny portraits of some of our favourite Dada artists in among the text, as well as miniature renditions of some of the most famous Dada readymades, including the most notorious of them all, Duchamp's *Fountain*, which famously consisted of a toilet bowl turned on its end, exhibited in the

1917 Society of Independent Artists show in New York under the name R. Mutt.

In the centre of each of the five drawers of the chest, between the simple art-deco steel handles, we constructed the name of five different Dada cities of significance from a mixture of rusty garden-rake teeth, old paint-brush handles, broken-up scissors, bird feathers and pipe cleaners. The cities we selected were Zurich, Hanover, Cologne, New York and Paris.

When you opened the drawers (being extra careful not to cut your hands on the dangerous names of the Dada cities), you would find a vivid riot of information about the exponents in each city, written and drawn onto the original flypaper inside.

The top drawer was of course the Zurich drawer, the birthplace of Dada, and its contents focused on Hugo Ball, Emmy Hennings, Hans Arp and Tristan Tzara, and the amazing groundbreaking performances that took place in the Cabaret Voltaire in 1916. The Hanover drawer was next, consisting largely of a loving and appropriately nonsensical ode to the greatest collage artist who ever lived, Kurt Schwitters. The Cologne drawer underneath that explored the connections between Dada and Surrealism through the junk-work of artists such as Max Ernst and Johannes Baargeld. The New York drawer was all about Duchamp's *Fountain* and the paintings of that relentless Italian, Francis Picabia, while the Paris drawer, which was at the bottom of the chest, told the obscure and extraordinary story of my personal favourite of the Dada artists, Arthur Cravan.

As much as I'd been enthralled by the goings on at the Cabaret Voltaire, the po-faced ironies of Duchamp and the joyous assemblages of Schwitters, the story of Arthur Cravan's freakish life had a physical reality to it that connected with me beyond the world of ideas and art. Cravan was not only a major Dada artist but amazingly he was also the heavyweight boxing champion of France and had actually fought against the great American Jack Johnson! Added to that he was Oscar Wilde's nephew. Cravan's crowning glory, however, was his death, which in all probability was by his own hand given that he sailed off the Mexican coast in a tiny boat, into waters known to be thoroughly shark infested, and was never seen again.

As a country boy studying in the city, I related to the contrast between Cravan's artistic creativity and his intensely physical life. The boxing, the sailing, even just the enormous size of the man seemed to set him apart as someone from out-side the square. He was raw, unavoidably physical, and unlike his famous uncle was only ever urbane when he chose to be. I remember spending hours lovingly attending to the drawer in his honour, writing out long enthusiastic quotes from his magazine *Maintenant*, which ran off the flypaper and up the sides of the bottom drawer, interspersed with small portraits of the bare-chested Cravan shaping up to the great Jack Johnson in his baggy boxing shorts and sailing off into the Pacific Ocean with sharks snapping at his boat's timbers. I spent hours making a large heading in Lissitzky-style block type, announcing that the great Arthur Cravan was in fact still alive and living in Australia. Rumours had abounded in Dada circles ever since he disappeared that he was still alive and kicking, and living under pseudonyms in New York or Berlin. Some had even gone so far as to claim that his enigmatic life continued even now, and was some miraculously defiant triumph of art over life, the ultimate rule-breaker, the greatest living Dada readymade of them all.

As late as 1987, a full seventy years after the Dada freedom virus was first unleashed in Zurich, the chest of drawers Veronica and I made caused quite a ruckus in the supposedly progressive art school on St Kilda Road in Melbourne. Of course all our friends thought our 'readymade essay' was inspired, but our immediate supervisor made the strange decision to refrain from marking it, thereby disqualifying us from that aspect of the course and jeopardising our results overall. In her typical style Veronica complained loudly about this and eventually our teacher was overruled by none other than the director of the college. We were given top marks for our 'thorough and felt understanding of the spirit of the Dada movement'. I'll never forget those words.

Not surprisingly this tiny scandal, and our ultimate victory, put a hot blast of wind in our sails, and for a time we felt self-initiated as members of the international Dada clan. We believed that we'd experienced our very own bonafide Dada moment, not just as voyeurs or mere students but as actual exponents, and looking back, in a small way, I suppose we had.

But now, after all those years, we were about to experience another Dada moment, and this time on a larger scale, outside the protection of an art institution, and supposedly as mature, fully grown adults. We were not in Paris or New York, or in Zurich, Hanover or Cologne, or even Sydney or Melbourne, but down south in the salty sticks. Understandably we were both incredibly excited and a little nervous about what was ahead.

Our idea for 'Duchamp' was that the urinal would talk when the piss hit the tin. And the words it would say would let it be known that, among other things, this was a hotel that did not suffer fools. In time out between drinks, between ravings and games, between drowning sorrows or arguments, the male patrons of The Grand Hotel would stand side by side to relieve their bladders to a soundtrack of the follies of the human world around them. There would be a talking-urinal audio archive, which anyone could contribute to, the only proviso being that the contribution had to in some way embody the effervescence of the Dada spirit. I'd already assembled a few samples to give everyone the idea and get the ball rolling, and on the day that Veronica's friend Seb from Bells & Whistles came to install the sensors and wire the room, I used one of my favourite items, 'The Irridex', for the demonstration.

'The Irridex' was a verbatim extract from the two-inch-thick annual *Tourism Management Manual*, and I'd had Kooka read it aloud into his old Grundig recorder. In a chapter of the manual dedicated to 'local disenchantment with tourism operations' and 'backstage lifestyles', a five-stage graph called 'The Irridex' is shown, to illustrate the process by which aspiring tourism operators could overcome local obstacles. It was explained in the manual that the word 'Irridex' was simply shorthand for 'Index of Local Irritation By Tourism'.

In his newsreely reading voice, Kooka had recited 'The Irridex' into the Grundig, which Seb from Bells & Whistles then transferred onto a digital loop that was hooked up to the sensors behind the urinal surface and could conceivably run for days on end. As Seb knelt by his equipment and gave the thumbs up, myself and Gene pulled out our willies and began to piss.

Voila! There it was:

The Index of Local Irritation By Tourism
or, put simply, THE IRRIDEX

THE IRRIDEX Stage One – EUPHORIA
Tourists provide good company and good monetary
returns for the local community.

THE IRRIDEX Stage Two – APATHY
The flow becomes larger, tourists are taken for granted,
interactions become formal and commercial.

THE IRRIDEX Stage Three – IRRITATION
Irritation is at the heart of the Irridex.

THE IRRIDEX Stage Four – ANTAGONISM
Social, cultural, and environmental carrying capacities
of the destination are exceeded.

THE IRRIDEX Stage Five – RESIGNATION
Resignation sets in. Residents realise they must adapt
to a drastically altered community setting.

I've got to admit that right there and then you could've read the phone book onto the loop and it would've been funny, just from the crazy buzz of getting Duchamp to work. Big Gene's eyes were popping as he pissed, and he kept shaking his head in wonder. Eventually, when we zipped up, Seb himself couldn't resist having a go just so we could hear it again. He kept nodding and smiling as his bright-yellow stream re-triggered 'The Irridex'. As he stepped down, he said he was quite happy with the technical quality but thought the volume of the loop could be raised. He pointed out that, given it was a unisex toilet, the loop had to be loud enough for the women to hear it clearly from the cubicles. 'Otherwise,' he said, with an effeminate flourish, 'all that eloquence will just be wasted on the men.'

That night, when the usual visitors came round to continue sampling the beers, Duchamp the Talking Urinal was a big hit. Everyone kept heading off through the sunroom to try it again, and at one stage Oscar, Nan, Veronica, Darren, Ash and his wife, Vita, were all in there drinking in the toilet, while Gene and I were alone with Frankie in the new bar, giggling and dipping our fingers into the peanuts.

No Sheep No Shenanigans No Service

LIKE A GOOD OMEN THE FLOWERING GUM NEXT TO MY barn was miraculously ablaze with red flowers when I woke up on the day of The Grand Hotel's reopening. I went straight outside and hoisted Dad's telescopic aluminium ladder up against the tree to pick top-branch flowers for the vases. They were iridescent, fibrous, supreme. Then I took my time over breakfast – a boiled pullet egg, abalone splashed with lemon juice and champagne – and pottered around the old place with Pippy on my last day of relative privacy.

From the outside on that first morning nothing much looked different. We hadn't painted the house, nor cleaned up the yard. Joe the old palomino still hovered near the disused aviary where I kept his chaff, the wire clothes line and bean trellis still ran along the apple and blackwood trees on the eastern boundary, and around the front near the hedge all we'd done was put in a few striped gymkhana wheels as beer-garden tables, and sturdy old couta boxes as seats. The only noticeable changes from the outside were the new coolroom on the Dray Road side of the house, and the blue and yellow floral curtains Nan insisted on putting in the windows of the upstairs bedrooms; oh, yes, and also the little wooden sign Darren had carved in beechwood and tacked above the door:

THE GRAND HOTEL. LICENSEE: N. LEA
NO SHEEP NO SHENANIGANS NO SERVICE

The first interesting thing that happened on the opening night was when Kooka unwittingly changed Gene Sutherland's name to Joan. We'd been open since three and, what with the word around town and the instant success of Duchamp the Talking Urinal, the place was nearly full only half an hour after the tradesman's knock-off of 4.30. I soon realised that the sunroom was gonna become a favourite hangout, running between the bar and Duchamp as it did. Men and women kept emerging from the dunny doing up their overalls or rearranging their hair with either astounded or amused looks on their faces at what they'd just experienced. The stock country phrase was 'Well, it's different'.

Of course they couldn't quite get their heads around us boarding up the ocean-facing windows in the bar either and when Happy Hour began at 5.30 with Pope Benedict's angelus live-streaming on Vatican Radio from St Peter's Square in Rome, the heads were shaking thick and fast. But the drinks were going down fast too. Rennie Vigata's Dancing Brolga Ale was much approved of, and everyone seemed genuinely happy to have somewhere local to drink again.

As the early hours of that first afternoon passed and people stopped to look at some of the stuff we'd put up around the walls, and as they talked to Darren or Nan or me about what was going on, the goodwill was beginning to turn into good cheer. By 6.30, when the Vatican Radio was exchanged for Jacques Delors videos on YouTube and the first plates of our opening-night entrée, whiting rollmops, were being handed around, the good cheer was really taking off. At 7.30, as new locals kept turning up to check it all out, we paused the proceedings to read out The Grand Hotel Charter. It was brief and to the point.

Kooka stood in front of the bar, his bronzed shoulders shining under the bleached hoops of his white singlet, and as he flicked the 'record' switch on the old Grundig we called for a bit of shoosh.

'The Grand Hotel Charter has four main components, each of which commence from tomorrow,' Kooka began. 'NUMBER ONE: in keeping with the original Grand Hotel that stood right here on this site, and that caught fire over one hundred years ago, no light beer will be served. The Dancing Brolga it is, ladies and gents. And stubbies of your choice, within reason of course. NUMBER TWO: as there is no car park provided on the grounds, drinks will be twenty per cent cheaper to those customers who have walked or ridden their bikes. This has nothing to do with political correctness and everything to do with lack of space. NUMBER THREE: The Grand Hotel, at the discretion of the owner and his committee, will close during long weekends and holiday periods. Make of this what you will but consider that the architecture of Noel's old house is hardly equipped to cope with the summertime hordes of the Showcase Coast. And lastly NUMBER FOUR: in The Grand Hotel mirth is the object and liquor the licence. Gentlemanly conduct is considered preferable and the more good natured the conversation the more nuts will appear in your bowl. The licensee, Noely here, has asked me to pass on that any objections, enquiries or even commendations on the way the hotel is run should be directed to Frankie the Canary or his spaniel, Pippy. Each evening after stumps Noel has promised he will sit down with Frankie and Pippy, share a few cuttle and chop bones, and discuss the issues. Thanks, ladies and gents. Enjoy yourselves and please let's raise a toast to the reopening of The Grand Hotel, Mangowak!'

As the throng crowding the bar and spilling out into the sunroom raised their glasses and began to discuss the charter, seriously debating its points and laughing at what seemed a preposterous situation, Kooka turned with a beaming face to Gene behind the bar and called, 'A claret please, Joan.'

It was a numinous moment, also an unwitting augury of events to come. The natural historian had forgotten where he was, or rather, in the excitement of his unlikely but bright idea being realised, of history being made and him being part of it, he'd forgotten what year we were in. For a split second time had vanished in his midst and Kooka had been back in the original Grand. Perhaps it was 1893, perhaps it was 1897; either way he was ordering his drink not from big Gene Sutherland but from Joan Sweeney.

Veronica pounced. 'Of course!' she cried, turning her back from the stove full of sizzling pappadums. 'Joan Sutherland. What could be a more fitting name for the barman of The Grand?'

In the hubbub and noise only a few thirsty drinkers near the bar heard this exchange but it was enough to make the nickname stick. Much to his own amusement, and to the embarrassment of his two young boys, Dylan and Doug, from that day on Gene Sutherland became Joan Sutherland and The Grand Hotel had a dairy-farmer diva as its head barman. And as for Kooka, well, he couldn't believe his luck.

Whether it was The Grand Hotel Recommended Looseners, the talking urinal, or simply the fact that the hotel still felt and looked as relaxed as a house, things went from strength to strength on that first night. The weather was calm, and by 9 pm we'd opened the boarded-up double doors and spilt out into the garden behind the tea tree hedge. We had no PA so Jim and Oscar's ragtag band of local mates, The Barrels, who were well used to improvising at weddings and surf-club events, just played through amplifiers out on the grass and the dancing began.

We cooked cayenne rabbit as the main course, in three huge pots on the stove behind the bar, and you wouldn't believe how many people kept saying they hadn't tasted rabbit for years. They thoroughly approved of the recipe and thought it went down well with the Dancing Brolgas. Speaking of which, Rennie Vigata turned up in his monstrous black Chevy van on that opening night. It looked like a cross between a vehicular version of an Anselm Kiefer painting and something straight out of *Mad Max*. Rennie was equally as scary and as a joke he pinned me up against the wall in the bar and dared me to charge him full price for a Laphroaig whisky on account of the fact that he'd driven to the pub and was thus ineligible for the walker's discount.

In the raspy baritone of a man who at some point in his past had experienced a deft karate chop to the vocal cords, he said, 'You're prejudicing the hills, Noel. Do you know how long it would take for me to walk here?'

Angling his powerful bodyguard's forearm, he held me tight in under the cuckoo clock and the catfish skeleton on the wall. One thing was for sure: he didn't know his own strength. Surely, I thought, he would realise from past experience that I was about to choke.

Eventually Rennie let me go with a sneering smile. I gulped in the air. There's nothing like the fear of a premature death to inspire you and I had an inspiration right on the spot. Feigning great forethought, I explained to him (and to myself I might add) The Grand Hotel's very own Bonafide Traveller scheme. In the old days, of course, when hotels shut with the six o'clock swill due to the wowserish early licensing laws, a bonafide traveller was allowed to drink to his heart's content in any hotel beyond closing time. Now, as I explained to Rennie, The Grand Hotel had revived the concept but with a twist. Anyone drinking at The Grand who'd come from over fifteen kilometres away was exempt from the price penalties of driving their car.

'There you go,' I said to Rennie, feeling some normality coming back into the area of my larynx. 'As if we'd ever not think of you hillbillies up there. You get the discount. And an extra feed as well, being our main beer supplier.'

I stood with Rennie and his tall dark girlfriend, Lee, at the bar then, as Joan Sutherland poured the Laphroaig for him and a Bundy and Coke for her. Joan and I bashed their ears about how well The Dancing Brolga Ale was going and Rennie seemed quite chuffed. He skulled his dram, stood back, and looked around the room from his great height. 'Pretty weird bar you got here, Noel,' he rasped.

'Yeah?' I replied. 'What's so weird?'

'Well for a start it just looks like a living room with extra tables and chairs. There's no TAB, there's weird shit all over the walls, you've boarded up the fuckin' windows and, for once, everyone looks like they're having a great time.'

'It's the beer, Rennie,' said Joan, as he poured him another Laphroaig. 'The Dancing Brolgas.'

Rennie snorted and gave Lee a smiling wink. 'Thought as much,' he said, proudly. 'Well, there's plenty more where that came from.'

Big Rennie'd come to regret those words.

Despite the announcement that any feedback should be addressed to Frankie and Pippy, as the night progressed into the late hours people started to come up to me to talk about what was going on. I was uncompromising in my answers, stressing the fact that without The Grand Hotel there would be no hotel anymore in Mangowak and because it was my hotel I'd run it how I liked. The only concession I made was when Joan Sutherland's wife, Jen, quietly suggested that the 'no light beer' rule was a bit hard on the oldies. She said they drank light not only because of drink-driving concerns but also for health reasons. She said some of them were diabetics, some had dodgy tickers. I said that was fair enough and that not everyone could put it away like Kooka. We agreed right there and then to amend the charter to include light beer for people born before the Black Friday bushfires of 1939. It was as good a cut-off point as any.

Most of the discussions I had, though, were positive, and inebriated. Givva Way for one was inspired. The town earbasher had been a bit quiet of late, bewildered as he was by the Plinths, the indoor creek and Wathaurong Heights, but now he was off, full of praise for The Grand and swooning reminiscences of the old Mangowak pub in the 1970s. He raved on about all the bands that used to come through on their tours to Adelaide. He brought up the time that he and my brothers Walker and Jim had smoked bongs all night with Colin Hay from Men At Work. Their famous song 'Down Under' had twenty-seven verses back then, Givva told me, not for the first time. Eventually, after slapping me on the back with his thick house-painter's hand, he said, 'Better go off and have another chat to Duchamp.'

It is proof of my simple pleasures in the days of The Grand Hotel that you couldn't wipe the smile off my face after hearing Givva Way say those words.

By midnight I was dancing with Nan Burns to The Barrels' version of the theme from the cartoon *Top Cat* and couldn't care less about anything. We were already an hour over the licence, Dylan and Dougie Sutherland had taken to pouring beers behind the bar under their father's guidance, and the general mess was incredible. I could see Veronica and Darren and Jen Sutherland busily trying to tidy up. Plates and glasses were strewn everywhere, beer and wine were spilt and ashtrays were overflowing in the sunroom and beyond. It was obvious we had a bit to learn but for now I was content to dance with Nan, to watch the new grey strands in her red hair fall across her face, to smoke her rollies, and to think about it all tomorrow.

The Blonde Maria

THE MORNING AFTER THAT FIRST NIGHT I WAS AWOKEN in my barn-loft at six o'clock sharp by wattlebirds doing power-saw impersonations. Groaning, I waited for them to stop but no, they were in for the long haul. So I propped myself up on some pillows, got comfortable, and ran the last night's events over again in my mind. Somewhere along the line the wattlebirds must've stopped, because I dozed off, and when I awoke it was nine o'clock and I felt grateful for the extra sleep. I climbed down the ironbark ladder, got dressed, and like some honorary treasurer of old decided I had better attend to the banking.

There's never any mention in Hugo Ball's diary account of the Cabaret Voltaire of who managed the Dada money and how. Presumably they just cut all the banknotes up for collages and used the coins as gypsy necklaces. For The Grand Hotel, however, the money was siphoned off into a black Aquila shoebox at the end of each night. This shoebox was then taken under my arm out to the barn when I went to bed, where I placed it inside an old canvas fishing bag flung into a corner full of rods and nets and reels. I dimly remembered now that when I did this the night before for the very first time, the shoebox was immediately filled to overflowing.

After counting the money and placing it in its denominations, a sudden wave of emotion hit me where I sat at my desk. Before I knew what was happening, giant teardrops had begun to fall from my eyes, running down my cheeks and rolling off my jaw and onto the money. I was silent – there was no whimpering, not even a sigh – but the tears were giant sized and kept coming nevertheless. After a good ten minutes of this I felt just like a cow who'd been milked. Those tears obviously had to come out. Otherwise, given all the excitement of the time, I might have foundered or developed mastitis and ruined things for everyone.

By the time the globulous tears had stopped, the top layers of that first night's takings were drenched. I lifted a dripping 'crayfish' – our local nickname for the orange twenty-dollar note – to my nose. It smelt salty, like the sea. 'Oh well,' I reasoned, trying to flick some moisture away with my finger. 'It's still legal tender – whether it's bathed in tears or not.'

I gathered it all up, placed it back in the Aquila box in its piles and headed off in Kooka's Brumby round the coast road to Minapre to put it in the bank.

By the time I got back home, I felt fresh as a wild freesia. Pulling into the drive, I switched off the ignition and immediately heard the bells clanging on their Plinths at the rivermouth. But then I heard laughter and singing from around the front on the verandah. I made my way inside, popped the empty shoebox into the cupboard under the cutlery-drawer cash register, and went out the front to investigate the mirth.

Seated around the table on the verandah, where a thirsty clique of Boat Creek lifesavers had been ensconced in their bright polar fleeces and zinc cream the previous night, were Joan Sutherland, Kooka, and the musical and housekeeping saviour I'd been waiting for: The Blonde Maria.

The last thing I had wanted was for the original edge of The Grand Hotel to be blunted by The Barrels' endless homages to Dick Dale, 1960s cartoon themes, and the *Morning of the Earth* soundtrack. So, after running it by Jim the week before we had opened, and not realising I was about to kill two birds with one stone, I had rung my friend Dean Kelly up in Dookie to locate his little sister Mary, who since leaving the family farm had become quite a sensation in the most high-cred pockets of the Melbourne music scene. My perhaps fanciful idea was that Mary might like to come down to The Grand from time to time to front The Barrels and keep us and them on our musical toes.

When I got hold of Mary on the phone, she explained to me how she only made ends meet by cleaning big houses around Brighton and St Kilda during the day while performing under the name of The Blonde Maria at night. Sounding a little burnt out by the hectic pace of her city life, and being a country girl at heart, she unexpectedly jumped at my offer. In fact she asked me right away if I thought there was any chance of it becoming a permanent arrangement! Then, to sweeten the deal, she suggested that she could help us out by doing a spot of cleaning around the hotel during the days as well.

When I'd put the phone down, I could've jumped for joy. But when she didn't turn up for the opening night as she'd promised, I'd written off the arrangement as just a momentary flight of bohemian fancy on her behalf. Now, however, out on the verandah, Kooka had the Grundig propped up on the table, with its Bakelite 'record' button on, as The Blonde Maria, dressed in a three-quarter flared floral dress, with jeans on underneath and a pale green headscarf, was in full song. She had a half empty stubby of Heineken in front of her, a half dozen or so empty ones standing beside that, a cigarette poised between her fingers in mid-air, and her voice was pipey, in a tremulous way, but strong, a throaty flute. Kooka and Joan both were loving it.

I hadn't seen Dean Kelly's little sister since she was seventeen but now, ten years later, she had not only changed her name but also grown into an attractive young woman, with a big-jointedness about her that would have appealed to the bullockies back in the droving days. She had quite the presentation too – let's just say she was not afraid of showing off her attributes, which of course would have also appealed to those bullockies of yore. They say some women have a way with men, the common touch, but often it's just big breasts. And if they can sing as well, wow, the cocktail can be genuinely explosive.

A man like Joan Sutherland, for instance, can get confused in the crossfire. I could see at the table that he was having trouble choosing exactly what it was he wanted to concentrate on, the song or the freckled cleavage. In the end I think he realised that if he didn't waver too much, if he just locked his stare on the freckles and left it there, then his ears would be freed up to listen as well. Nevertheless it was quite a strain and by the time the song was finished I think the big boy from the banks of the Barroworn was well and truly exhausted.

The Blonde Maria stood up and opened her arms wide to embrace me. 'Young Mary Kelly,' I said, whispering in her ear, 'you're a sensation.'

'Noel!' she cried. 'The Grand Hotel is amazing. These two lovely fellas have already given me a guided tour.'

'You like it?'

'Oh yeah, it's glorious. I rang to tell Dean and he said to say you should think about a franchise.'

I scoffed at her brother's joke. He'd always enjoyed having a lend of me. 'How long have you been here?' I asked her.

Kooka piped up. 'Since the crack, Noel. She let herself in and woke us upstairs with her whistling around seven. Joan had flopped here after the big night but we were happy to have an early breakfast, weren't we, Joan? And we haven't regretted it. We've already recorded an account of her family connection to Ned Kelly.'

'Is that right?'

'Oh yeah,' Kooka said, hardly able to contain his enthusiasm for a buxom lass from the normally health-conscious younger generation who was prepared to drink with him from daybreak. 'The Blonde Maria's great-great-grandfather gave Ned the horse he rode to Glenrowan.'

The Blonde Maria beamed my way. 'Dean's told you that, hasn't he, Noel? Why are you looking so surprised?'

I smiled and shook my head. 'Oh no, it's not that. I'm just amazed at Joan and Kooka's resilience. We had a pretty huge one last night, you know, and I would've thought . . .'

'Oh there's no fear there,' Kooka interrupted. 'This girl's a tonic. She makes me feel like the state of Victoria's just a tiny little community again. Listen to this.'

Kooka's thick bent-knuckled fingers fumbled with the buttons on the Grundig, rewinding the tape until the numbers on the time-code meter settled in the right combination. He pushed 'play'.

'Yes, my dear fellows, our great-great-grandfather, Black Jack they called him, played cards right through the 1870s with Ned on the family farm. From before he was on the run until right at the height of his fame.'

The Blonde Maria's voice on the tape was full of theatrics, as if she was holding court to rapt attention in a hollow windowless cairn on a windswiped peat bog.

'We're a horsing family, going way back to Tipp, and the story goes that Ned made a special trip to our farm to find a horse *reliable* enough, and with enough *pluck*, to help him declare the Republic of North Eastern Victoria on that fateful day at Glenrowan. Of course it's not all family folklore. It has been recorded *officially* that the horse that Black Jack gave to Ned was found making its way back to Dookie in the days after the siege.'

Kooka clicked off the Grundig, saying fervently, 'And that's a bloody long way, Noel, from Glenrowan to Dookie, a bloody long way for a horse on its own.'

'Yes,' said The Blonde Maria. 'And what I didn't say on the

tape is that when the horse arrived back at the farm, Black Jack changed its name to Pigeon, for two very obvious reasons. One, because it'd made its way home by its own instinct, and two, because he suspected the police might come sniffing around, looking for clues. Some people were saying that Ned called for the horse as he fell to the ground in his suit of Cantonese ploughshares.'

'Pigeon, eh?' said Joan, fascinated and approving. 'Good name for a horse too. Can I get you another drink, Maria?'

The Blonde Maria glanced quickly at her Heineken, saw it was only a quarter full and said coquettishly, 'Yes please, my dear. And I hope that you'll join me.'

On top of all her other attributes it seemed The Blonde Maria also had a prodigious capacity for drink. If I had half a dozen Dancing Brolgas as we sat on the verandah that morning, she must have had at least that amount, plus the Heinekens she drank before I arrived. I'd never seen anything like it in a girl her age. By one o'clock, after a solid three hours' drinking, I could see that Joan and Kooka were positively over the moon about the arrival of our capricious new chanteuse and cleaner. But with opening time approaching, I decided that I'd had enough and coaxed Maria away to show her upstairs to her room. As we headed for the narrow stairs, she refused help with her heavy pack, and she didn't miss a single step as we ascended.

We reached the second storey of The Grand Hotel unharmed and found the wide airy hallway punctuated with shafts of northern light, spilling out from the open doorways of the three bedrooms. The shafts of light fell in rhomboids, half upon the decorous old carpet and half up the willow wallpaper opposite. With The Dancing Brolga Ale coursing through my veins, it seemed the old swirl of platypus and duck in the carpet had come to life in the animating light – the hallway was in motion, with the ducks at play in the eddies and whirls of creekwater, the platypus dunking and flipping on the surface and the willows of the wallpapery banks rustling ever so gently in the breeze.

We waded across this scene, The Blonde Maria peering into each room as we went, until she chose the farthest one along next to The Sewing Room, as I was sure she would, it being the most private.

We stepped into the room through a grainy shaft of sun. She slung her pack onto the single bed and looked around delighted. I went over to the sash window and raised it with its customary shudder, then propped it in place with a three-inch nail.

Up there on the second storey, at the same height as the two big driveway pines, the sappy perfume of the old trees was close and sweet. They'd been planted way back in the days of the original Grand Hotel, and as a child I used to clamber out of the upstairs windows and risk my limbs jumping from the hardwood sills onto the branches of the tree closest to the house. High in that tree there'd always be some bird nesting, a magpie, or a nankeen night heron; if time existed at all up there, it was only as a cycle of nature. Now as I looked out, there was no activity in the heavy green fronds and flaky old branches, just the eternal stillness of the needles and the cones. I let myself drift for a moment in a kind of happy swoon until from the spouting above me came a light sprinkling of rainwater. A trio of honeyeaters were taking their afternoon wash.

I turned back into the room and found The Blonde Maria suddenly, instinctively, sound asleep on the bed.

I stood for a minute, looking at her. She was no longer the teenager I remembered sulking on the farm at Dookie. No, she was quite something, and I was so glad she'd arrived.

I checked that she'd have everything she'd need when she awoke: a jug of water, an ashtray, some tea near the kettle on the dresser, a towel, and some old records she might like. In the cabinet space provided under the old three-in-one turntable I saw a few things that might take her fancy: *Charles Aznavour Live at Carnegie Hall*, *Different Class* by Pulp, Tim Buckley's *Starsailor*. Then I quietly slipped out of the wallpapered room and back into the hallway, closing the door quietly behind me.

A New Use for Frankincense

FOR THE SECOND NIGHT OF THE HOTEL WE CHANGED THE recording in Duchamp, swapping 'The Irridex' with a piece called 'Lifeline to the Perfect Man'. Like the night before I got Kooka to read it onto tape in his warbly old-timer's voice:

> If you experience no sexual problems whatsoever or are
> living happily in a loving long-term relationship, you
> could well be feeling isolated in contemporary society.
> This could pose all types of problems but is nothing to
> be ashamed of; we all want to feel like we belong.

> Please call our free number here at The Grand Hotel
> to talk with us and work through your issues.

> And remember: true happiness is a lonely place.

Once again, when we opened at three, people were hell-bent on drinking fast just so they could hear what Duchamp had to tell them. And like on the opening night, when the tradesmen arrived after knock-off at 4.30, you could have sold tickets to get into the toilet. They thought 'Lifeline to the Perfect Man' was, once again, a pisser.

On the verges and banks of the grassy ditches all around the house there were half as many cars and utes as the previous night, but just as many people inside the hotel. The cut rate for walkers and cyclists had chimed in nicely and an unexpected by-product was that Greg Beer, our local coppa, congratulated me on what he thought was a masterstroke in the battle against drink-driving.

Greg Beer's personality will always be defined for me by the fact that back at primary school he chose to spend his lunchtimes picking up papers in the yard while the rest of us were hounding bluetongue lizards or throwing water bombs. 'Before you get too carried away,' I said to the wiry sergeant in the bar, 'tonight we're calling for contributions towards our "Clippin' the Eucalyptus Film Night". We're gonna show as many examples as we can get of legendary drink-driving escapades captured on people's home movies. You know, picnics being sideswiped, bogged Holden station wagons, utes in creekbeds. And plenty of people just driving along, without a care in the world, playing a tune with their zigzagging vehicles on the leaves of the roadside gums. You'd be aware yourself, Greg, that there's bound to be a bumper crop.'

Greg Beer frowned at me. 'And why would you wanna do

that for, Noel? Just when I thought you were making some kind of valid community contribution.'

I laughed. 'Oh this'll be a great contribution, Greg. It's the gathering of local history. Speak to Kooka about it, he'll tell you. You shouldn't deny your past after all. You shouldn't cover over your history, should you? Well, there'll be none of that at The Grand Hotel, I can assure you of that, Sergeant.'

Greg Beer gave me one of his squinty looks, as if he thought I was barking mad. In actual fact we both knew the truth was a little more complex. I had just touched a raw nerve. Greg Beer and his sister Susan had had a hard time being raised by their alcoholic mother, Meryl, in their fibro house up on Carroll Street, and at times Greg's whole subsequent life as an abstemious policeman seemed like one hugely determined effort to erase the memory. No doubt the image of his poor mum slumped over the green Coolabah cask in the Carroll Street kitchen was in both our minds as we agreed to disagree over the drink-driving question in the bar.

That second night was packed, uproarious, with The Blonde Maria thoroughly enjoying meeting everyone in the bar, particularly the members of The Barrels, and all the locals seeming to enjoy encountering the oddities of the establishment. I actually spent a lot of that night in The Horse Room playing pool. This was the room at the bottom of the stairs beyond the sunroom, where my elder brothers had slept when we were young. It was called The Horse Room because in the days before my grandfather built the barn he used to mend saddles, bits, bridles and halters in there on an unusual myrtle-beech bench he had fixed under the high strip of louvre windows running all the way down its eastern wall. Even in later years, when Bernard and Walker slept in there, Papa liked to keep all the paperwork concerning the horses in a trunk under the bench, as well as his meteorological records, and he'd sit in there of an evening after dinner, mumbling to himself and poring over the contents of the trunk, telling my brothers stories when they were meant to be doing their homework, tales of bogged horses and rogue waves and legendary runs of weather on the coast, until Mum or Dad would come and shoo him out, back to the fire in the living room or to his own bedroom upstairs.

For the sake of the hotel we'd decked The Horse Room out with Papa's old prints of dogs playing snooker, his Common Seabirds posters, and a few other choice pieces, like the collage Donny Johnston from Minapre had made with a mako shark's jaw framing a picture of unsuspecting swimmers at the starting line of the 1997 Mangowak to Minapre Ocean Swim. In the corner of the picture Donny had scrawled in fat Artline texta, 'Yum Yum!' He had this piece along with a few other of his parochial creations stored in a back room behind the freezers at the Minapre Fishermen's Co-Op, and I'd persuaded him to let us have it on loan. First-timers at The Grand always got a good cack out of it and of course shark stories became a talking point.

I'd moved our old couches into The Horse Room too, and Dad's old dragnet hung from the roof, with the corks still down one side and the sinkers down the other, and still with the dried strips of sea lettuce tangled in its web from the last time we'd ever dragged it: 16 March 1994. That was the night Greg Beer told us we'd had our last warning – one more time and we'd cop a big fine. Not that that stopped him from accepting the three mullet we gave him to take home and cook for himself and poor old Meryl.

Both the legendary dragnet on the roof and Donny's Yum Yum picture on the wall acted as tall-tale triggers in The Horse Room, as did Kooka's ingenious and colourful map of what the local area would look like after the projected sea-level rises due to global warming. Kooka's map was especially curious from my point of view as the big transparent pink sprawl of his reckonings with the highlighter pen showed that if you were up on the ridges on either side of the valley in years to come you would still be high and dry, whereas the riverflat itself, including the five little shops, the old plasterer's shed and the woodyard, not to mention the main road, would be well and truly inundated. A pink-highlighted mass of new water surged across the gradually thinning blue river as well as the green catchment area of the flats, showing clearly that if you expected to look at that exact same map on that exact same wall of The Grand Hotel in fifteen years' time you'd need a pretty decent snorkel.

Kooka's big map dominated Papa's long bench wall in The Horse Room, but right alongside it was a smaller picture, tiny in fact, hung in an *el cheapo* chemist-shop frame, which attracted just as much attention. This picture quickly came to be known in the days of the hotel as 'Where's Wally?', and it had arrived mysteriously as a JPEG in my email inbox one day from an unknown source. It was a photo of the town, reconstructed in Photoshop to look like it would have before, or just after, white settlement. Whoever made the image must have had horticultural knowledge, because where nowadays the five shops sit between the main road and the riverbank, all had been erased and replaced with very complex, authentic looking flora. Running down the slope from the meteorological station headland (in the picture, of course, there was no meteorological station, nor any navigational light), the bearded heath bunched into a valley devoid of today's infrastructure. Where the bottom shops terminate at Bon Thompson's brown-brick glazier's business, all you could see was a tongue of the heath giving on to the chartreuse reeds and rushes around the inlet. There was no road, no cars, only tufted sedge. No 'Total Fire Ban' sign swinging in a northerly, no mown verges, no gratuitous bollards, just the river running seawards with the sky in its surface, the egret's backwash in the foreground, and in the background, on the treeline of the headland, the only giveaway that the picture wasn't real: the spiky outline of a non-native cypress tree silhouetted against the blue sky.

It quickly became a game in The Horse Room for people to test each other to find this telltale cypress in the picture, hence the 'Where's Wally?' nickname. I'd wondered ever since I'd received the email if the cypress was left there on purpose, like the Amish always leave one mistaken stitch in a quilt to acknowledge that only God is perfect. It was reassuring to think that someone in Mangowak had the combination of spiritual and technological savvy required to not just reconstruct the inlet but also include the intentional flawed stitch of the cypress.

I came and went from The Horse Room on that second night, between shifts helping Joan in the bar or doing the rounds picking up glasses or restocking fridges from the coolroom. As stumps approached, I sat on the orange couch in there just taking it all in. Occasionally people would sit down beside me to give me their two bob's worth, and most of them had already picked up that The Grand Hotel represented a new way to cope with not only the absurdities of life but also what was happening in the town in particular. I must admit I found it peculiarly Australian how even people who'd always been pro-development seemed to be enjoying the Dada vibe of the pub. The existence of a new waterhole seemed to override any philosophical differences we might have had. Well, it is a dry country after all.

It was the very next night, however, the third night of The Grand Hotel, when we encountered our first real challenge, not so much to the existence of the place but to the idea and philosophy behind it.

With The Blonde Maria still upstairs snoring off her huge first day of drinking, we opened again at three, despite Joan running a little bit late due to his own Maria-inspired massive hangover. Kooka and I looked after the bar until he arrived. The loop in Duchamp had been refreshed again, but this time I had changed tack. 'Lifeline to the Perfect Man' was replaced with a subtle bleating quote about the proliferation of laziness and the lack of farming craft in the early days of the colony of Victoria:

> The furrows are ill-drained, the wheat is ill-thatched,
> thrashing is performed in open air on the ground, much
> corn is shed in the field, rotation of crops is never
> observed, variety of produce is not recorded, roads are

left unattended, and worst of all, no economy of labour
is observed . . . I once saw five men merely standing
around, looking on at a bee swarming!

Not surprisingly this offering from Duchamp produced more bewilderment and confusion than hilarity, and in fact I did overhear some of the tradesmen express outright disappointment at it early in the night. None of us had any way of knowing, however, just how pertinent the loop would become only a little later that evening.

It was around 7 pm – I know that because Happy Hour had finished half an hour earlier – when the posse from Wathaurong Heights arrived. There were six of them, two in grey suits, one in a blue suit, another in a mustard double-breasted suit and the other two dressed casually in chinos, polo shirts and jackets. The two in the grey suits carried hard plastic folders under their arms, the guy in the mustard suit had a laptop, the blue-suited fella carried a sheaf of papers rolled into a cylinder and the two casually dressed guys held only their mobile phones.

The posse went straight up to the bar and asked for a table. Joan Sutherland, a little less genial than normal due to his Heineken headache, merely said, 'Take your pick.'

The posse turned at the bar and cast their eyes around the room. All of the four-seater laminated tables were full, but one end of the big communal dining-room table was free nearby.

The shorter of the two casually dressed men turned back to the bar and said politely, 'Do you serve meals? We'd like to sit down and have dinner.'

He was in his mid to late forties, well-built, tanned and

with the rounded vowels common among successful Melbourne businessmen with an interest in yachting.

Big Joan managed a smile and said, 'We do meals but not by request, mate. There's a set dish every night and later on in the evening we fire up some snacks on the house – you know, toasted sangers, smoked-trout pastas – just as ballast against the grog. I think tonight's main course is fricaséed bandicoot. No, only joking. Tonight we've got baked lemon lamb with Greek salad. You're more than welcome.'

The posse's elegant spokesman raised his eyebrows, smiled thinly and glanced towards his friends. After a quick consultation he turned back to Joan and said they wouldn't mind paying for their food if we could offer them a menu.

Joan Sutherland let out one of his loud good-natured country laughs and simply reiterated what he'd already told them.

Once again the posse consulted, and the tanned yachtsman turned to Joan and enquired as to what time the lamb would be served.

'Pretty darn soon I think,' said our head barman, turning to Veronica at the stove behind him. 'How long, Ronnie?'

Veronica didn't answer, and I could see from where I was standing under the window near the sink that her profile was in full scowl.

Joan turned back to the posse, nonplussed. 'Look, I know it's a slow cook this dish but geez, it's already been in there four hours. So anytime now I'd say. Why don't you order some drinks, take a seat and relax? We'll look after you.'

Once again the suits consulted with the polo shirts and eventually, after much head-swivelling and squinting at the pictures and maps and slogans on the walls, they conceded to take up Joan's offer.

Next they asked about the beers and the fella in the mustard suit said he'd actually heard good things about The Dancing Brolga Ale. That was interesting. Nevertheless the others were keen on a little more research and began quizzing Joan at length about what else was available. Eventually, with the mustard suit's encouragement, they decided against the monastery-brewed Belgian Pilsener and agreed to sample The Dancing Brolga. Fortuitously for them the whole dining-room table had been vacated by the time they turned to sit down.

As soon as the posse had settled in, they began to spread paperwork across the table. It became obvious that they had availed themselves of the Grand Hotel bar for the purposes of conducting a business meeting. Mustard Suit flicked open his laptop and began talking in a deadpan dialect easily recognisable as planning-department legalese. This seemed as incongruous in the Grand Hotel bar as aftershave on a bush track. Before long anyone with ears had worked out that the two casually dressed blokes were the architects of the Wathaurong Heights housing cluster, the two fellas in grey suits were from the Brinbeal shire, and the fella in the blue suit was the owner of the land. Mustard Suit was, without a shadow of a doubt, the legal eagle.

I can't say that the hackles were rising on the back of my neck at the presence of these people in the hotel, but as Veronica turned away from the food in the stove and headed out through the sunroom it would be safe to say that hers were. Was I dreaming or had she suddenly taken on the spiky protruding backbone of one of our long-ago local dinosaurs? When she hadn't come back after twenty minutes and the posse were re-investigating the possibility of dinner, I surmised that like the dinosaurs she'd gone on temporary strike. She wanted nothing to do with these blokes.

I popped open the oven door and checked under the foil of the three huge baking dishes to see where the lamb was at. I prodded it with a serving fork and the meat fell lasciviously off the bone. It was perfectly cooked.

As Darren Traherne appeared from The Horse Room with a tray of empty glasses, the two of us set to carving the lamb and sluicing it with salad onto the old Coalmine Creek Golf Club green and white plates. Joan did his quick whiparound of the patrons to see how many takers there were for food. He was gone for a good ten minutes, off into The Horse Room, back through the sunroom, out onto the verandah, and back through the bar until he declared that there were thirty-seven hands up for dinner. Darren and I looked at each other and then down at the food. 'Easy,' we agreed.

By this stage the Wathaurong Heights meeting was rais-ing a few eyebrows among other people in the hotel. Their dis-cussion, complete with architectural spreadsheets, procedural bullet lists, PDF flowcharts, planning caveats and the like, was becoming a bit heated. It seemed that the shire suits were disagreeing with the blue-suited owner and his architects on heightlines, sightlines and particularly on plumbing arrange-ments in the 'eco-cluster'.

The shire suits were put out because after approving the development as an eco-cluster it seemed that now the intended grey-water scheme and on-site sewerage treatment plants had vanished from the plans. For their part the architects were claiming that the density of the proposed occupancy on the land, complete with some three- and even four-storey apartment buildings, simply disallowed for some of the green components of the original plan. As a sweetener, however, the architects were promising to ramp up the use of photovoltaic solar cells in the buildings and also to investigate the possibilities of the whole Wathaurong Heights estate becoming carbon neutral somewhere down the track.

At this suggestion Mustard Suit the Lawyer looked up from his laptop screen and raised his hand with emphasis. It seemed he was recommending extreme caution in regards to such spontaneous proposals on behalf of his clients. As his discretionary palm returned to rest near the mousepad of his Hewlett-Packard, the senior of the two shire representatives seemed suddenly to lose his temper.

'Oh this is very unclear,' he spat out crossly, 'very unclear indeed. What you presented in the proposal *must* take place. And if you find this architecturally impossible, then you must reduce the number of apartments, not abandon the green components of the cluster. This is all highly unprofessional.'

During this outburst the owner of the land and financier of the whole Wathaurong Heights development sat impassively on the red cedar pew on the sunset window side of the table. His face was stony but calm, almost as if he was thinking of something else entirely.

It was at this point, just as Nan Burns and Ash Bowen were beginning to hand around the plates of lemon lamb, cooked superbly to the traditional recipe, that I noticed Veronica re-enter the bar through the verandah double doors. Ever so slowly she headed around the room, ducking in and out of the furniture and leaning politely but silently across conversations, all the while placing small silver disc-shaped objects on every available surface. One by one as she went she lit these discs with a large kitchen-box of matches.

Looking out through the sunroom, I could see wisps of smoke wafting about – she'd obviously made her way through The Horse Room already – and before long the delicious aromas of the slow-cooked lemon lamb were being gradually replaced by the unmistakable scent of frankincense.

Of course different cultures have different purposes for frankincense, depending on the history of its ritual role in their society, but for me personally it has only ever been associated with one thing: funerals. As Veronica moved around the bar with her jaw set, lighting countless of her frankincense discs, and as the smoke from The Horse Room and sunroom started to billow through the doorway, Joan Sutherland began coughing behind the bar. Before long the air was absolutely thick with the stuff and so pungent it was as if there was a funeral pyre set alight in the middle of the room.

Chaos ensued. Some people started shouting in anger while others were spluttering and cackling in amazement. Suddenly it occurred to me what was going on. Veronica had decided that evil spirits had inhabited our hotel and was using her own hybrid of Lebanese and Argentinian understandings of frankincense to cleanse the space. It was brilliant – entirely symbolic, of course, but practically effective as well.

Quickly covering the plates of food on the benches behind the bar so they wouldn't taste of death, I watched as the posse from Wathaurong Heights simultaneously reached for their snowy-white handkerchiefs and placed them over their mouths. Cries of 'outrageous' and 'unprofessional' came muffled from behind the hankies as they gathered up their documents and charts and made for the door. Did they have any idea, I wondered as I watched them go, that they were being fumigated?

Within no time the whole hotel had emptied out into the backyard; the frankincense smoke was so thick inside that you could hardly see, let alone breathe. Clientele who up until that point had been prepared to go along with the anomalies of the establishment now took off in a bewildered huff towards their houses. Some of the more asthmatic among them never ever returned. Others loitered around under the pine trees, still unsure as to whether or not the building had caught fire.

Veronica, meanwhile, was standing alone by my giant aloe vera plant down near the barn, glowering in my direction. I ignored her, not because I disapproved of what she'd done but because I was intimidated by the ferocity of her mood, the sheer willpower of this woman. With one lateral step she had not only got rid of the Wathaurong Heights delegation but had also revealed the extent to which The Grand Hotel was prepared to go to emulate its original predecessor. If Kooka was right and they did let a one hundred and forty pound black pig into the original Grand every evening to clean up the scraps, then using frankincense as a bouncer to remove riff-raff from the premises seemed somehow quite apt.

After about half an hour, of the seventy or so people who

were in the hotel when the frankincense was lit, about twenty
remained on the grass in the yard. Joan, Darren and myself
made our way back into the building. Quickly we opened all
the windows and doors to help the ritual fog subside. Then,
waving our hands to clear a path, we raided the coolroom for
slabs of the Belgian monastery beer, which we took outside and
distributed among the crowd. Given the religious atmosphere
caused by the frankincense, it was an appropriate choice.

'What about the lemon lamb?' someone cried.

'Great idea,' said Joan, and together he and I headed back
through the smoke to grab the oven dishes, the bowls of salad,
and an armful of cutlery and plates.

When we returned outside, we placed the food on the
upturned boat under the blackwood trees and everyone helped
themselves. All the fuss had obviously awoken The Blonde
Maria upstairs, because as we washed the lamb and salad
down with swigs of the monastic Pilsener, strains of *Charles
Aznavour at Carnegie Hall* could be heard coming through her
open window. I must say it was quite a celebratory soundtrack
to what in the end was a lovely al fresco meal.

Later that night, when most of the frankincense had
cleared and The Blonde Maria had come down from her room,
she and The Barrels, who now announced they were to be called
The Blonde Maria and The Connotations, played an astonish-
ing inaugural set of blues and jazz riffs and rhythms, with The
Blonde Maria medleying through old delta woes, bog-Irish
lamentations, and joyous and dexterous improvisations on her
luck in arriving at The Grand Hotel.

Jim and Oscar and the other boys in the band were feeling

lucky too, as The Blonde Maria was saving their skin, releasing them from their hackneyed west coast surfer's repertoire and directing their very capable musical abilities into previously unknown territory. To a man their grins were a mile wide as they rumbled along behind her pipey voice and torch-song charm. As a band they seemed to arrive at textures and to risk dissonances that they never before would have dreamt of. For the small audience dancing behind the front hedge under starlight, it was a memorable gig indeed. Veronica, of course, had no doubt as to what it was that had released the band's creative juices. As far as she was concerned, the smoking of the hotel with frankincense was its true beginning, and The Blonde Maria's work with The Connotations was just a part of it.

It has to be said that although we never again had the numbers in the place that we'd had on those first three nights, the fumigation of the posse from Wathaurong Heights really crystallised the essence of the hotel. From that point on you were either in, or you were out. A bit like the old days in the pub back up on the hill, when given the opportunity to kick on after stumps you could only accept if you were prepared to go the long haul and stay until the magpies started singing up the dawn.

False Alarm

AT NINE O'CLOCK THE NEXT MORNING I HAD SERGEANT Greg Beer slamming on my barn door. I'd been enjoying a long satisfying sleep after a terrific night and was rudely awoken.

I threw open the timber shutter of my loft and looked below. There was his freshly showered scalp right underneath me, the skin the colour of strawboard under fastidiously combed wet wisps of hair.

'What do you want, Greg?' I called down.

He stepped away from the double doors below and tilted his head back to see me. 'Good morning, Noel. Sorry to wake you – but it is 9 am.'

'Yeah. We had a late night. You keep different hours when you're running a pub, Sergeant.'

'Yes. I suppose you do. But, Noel, I need you to come down

and talk to me. There's an issue I'd like to discuss.'

'It can't wait?'

'No, it most certainly can't.'

I closed the shutter and groaned. Of course Greg Beer and I had never got on, even as kids, and I could sense now that The Grand Hotel was going to be his opportunity to make my life difficult.

After climbing down my ladder, I pushed the button on the barn kettle and then flung open the double doors, letting the bright morning light hit my face.

'Would you like a cup of tea while we chat?' I asked him, in a friendly enough way.

It took him a moment or two to answer as his eyes absorbed the chaos of equipment in the barn behind me: half built frames and half finished pictures everywhere, scattered tubes of paint, lopsided high shelves loaded with manuals and books. There was refuse from the land and seascape covering every surface: fronds of mistletoe, switches of moonah, cereal bags full of pollen fibres, broken road signs, swan-down and heron feathers, scraps of wallaby hide, rusted farm axles, albatross mandibles, sheaves of dried sedge and clubrush, clusters of horny conebush, washed-out stacks of all the different coloured plastics the ocean offers up. The sergeant's analytical squint betrayed the fact that the inside of my barn was helping him complete a picture he'd long ago begun to compose – of Noel Lea as a slob, as a slackarse and a madman, a dangerous variant to everything decent, clean and respectable in his home town. His distaste for what he saw warped the narrow features of his face and I couldn't help but surmise that it all may have reminded him of his own childhood home up on Carroll Street, where chaos always reigned and stuff was always strewn around his poor mum as she sat wrestling her cask of demons at the kitchen table.

Eventually he curled up his nose at the scent of turps and sea wrack and said, 'No, no tea for me thanks. I've had breakfast, Noel. I was actually wanting to have a look around your hotel. Apparently you had quite a deal of smoke in there last night and I've had a report that no alarms went off. You're aware of course, Noel, that to run a hotel without smoke alarms is a serious offence – not to mention an extremely dangerous course of action. I thought you might like to show me where your alarms are, and together we could ascertain why they failed to work last night.'

Bloody smoke alarms! I should've known. Some pissed-off victim of Veronica's frankincense fumigation had gone whining to the cops. Probably one of the Wathaurong Heights posse – most likely one of the suits from the shire. I flicked the kettle back off and stepped out of the barn. All I could do was feign innocence.

'Yeah,' I said casually to Greg Beer as we walked across the yard towards the hotel. 'I thought it was funny they didn't go off. There was quite a bit of smoke after all.'

The truth was that as soon as the health-and-safety inspections had been completed, I'd taken the batteries out of all the smoke alarms before we'd opened the hotel. None of them were active.

The thing with smoke alarms is that if you're cooking with any degree of flair at all, or smoking cigarettes like it's 1958, the bloody things go off unannounced! It's too annoying, not to mention damaging to the eardrums. I wasn't gonna have that nerve-tingling racket going off all the time. But now I had to explain that to Greg Beer.

As we stepped into the sunroom of the hotel, I bought myself some thinking time by opening all the louvre windows one by one, to let the fresh air in from the garden. Beside me I could feel the sergeant developing a relish for his task. He was sure he was onto something, and I knew that as far as the law went smoke alarms without batteries are just the same as no smoke alarms at all.

'Okay then,' Sergeant Beer said, as I ran out of louvres. 'If you could please point out where your alarms are located, we'll see what we can find. I presume you do have alarms installed, Noel?'

Nice try, Sergeant, I thought, but it's not going to be that easy.

'Yes,' I said, 'we've got sixteen in total. Let's go through to the bar and see if we can solve the mystery.'

As we walked through the sunroom, I was racking my brains for a solution but needn't have bothered. Behind the bar we found big Joan Sutherland in a pair of green cargo shorts and a flannelette shirt, standing on a stool with a plastic bag of AAA Duracell batteries hanging from his wrist. Directly above him on the ceiling the white plastic lid of the smoke alarm was hanging down.

'Morning, Noel. Morning, Sergeant,' Joan said, smiling broadly as he saw us. 'Noel, I've just been swapping the batteries over in all the alarms. Must've been duds in them last night, what with all that smoke and them not going off. I got some Duracells from the store. They're the best. Those no-name ones that were in there are next to useless.'

With his right hand he selected two batteries from the bag, clicked them into place and then closed the lid of the alarm. Then he fished out a Winfield Blue from his shirt pocket, lit it with a match and took a big drag. With his huge ruddy frame only centimetres from the device, he exhaled the blue smoke all over it. Straightaway the unbearably high pitched BEEP-BEEP-BEEP-BEEP began. Greg Beer and I dived for cover, blocking our ears.

Nonchalantly Joan unclipped the lid of the alarm and switched it off. 'There,' he said. 'That's more like it. So what brings you here before opening hours, Sergeant?'

Greg Beer took his hands from his ears and grimaced. He ignored the question.

'Great minds must think alike, Joan,' I said. 'Greg had come round to check on our alarms after last night. He was concerned for our safety. But you've had the same thought. And what's more, you've done something about it. Have you replaced all sixteen?'

Joan stepped down gingerly from the bentwood stool, which miraculously hadn't folded under his frame. 'Yep, all except the one in The Blonde Maria's room. She's still sleeping. I wouldn't dare wake her after the show she put on last night. You should've seen it, Sergeant,' he said, turning to Greg Beer. 'The girl's magnificent. Everyone who stayed after the smoke had an absolute ball!'

It was now Joan's turn to offer Sergeant Beer a cup of

tea or coffee but once again he refused. Muttering something about paperwork back at the station, he made his farewells and promptly left through the sunroom door.

I turned to Joan and positively cheered. 'How the fuckin' hell did you know he was here for the alarms?'

Joan shook his head from side to side in wonderment. 'I didn't, Noely. I was genuinely checking the bloody things. Couldn't work out how come they hadn't gone off. Woke up in the middle of the night worrying about it. Then I find there's no friggin' batteries in any of 'em! But of course I couldn't tell the sergeant that. I twigged right away that he wasn't here for bacon and eggs.'

'Certainly wasn't,' I said. 'Now take those bloody batteries out again, will ya? You can't even suck a cigarette in here without the silly things going off. And you just proved it.'

Although we never had to fumigate property developers from the hotel again, if we left those batteries in the alarms they would've been sure to go off over the following weeks. Especially on those lucky nights when my brother Jim would agree to cook up his famous west coast bisque for the patrons. As he poured the St Agnes brandy over the charred crab and crayfish shells, the crowd in the bar, nicely sluiced on the Dancing Brolgas, would stand around in keen anticipation. And then the moment would come. With a flourish Jim would ignite the dish, which roared into flame. The crowd would hoot with excitement, all the while licking their lips at the thought of the dinner ahead. The flames would re-settle, giving off the rich aromatic smoke, and Joan Sutherland would do his nightly whip around to see how many takers there were. Who would ever want to ruin such a dramatic, oceanic, culinary moment as that with an earbashing siren from some electrical shop?

Nan's Towering Inferno

IT WAS ONLY TWO WEEKS AFTER WE'D OPENED THE HOTEL, with the wheat sorted from the chaff by Veronica's frankincense fumigation, when tragedy struck the town. The spring rains had come on strong – we hadn't had such October downpours in years – and I remember thinking that if it wasn't for the intense humidity accompanying the rains, you could almost believe the local climate was reverting to its patterns of yore, to keep in step with the reopening of The Grand Hotel.

A strange upshot of the rains, however, was that the shire's controversial indoor creek, which had never been embraced by the young mothers it was intended for, had finally found a niche in the culture of the New Mangowak. Every day after school kids would gather in the pouring weather, to swim untroubled by the heavy downpours that came in chaotic rhythms from both the inland and far out to sea. On any weeknight you could find eight or ten teenagers under that newfangled retractable structure overarching the creek. They would huddle in there as if in an adolescent clubroom, smoking, texting, tagging the tin, listening to their iPods and swinging off the high-tensile polypropylene rope that had been attached to a specially installed gantry designed for the purpose.

This re-installed swing-rope had a history and was viewed by some in the town as an example of the benefits of community consultation and compromise. It all came about because the original swing-rope, which hung from an old manna gum on the riverbank, had been deemed unsafe by the shire. This was only possible due to the fact that once public infrastructure, such as the indoor creek, was installed on the river, by law the shire then became legally responsible for any injuries that occurred in its new 'riparian precinct'. Of course there was such an outcry when it was revealed that swinging from that thirty-year-old farm rope hanging from that one-hundred-and-twenty-year-old manna gum was going to become illegal that the shire just had to act. Meetings were conducted on the riverbank itself to sort out the problem and finally the powers that be agreed to incorporate a new swing-rope in the design of the indoor creek, which they promised to be bigger and better than ever.

As it turned out, the indoor creek swing-rope was higher than the old manna gum version, and the polypropylene and Kevlar rope was apparently made of the same material that climbers of Everest used when they were ascending the mountain. From the day it was installed, though, the kids showed no interest until suddenly, with the October downpours, they'd finally taken to it. Sadly, however, the hi-tech shire-endorsed swing-rope came to its tragic demise on a completely unsuspecting Tuesday afternoon, as the kids gathered there after school in what felt like a very unseasonable tropical North Queensland storm.

The indoor creek structure was built firmly into the bank, with pile-driven pre-rusted steel foundations, but as the thunder began to grumble from far out over the hills of Minapre, and the wind began to lash from the south along the course of that stretch of the river, whipping up under the roof of the indoor creek and thrumming loudly on its fashionable corrugations, the river-rope gantry that had been affixed on the eastern wall of the structure came loose. Givva Way's boy, Alex, was swinging from the rope at the time and with the unexpected collapse of the gantry fell awkwardly onto the water, injuring his spine.

For a time the town was in shock, as it looked like Alex Way was never going to walk again. The recriminations over the accident were running thick and fast. Alex was in the spinal ward at the Austin Hospital in Melbourne, and his mother, Christine, had taken a flat in Heidelberg to be nearby. Givva, though, remained in Mangowak to work and visited his wife and only son on weekends. He spent his weeknights in The Grand Hotel, furiously drowning his sorrows and talking to anyone who would listen about what had happened to his son.

Everyone was sympathetic, of course, despite the fact that Givva had always had a reputation in town as being loose with his mouth and liable to bullshit. But now he was a man in pain and I was determined, despite my traditional wariness of him, that the hotel would be his shelter from the storm. He could offload onto sympathetic minds, particularly in relation to the culpability of the shire, and we could watch him closely and make sure he didn't drink himself into an oblivion from which he wouldn't be able to work, or travel to Melbourne every weekend to see his son.

Veronica and Nan both had no time for Givva Way and found it difficult to have him in the hotel night after night, alternately venting his spleen or overbrimming with bitter mirth at the brutality of life. I found it difficult to accommodate Givva also, especially as my modus operandi for coping with the New Mangowak had become a creative type of humour. There was, after all, nothing at all funny about Alex Way's accident. But, as I was at pains to explain to Veronica, and Nan, whose distaste of Givva went right back to when they lived together in a surfers' share-house on the inlet, a good pub as I had been brought up to understand it could cope with tears as well as laughter. And a good publican would always see that the local loose cannons were safe from harm. 'If we don't look after him,' I told them both on more than one occasion, 'the cops will. And you know his history with Greg Beer. It'd get ugly for sure.'

So Veronica and Nan tolerated the situation, and often at stumps, after a hard night on the turps, I would help Givva up the narrow staircase to the middle room, unclip his paint-spattered working overalls and sling him onto the bed. I'd put a laundry bucket on the floor next to him and leave him to his drunken blur. In the mornings he'd come down for breakfast with a blank expression and together we'd sit over unseasonable mushrooms on sourdough, sometimes with Kooka or The Blonde Maria, and talk more rationally about his situation and the world at large. By the time breakfast had finished, Givva would invariably be feeling better, after good counsel and the delicious climate-change mushrooms. He'd wander off home to jump in his ute and head off to work, where he'd spend his days painting house sides at the top of telescopic ladders, before turning up again around 5 pm for yet another session of grief and recrimination.

This went on for quite a few weeks until the good news started to filter out of the spinal ward at the Austin that Alex would recover fully from the accident and Givva and Christine plucked up the hide to lay an accident insurance claim against the shire. By the time young Alex was discharged and back at home, Givva had thrown off his cloud of woe and resumed his traditional role as the town earbasher. He still drank at The Grand, of course, and was in his own way grateful for what we'd done for him, but he'd tell any unsuspecting stranger who'd listen that as soon as Alex's insurance money came through he was packing up and moving to Western Australia. 'Fuckin' hole this town these days,' Givva would bleat, holding court in his spattered overalls at the bar. 'No fuckin' peace and quiet anymore. People don't look out for each other like they used to. Cunts have wrecked it.'

Joan and I would listen to him as we poured the Dancing Brolgas, look at each other and roll our eyes. We knew Givva would never leave town and that the insurance money wasn't his to spend anyway. But off he'd go on a longwinded diatribe to whichever Swedish or Italian backpacker he'd managed to bail up. He'd regale them with descriptions of the beauty of the west, tell them about the times he'd spent over there crayfishing in Geraldton in his thirties. But always, after he'd reached a certain threshold with the Dancing Brolgas, he'd end up singing the praises of the old days in Mangowak, the 1970s, and yes, he'd wheel out the old chestnut about singing the song 'Down Under', all twenty-seven verses, with Colin Hay from Men At Work when he was passing through town on tour to Adelaide. Some of the backpackers, of course, would know the song – it was a hit all over the world after all – and Givva would get his mileage. 'Yeah, good bloke, Colin,' he'd say, taking another sip. 'Scottish he is. Not many people know that. Doesn't mind the hoochy cooch either. No, doesn't mind it at all.'

It was during the time that The Grand Hotel was Givva Way's shoulder to cry on that I threw the Happy Hour entertainment open to the clientele. It's a little known fact that people who live in country areas like ours are often more technologically savvy than city dwellers. People in Mangowak and in the surrounding hills use the internet like people in Melbourne use the trams and trains. There's no cinema or bands to go to see at night, so invariably people here are involved in some clandestine activity or another on the net. Some are researching surfboard design, others are listening to Alaskan fishing reports, some are co-writing graphic novels with schoolkids in Kyoto, while others are uploading local video grabs onto YouTube. Some, as was evident on the wall of The Horse Room, are using Photoshop to reconstruct the landscapes of the past, while others are connected to research networks monitoring banded seabirds as they fly magnetically across the globe. There're locals into the gaming scene, global embroidery guilds and of course more and more people around here doing what the Europeans call 'telecottaging' – working online from home.

The idea of handing over the live-streaming from the internet during Happy Hour brought a lot of these bush-technos out of their huts and bungalows. I figured that whatever they did, as long as they weren't broadcasting free-to-air TV, would be somehow interesting enough to fit The Grand Hotel Charter. There'd be no outright expressions of art, of course – no, the idiosyncratic hobby and the furtively anarchistic fetish would be brought to the fore.

Luckily for us first cab off the rank was Nan Burns, who, as one of the most vocal critics of the nightly streaming of the Vatican Radio, which had been the staple absurdist fare during Happy Hour since we'd opened the hotel, had taken up the challenge.

Nan lives by herself these days, on a farm out the back of town, where she spends a lot of time in the warmer months up a fire tower the Country Fire Authority installed on the property years ago. She's got a very comfortable arrangement up there in that tower, with a kitchen, a bed and shower, and of course beautiful views across the east Otways. With a wireless computer, a telescope, and two huge mounted sets of binoculars she keeps an eye on the landscape around her for wind shifts, for glassy glints and wisps of smoke, and is paid a nominal fee to maintain a webcam and report on fire-related matters to the authorities. Now, with her characteristically biting humour, she displayed her subversive contribution to Happy Hour on the big screen in the bar.

It was called 'Nan's Towering Inferno' and consisted of wobbly but high-powered footage of all the properties within view of her tower, complete with a voice-over describing how pathetically reprehensible her neighbours were when it came to preparing themselves for bushfire. The catch was she didn't talk about the clearing of their properties or their sprinkler systems or whether or not they'd built bunkers. Instead, in a deadly serious voice, she talked about the quirks and foibles of the residents themselves, their fondness for the bong or the bottle, their tendency to either blather on or remain monosyllabic, their penchants for not answering the phone and not listening to the radio, their liking for keeping their watertanks empty so they could sing into them instead of drinking or hosing from them, or the men's fondness for 'freeballing', as she called it – i.e. not wearing underwear – and how all these attributes would hamper or hinder everyone in a fire crisis. Basically it was Nan's shot at the level of emergency-style surveillance that had become expected in our area of late. And because a lot of the people she was talking about were either in the bar watching or known to those of us who were, 'Nan's Towering Inferno' brought the house down.

A bit later that night, after The Blonde Maria had sung yet another lascivious set of scalding-hot blues songs with sexual subtexts, songs such as 'Let Me Play with Your Poodle', 'Pig Meat Papa', 'The Best Jockey in Town' and 'Keep On Eatin'', I was standing in The Horse Room feeling pretty pleased with myself when Maria herself came down off the stage, marched through the bar and flung herself down onto the couch beside me. She let out a heartrending groan.

'All these songs are driving me crazy, Noel,' she said. 'You do realise I left a perfectly good young man back in Melbourne, don't you, a sweet young Goth with blue hair? I'm a goddess to him, Noel. All I have to do is ask, and he'll do anything I like. And I mean anything! I was expecting some real man-action down here in the wild west, some vigorous country fare here at The Grand. And all I'm seein' is a bunch of old farmers and tradesmen farting at the tables, and sunburnt surfies half spent and dribblin' into their beers. And what's more they won't take their eyes off *moi* coz my physical attributes are just about the only thing they recognise, due to the weird shit you're dishing up in the rest of the pub. You'd have to admit that things are pretty odd if my cleavage represents the mainstream around here. Where in God's earth did that fella Givva Way come from? I mean, is he for real?'

She threw her head back on the couch and lit a cigarette, then let out another deeply frustrated groan.

I was taken aback. 'Geez, Maria,' I said, sitting down beside her, 'I thought you were enjoying yourself. You've been in such good voice. And anyway, there's plenty of nice fellas here. What about my nephew Oscar over there? He'd give you a run for your money.'

'What, the bass player kid with the big smile?' she spat out. 'Are you kidding me, Noel? Granted, I've always had a thing for younger men but I would've thought you could have picked my type.'

I gave an ironic frown. 'Yeah, well maybe you should just try singing a different kind of song. You've been mining that "Bed Spring Poker" stuff ever since you got here. It's gettin' you all het up. Why don't you go a bit political? Sober yourself up a bit. Do some protest songs. Get your mind off things.'

The Blonde Maria took a drag of her cigarette, thinking. Then suddenly she broke into a cheeky smile. 'There is actually one fella here who I quite like.'

Naturally my mind started ticking over, considering all the likely candidates.

'Not my brother?' I spat out in a twisted voice, squeamish at my conclusion.

'No,' she laughed. 'No way. That'd be like, I dunno, incest or something. And your brothers are like *old*. No, Noel, someone else. You'll never pick it.'

'Well, how about I don't even try?' I said, facetiously. 'Though I must say I'm relieved that there's at least one candidate you could consider unleashing your talents on.'

The Blonde Maria looked up at me, fully grinning now. 'He'd be a challenge, Noel, this one. A real challenge.'

'I see. Is that so?' I said. 'Well, I'm sure you're up to it. Meanwhile can I get our very own Umm Kulthum another drink?'

'Oh you're a darling, Noely. Make it a Laphroaig. Neat.'

By stumps later that night The Blonde Maria was holding a party upstairs in her room, with not a hint of her previous frustration. The air was thick with smoke, even though the windows were wide open to the night pines. She was playing the DJ, spinning old LPs as the boys from The Connotations, and Joan Sutherland, Givva Way, Darren Traherne, Kooka and a burly Italian tourist named Guido gathered around her. I had to hand it to Maria: she could make the dreariest, most browbeaten and mortgage-pressured men come to life again. She was in fact a genuine flesh and blood bohemian in an era where typically they can only be found in coffee-table books. And because of her insatiable need of drinking partners The Blonde Maria would sup with absolutely anyone, without changing herself a scrap. She'd carry on regardless, as if no matter where she was, or who she was talking to, the centre of the universe was just nearby. She could make even Givva Way feel like he was a part of a seminal cultural underground. Which might go part of the way to explaining how resolutely Givva's tedious nostalgia for those old bands who toured along the coast in the 1970s would keep surfacing in her midst. Oh man, *could he go on about it*! But that night, between the acacia wallpapers of her bedroom, with the prerogative of the sexually powerful female, Maria went where no man or woman in Mangowak had gone since young Alex's accident in the indoor creek. She took to ribbing Givva Way about this godforsaken boring habit of his.

It started around 2 am, with everyone well and truly sluiced. The Blonde Maria was leaning over the turntable changing records, wiggling her arse like a cancan girl as she did so. As the needle skew-whiffed onto the vinyl, she quickly turned back into the room and said, 'Oh Givva, can you tell me again about the night you smoked the spliff with Colin Hay?'

As applause from *Charles Aznavour at Carnegie Hall* rang out of the speakers, the rest of the room groaned. For a moment Givva looked confused. Then Guido the Tourist piped up: 'Who eez theez Coalen Ay?'

At that Givva collected himself and went straight back

into gear. 'Aw, mate, come on. Colin Hay? Haven't you ever heard of "Down Under"?' He began to sing the song.

Guido's jowly face took on a look of recognition. 'Oh yeez, I haff, of corz,' he said.

'Yeah, well Givva helped him write the lyrics,' said Jim.

Before Guido the Tourist could begin to weigh up whether or not this was possible, the room burst into laughter. And soon enough they all began to speculate as to what some of the co-written verses might have been, the ones that Givva had always assured us the cappo pigs from the record company had rudely edited out of the final famous version of the song:

> *Sittin' stoned in a west coast hotel*
> *Bored to tears in a living hell*
> *I got up to leave for the next show*
> *But some mad bastard called Givva Way wouldn't let me go*
> *He was singing, 'I come from a . . .'*

Oscar began to play the iconic flute riff from the song on the mouth of his stubby. And the banter continued:

> *Travellin' in an EH Holden*
> *In the years gone by so golden*
> *I said, 'Givva, will you please piss off now?'*
> *But he just smiled and said, 'Sorry, Col, I don't know how.'*
> *And we were*
> *Livin' in a land . . .*

Before long a torrent of hypothetical verses was ringing out, with The Connotations tinkling the wine glasses along with Oscar's stubby-flute and everyone joining in on the chorus. Givva was the butt of them all, of course, and over in the corner on the bentwood chair, quite blotto and still in his working overalls, he was shaking his paint-flecked mop of black hair and looking glum. Eventually, though, after things got so drunken and ridiculous that even Guido the Tourist had a go at a verse, Givva perked up, seemed to get the joke, and began happily singing along in the choruses at his own expense.

It was a good hour at least before this joyful musical carousing calmed down and someone suggested it was time for more food. In typical fashion Joan Sutherland volunteered, and as he lifted his heavy frame up to go down to the bar everyone took a breather. They reached for their drinks and cigarettes and began to sip and sigh happily in the aftermath of the laughter.

It was in that pleasant lull at 3 am that the resolute Givva Way was heard to say, 'Nah, but fair dinkum you should have been there, Maria, back then with Colin Hay and the musos and that. You would have loved it, you really . . .'

A torrent of howling abuse burst through the upstairs windows of the hotel and into the night sky. It rained down on the poor house-painter where he sat innocently on his bentwood chair. The cries of astonished disbelief were so loud in fact that they were heard all the way down the starlit Mangowak valley. Even Big Ted, the laconic doyen of the riverflat kangaroos, swivelled his old grey ears southward to catch the sound.

As two ringtail possums peered into The Grand Hotel from high up in the pine tree beside The Blonde Maria's window, they witnessed a chaotic scene. For the howls of astonishment were not the only things hurled in the direction of Givva Way at that moment. Along with them came thrown shoes, rolled-up magazines, disposable cigarette lighters, LP covers tossed like Frisbees, abalone-shell ashtrays, car keys, an empty cigar box, indispensable guitar capos, a tennis ball and a mug half full of sarsaparilla – anything at all in fact that his uproarious fellow drinkers could find to throw at him.

The Lazy Tenor

FOR THE LIFE OF ME I COULDN'T WORK OUT WHO IT WAS that The Blonde Maria had set her sexual sights on, and I wasn't completely sure whether or not I cared. But only a week or so after her groaning confession in the sunroom, a week in which Sergeant Greg Beer made not two but three separate inspections of the premises (apparently he'd had complaints about the noise from a couple of kangaroos down on the riverflat), a strapping visitor in a bottle-green suede coat, who was to have a romantic and a cataclysmic influence on both Maria and the destiny of the hotel, turned up from the city. I took one look at him and was sure her pent-up frustration would be cured.

When I say this was a visitor from the city, that is not exactly true. In fact Louis Daley, or The Lazy Tenor, as he came to be known to us, was born and bred in a broken-down scrubland of central Victoria that to this day still goes by the name of Blokey Hollow. He was patient with his parents and brothers on the windridden family farm but as soon as it was physically and linguistically possible he had fled, tripping over tractor parts and shingleback lizards as he went, in search of, to quote the man himself, 'whatever the fuck was on offer in the big smoke'.

His departure from Blokey Hollow had subsequently set many adventures in train. Not only that, he had managed to find himself a few good square meals in his travels as well, which had seen him grow from the malnourished rag of thistledown he was when he left the crumbly asbestos home of his childhood into a six-foot-four, broad-shouldered, honey-voiced exemplar of the male species.

Louis Daley's arrival in The Grand Hotel was greeted with warm aplomb, for not only did he have a twinkle in his royal-blue eyes but he also announced that news of the good cheer and virus-like freedom of The Grand had begun to spread.

'So,' bellowed the new arrival, heaving a tattered red Adidas sports bag onto the bar, 'this then is the famous Grand Hotel.'

Darren Traherne, from where he stood at the sink twisting dirty beer glasses onto an upturned bottlebrush, looked at him querulously and said, 'Famous? I dunno about that, mate. We've only been open five weeks.'

'Well you're quick workers then,' said Big Lou Daley.

Immediately sensing a colourful new ingredient for his archive, Kooka hit the record button on the Grundig where it was propped up at the other end of the bar. He plugged in a microphone and ran the lead down along the floor ashtrays until the mic itself was lying on the bar right under the big man's nose.

'Go on?' said the old-timer.

'Oh, God, yeah,' continued our new guest, glancing down at the microphone and rising to the occasion. 'I had two different floozies going on to me about it the other night in Melbourne. They had big raps on this place, though they did admit it was a tad unusual. But that's what got me interested. I gathered it was in a nice quiet spot on the coast and had cheap accommodation. And so, I said to myself, Lou, your shaggin' days are over, it's time to write your life story. So here I am. I've got this bloody crappy laptop in this here bag, I'm cashed up, and I'm here to knuckle down. By the way, I couldn't get a drink could I, mate? Thirsty work that bloody highway.'

Darren poured Louis Daley a nice crisp Dancing Brolga, and with barely a 'here's health' Lou wolfed it down. 'Aah,' he burped. 'That's better. So then, have you got a spare room? I'll pay up front. I'll be here for as long as it takes me to write the book.'

'How interesting,' said Kooka, beside him. 'You're a writer are you, big fella?'

Lou Daley just laughed, running an enormous hand over his face and through his bright red hair. 'Who me? A writer?' he scoffed. 'No fear. But I reckon with the things I've seen, and particularly the ladies I've got to know over the years, I've got some kind of blockbuster in me for sure. But no, mate, I'm just a mechanic, if the truth be known.'

He looked around the room with a big grin on his face,

then he leant down towards the microphone and added, 'Specialising in ladies' parts.'

Standing up straight again, he waved his hand dismissively. 'Nah, I love a good time, good music, and well yeah, life's been kind enough to me that I reckon I could tell a few stories. Give a few sad-sacks a clue. Anyway, my name's Lou Daley. Some people call me Big Lou, others call me Louie the Lip, but those who know me well, they call me Lazy.' At this he opened his mouth wide and let out a huge narcissistic guffaw, slapping his palm down on the bar mat. 'Hey?' he said through tears of mirth. 'Those who know me call me Lazy. Hey? If only it were true.'

This surprising new guest looked to be in his late thirties, and the old green suede jacket he wore looked like it had accompanied him on most of his escapades. His arrival gave the bar an unexpected charge, so much so that for the first time Happy Hour was technology free that night. Once he'd established that a room was available, Louis Daley propped up the bar for a good two hours, telling anyone who did or didn't want to listen about the book he was going to write.

'I needed somewhere real quiet, but somewhere I could get a good feed, and a decent drink. Coz this is gonna be a flat-out masterpiece this. It's gonna take some doin'.'

Nan had arrived for her evening shift still wearing a pair of farm overalls, and she and Darren were working the bar. By the look on her face I could see she was taking this new guest with a grain of salt. 'So has this "masterpiece" got a title yet?' she asked Louis Daley, pouring him another drink.

The big man from Blokey Hollow's face creased with

pleasure. 'I'm bloody glad you asked,' he replied. 'Too right it's got a title. You ready for it? "The Tradesman's Entrance". Yep. That's what this book's gonna be called.'

On two separate occasions on that evening of The Lazy Tenor's arrival I was taken aside with conciliatory gestures for 'a bit of a chat'. Firstly by Veronica. She nabbed me upstairs while I was making up Room One for our new guest. She demanded some answers.

'You're not going to let that big idiot stay here are you, Noel?'

'Well, what else am I meant to do? I've told you, Ronnie, any pub of mine has to have open doors.'

'But he's gross! What a pig! He's in the bar now telling the whole world about his sexual conquests back in Melbourne. "The Tradesman's Entrance"! He's a sick mind.'

I quietly puffed up the pillows of The Lazy Tenor's bed to be – a white cast-iron cot from the long defunct Birregurra Hospital, where my aunt had been a matron. I flicked on the bedside lamp to make sure it was still working, then simply shrugged my shoulders. It wasn't much of an answer but what could I do? Our new guest had come a long way; I could hardly just throw him out on the spot.

'Look,' I said, 'he's probably just a bit excited to be out of town. Let's see if he settles down a bit.'

She looked at me dubiously.

'But in the meantime,' I continued, 'don't forget Arthur Cravan, the Dada boxer. He was a complete oaf probably, but he was a free agent. He got thrown out of just about every joint he entered didn't he? And what for? Just for being a different ingredient in the pot. Maybe this red-headed fella's a bit like that.'

'I think you're being a bit optimistic there, Noel.'

'Maybe so,' I replied, 'but I'm not ruling anything out.'

Later on that night at around ten o'clock I was ushered in to stand in front of Duchamp with Joan Sutherland. As our genial barman unzipped his Yakkas, he told me he was 'a little concerned' about our new guest. 'It's just Jen and the kids, Noely,' he began. 'I can't have Dylan and Dougie in the bar with a fella carrying on like that. He was just telling the whole world how his book's gonna begin with him shagging some chemist girl who'd come to his garage to have her car looked at. He reckons he got into the front seat alongside her and then his mate hit the hoist button and up they went. The two of them were up there near the ceiling, rocking her little Hyundai for hours. But he went into too much detail, Noel. I told him to leave off, I tried to be nice, suggested he keep the juicy bits for the book, but Givva and a couple of others were encouraging him. And Kooka, the filthy old mongrel, was recording the lot. I had to send Jen and the kids home. I don't want to tell you what to do or anything in your own pub, but I reckon you'll have to send him packing. That's if it continues of course.'

Because we were standing right where we were, I decided to join Joan and empty my bladder. Before I could reply to his concern, the loop on Duchamp the Talking Pissoir was doing it for me:

The Lifestyle Republic
Democracy means freedom. Freedom to follow your dreams,
to speak out on issues that concern you, to laugh and cry with

loved ones in your own cherished home. Here at Rockpool Interiors (www.rockpoolinteriors.com) we're democrats through and through. Come in and see our newly imported panoply of antique voyeuse and shepherdess chairs, hand-picked from the flea markets of France, the home of style and liberty. Or what about our range of elite bedding ensembles, complete with scintillating free-to-speak customer testimonials? Come on, Australia, enjoy your right as citizens of the lifestyle republic. Come in and *feel the freedom*. At Rockpool Interiors there's no horizon when it comes to comfort.

The loop had been put in Duchamp to take the piss out of the lifestyle set but now, as Joan and I shook ourselves down, the word 'freedom' was all I could hear.

The night drifted on like a cloud in the sky or, to be more precise, with the dogged persistence of a bad rumour. Somehow, for the rest of the evening, the usually crisp and salient tempo that could be found in The Grand was sullied. Kooka and Givva Way stayed perched at the bar listening to The Lazy Tenor's stories. (Kooka, of course, could almost be excused due to his vocational ulterior motive. Givva, as usual, had no excuse.) Everyone else hunkered in the corners and pokey shadows of the building. Many clustered sulkily in The Horse Room playing perfunctory games of pool, some nestled disheartened on the verandah and listened to The Blonde Maria and The Connotations sarcastically mocking early Bob Dylan covers (the chanteuse had taken my advice about her singing political songs, but with a grain of salt. Bob Dylan was God to a lot of the old surfie types, especially to the boys in the band, and she was really digging the knife in), while others, like Veronica and Nan for instance, took the opportunity to go home early. They weren't needed, it was true; the amount of beer consumed that night in The Grand was only a fraction of the usual, but I for one was disappointed at the small town conservatism or, dare I say it, the wider-world political correctness that this big red-headed stranger had triggered merely by turning up and announcing himself. Sure he was loud, sure he was an earbasher and yeah, he had a dirty mouth, but we weren't at a meeting of the Presbyterian Quilters Guild! This *was* a hotel after all.

But what a difference a good sleep can make, especially when there's melaleuca and music in the air. On the day after The Lazy Tenor's arrival I woke up to the blessed and freakish delivery of an authentic bit of local spring weather. I'd been dreaming of the sap and the sea. In days gone by my brothers and I would help our parents harvest melaleuca oil and mussels on mornings rich with the scent of flaky timbers. As caterpillars moseyed lazily over the rose-gold clifftop pathways, and new crafts of life emerged from every dusty dangling cocoon nearby, deep in the lilac tidal beat and the dark lap-lap of the water around the jetty poles we'd float like pale jellyfish with improvised scraping tools: paint-strippers, discarded garage-door hinges, screwdrivers. We'd harvest the purple mussels from the old sea-blonded uprights. Then we'd come out of the water and slash the twigs off the whippy tea tree spars of the dunes to take home for Mum to distil and extract the oil. The melaleuca oil was a cure-all then and of course remains so now. But my mother was ahead-of-her-time mad for it. She not only prescribed it for our cuts and colds but used to have us shine our school shoes with it as well. We must have entered the already salty classroom pungent with the stuff.

Looking back, of course, they seem like golden days, when the notion of an indoor creek would have been as strange as a tall ship sailing into Botany Bay. But now as I rolled languidly in my dream towards the familiar scents coming through my loft shutter-door, I felt as though I'd returned to the timeless harvest of my childhood, or as if somehow it had returned to me.

There was a tingling on the perimeters of my waking state. Still half in the dream I could only feel the essence of what it was, an essence so pleasurable, so effortless and heartening that the bridge between golden dream and present day reality seemed no bridge at all. As I emerged, it was as if I was making my descent from high up in the air, and with a pelican's stable wings. The romantic gliding feeling has never left me to this day, nor has the memory of when my eyes opened and I finally registered, albeit unbelievingly, the ingredients that were making up my pleasure.

It was hard to fathom at first – not so much the familiar perfection of the perfumes but the unexpected beauty of the sound. Others described it later to me as their musical awakening. The Blonde Maria for one was humbled, almost beyond recall. She flat out refused to sing in The Grand Hotel for weeks afterwards, thereby setting in train the hotel's most miraculous moments but also perhaps its eventual demise.

As my eyes opened from the dream of golden harvests, I breathed deeply through my nose and lay still. Along with the rhythmic healing wafts of riverflat melaleuca drifting into my loft came a song, a song like no other.

It really was a *song*, in the purest sense. And it came from a voice at once so beautiful and ordinary that it seemed both as substantial and ethereal as the sky. In fact, to be more accurate, it was a voice that seemed to contain all the dark heaped-up soil of the earth as well as the endless consolations of the sky's blue light. In the gentle gusts of our local wind this song sailed like the sun itself from an upper-storey window of the hotel out into the morning air of the backyard, convincing everything it touched and anything that heard it that time itself was no more than a sighing, loving, somehow wistful thing.

I learnt later that it was 'Di Provenza il mar', Germont's baritone aria from *La Traviata*, but that's to somehow trivialise what I heard at the time. I knew nothing of operatic names – I still don't. All I knew was the beauty of a lost world somehow restored to me. Awakening from my dream, it was as if monstrous and needless fissures had been healed.

I propped myself up on an elbow and the singer began the aria again from its beginning. It grew fainter and louder again, and the penny dropped. It could only be The Lazy Tenor, singing this extraordinary welcome to his first day in Mangowak as he moved about his room.

So I lay back again, flat on my pillow, staring joyously at the old barn rafters. What had I said to Veronica when she'd pooh-poohed my comparison of our new visitor with Arthur Cravan? I said I was remaining open to everything.

'Di Provenza il mar' has a gentle pulse rather than a time signature, more an aquatic current than a rhythm, but of course, as The Lazy Tenor sang it from his upstairs room that morning, any orchestration there was could only come from the weather itself. In an instant, and for the very first time, I understood all the fuss about operatic singing. I understood the word 'aria' for the first time too, the word 'air', and that this is the very beautiful thing that sustains us. This was a sound as superlative and fresh as low-tide abalone, a song with all the tangy nourishment of a December strawberry; it was as miraculous as a champion racehorse from a backwater town, as awe-inspiring as a giant Otway mountain ash. It seemed to capture all peace, hold all power, and at the same time set it free. It included all restless and aimless desires but it also had the certainty of a well struck hammer blow.

As The Lazy Tenor began the aria for the third and last time, a new certainty of my own had begun growing within my chest. There was no way, no way on heaven and earth, that this new guest would be turfed out of my hotel.

It took me a long time, but finally, after the singing had stopped, I managed to rise and climb down my ladder. Pulling back the big barn doors, I went out to investigate.

There was not a sound from the hotel now, either upstairs or down. I made my way through the sunroom into the bar. I fossicked in the cupboards and started to fix myself an omelette. As I cracked a large galaxially speckled Heatherbrae pullet into the skillet, I noticed that still lying on the bar mat was a pink business card from an Altona hairdresser, which The Lazy Tenor had been exhibiting the night before as a souvenir of one of his conquests. The likelihood of the singing I'd just heard coming from the very same man who'd brandished that card like a trophy of war began to seem more and more remote. By the time the fourth egg was in my hands and I'd split it on the cast-iron rim, I was convinced the aria just had to be part of my dream, along with the melaleuca and the mussel harvests.

I leant down into the old champagne bucket where we kept the cut herbs and threw them in with the eggs: parsley, oregano, French tarragon, thyme and Vietnamese mint. As I kept prodding the moist parts of the omelette into the centre of the pan and fluffed and finally folded it onto my plate, the everyday reality of food had almost convinced me that, yes, the super-real aria was from the dream. But then I heard a shifting on the furniture, a creak from near the ashes of last night's fire. And a quiet voice asked, 'Is that you, Noel?'

I picked up my plate and carried it to the other side of the bar. I looked around the corner of the L-shaped room. There was The Blonde Maria, seated at one of the brown laminated tables in her dressing gown, smoking a tailor-made cigarette, with a half eaten chicken carcass and a bottle of ouzo in front of her.

'An ancient Greek breakfast,' I joked, pulling up a chair beside her and putting down my plate.

She smiled mildly, then laughed quietly through her nose. She took a swig of ouzo, straight from the bottle.

'All we need is naked men,' she said.

I nodded, laughed quietly, then tucked into my omelette. My appetite was strong. Beside me The Blonde Maria just puffed on her cigarette.

Eventually she leant back in her chair, let out a deep chicken-scented breath and asked, 'Could it really have been him?'

My knife and fork stilled. I considered the question and then asked tentatively, 'Do you mean the singing?'

The Blonde Maria gazed into my eyes with a glazy look. 'It's the most beautiful thing I've ever heard,' she said.

I swallowed, filled my cheeks with air and blew. 'Well, you won't get any arguments on that from me. I was just beginning to think I'd dreamt it.'

'I still can't believe it,' she went on. 'I really can't. I'd just woken up from the most beautiful dreams. I was riding a grey mare on the indigo slopes back in Dookie. I opened my eyes, felt so free and relaxed, and was about to go down to the ocean for a swim when I heard a man's footsteps in the hallway and remembered he was staying. So I stopped, sat down on the edge of the bed looking out the window, and waited. And then it started. Oh my God it was beautiful.'

I began eating again. Tink, tink, went the knife and fork. So I hadn't imagined it, or dreamt it. And up there in the room above us the singer still sat, presumably hunched over a laptop, writing his ribald book.

'I know there were a few people unhappy with his behaviour last night, Noel, but you can't kick him out. Not if he sings like that!' said The Blonde Maria.

I didn't reply. I finished off the omelette and wiped my mouth. Then I reached over and grabbed the ouzo bottle and took a burst for myself. A hot course of aniseed rushed through my blood.

'You don't have to worry, Maria,' I said then. 'That fella can stay in my hotel any old time. Let's just hope "The Tradesman's Entrance" is a bloody long book.'

Italian Yoga

LATER THAT DAY, IN A MOOD SOMEWHERE BETWEEN happiness and bafflement, I was standing alone in the toilet, having just installed the day's new loop in Duchamp, when our illustrious singer himself appeared, busting for a piss. He looked dishevelled, he reeked of beer and seaweed, but although his boots and shirt were wet on his huge frame he was buttoned to the cuffs, just like a boy from the inland would be.

He told me gruffly he'd been drinking on the beach since well before lunch. As his pent-up golden stream splashed into the stainless steel, the new contribution I'd chosen for Duchamp sounded almost more apt than surreal:

Drunken Seals

Sometimes large seals climb into the vineyards at night
to steal our grapes, just like Christians on a bender.

Many people have had their grapes stolen that way.
And when the seals have had enough,
they fold themselves into a sort of ball,
like an orange, and roll back into the sea,
and drink and drink and drink . . .

I'd chosen this particular loop to inspire a greater intake of alcohol, after the paltry quantities that were drunk the night before due to the distraction of our new guest. Now, as he finished pissing and zipped up, he asked me with a big smile if we could hear the loop again. So I stepped up onto the pissoir and had a turn. When I finished halfway through the second repeat, he clapped his big hands together and crowed, 'Well fuck me! That is deadset weird.' He put a thoughtful hand up to his chin and broke into a broad grin. 'This pub is tops. I slept like a twit up there last night. Nice room, nice breeze, nice fartsack. Took myself down to the beach this morning after breakfast, thought I'd give myself a day to settle in before I began the book. Bloody beautiful. Gotta watch the sunburn though. Freckly bastard aren't I, hey? The red hair and that. Mate, I might be able to drink but I'm no bloody drunken seal yet, that's for sure.'

Seeing him so happy, I decided to test the waters. I had to – I just couldn't stand the cultural confusion. The guy was like a walking collage. 'If you like Duchamp,' I said innocently, 'maybe you could sing something for us and we'll put it on the loop one day? That was *you* singing upstairs this morning wasn't it?'

He thrust his lips forward, turned his head to one side

and began scratching his neck. 'Singing?' he said. 'Is that what you'd call it? You should hear me on a good day.'

'Well I'd like to. What I heard this morning was beautiful.'

'Beautiful!' the big man scoffed, loudly, with a full horsey snort. 'No, mate, let me tell ya, only women are beautiful, only women. Well, maybe a recording or two of Tito Gobbi, in his prime mind you, but that stuff this mornin', nah, I was just stretchin'. Italian yoga I call it.'

I laughed. Italian yoga. That was a good one. But I couldn't work out whether he was serious or not. Surely he'd been told all his life how amazing his voice was, and surely somewhere along the line he'd put a lot of effort into getting it to sound like that. 'So are you a tenor?' I asked. 'Excuse my ignorance.'

'Ignorance!' he scoffed again. 'Come off it would ya! Don't worry about that, mate. This is your fuckin' joint isn't it? You can ask any question you like.'

Suddenly then his face took on a different cast. It settled, became more considered, and he said, 'I am a tenor actually, but I'm what they call a *lazy tenor*. Can't be bothered with the high notes you know. Most of the time I end up singing baritone parts. They're more solid anyway – you know, richer tone, more manly. Like that thing from *La Traviata* this morning, "Di Provenza il mar". Magnificent piece of music that. They say Verdi wrote it but it's more like an act of nature.'

The Lazy Tenor began to hum the aria right there in the toilet, and straightaway I could hear the honeyed resonance I'd encountered when I'd woken from my dream. Even with his lips closed, just humming, I could hear it.

He stopped as quickly as he'd started. 'My pa back in

Blokey Hollow used to sing that piece when he was fixin' his bikes. Heavily into pushbikes my pa.'

'Is that right?' I replied, deciding to tease out a bit more information. 'Did he have a good voice too?'

'Pa? Nah, you couldn't really say that. But I liked it, as a kid and that. He was a smart bloke, Pa. Made my first violin with his own hands. It was rough as guts lookin' back, probably sounded like a shot cat, but he made it himself you know. In his pushgrunt workshop.'

'In his what?'

'His pushgrunt workshop. Pushgrunt's what we used to call bikes in our part of the world. Pa had dozens of 'em there in his workshop. And old wheels and bits and pieces lyin' about.'

'So you play the violin as well?'

'Not anymore. Don't ride bikes anymore either. Used to though. Used to race 'em as a real young fella. And then when I got a bit older I used to chase sheilas on 'em. Geez, the miles I've pedalled a pushgrunt after the hairy magnet! Hey? Fuckin' miles alright. Most of central Victoria I reckon!'

'Is that right?' I said, poker-faced.

'Yep, I reckon. Used to go down to Harcourt, Castlemaine, up to Boort. Went as far as Mildura once. Folks thought I was going to sing in church choirs but nuh, I was pedallin' after the skirt. Now tell me, would ya, who was that sheila I saw here last night? With the dyed hair and the big brown eyes? She went home early.'

'You mean Veronica?'

'That's it, that's the one. They were callin' her Ronnie.

Nice lookin', bit exotic. Not that I'm here to shag. Nuh, I'm here to write – I've told you that.'

'Yeah, "The Tradesman's Entrance".'

At the mention of his book The Lazy Tenor's face opened like a child's. It was the first signal I had that he wasn't completely cocksure.

'That's right! You remembered!' he cried.

'Well, I could hardly forget.'

'Nah, I suppose not. Great title isn't it? Titles are important you know. They gotta sound good. Otherwise you're stuffed. That's why the Italians write the best operas, mate. The language just sounds so grouse. Virtually everything rhymes you know. *La Traviata, Il Trovatore, Rigoletto, Otello* . . . I mean "The Tradesman's Entrance" doesn't sound as good as that but it's funny you know, like a punchline to a joke.'

'You don't reckon it's a bit *off*?'

'What do ya mean "off"? Like too dirty or somethin'?'

'Well, yeah.'

He wiped a polyester cuff across his brow. 'Oh geez,' he said, in a mildly depressed tone. 'I didn't pick you for an uptight prick. You are the publican here aren't ya?' He nodded towards Duchamp. 'You obviously don't mind a bit of a laugh, hey? So, what the fuck?'

I giggled through my nose; it's all I could do. Without going right back through the history of the oppression of women and dragging out the worthy clichés about the objectification of the female body, there was nothing I could say. He had me stumped. Plus, I was cornered by my sheer amazement at what this bloke entailed. By the pure and natural qualities of both his singing and his boorishness. He was nothing if not well and truly *alive*. If I was ever gonna try to rein him in, I'd have to take a few deep breaths first. But now wasn't the time, I decided. No, I certainly wasn't up to it there and then. And besides, I was having too much fun.

The Little-Girl Voice

I DIDN'T SEE THE LAZY TENOR FOR THE REST OF THE DAY, but at 5 pm sharp he was standing at the bar, leaning on his elbow with a glass in his hand, his jaw jutting out and a sociable twinkle in his eye.

First he started talking to Joan Sutherland behind the bar, but instead of small-talking his way towards familiarity or exchanging pleasantries in order to establish a healthy and inde-fatigable drinker-to-barman relationship, he launched straight into describing his own purpose in life, which, as he said, was once to 'shag anything that moved' and now was simply to tell people about it by writing his upstairs masterpiece.

But of course, after Jen and the boys had had to go home early the night before, Big Joan was not as genial as he normally would've been. In fact, declaring his ground straightaway, he suggested to The Lazy Tenor that The Horse Room might be a more suitable place for the retelling of his exploits. 'Plus,' said Joan, 'tonight for Happy Hour we're reverting to Noel's old favourite, live-streaming Vatican Radio from Italy. I think you and the Pope might be at cross purposes.'

On hearing this information The Lazy Tenor beamed, just like he had when he'd heard the 'Drunken Seals' loop on Duchamp. It seemed that the crazier the pub was the more he liked it. When Guido the Tourist and a friend walked in during Happy Hour, I watched closely for their reactions. As they ordered their drinks from Joan, they had Pope Benedict on one side, whining away at his digital angelus, and The Lazy Tenor on the other side, describing 'shoehorning a salesgirl in a back room at Northland'. I don't know quite whether you would call the scenario Dada but it was certainly uproarious, contradictory and atypical, as the look on the faces of the two out-of-towners showed as they took their drinks and sat down at a table.

Once again Veronica was aghast at The Lazy Tenor's narratives. She kept glaring at me as she moved about the hotel, picking up dirty glasses and plates and emptying ashtrays. She had a point, of course. It wasn't as if The Lazy Tenor's exploits made for brilliant entertainment – most of the tales were told purely to the advantage of his own sexual prowess and for that they lacked both charm and imagination. The thing was, though, he very seldom actually swore. His language was too euphemistic to be foul, and therefore it required a certain amount of interpretation along the way. Because of this it seemed almost possible that children could've stayed in the bar after all, as he spoke of the 'hairy magnet' and the 'shoehorn'.

In the end, however, it's always too difficult to tell just how much your average nine- or ten-year-old does understand about sex. And so, for that reason alone, with The Lazy Tenor as a Happy Hour fixture I feared that the public bar of The Grand Hotel was about to become like a typical Australian public bar of old, full of men and men alone, all clutching their beers for dear life as over in the lounge, or outside in the beer garden, or back at home, their wives and kids left them alone to their shickered shadow life. Any inkling of such a scene in a hotel of mine had to be stopped. We had both a tradition and a new charter to uphold, a tradition going back to the original Grand Hotel, of true and open hospitality in Mangowak, and a new charter that called for a different type of open slather, for the spreading of the freedom virus and a new knockabout rendition of the end of the world.

This of course was where the problems lay. On the one hand, yes, an eight-year-old could no longer pour beer in the bar with The Lazy Tenor in full swing but, on the other hand, the very idea of such a wildcard turning up to stay was very much in the spirit of our charter. Struck by the dilemma, I poured myself a Dancing Brolga and sat quietly on one of the old church pews at the big table to ruminate. 'If only he wasn't so boorish,' I was thinking, when Oscar stepped through from the sunroom looking for me.

The kid had a worried look on his face and sat down beside me on the pew. He whispered up close, 'What the hell have you done to The Blonde Maria?'

'What do you mean?'

'Well, she's up in her room, still in a dressing gown and

refusing to come down and sing. And people keep on coming up to me wanting to know when we're starting. They're sick of listening to bozo over there.'

He pointed in the direction of The Lazy Tenor, who was midstream with his hands out wide, re-enacting another scenario for Kooka, the Grundig, Givva Way, and a frustrated Joan Sutherland behind the bar.

'Well why won't she come down?' I asked Oscar.

'She won't say. She's totally different all of a sudden. She's talking in a little-girl voice like Marilyn Monroe and drinking ouzo out of the bottle. And she won't budge.'

'Shit.'

'Yeah, shit, Uncle Noel. Me and Dad and the boys are ready to roll, and believe you me if we don't play something soon that bloke over there at the bar's gonna get lynched.'

I frowned and drained the rest of my beer. 'I'll go and have a word with her,' I said, getting up off the pew.

I stomped upstairs, giving The Blonde Maria plenty of footfall by way of a warning that I was coming. At the top of the stairs, however, I found the platypus and black ducks floating happily in the hallway carpet and the willows of the old unrevegetated wallpaper rustling blithely above me. The air was soothing, cool and quiet after the dynamics of the bar.

After knocking gently, I entered the room to find her sitting, just as Oscar had described, on a chair by the window table in her dressing gown. Looking up at me, she smiled meekly.

In front of her on the table was a bottle of ouzo, a packet of Peter Stuyvesants, and a half finished jigsaw of the Bavarian Alps. I pulled up a chair and sat beside her, facing the pine trees out the window. She bowed her head but said nothing.

I don't know why I didn't come straight to the point. I just sensed that the situation was suddenly very delicate and that our previously bawdy chanteuse had now to be treated with kid gloves. Idly I started flicking through the pieces of the jigsaw, looking for the solid block of pale blue that the jigsaw lid showed the alpine light was reflecting in the window of the mountain hut.

The Blonde Maria took a swig from the ouzo bottle and silently the two of us looked at the little hut in the foothills, dwarfed by the great Bavarian mountains behind. The Blonde Maria lit a cigarette. She offered me one by pushing the pack towards me, but I declined.

'So what is it?' I asked gently. 'They're all expecting you down there.'

In a tiny tremulous little voice she replied, 'I know.'

I frowned. She was in a very strange state.

'So what's wrong, Maria? Why won't you get dressed and come down? Jim and Oscar and the band are itching to start.'

'I don't know,' she said, again in the frail little-girl voice.

'Well you must have some idea.'

She shook her head, with an ashamed look on her face.

I leant back on my chair and stared out at the pine trees. 'The thing is, Maria . . . you can tell me what's on your mind, whatever it is that's troubling you. I can take it.'

She took a drag on her smoke and looked sheepish again, but apart from that nothing, just silence.

Out in the hallway now I almost thought I could hear the river lapping at the door.

'Look,' I said, a bit more firmly. 'If you don't come down and sing, The Connotations are gonna become The Barrels again. They'll bore everyone senseless.' I laughed, to make light of things. 'And someone will bop The Lazy Tenor right on the nose. Probably Joan Sutherland I reckon.'

At this apparently innocuous remark the ouzo-swilling jigsaw player just crumpled in her dressing gown. She began sobbing uncontrollably.

I got the shock of my life. What the hell was going on? Instinctively I put my arm around her, comforting her, while trying to nut it out.

She sobbed and sobbed, her body rocking to and fro on the chair. Finally, and still in the little-girl voice, she said, 'I'd like the night off, Noel, please, if that's okay. I need the night off.'

Her pain was so demonstrative and her voice so fey and eerie that I had no hesitation. 'Okay, Maria,' I said. 'That's absolutely fine. Take the night off. You've been going hard haven't you? You've been a trooper. I'll tell Jim and the boys to go back to the stuff they were doing before you showed up. Who knows, we might even get The Lazy Tenor to sing. Did I tell you how come he's called The Lazy Tenor?'

With this question she started sobbing uncontrollably again and didn't answer. I rubbed her back and cooed. 'There there,' I said. 'Calm down. It's alright. You're just tired. Why don't you get into bed?'

Ten minutes later I left her still in the chair, having settled down a bit after I changed the subject back to the jigsaw. I told her I'd pop back up later in the evening to check that she was alright and that I'd even bring her a plate of Nan's mushroom moussaka, which was on the menu that night. The Blonde Maria nodded and smiled at me weakly. For the moment there was nothing more I could do. I clicked her door shut and headed back down the stairs.

Kooka Falls Off His Perch

WHEN I GOT BACK DOWNSTAIRS, A ROW HAD ERUPTED, but not the one I was expecting. The seemingly innocuous Italian tourist Guido had turned up with a T-shirt that had 'Skinheads D'Italia' written on it, and when someone had asked him about it all hell had broken loose. Guido had gone on a long and obscure political tirade about the glacial inadequacies of democratic processes in the climate-change era and the can-do powers of neo-fascism.

It seemed Skinheads D'Italia was a far-right cult who worshipped at the shrine of Mussolini. Guido had obviously had quite a few Dancing Brolgas, and his normally sociable and gregarious personality had warped into a defiant stance. Challenged by a cluster of locals on the philosophy of the Skinheads D'Italia cult, he grew increasingly arrogant. As Ash Bowen started accusing him of anti-Semitism, Guido took a patronising tone, dismissing not the Jewish peoples but rather Australia and Australians as the idiot children of the global village. 'Yoo are sheltaired. To yoo laiff iz a plything,' he was saying, as I made my way behind the bar to stand beside Joan. 'But, een Yoorope we mast faize ther chairlengerz. We mast be ztrong end see ther sityooaijen en howl eet ken be kyewered.'

Of course neo-fascism was one thing but saying that Australians were irrelevant innocents was another. People really started to get their backs up, and the more riled they became the more supercilious Guido's smile of certainty became. Even The Lazy Tenor interrupted his own monologues to tell Guido to 'put a sock in it'. Well, that was a turn-up. Eventually Veronica and Ash Bowen engaged Guido in some serious analysis of the Skinheads D'Italia platform and the three of them went over to the pews to argue it out.

The bar was quite full by this stage, and noisy as all get-out. What with The Lazy Tenor still bar-slapping about his exploits to a small but appreciative crowd and the declarations of Guido raising the room temperature, and of course with Jim, Oscar, and the rest of The Barrels impatiently tuning up and noodling on their instruments, not to mention Pope Benedict's whining incantations from the speakers at the bar, the scene was quite chaotic.

I poured myself a Loosener and went over to tell Jim that The Blonde Maria wasn't coming down. He was demoralised by the news. I tried to cheer him up. 'Come on,' I cajoled, 'it's only one night. You played plenty of gigs before she ever showed up.'

'Yeah, but we had no idea what it was to play great live

music then,' Jim declared. 'She's showed us, Noely. She's raised the bar. We can't go back to *Top Cat* and *Morning of the Earth* now. It just feels backward.'

I rolled my eyes. That was all I needed. 'Come on,' I said. 'If you guys don't start up, everyone'll be stuck with either bozo at the bar or the Nazi in the corner. You wouldn't want that would ya?'

Jim peered over at The Lazy Tenor and then across at where Guido was gesticulating at Veronica and Ash. He shook his head slowly. But he said nothing. Eventually he just blurted, 'It's a fuckin' mess, Noel,' stood up and began putting his guitar back into its case.

'Hey, wait a minute,' I said, alarmed. 'Don't put that away yet. I'm relying on you.'

Jim swung back around angrily and brought his face up close to mine. Our noses were nearly touching as he pulled big-brother rank over me.

'Now you listen here, kid,' he said. 'Don't you dare lay that trip on me. You're the one who's dragged everyone into this weirdo freakshow you're calling a hotel. What do you reckon Mum and Dad would say about this place? Hey?'

I wiped the spittle of my elder brother off my cheeks and scoffed. 'What, and you haven't been having a good time? Don't give me that.'

At which point Jim pushed me in the chest. But just as we were ready to have our first fist fight in many a long year, a loud resounding CRACK was heard from across the room. Jim and I forgot our disagreement and looked over to see old Kooka falling from his bentwood bar stool onto the hard wooden floor.

Everyone stopped their conversations and immediately hurried to Kooka's aid. The old bloke with the bronzed bull head was lying pale and crumpled in his slacks and white singlet on the floor. His mouth was pursed and his eyes pinched, closed tight in pain. Veronica and Joan leant over him and checked his pulse and breathing. He was still alive but his complexion was ghostly white and he looked to be in some degree of discomfort. What was going on? Had the stool collapsed under him, or was he having a heart attack?

From the beer garden Jen Sutherland miraculously appeared with a first-aid kit and, grabbing a cushion from one of the bar-room couches, propped it under Kooka's head and made him more comfortable. As I leant across and clicked off the 'record' button on the Grundig, it seemed that Kooka was coming around. Maybe he had just fainted? Joan took two white towels from his wife and ran them under a cold tap behind the bar. He handed them back to Jen, who wiped the old-timer's brow and told everyone gently to stand back.

After a few minutes it seemed that Kooka was quite stable. He still hadn't opened his eyes but he was breathing evenly and responding to questions. When Jen offered him a glass of water, he shook his head and asked for a claret. Jen suggested that mightn't be such a good idea but Kooka was adamant. 'A claret. Lovely,' he said, in a hoarse but calm voice.

As the licensee of the hotel and a great supporter of Kooka's historical activities, I cut straight to the chase. I reached up above the bar into our claret store and popped the cork on a 1971 Hardys Red. Slopping a bit into a glass to check that it hadn't turned, I took a sip and then filled up the remainder.

What a drop! It was full, complex, a tonic for even the healthier among us, let alone those who'd just fallen off their perch.

'Here you go, old fella,' I said, leaning down and putting the claret to Kooka's lips. Still he didn't open his eyes. But he took a sip and breathed easy.

'Been known to cure a broken leg,' he said quietly.

He took another sip and ran his tongue across his lips. But then his eyes pinched again and he grimaced, obviously still in some kind of pain. 'Nice drop,' he said in a whisper, and then, 'Hit "stop".'

'What's that, Kooka?' I said.

'Hit "stop",' he said again, but still I couldn't make out what he meant. I looked over my shoulder at Jen to see whether she heard it more clearly. Jen just shrugged.

'Sorry, Kooka, I didn't catch that,' I said, leaning in towards him with my right ear.

'Hit "stop",' he said again, but this time added, 'on the Grundig.'

'Oh,' I said. 'It's already done, Kooka. I stopped the tape just after you fell.'

Kooka nodded slowly. 'More plonk,' he said then.

Before long he had drained the glass but was still wincing occasionally with pain and hadn't opened his eyes. What were we going to do? At some point he'd have to see a doctor, but he didn't look like he wanted to be moved far right then. The Lazy Tenor, who'd been waiting patiently at the corner of the bar to resume his narratives, suggested we carry the old fella upstairs and pop him on his bed in The Sewing Room. It seemed like a sensible idea.

'Would you like to lie down upstairs for a while, Kooka?'
Jen whispered in his ear, as she stroked his brow with the cool
towel.

The old man nodded. 'Yairs,' he said. 'A little lie down.'

The problem was he couldn't walk. We weren't even sure
he could stand. Eventually we decided we'd have to carry him.

Immediately The Lazy Tenor left his talking post at the
corner of the bar and moved towards Kooka. 'Here,' he said.
'I'll carry him upstairs.'

Before any of us could protest, The Lazy Tenor had bent
down on his haunches and carefully, even tenderly, lifted Kooka
up off the hotel floor. In one fluid movement he hoisted him
over his left shoulder, just as you would a bag of Yeo potatoes.
Kooka didn't even flinch. He just hung there, claret-lipped,
slack-mouthed, draped over The Lazy Tenor's towering frame,
where he promptly fell fast asleep.

The Lazy Tenor marched out of the bar, through the
sunroom, past The Horse Room and Duchamp and up the
stairs. I followed with Jen, the first-aid kit and the bottle of
1971 Hardys. As we reached the Sewing Room door, I could
hear the opening strains of 'Peace in the Valley' coming from
downstairs. It seemed that Kooka's turn had changed Jim's
mind. The Barrels were up and running again.

Since Kooka had moved into The Sewing Room, I'd
paid little attention to it. In fact I'd hardly even been in there
since the day we helped him move. To my surprise now, as
we entered, I found the room just as we'd left it that day. The
boxes and crates of the archive sat unopened near the ocean-
facing window, and the only furniture was the single bed in

the middle of the large room, the wicker chair beside it, a small bedside table and Mum's two old standard lamps. Apart from that the room was empty and as always seemed quite a vast and cavernous space.

Gently The Lazy Tenor eased old Kooka down onto the bed, and Jen removed his shoes. We let him lie there above the blankets for a time, just to observe how he was faring. There was a little bit of colour coming back into his face but even so he had still not opened his eyes. He was obviously exhausted. The Lazy Tenor stepped back out of the room without a word, no doubt keen to get back downstairs, and left myself and Jen to attend to the old man.

Jen started asking Kooka questions, trying to ascertain whether he'd broken any bones or was feeling any physical discomfort, but he would just shake his head and finally she stopped asking. The two of us sat there with Kooka under the high pitched roofs of The Sewing Room and shrugged our shoulders. We discussed the possibilities in a whisper and agreed that we'd call our local doctor, Bernard Feast, first thing in the morning. For the time being it seemed as if Kooka was happy to rest.

Jen had left her two boys at home with her sister, and so she stayed beside Kooka's bed for the rest of the night until stumps. Downstairs in the bar The Barrels seemed to have found a way to enjoy just being an old surf band again and The Lazy Tenor had retired to The Horse Room so his stories could be heard without the racket. At closing time, when I went upstairs and took over from Jen, she assured me that Kooka was quite calm. I sat there falling in and out of sleep right through the small hours. Even though I was meant to be keeping an eye on the old bloke, I have to admit that sitting in the quiet of The Sewing Room in the middle of the night flooded me with memories, not only of my goodnight chats with Mum as a kid but also of all the old stories she used to tell us about growing up with Papa in the meteorological station.

When the next morning dawned with the warbling of magpies, Kooka didn't wake up. Well, he did briefly – he even opened his eyes at one point and looked around the large room – but he closed his eyes again straightaway, rearranged his body among the bedclothes and began to snore.

When Dr Feast arrived after breakfast, he stood at the end of Kooka's bed for quite some time, just observing him. Eventually he woke the old fella gently, felt his pulse with his finger, checked his heart rate with his ear, before declaring that there seemed nothing much the matter with him. Dr Feast, as thorough and old fashioned as he is, could only describe what had happened to Kooka as 'a turn'. He suggested he have a break from alcohol and just lie in the bed in The Sewing Room and rest.

After the check-up I did the usual thing and asked Dr Feast to join me downstairs for a cup of tea and a biscuit. We sat in the bar talking casually about the town, and of course about the progress of the hotel. Then, just as he was finishing his tea and getting up to leave, we heard that honey-toned morning voice again, singing from upstairs in Room One.

At hearing the opening words of the famous aria from *La Traviata*, Bernard Feast's eyes opened wide at the bar. Without so much as a word to me he put down his Gladstone bag and walked slowly into the sunroom, where he stood listening. Then, as if in a trance, he stepped out of the sunroom and into the backyard. I watched him stop there under the pine trees, looking up towards The Lazy Tenor's window quite agog.

The Lazy Tenor sang the aria over and over again that morning. The weather was still fine, the pollen still drifting, and with his voice in the gauzy air, time, as we have grown accustomed to it, once again ceased to exist.

I sat down on the two-seater couch in the sunroom and experienced the double pleasure of listening to The Lazy Tenor's morning song and watching Dr Feast's enjoyment of it. He obviously knew the piece, because after a while he started mouthing the words. When finally The Lazy Tenor concluded his morning session, the good doctor, whose sure hands and safe judgement had brought nearly the whole population of Mangowak and Minapre into the world over the years, shook his head slowly from side to side and began to applaud.

It's funny but I immediately panicked, fearing The Lazy Tenor mightn't respond well to applause for what seemed to be just a personal habit of his mornings. Abruptly I raised my hand in the air, gesturing urgently through the window to the doctor to stop.

Dr Feast's hands fell immediately to his side, but unexpectedly applause could still be heard. It was coming from upstairs. And along with it came muffled cries of 'Bravo! Bravo!' through the walls and the floorboards. It was The Blonde Maria, enraptured in her room. She clapped enthusiastically for a few moments longer, and with an ecstatic cry of 'Magnificent!' she ceased. The quiet of the riverflat once again reigned over the morning.

A little later, as I stood in the backyard listening to Dr Feast's Peugeot purring away along the Dray Road, I looked up at the second-storey windows for signs of life. The Lazy Tenor's window was flung open, with Nan's floral curtains shifting in the subtle currents of the air. But there was no other movement. Finally, upon hearing a footfall and a shifting of furniture from The Blonde Maria's room, I decided that the poignant aftermath of the aria had disappeared. I made my way back inside for breakfast, reflecting on the pros and cons of our current lodgers. There were definitely marks on both sides of the ledger.

Holy Bohemian

DURING THE COURSE OF THAT DAY KOOKA'S HEALTH stayed much the same. I'd check in on him from time to time to find him sound asleep, with a peaceful look on his face, and no sign of any discomfort. The Blonde Maria's situation, however, seemed to be worsening. She still wouldn't budge from her room, nor would she even change out of her dressing gown. She'd completed the jigsaw of the Bavarian Alps and was now chewing through the eclectic collection of my mother's books she'd found on the lacquered Oregon bookshelf in her room.

It was the life of St Thérèse of Lisieux that The Blonde Maria was reading when I knocked on her door just before lunch. Once again I found her sitting at the table in front of the window. This time she was more prepared to speak, although still with a trace of the little-girl voice of the day before.

She asked me straightaway if I'd heard The Lazy Tenor's singing again that morning. I told her I had and explained that it was Dr Feast who was applauding in the garden. 'It was beautiful alright,' I said. 'But I don't know whether clapping him might make him go back into his shell.'

The Blonde Maria raised her finger to her mouth in horror. 'Oh my God, I hadn't thought of that,' she exclaimed.

Clearly she was still a little unhinged. But somewhere inside me a tall bird fluttered its wings and I finally realised that her retreat to the room had something to do with The Lazy Tenor's singing.

'You know,' she said, with a sudden change of tone, and holding up the saint's life in her right hand, 'this is an interesting book.'

'Yeah. I think I read it, but years ago now.'

'Mmm,' was all The Blonde Maria said.

'From memory, though,' I added, trying to fill the gap in the conversation, 'Thérèse had a lot of insight.'

'The point is, Noel, it is impossible for a bird to sing a wrong note.'

Rather than explain this remark, The Blonde Maria promptly lit a cigarette. Then, as if she couldn't focus on any one thing for long, she changed the subject again. 'Was that Kooka I heard calling in the night?'

'It could have been,' I said. I told her about his falling off the stool and how he had to be carried up to bed.

She nodded happily. 'Yes it was him then. I thought so.'

'Did he sound okay? He wasn't distressed was he?'

'Oh no, not particularly. It was more as if he was dreaming.

Calling out to people he knew. But quite happily I think.'

'I see.'

The Blonde Maria's expression changed yet again and she stared at me gravely. 'I'll never sing again,' she blurted out.

Inside I frowned but externally I tried to look calm. 'Why not?' I asked.

'I'm not a singer,' she said. 'There's something I am, but it's not that.'

'I see. Well, what is it you are then?'

'I don't know.'

I breathed through my nose, a bit impatiently now. 'Well, I'm not a publican, Maria, but look at me.'

'What do you mean by that?' she asked.

'Well, *I'm not a publican*!' I said, finally exasperated. 'We're all doing things we're not necessarily suited to.'

The Blonde Maria smiled at me patronisingly. She was once all good times and insouciance but now the vaudevillian had taken another role. 'But that's my point, Noel,' she said. 'Who wants to continue as a fraud? Not me. You can count me out on that score. At last I've encountered a human being who is on the one undivided path. I've woken to the living proof the last two mornings. I know now, for the first time, what music is. What it *really* is. That's good enough for me. We can't go on like this.'

'Can't go on like what?' I said. 'It's a beautiful voice, but hey, so is yours.'

As soon as the words had come out of my mouth, I winced. The Blonde Maria's voice was good – as an entertainer she was fabulous – but when all was said and done The Lazy Tenor worked on a different plane. We both knew I had proved her very point with the lie.

Slowly I straightened my face and stared at her. She had a different look again now, a zealot's look, a look of shining realisation. She sat before me like some reformed harlot of song, smoking in a dressing gown. I heard my brother Jim's words ringing in my ears. What would my mother and father make of this hotel their old house had become, with the author of 'The Tradesman's Entrance' in one room, a sick old man taken to his bed in another, and a holy bohemian in between?

For a precipitous moment, sitting there at the table with The Blonde Maria, my humour grew slipshod, my inner vision went blank, and I retreated to the dank loneliness that had exiled me from town. With a psychiatric urgency I clasped my left wrist with my right hand to see if it felt wooden and numb. But no, there was warmth there, there was life. I could still feel the blood coursing through me. I hadn't reverted. I wasn't the Reverse Pinocchio. Instead I felt those globulous, tremulous, giant-sized tears welling up in my heart. 'Oh dear,' I said aloud. And then, shaking my head in a way that immediately reminded me of my mum when she couldn't see the lighter side of one of my world-shattering childhood dilemmas, I said it again. 'Oh dear.'

By the time I'd said it for the third time it was with a hint of irony and a smile. A little laugh of gladness spluttered out of me for the knowledge that despite the madness of the human world I would always remain sane as long as those globulous tears were welling up beside my laughter. As long as they were there, I knew that the garden of my life would have both the sun and rain it required.

Sensing my transition from uncertainty to humour, The Blonde Maria grew a little uncertain herself and retreated back into her shell. She picked up the book of the saint again and buried her nose in it haughtily.

'Oh dear,' I said. Yes, I said it again, realising what a debilitating effect The Lazy Tenor's voice had had on The Grand Hotel's chanteuse.

Finally getting up to go, I put my hand on Maria's shoulder and asked her if she could check in on Kooka from time to time, seeing as though they were both confined to their rooms. She nodded into the book, still haughtily, and almost as if I didn't have to ask.

Kooka Stays Put

THE NEXT FEW DAYS PASSED SMOOTHLY, IN THE NEW rhythm created by the upstairs inhabitants of the hotel. The Lazy Tenor would entertain some and upset others every Happy Hour. Jim and The Barrels would stoically ride their way through their sets, and up in The Sewing Room Kooka would lie with eyes shut in the big space, snoozing and farting and being attended to by myself, Jen and Joan, and in the wee hours of the night by his new saintly companion, The Blonde Maria.

It was early November and all through the valley the mushrooms were still sprouting. They remained on the menu right through the month. Dishes such as 'Japanese Rising Tide Soup', 'Endless Autumn Pasta', and 'Perennial Mushroom Pie' were constantly being invented. It was disconcerting for people, even subtly terrifying, this surfeit of fungi, but nevertheless

The Grand Hotel's purpose seemed stronger than ever – to cheer people up. In this respect we were remaining faithful to the much loved tradition of hospitality in Mangowak.

Each morning The Lazy Tenor would fling open his window and regale the riverflat with his gift. In essence it became a form of metaphysical rent he was paying to the likes of myself in the barn, The Blonde Maria in her increasingly monastic room, and anyone else who bothered to drop by to hear the arias. Even Kooka, whose eyes like a newborn pup's were gradually beginning to open more and more, remarked to The Blonde Maria that he hadn't heard anything as good for a long time. 'It's like eavesdropping at the doors of nature,' he told her one evening, when she'd asked him what he thought.

About ten days after his turn on the stool in the bar I took a plate of Endless Autumn Pasta up to Kooka for his lunch. When I'd placed the tray in his lap and opened the ocean and inland windows to circulate the salty air, he asked me if it was possible if lunch could be accompanied by a drink. Well, he was sitting up quite chipper in his single bed, and despite Dr Feast's recommendations I couldn't see the harm in it. I went downstairs straightaway and returned with a carafe of red wine.

'Well, Kooka,' I said, pouring the wine. 'I reckon you'll be up and about again soon. You've got good colour. And anyway, it's time you got that whodunnit game going downstairs.'

Before he'd fallen off his perch, Kooka had been concocting a barroom game based on the hushed-up mystery of why the original Grand Hotel had burnt down. The game was to be his fun way of exposing everyone to his particular obsession for our long-ago predecessor, and also maybe to nut out once and for all what had brought it to an end. Why had Joan Sweeney shot through to Chicago and refused to answer the police's questions? And why were the authorities convinced it was arson yet they couldn't find a culprit? Basically the game would work like a TV whodunnit. From his research Kooka would provide us with the scenarios and the characters, and each player would try to patch together the most plausible story to explain the fire.

Kooka had been very excited about it. In fact, around lunchtime on the day of his fall I'd found him sitting alone at the communal dining-room table in the bar, surrounded by an assortment of the different coloured shards of time-smoothed glass from the tartan shortbread tin I'd seen in his shack. He fondled these cast-offs from the old Grand Hotel bottle dump with a reverence usually reserved for religious relics. With great enthusiasm he showed me the broken decorative lettering and the ingenious nineteenth-century graphics of the brands embossed on the softened pieces of hand-blown glass, and began to tell me how his whodunnit game would work, who he considered the main protagonists to be, and how each player would get his or her own different coloured piece of glass at the outset, which he would add to as their scenarios and scores progressed over the coming rounds. He also planned to make up special cards, complete with a map of the old Mangowak, for each player to concoct his or her scenario with. Next to the tin and the glass on the table in front of him there was a sheet of adhesive labels with the names of the current regular clientele of The Grand Hotel and other names that I presumed to be the protagonists in the hotel of the past. He had seemed quite possessed by the concept on that afternoon in the bar but now, when I brought it up, it didn't seem to register at all.

As he looked at me blankly, I didn't want to press the issue. He was getting on, after all, and maybe his falling off his perch was the first sign of a coming decline. Instead we clinked glasses and wished each other a ritual 'good health'. Kooka took a sip and smacked his lips. 'Terrific,' he said. 'Bloody nice drop.'

'Yep. Well you can blame the Balts for this one, Kooka. It's from Finland.'

'You don't say!'

'Yep. I do.'

Kooka licked his lips again and nodded in a surprised re-affirmation of the wine's quality. It was a light summer-berry wine recommended to me by our wine supplier. He'd thought the novelty might appeal to me, as Finnish wines had only recently been imported into the country.

'Now, Noel,' Kooka said, adjusting his bedclothes, 'there's something I've been meaning to talk to you about.'

The old fella's big birdlike head took on a serious cast so I leant in a bit closer out of respect. 'Yeah, Kooka?'

'Yes, well, I was wondering how you'd feel if I just propped here for a while. Instead of, well, you know, getting back up on the horse?'

I stayed poker-faced, careful not to betray any surprise. 'You're comfortable here are you, Kooka?' I said.

'Too right,' he replied enthusiastically. 'I like this room, Noel. And the bed itself is nice and soft, just how I like it. To tell you the truth, I don't think I can be bothered with anything much anymore.'

Kooka looked at me sheepishly and took a sip of the wine. I took a sip too. It was a nice drop indeed. Then he said, 'Well I'm gettin' on a bit you know, Noel, and –'

But I cut in. 'You don't have to explain, Kooka.'

'No?'

'No.'

'It's just that I've been on me Pat Malone for years now, since Mary died, and what with one thing and another, falling off that stool the other night made me realise it's time I gave it a spell.'

'Kooka, it's alright. You don't have to explain.'

'Well, Noel, I've been lyin' here snoozin' and thinkin', looking about at this old room where your mum, Audrey, used to fix up my shirts and trousers and run up dresses for Mary and the rest of the Mangowak lasses, and I dunno, I just have a notion I could be content here. That it'd be a good place to finally prop and maybe have a bit of a think about things.'

'Fair enough, Kooka, if that's what you want.'

'Yairs, well to tell you the truth I feel like I've been runnin' around like a blue-arsed fly almost since the day Mary died.'

I nodded, sympathetically. 'But what about the Grundig? It's still downstairs on the bar you know.'

'Is that so? Well, to be perfectly honest, Noel, I think the days of the Grundig are over for me.'

He let out a deep sigh, a tired sigh, as if the very thought of the portable recorder exhausted him. 'You do what you think best with it,' he said. 'And that tape that's in it, well, it's all monkey business anyway. That big fella's stories, down at the bar. That's about all I've recorded for the last little while.'

He took a last and demonstratively savoured sip of the Finnish wine and placed the glass gently on the bedside table. Through the inland sash window flickers of light were playing on Kooka's unshaven face as he turned on his side to go back to sleep.

'Bit weary now, old fella?' I said, fondly.

'Yairs,' he said, in a hoarse whisper, 'nicely so. The food and the grog. From Finland, eh?'

'Yep. Who would've thought?'

'Like bloody nectar, Noel,' he said, almost inaudibly, his eyelids beginning to grow heavy and close.

'Yep,' I said sadly, 'like nectar, Kooka. Now you just rest. Don't worry about a thing. You can prop up here for as long as you want, old-timer. You can stay for keeps if you like.'

As Kooka's breathing deepened and he sank away into a deep sleep, I added quietly, 'Yes, my old friend, you can stay till stumps, till the last drinks are called and even beyond. You can stay till all your local histories are finally said and done, old boy.'

And with that I got up, took the half empty carafe of wine and tiptoed out of the room.

Lovesick

AS THE WORD GOT AROUND TOWN THAT KOOKA HAD hung up his boots and was lying in The Sewing Room, a few locals took the trouble to visit during the daytime and see if he was okay. In fact for a few days there I was quite flat out before opening hours with showing these familiar faces up the stairs. Joe Conebush, whose grandparents had taken Kooka in as their orphaned cousin from the city in the 1930s, was one who stopped in for a stickybeak, and also Dusty Miller, Prickly Moses, Penny Royal, Old Jack Heath and his daughter Erica, and even David Baird, Minapre's fitness-fanatic postman, came running by one day to pay his respects.

Everyone was quite concerned about the dear old fella, until of course they saw how contented he was in the big lumpy bed in The Sewing Room. Propped up there, with his broad tanned head poking out of his light-blue collarless pyjamas, he'd welcome everyone in quite cheerily, enquire as to the health of themselves and their families, and chat pleasantly enough until they'd seen what they had to see and could happily go about their business, knowing Kooka was perfectly alright. Sometimes on these visits they'd talk a little history with him, offering tidbits that they were sure he'd add to his archive, even though it still sat unpacked in its boxes over near the ocean window. They were surprised when he'd nod and say 'go on' but not reach for a notebook and pencil to record a precise account of the information. Later on, as we descended the stairs, I'd explain that he'd not only hung up his walking boots but his history ears as well. 'Is that so?' the visitors would say, or, 'You're kidding surely?', and some of them would grow almost anxious at the thought. 'You're sure he's alright, Noel?' they'd ask, to which I could only reply that his appetite for food and drink was as healthy as ever and he seemed far from depressed, just a little more thoughtful if anything, and occasionally perhaps a little weary of the trivial things in life.

So we went about the daily business of the hotel, serving drinks and food, balancing out the demands of the clientele with our own idiosyncratic foibles. Sergeant Greg Beer kept a close eye on things as usual, occasionally we'd have another paying guest upstairs in Room Two between The Lazy Tenor and The Blonde Maria, and of course Dr Bernard Feast made regular morning visits, ostensibly to check out Kooka but always in perfect time to catch some of The Lazy Tenor's arias. After every visit he'd leave shaking his head and smiling with an enchanted disbelief.

One morning I explained how if he was ever to show up

for a drink at the other end of the day, during Happy Hour, he'd experience a disbelief of an altogether different order. 'How do you mean, Noel?' he asked. I explained that in fact The Lazy Tenor was in residence at The Grand Hotel because he needed somewhere quiet to write up his memoirs, and that every evening around five the bar was treated to an account of what he'd been working on that day. I explained that many in the bar found The Lazy Tenor's stories extremely distasteful, and that if he himself was to hear some of the ribald details he'd have trouble believing it was the same man who could sing like an angel.

The doctor shook his head knowingly at this. 'Ah, but that's where you're wrong, Noel,' he said. 'The extraordinary thing about his song is that he sings not like an angel but like a man. That's why it breaks my heart you see, and why it makes me so happy. The voice sings, Noel, the note is true, but the timbre and the emotion are textured with real experience. An ability like that almost goes beyond music – it's a rare gift – and whatever else he gets up to is obviously good for it. With artists such as that it's often as if they are two people. A little bit like being a doctor perhaps.'

'A doctor?' I said, confused.

'Well, yes. As old Bill Dwyer used to tell me when I first showed up as his young understudy in Minapre, we all have our private lives, Noel. We minister to the sick *and* lose our temper at home. We listen patiently to the obsessions of the town's hypochondriacs *and* stop in ourselves for a gloomy afternoon playing the pokies in Colac.'

'You play the pokies?' I asked him.

Dr Feast laughed, and waved his hand dismissively. 'Oh, don't take me literally, Noel. You know what I mean.'

By this time The Lazy Tenor had been at The Grand Hotel for over a month, but as yet I'd seen no sign of the manuscript of 'The Tradesman's Entrance'. Of course we were all still enduring the anecdotes that were to make up the book every evening at Happy Hour, although I had finally convinced him to tell these lurid yarns in The Horse Room on a permanent basis, for the sake of the other patrons. But I was beginning to grow curious, given his propensity to big-note himself, that we hadn't yet been shown even one page from his illustrious manuscript.

One day after lunch I climbed the stairs to check the linen in the vacant middle room. When I got to the top, I found the hallway trees and ducks and platypus alive as ever in the afternoon light. Down the far end I could see the door of The Sewing Room shut fast, with Kooka no doubt snoring behind it. I knew that sometimes The Blonde Maria would sit with him in the afternoons, and seeing that her own door was flung wide open I imagined that was the case.

The Lazy Tenor's door, however, was shut. Craning my neck forward like the brolga in the clearing, I listened for a telltale clicking sound from his laptop keyboard. I heard nothing. The whole hotel was quiet and peaceful, with almost the air of a hermitage. Very gently the willows of the wallpaper rustled in the light breeze coming through the open doorway of The Blonde Maria's room.

I knocked gently on The Lazy Tenor's door and waited. There was no answer, and still no movement from within. I found myself standing there indignantly, questioning whether the book we'd heard so much about was actually being written at all. So I knocked again, a little bit harder. But still no response. I wondered if he'd gone out but felt sure I would've seen him if he had. I'd been cleaning in the bar and in the sunroom all morning and he would have had to pass me to leave the hotel. I popped my head through the bathroom door next to his room to make sure he wasn't in the bath but no, he surely wasn't. And then, perhaps irrationally, given how happy and confident The Lazy Tenor always seemed and how quiet his room had always been in the afternoons, I worried that perhaps he might have done away with himself in there. Yes, the mind plays tricks, particularly in the memorial stillness of night or on a dreamy afternoon in an empty hotel. But, suddenly convincing myself that it was my proprietorial right to make sure things hadn't gone astray in one of my rooms, I turned the door handle and pushed it open.

The room was dim, the curtains pulled across the partially opened sash window. Straight ahead at the desk under the window there was no sign of a laptop, just a half empty bottle of Laphroaig and a newspaper opened at the crosswords. The Lazy Tenor's green suede jacket was on the back of the desk chair and his packet of cigarettes had fallen out of the pocket and was lying on the carpet beside the chair. There was a smell of cigarette smoke in the room but not a stale smell, rather an old attractive smell, with a hint of cigar about it.

Then, looking towards the bed against the wall to my right, I saw what I was in no way meant to see. Sleeping peacefully, with naked limbs entwined on top of a single sheet, were The

Lazy Tenor and The Blonde Maria. Their bodies were glowing through the gloom, still luminous with sweat, The Blonde Maria's spent form splayed languidly like a figure in a Bonnard painting across The Lazy Tenor's rufous stomach and thighs.

It was a scene of great repose, great sensuality, and, needless to say, great privacy. I quickly stepped backwards through the doorway and hurried down the stairs. I felt foolish, and intrusive. I couldn't believe that I hadn't put two and two together. In my naivety, misled by The Blonde Maria's recent monastic air, I hadn't considered it possible that these two highly sexual musicians, alone in the upstairs floor of a country hotel, day in, day out, with only a sleeping local historian as chaperone, might somehow find their way into each other's rooms. Well, that was exactly what had happened. I shouldn't have been surprised, but I was. And yet that was nothing compared with the complicating surprise I was presented with later that same evening by Joan Sutherland.

It was a busy night, and now that The Lazy Tenor had agreed to hold court in The Horse Room rather than in the bar we all had a good time during Happy Hour with my brother Jim's first non-musical contribution to the entertainment. He had put together a short mockumentary film, which we accessed on the big screen via YouTube, called 'The Dying Gardens of the Great Ocean Road'. In it Jim posed as a celebrity gardener touring the private gardens along the coast, delivering an earnest narrative about the supposedly catastrophic effects of the Great Australian Drought. The joke was that despite him being dressed comically for ultra-parched conditions, in park ranger shorts and a bush tucker man hat, he described the devastation of the Great Drought with a background of Otway drizzle and from a series of lovingly cultivated and obviously flourishing green gardens.

The locals in the bar lapped up this piss-take of Jim's. They were always ready for a parochial poke at the mainstream media's expense, so the film set the mood for the night. The food was top-notch too: kangaroo steaks with mushroom sauce for the carnivores and leek and mushroom vol-au-vents for the vegetarians.

Around eight o'clock, after the fun of 'The Dying Gardens of the Great Ocean Road' and a hearty meal, Jim had happily swapped his cinematic for his musical hat and The Barrels were in full flight. I'd confided to him only the day before that I'd given up on The Blonde Maria ever descending the staircase again, and the new certainty of that unfortunate situation seemed to have relaxed the band. They were no longer anxious for her return, even though they would always long for another late-night party in her room. As far as their music went, well, they were not quite up to what I would have liked, but nevertheless they had improved since playing a few nights with an inspired expert. Either way both Jim and I were resigned to our self-sufficient fate.

Near the end of The Barrels' first set I noticed Joan and Jen Sutherland having a disagreement just outside the door of the hotel. I could see Dylan and Dougie waiting forlornly under the pine tree and could feel the whole family's tension. That was unusual, I remember thinking, they were typically a very harmonious outfit.

Before long Joan was waving his arms about and kicking

the empty beer barrels near the back door. He shouted and ges-
ticulated until eventually Jen took off in a huff with the boys.
Big Joan stepped back into the hotel, shot a gruff 'Don't ask' to
me as he entered, and headed back to the bar.

Something was up so I followed him back into the bar only
to find him pouring a double whiskey in a corner with his back
to the clientele. He normally only drank Dancing Brolgas but
he skulled the whiskey and turned around to continue serving, his face flushed, a barely suppressed look of anxiety in his
eyes. I had noticed he'd been a bit tetchy of late but what with
everything else that had been going on I hadn't had the time
to think about it. But now I made a mental note to talk to him
when the time was right. The fact was I loved Joan Sutherland
like I loved few men. He was a big giver, a loyal heart, who also
had the indispensable knack of always seeing the best side of a
situation.

Later on in the evening Rennie Vigata showed up with
Lee, his girlfriend, which I was happy about because I'd been
ringing him for the past week to come and take away the empty
Dancing Brolga barrels that were piling up in the backyard.
Rennie's supply of the grog had been fantastic, and I let him
know now once again what a consistent hit our Recommended
Looseners continued to be.

'You must be flat out up there, mate, coz they're certainly
drinkin' the stuff down here,' I remarked.

Rennie's black underworld eyes and bushy single eyebrow
sneered at me, somehow offended by my compliment, as if my
surprise at the success of his beer implied some deeper doubt
about his abilities. Lee, tall, skinny, in stretch jeans and leather

jacket, replied for him, 'He knows how to work, my Rennie. And beer's in his blood.'

Rennie Vigata's scary face broke out into a big smile at his girlfriend's joke. It was obvious he adored her. They left me then to hit the dance floor in front of The Barrels. Tommy Collins, the keyboard player, was singing 'Bend Down the Branches' by Tom Waits. Rennie and Lee went into a tight black clinch in front of the band, their hips close and moving imperceptibly. They were a dark smouldering pair and I couldn't help but wonder about all the wild nights they must have enjoyed up in those rainsoaked Poorool hills.

Rennie and Lee danced for ages, and The Barrels didn't dare pick up the tempo, for fear of putting them offside. I left them to it and made a round of the premises, gathering up ashtrays and empty glasses, wiping tables and checking that everyone had had enough to eat. The lifesaving set from Boat Creek were ensconced as usual out on the verandah and called for more steaks, saying they were first rate. In The Horse Room I found The Lazy Tenor and four or five others sitting in silence as they listened back to the big fella's latest oral instalment of 'The Tradesman's Entrance'. I groaned inside. Kooka's abandoned Grundig had opened up a can of worms. The Lazy Tenor had purloined it from the bar and not only was he telling his nightly tale but now he was also getting whoever was in The Horse Room to spend the rest of the night listening back to it on tape, entranced by his own prodigious sexual capabilities and his brilliant ability to narrate them. Just to rile him, I put a dollar coin in the pool table and pushed the slot in. The balls came crashing down, drowning out his voice on the Grundig.

He swivelled around on his chair, furious at the interruption.

But I was having none of it. 'Cut it out would ya, Lazy? This is a pool room after all. Who's for a game?'

'Aw, come off it, Noel,' he cried. 'This is the best bit. I'm shagging this office girl from Bob Jane T-Marts. She's half my age and boy has she got some unusual piercings!'

'Well there's a free game here if anyone wants it,' I said, annoyed, picking up a pile of plates and leaving the room.

After returning the plates to the bar, I headed upstairs to check on Kooka. He was sleeping soundly, with his innocuous looking black tranny playing country songs on the bedside table. I took his empty dinner plate and, heading back past The Blonde Maria's room, didn't hear a sound. I snorted through my nose. Our holy guest was obviously busy praying in there.

When I got back downstairs, it was clear that Big Joan had partaken of a few more double whiskies. He had pulled a bentwood chair in behind the bar and was just plonked on it, his Otway dewlaps hanging morosely over the collar of his flannelette shirt, his big sideburns sagging, as he repeatedly smacked his lips and muttered to himself. Poor Darren Traherne kept pouring beers but didn't know what to make of it. Without saying a word, he threw a querulous look in Joan's direction, as if to enquire as to whether our head barman had lost his mind.

I shrugged. There was nothing I could do right then because Rennie and Lee had finished up dancing and were keen now to get a move on with the barrels so they could head home to the hills. They were expecting me to help load them into their van and, well, who was I to argue with Rennie Vigata?

We stepped outside and I laid the corduroy rolling planks out between the door and the driveway where Rennie had backed the van in. We set to work. Rolling barrels was usually first-thing-in-the-morning work, so it took a bit longer than usual, even with Lee's help. There were about eighty empty barrels there, after all. By the time we were done and I'd said toorah to Rennie and Lee and headed back inside to check on Joan, he was a total mess.

At first, when I entered the bar, I couldn't even see him; he was no longer on the bentwood chair. Discreetly Darren nodded down towards the back kitchen corner of the bar and said, 'It's hard to work with that in here.'

I peered down to see Joan Sutherland's massive frame sprawled over the black and white checked lino. I was shocked. He'd taken his big Blundstones off and his socks stank. He was shaking his head disconsolately from side to side, tears were falling from his eyes, and he was muttering away to himself like a madman.

With Joan's legs halfway across the floor behind the bar Darren was right when he said it was hard to work. Every time Darren turned around to get a spirit or a soft drink from the dispensers on the back wall, he'd nearly go flying as he tried to avoid the dairy farmer's big red socks.

I knelt down and grabbed Joan by the hand. 'What the hell has got into you?' I said into his ear. There was no reply. 'Come on, mate, you can't stay in here like this,' I said. 'You're in everyone's way. Let's go for a walk.'

Joan put up no struggle and, with Darren's help, I hoisted him off the floor. He stood tottering like a power pole in an onshore wind, before sucking in a long whistling breath and letting me lead him out of the bar, through the sunroom and outside. I didn't even bother trying to get his boots back on, and I figured he wouldn't die without them.

We walked out under the pines and along the dirt road to the river, between the silent grassy ditches. On other nights walking between those ditches the natural world seemed to be in full chorus, but this time there was not even the intermittent hoot of an owl, just Joan's histrionic breathing and the inexplicable gibberish he was muttering beside me.

We rounded the bend of the road and made it onto the riverbank proper. The river was flat and sheeny, slate-like, in an optical merger with the depth of the black moonless night. Ever so faintly I could still hear The Barrels playing off in the distance. I marvelled briefly to myself how we had never had even one complaint about the noise since we'd opened the hotel. Either people were scared of upsetting us or we'd gathered together quite a degree of local goodwill.

By the time we arrived under the canopy of the two old river red gums that my mum used to call The Twins, the big fella's muttering had slowed down and the fresh air was beginning to have a beneficial effect. I couldn't get him to prop under The Twins, though; now that he'd started, he seemed to want to keep going. So we continued along the bank and on towards the indoor creek.

Arriving at the infamous roofed section of the creek that had caused so much controversy and grief, we found Joe Conebush's youngest boy, Kim, smoking a spliff with a teenage girl under the new gantry. As we approached, they pretended they hadn't seen us but as soon as we actually entered under the roof they took off into the night like a pair of wood ducks.

Perhaps because of the air of vacancy left by the teenage departure, or more likely because of the broad bench seats the shire had provided under the roof, Joan all of a sudden decided he'd had enough of walking and flopped himself down.

If I thought it was dark out in the moonless night, it was even darker under the Colorbond roofing of the indoor creek. The lights under there had long ago been smashed, and without the radiance of the Milky Way I was struggling even to see my hand in front of my face.

I sat down beside Joan on the seat and for a few seconds listened to the poor fella just sniffing and breathing. Eventually I said, 'Bloody shit in here hey?'

'Can't see a fuckin' thing,' was his reply.

'Do you wanna sit somewhere else?'

'Nah,' he said. 'This is as good a place as any to hide.'

I reflected on that comment for a few seconds, then took up the challenge. 'What do you want to hide from?'

More sniffing came from beside me in the dark. Then silence. But then, 'I want to hide from Jen. Nah, from myself more like it.'

'Why? What's wrong?'

More sniffing. 'You don't wanna know. Believe me, you don't.'

The indoor creek smelt of cheap paint, piss and marijuana. I knitted my brow in the darkness, trying to ignore the aromas, concentrating hard. 'Well, actually I do want to know, given that I've just had to scrape you up off the floor of the bar like a spilt parmigiana.'

A hint of mirth issued from the pair of nostrils beside me. Ah, I thought, that's a bit more like it.

'Have you got a smoke?' he said then.

'No,' I answered. 'But anyway, you don't smoke.'

'Well, I've really fucked up this time.'

'Yeah?'

'Yeah.'

More sniffing. Then he said something under his breath.

'What was that?' I asked.

'I said she doesn't fuckin' deserve it.'

'Who?'

'Jen. Who else?'

I rolled my eyes in the darkness. I was getting sick of the riddle. 'Well, what doesn't she deserve?'

'Can we walk again?'

'What, now?'

'Yeah. Do you mind?'

Fifty yards further down the bank we came out from under the roof to the galaxies blazing above us. It was as if a celestial jewellery box had been opened wide, purely to fling radiant stars across the universe to light our way. I could see Joan plain as day now, walking beside me in his socks. He no longer looked so messy either; rather, he looked as solemn as when he'd been a pallbearer at the mud-brick Barroworn church on the day of his father's funeral.

We walked a little more along the bank in silence. The previously slatey rivertop now had creases of starlight reflected in it. I thought perhaps those lovely tricks of the light would relax Joan enough to tease the story out of him; but no, there was nothing forthcoming.

'So why don't you tell me what's upsetting you?' I said, eventually.

'I'm rooting The Blonde Maria,' was the big dairy farmer's sudden reply.

Was it the tricks of light in the river or the sharp transition from dense blackness to the Milky Way that had me doubting whether I'd heard him right? After a few steps, however, an involuntary shudder went through me, and I knew I was not mistaken.

I couldn't speak. Thoughts began splintering off in my brain like the space junk of some kind of small town Big Bang. How long had this been going on? What the bloody hell was he thinking? And had he any idea of what I'd discovered in The Lazy Tenor's room just a few hours earlier that afternoon?

'Well aren't you gonna say something?' Joan said eventually, in a bleak and desperate tone, as we reached the riverbend slope where a spiky layer of euca-mulch had been strewn by the shire.

I breathed out. 'Fuck, mate. I don't know what to say. Is that what you and Jen were fighting about earlier tonight?'

'No,' he said heavily. 'She still doesn't know. But I've been that stressed out about it I've been treating her like a dickhead.'

'Well can I ask how long it's been going on?'

'For a while.'

'What's a while?'

'Oh I dunno. Probably since that night we had the party in

her room with Givva Way. She's a great girl, Noel.'

'Yeah sure, but that's no reason to ruin your life.'

We rounded the bend in thoughtful silence. Now we had a choice. Either we continued along in a straight line on the ragged bitumen of the Dray Road or we straddled the paddock fence and followed the eely course of the river through the pasture of the flats. One thing was for sure, we both now needed to walk a little while longer.

In the end we straddled the fence, preferring the privacy of the river to the publicity of the road, even at night time. Immediately on our left the ducks that sleep in the open by the little soak there woke up and flew off, with tiny bird hearts beating fast. At the far end of the flats I could just make out a herd of steers bunched together under the red gums. I prayed they wouldn't take exception to our nocturnal meander.

We followed the straight stretch of the river running westward from the bend. We clumped along over soft ground dotted with kangaroo poo, cowpats and shaggy-caps, and with occasional patches of pigface. Joan's socks were no doubt getting a little dirty and moist by now but he wasn't worried; he had other things on his mind.

As we walked along, he began to explain. Or tried to. 'I've never, in all the years with Jen, even looked at another woman, Noel. I mean why would I? We've always been happy. But Maria, well, she's a different kettle of fish. That first night up in her room, you fellas had all wandered off to bed. There was only me and her, and Givva and that Italian bloke Guido, just sittin' in there with the lights out and the window flung open, waiting for the dawn. She started telling us how she loved to see the dawn but, to tell you the truth, I was the only one listenin', coz Givva was sound asleep on the chair under the window and the big Italian bloke was slumped against the cupboard, obliterated by the booze. So it was like me and Maria were all alone.

'Anyway, I was sittin' on the end of her bed with me back against the wall and she was lying on the bed with her feet restin' across my legs. And we were just talkin'. And smokin'. Yeah, I was smokin'. She makes it look so good, Noel.

'She started telling me a few stories from the city, talkin' too about how she loved the country life, and I was fillin' her in about how we got off the dairy, and how Dad was the tallest bloke ever to run a place in the Stawell Gift. I even told her a bit about Jen and the kids. I felt so good, Noel, up in those second-storey rooms it's bloody tops, and it was a beautiful still night, and she's, you know, real familiar, like a little sister except totally exotic at the same time.

'Anyway, we started talkin' about the pub and that and I was fillin' her in how I'd never been a barman before and she couldn't believe it. She reckoned she'd played music in loads of pubs across Australia and never seen a better barman than me. Then she asked me if I'd like a foot massage while we waited for the sunrise, coz of being on my feet all day and that, and well . . . anyway . . .'

Joan's voice dwindled away as we trudged along the bank. He was devastated. I had to feel for the big bloke.

'I shoulda said no to the massage I suppose.'

'It was probably hard to resist,' I said.

'Too right it was. She's such fun, Noel. It's all so easy and natural with her. You don't even have to try you know.'

'Does anyone else know about this?'

'No. No way. Definitely not. At least I hope not.'

'So, if you don't mind me asking, has it all been going on just in her room? Or elsewhere as well?'

'For the most part in her room, yeah. Although with The Lazy Tenor and Kooka around it's been a bit awkward at times.'

'How do you mean?'

'Well, you know, you have to watch your noise levels. You have to keep a sock in it.'

'I see.'

'Yeah, so a few times we've nicked off down to the caves after stumps.'

'To the caves?'

'Yeah. Well no one's gonna bust us in there, eh? Remember those fires we used to have in the caves as kids, Noel? After climbing out our windows at midnight. Remember Spin the Bottle?'

'Yeah, I remember.'

'Anyway, come the cooler months we'll have to find somewhere different.'

'Hey?'

'Yeah, well it's bloody freezin' in those caves in winter.'

For a moment Joan's last remark didn't compute. How could he be in a state of shame one minute and then planning their winter rendezvous the next? This was totally contradictory. But then, of course, I realised the obvious. Joan Sutherland was in love. Or, as the first whalers and sealers around these parts used to say, in a phrase not so much well worn as twisted with isolation, he was 'cunt struck'.

It was obvious now that part of his depression was coming not only from his shame but also from the knowledge that it was destined to continue. He was helpless, flailing about between extremes of despair and bliss. I also understood now why he hadn't wanted to talk about it. What was the point, if he wasn't looking for a way back onto the straight and narrow?

Now, purely from expressing some of his pleasure with The Blonde Maria, he was all of a sudden a little buoyed up as he walked on the starlit bank beside me. For a moment the shame had been displaced. He started to talk, sixteen to the dozen, but I wasn't listening. I could only feel disturbed at what The Grand Hotel had done to Big Joan's life.

I realised that I couldn't break it to him about The Blonde Maria and The Lazy Tenor. The mere fact that she was two-timing him made me feel coated in muck. If you wanted to talk rain, grass, cattle, or milk, Joan Sutherland had definitely not come down in the last shower – he knew the simple brutality of the food chain and the practical world of creatures – but I feared that when it came to romantic love in the big wide world, if you want to call it that, and the enticement of a thrilling new sexual experience, he was most certainly a babe. To tell him what I saw in The Lazy Tenor's room earlier that day would be to change him. And frankly, at this point, I'd had just about enough of change.

So we walked along and I listened in silence to Joan's effusions about his new romance. Eventually, probably because I didn't sustain him by a response, his enthusiasm began to dwindle again, his mind turning away from the delights of The Blonde Maria and back to the betrayal of Jen.

As we rounded another curve in the river, we were now quite a distance from any houses, right smack in the middle of the riverflat, and he started to dwell upon his boys as well. Oh my God, it was torture. He was caught in a vice he couldn't get out of. I began to try to dissuade him from his passion for Maria before it was too late; I even went so far as to betray Maria by intimating that she had a bit of a chequered history and perhaps would just leave him for dead. Her current shenanigans with The Lazy Tenor allowed me to justify the lie to myself. But Joan was having none of it anyway.

'If I had a choice, Noel,' he said, 'I'd take it. But I don't feel like I have. When I fell in love with Jen, I was a kid. Seventeen years old. But now I'm a man. I've never fallen in love as a man before. Doesn't everyone have to fall in love as a fully grown adult?'

I scoffed. 'The irony of that, mate, is that you're not behaving like an adult. You're carrying on like a seventeen-year-old. But worse. Coz of Dylan and Dougie.'

I felt him shudder beside me. 'Oh the boys,' he groaned.

We were out on that riverflat until three o'clock in the morning, walking, arguing, confessing, not even noticing the lightest of northerlies as it sprang up in the trees of the western hill on the other side of the river. By the time we'd said all that could be said, the warmer air was gusting in waves all about us and Joan in his fervour had stripped off and dived into the river near the old Bootleg Creek pontoon. He splashed and swam about in that unmistakable fashion of a man in love, sober now in terms of alcohol but drunk on the new quickstep in his heart.

He prowled around and shouldered himself through the

water, eventually floating on his back and calling out to me on the bank to join him. I said, 'No way.' So he said he was gonna lie on his back in the river for as long as it took to see a falling star.

'You look up too, Noel,' he called, 'and if we see it together we can both wish for the same thing.'

'Oh yeah. And what would that be?'

'For a cure, mate. I'm lovesick.'

As crazed as it was, it was the first sane thing he'd said all night. I lay down on my back on the bank, partly from exhaustion I must admit, and used Joan's clothes for a pillow. Above our heads the galaxies seemed even brighter than before; the Milky Way could easily be defined in its cloudy clusters. There was Venus and Jupiter out in the west, the Pleiades low in the northwest, and the Southern Cross, of course, draped like a celestial beach-kite over the ocean sky to the south. Even without a moon the radiance of the night had managed to unite the land and sky. I marvelled again at the unpredictable nature of things, how something that at first could appear so dim was, just a short time later, as obvious as the nose on your face. And so together we lay, he in the river and me on a patch of kikuyu grass wildly sown, staring up to the heavens in the hope of a sign.

Confronting The Blonde Maria

I WOKE UP IN THE LOFT OF MY BARN THE NEXT MORNING TO The Lazy Tenor singing both parts of the duet from Bizet's *The Pearl Fishers*. I exhaled with relief and lay listening in bliss, swooning again in the embrace of the voice and marvelling at his improvisations. The *Pearl Fishers* duet was a favourite of my papa's when I was a child, and as such was the only operatic music that featured strongly in my childhood. Despite The Lazy Tenor's lack of a singing partner it was a revelation to hear each vocal part separated from its pair.

As I lay there, I nudged my loft shutter open with my foot and looked out. There was an ever-so-faint drizzle falling from an off-white sky. Inevitably I began to recall the events of the night before. As soon as The Lazy Tenor finished, I was gonna have to go and flush out The Blonde Maria.

Then I heard the sound of Dr Feast's Peugeot pulling into

the yard. Craning my neck out the loft window, I watched him get out of the car and gaze up through the drizzle at The Lazy Tenor's room. He made a dramatic gesture with his right arm, the racing-green elbow patch of his tweed jacket suddenly cocked, and his hand clutched passionately at the air, as if conducting the music.

Jen Sutherland emerged from the sunroom of the hotel with a broom in one hand and Frankie the Canary's cage in the other. The doctor's arm returned to his side. They greeted each other, before Jen hung Frankie's cage on the hook under the sunroom awning and began hosing down the beery concrete where the barrels had been standing for days before Rennie had come to pick them up. I lay back on my pillow and listened to The Lazy Tenor, and the doctor and Jen discussing Kooka's health. Then the talking stopped and all I could hear was the sound of the water washing the concrete and the singing over the top.

Later that morning I climbed the hotel stairs with a belly full of Eno, not knowing what my strategy was to be. In the hallway I found the atmosphere all ructious on a wind-ruffled creek. The ducks had taken shelter up in the willows and were dotting the walls in crisp symmetrical arrangements. At The Blonde Maria's door I knocked and received a polite 'Come in'.

Once again I found Maria seated at the window table. This time she was fully dressed rather than in her dressing gown. She had an open book in her hand, but it wasn't the book of the saint.

'I hope you don't mind,' she said. 'I've been making my way through the shelf here.'

She held up the book to show me. It was a novel called *The World of Carrick's Cove*, by Gerald Warner Brace. Then she said, 'I never knew, Noel, what a remarkable hotel this really is,' as if somehow it had something to do with the book. 'And I had no idea of just how special old Kooka is.'

I didn't answer. I suspected that Maria's native cunning had smelt a rat, that she knew something was up and my visit wasn't to be benign. There was no hint of the little-girl voice anymore; instead she spoke in a calm and intelligent tone, as if a full engagement with me on the merits of my hotel and its patron and historian could somehow see me off at the pass.

She lit a cigarette now and blew a blue cone of tapering smoke towards the open window. 'It's so easy isn't it, Noel, to presume that someone as old as Kooka has no sense of beauty or romance?'

Once again I chose not to answer. I could see by her brow now that she was thinking fast.

'But I've been reading to him in the evenings and he's quite something.'

'Oh yeah? He stays awake?'

The Blonde Maria's eyes lit up. By my asking this question, she figured she had me diverted. 'Sometimes,' she said, before rising from her chair and making her way to the sink. I saw a quick cast of desperation come over her face as she plugged in the kettle, but it disappeared just as quickly.

'So there weren't any other books on holy people on the shelf here?' I ventured wryly.

She answered me with a sheepish look.

I let her clatter around among the tea cosy and cups and

spoons for a while. Then I said, 'You know it's one thing for you to leave all the cleaning of the hotel to Jen Sutherland but it's another altogether to go shagging her husband.'

There, I'd said it. There was no avoiding the issue anymore. So I pressed even harder. 'Particularly when he doesn't know you're also having it off with the guy up the hallway. I presume Kooka's safe from your affections?'

Maria's face looked aghast. 'Noel!' she exclaimed indignantly, as if dragging Kooka into it was a lower moral blow than she could countenance.

I raised my hands in the air. 'Well, I don't know what to think anymore, Maria! Last time I looked, you were about to take religious vows and then, in the space of twenty-four hours, I find out you're screwing half the hotel.'

'Oh, Noel!' There it was again, that look of moral shock, as if Purity and Honour were her only true companions.

'Well you tell me!' I cried. 'I'm actually the novice here. You seem to be the one pulling all the strings. Joan's head over heels and he's a married man with kids. Did you ever consider that?'

'Of course I did.'

'What, and you just figured that nothing else mattered but your satisfaction?'

Oh dear, now I was really getting heavy, hectoring her like that.

The Blonde Maria sat back down at the window table with the pot of tea – and let me have it.

First things first, she burst into tears. I slumped in the armchair, sighing and scratching my head. The tears were really flowing, but after a minute or so she started to dry her eyes with a tea towel. But she was still sniffing and gulping a lot. 'I didn't know any of this was going to happen,' she eventually got out. 'How was I to know that he'd fall in love with me? He just seemed like a sweetie who needed a bit of fun.'

I said nothing.

'And then that bloody brute turns up out of the blue. With a voice like that! Did you hear him this morning, Noel, singing *both* parts of the duet from *The Pearl Fishers*?'

I nodded.

'Well you've got to understand my predicament. One day I was living freely in your hotel, with everyone very appreciative of my music and you very grateful for my cleaning, and then the man I've always been destined to meet comes into the bar.'

'Who, The Lazy Tenor?'

She scoffed. 'Well, who else? It's all I've ever dreamt of, Noel, you know that, to live the musical life. Even if I'm not singing, just to be around a voice like that means everything to me. But now I'm stuck. The thing with Joan is just frivolous, a simple mistake gone wrong. And I know it's gotta stop, but he's so insistent. He's up here half the night, either desperate with guilt for his wife or boiling with passion for me. I'm worried about him. I don't know what'll happen if I let him down. He could do anything. He's quite mad at the moment.'

'So I found out last night.'

'Yes, but can you see my position? He's madly in love with me but, Noel, I'm madly in love with Louis.'

'Louis?'

'Yes, Louis. The Lazy Tenor.'

'Oh. And how does he feel about you?'

A sad look came over her face at this question. Her tear-moist eyes scanned the leaf-dappled floor. 'He doesn't really say, but he's tender to me and now, in the mornings, I'm sure he's singing as if . . . for a muse.' She shrugged her shoulders. 'I tried, Noel. Why do you think I started reading St Thérèse? I have tried. But it's hopeless. Louis Daley is my destiny. Everything leading up to this was just like a soundcheck.'

'So is that why you won't come down and sing anymore?'

'Oh, Noel, how could I sing with that man in the hotel? I'd stand no chance at all. The only possibility I have with him is if I never sing again. We've all got to find our true path in life, Noel, and I'm sure mine is just to support him, to make him a household name.'

'A household name!' I exclaimed. 'Are you sure he wants to be a household name?'

'There's nothing he can do about it. You've heard him. With my devotion and musical knowledge I can make sure his gift is protected in the process.'

'Have you spoken to him about this?'

'Not exactly. But I've spoken to Kooka about it.'

'To Kooka?' I said, incredulous.

'Yes.'

'And pray tell, what does Kooka think about small town adultery in his old age?'

'Oh, I haven't told him that bit. But I've told him how I feel about Louis and he understands. He's a beautiful old man, Kooka, and he understands the heart of love.'

'I see.'

'He also understands how much love can hurt.'

'So does Jen.'

'Oh, Noel. I'm trying to be serious here.'

'Well, if that's the case then you've got to protect Jen and Joan. I refuse to let them become casualties in all this, Maria. Let alone their two boys.'

She grimaced.

'So you've got to tell Joan what's going on. And quickly. It'll cut him alright, but at least he'll see there's a reason it can't go on. Because you're devoted to The Lazy Tenor.'

'What? You want me to tell Joan I'm in love with Louis?'

'Yes.'

'Oh, Noel.'

'Stop that "Oh, Noel" business would you?' I said in frustration. 'It's what you've gotta do.'

'Do you think?'

'I don't think, I know. For Christ's sake, Maria!'

'Well, can I talk to Kooka first? I'd like a second opinion.'

I raised my hands in the air and slapped them down on my thighs. 'What the fuck has Kooka got to do with it?' I shouted. 'He's just an old man who can't get out of bed anymore!'

'Noel! Keep your voice down. Kooka understands life. And love. Have you ever stopped to think why he can't get out of bed?'

'I know why he can't. He's old, he's had enough, he's exhausted.'

'It's not as simple as that. He's going through stuff.'

'Oh, is he now?'

'Yes, he is.'

I blew out an exasperated breath. This was impossible. 'Pour us a cup of tea, would you, Maria?'

'Certainly, Noel,' she replied with a smile.

The Beautiful Story-Voice

IT'S EASY FOR A GENERALLY QUIET MAN A LITTLE STARVED of sex such as myself to take the high moral ground about other people's infidelities. On the other hand I had no idea what Maria had been experiencing at night with Kooka in The Sewing Room, how genuinely profound it was, nor that it would turn out to be the guiding force and overwhelming key to the fate of our increasingly unstable establishment.

What I found out later, and what I now understand The Blonde Maria couldn't tell me until she was absolutely compelled to do so, was that most evenings at around 9 pm, with the sounds of The Barrels pretty much muffled through the floorboards, she would gently knock on the Sewing Room door and enter to find Kooka sitting up in bed, gladly waiting for her. The air in the big room would smell not only of the increasingly musty boxed-up archive and the ocean spray ballooning down the riverflat but also of that timeless combination from the days of yore: old man and mushrooms. Kooka's empty dinner plate would be sitting on the bedside table with oily smears of whatever version of a mushroom sauce he'd been treated to that evening. Beside the dinner plate would be a small claret glass, a crinkled foil sheet of mild painkillers, and his transistor radio, waiting patiently, butler-like, to be put into service.

Maria would cheerfully sit down on the chair next to the bed and together they'd chitchat about the day just passed. Invariably this would involve a few light recriminations about the sameyness of the weather or the calibre of the clientele downstairs, and then Maria would take up whichever of my mother's old novels she was enjoying and begin to read aloud to Kooka. The old fella would lower himself down into the bedclothes a bit, and with a contented grunt turn his big bird head in profile towards the seaward window. And there the two of them would remain, in the little pool of light cast by the tassled standard lamps beside the bed, Kooka lying and listening among the blankets, and Maria sitting upright on the chair reading to him, just like in an old Rembrandt.

And so it was one evening, with The Blonde Maria reading *The World of Carrick's Cove* to Kooka, that their empathetic conversations about nature, and about romantic love, were set in train. *The World of Carrick's Cove* was well thumbed – it had been read countless times – and both Maria and Kooka had already commented to each other how much they were enjoying the tale of a fastidious eldest son's frustrations with the sloppy boatbuilding of his father on the Maine coast of New England. But, as Maria was reading a lovely passage to Kooka about some wowsery folks further up the coast near Rockford – who the author joked liked money so much they used to salt it – a remarkable transition seemed to take place in the old Sewing Room.

As Maria said, the joke about the Rockford wowsers was an innocuous enough little passage from the book; there was nothing in it to account for what happened next. As she was approaching the end of the chapter, Kooka slowly raised his hand for her to stop reading. Telling Maria her 'beautiful story-voice' was making him a bit sleepy, he asked her if she'd mind just sitting beside the bed while he had a little kip. She said she didn't mind at all, but as she explained it to me it seemed odd because Kooka's voice didn't betray any sleepiness at all. If any-thing, it was strong, awake, as clear as ever.

The old man reached over and clicked on his transistor radio. A country tune began to twang out from the station. Kooka pulled the sheets and blankets up to his chin and closed his eyes. Maria just sat there looking at him. Then, in the pool of light cast by the two standard lamps, with all activity abated, and stillness ruling the room, the transistor started to speak.

The country song had abruptly stopped, the tranny had glitched and static filled the room. Then a man and woman were in conversation, but it wasn't just normal radio chat, and not intended for public consumption. The woman's voice was light and happy, and she spoke the most; when the man replied, his voice was quiet, a little muffled, and with a broken-down sort of grief attached to it. Then, as quickly as they had begun, the voices changed again, and this time the sound of splashing and sucking water among rocks was in the background. Now a woman was swimming in the ocean, and sighing with pleasure as she did so. She was also reciting lists to herself, as if she was trying to remember what she had to buy at the store. But the contents of the list were from another time: rushlights, chicory, strawberries by the quart, pickled onions, bottles of digestives from W. G. Hearne, a gross of buttons, calico, rum and mattress ticking. The list went on and on, the recital of it broken only when the swimmer dived under the waves, at which point all Maria could hear from the transistor was bubbling and then hiss, and a low subaquatic hum. And then, just as she was trying to figure all this out, the sounds changed once more, this time back to the conversation of before, except with the man speaking rather than the woman.

Sitting by Kooka's bed, The Blonde Maria was confounded. Quite understandably, given the various other antics of The Grand Hotel, she wondered if she was listening to some prearranged piece of avant-garde radio drama. But no – it had a different quality; there was something entirely unique and unpremeditated about it. As the scenes kept switching between the man and woman's conversation – which took place over cups of tea at a kitchen table – and the woman swimming with her sighs and old-timey lists in the ocean, Maria found herself trying to make connections between the two scenarios. But try as she might, the man and woman, and the swimmer in the ocean, seemed to bear no relation to each other whatsoever.

Yet each of their scenarios held Maria's attention regardless. She gathered that the couple at the kitchen table were man and wife, and that their names were John and Mary. This was normal enough, of course, but their talk was strange – fluid and natural one minute and then disjointed and abstract the next. And then, every so often, the woman at the table, Mary, would reel off long speeches of consolation to the man, her husband, John, but it was unclear as to what she was consoling him about. And always, just as Maria felt she was about to find out what was upsetting him, the sound would crackle and switch on the tranny, there would be silence for a brief moment, and then the sucking sound of water and the swimmer's breath and sighs would re-emerge. The swimmer would dive under again and her pleasure in the swimming could be felt, intimately, almost as if Maria herself was duck diving amidst the pool of light in The Sewing Room. And then the swimmer's list would continue again: castor oil, candles, a hundred pounds of flour, Turkish Delight, feather-down for the pillows, a new cask for sundries, kerosene, brown rum, malt, whiskey, *crème de cacao*, ink for the portmanteau and heavy thread for the bellows. The swimmer would dive and then stroke through the slack of the water between waves, composing her list. And then a wave would crash, the sound of breaking water would fill the room, and John and Mary's voices would continue, and Maria would sink deeper into their thrall.

'It is not a blind alley. The apricots were worthwhile, John. You just needed proof, so I took them away. But, dear, only for one summer, for you to credit me with it, to see me in the fruitless vacant tree, but all you saw were the empty branches and the knobbly bits on them, and the visit I paid became your hollow. Dear John, it needn't be, and your mother agrees with me. She's weeping. Her tears put out the fire. Oh yes, she's still weeping alright, but the fire is out and she agrees with me about the apricots, and now . . . wait, who's that coming now?'

Maria's eyes would close tight, then open as she tried to make head or tail of what was being shared between John and Mary. And who *was* this coming now?

A new sound cut across the waves, and high drama began to issue from Kooka's transistor. There was a fire in a building, and a woman's voice was screaming FIRE FIRE and OH MY JOHNNY BOY and then FIRE FIRE again and OH MY GOD MY JOHNNY. Taken aback by the intensity of the cries, Maria looked across at Kooka for the first time since he'd fallen asleep. His big head was still on the pillow but his jawline was twitching, and in the pool of light she could see movement behind his eyelids. Apart from that his face was quite calm.

Maria could hear timbers falling and walls of the building collapsing, paint crackling and distant yells for help, but that was nothing compared with the distressing cries of the screaming woman. Obviously the heat was getting closer to her now, her breathing was becoming laboured, and she was coughing and gasping for air. Eventually her cries subsided into moans, and then, as if the flames took her over, her voice was gone altogether. For a brief time the only sound from the transistor was crackling flames and the shifting structure of the building, but eventually the sound of horses' hooves and the voices of what were obviously firemen could be heard, and then the sound of a hose and the fizzing noise of flames going out.

All at once Kooka made a sudden realignment of his head in the bed. He rolled over towards the seaward wall, and after a harsh rapid glitch from the transistor, to Maria's astonishment the country song that had previously been on recommenced, as if it had never stopped playing.

Maria sat stunned beside Kooka's bed in the pool of light. She couldn't see the whole of the old fella's face, only his shoulder and the profile of his beak-like nose and bulbous forehead. She couldn't fathom what had happened. She considered right there and then, and despite her new found passion for Louis Daley, leaving The Grand Hotel for good. She feared she'd become unhinged by holing herself up in her room all day and night. Was she finally, and properly, going mad?

Later she told me she'd tried to rationalise it for a while but couldn't get around it. Kooka's sudden movement in the bed had definitely seemed to terminate the dousing of the fire. It was as if he was affecting what came out of his tranny.

Eventually the drowsy country song had reached its final verse, ended with a melancholy twang and then was back-announced. But there was no mention of apricots or a house fire, just a song called 'Sally Mae'. Nothing was said about a woman swimming with a list of things from long ago. This was a normal weekly country-music show, with no doubt a regular audience of insomniacs listening through the night.

The Blonde Maria got up off the chair beside Kooka's bed and immediately switched off the standard lamps. The pool of light vanished. Quietly she made her way across the floor to the seaward window and looked out. She waited in the darkness. Behind her she could still hear the tranny, but through the window now she could also hear the Plinth bells ringing down at the rivermouth. Oscar must have forgotten to tie them down again. She was thankful. The sound of them calmed her. She took a few deep breaths. She waited at the window for a long time, through four songs and the beginning of an interview with Troy Cassar-Daley. Then she quietly tiptoed out of the room.

The Blonde Maria didn't sleep that night and found herself just after the dawn roaming around Kooka's old place, looking for an apricot tree. She missed it at first but after searching the back and side yards thoroughly and almost giving up, she spotted it on her way back towards the front gate. The tree was laden with fruit.

She stood beside it, considering the possibilities. Then she spied a blue ice-cream container catching drips under an outside tap on the house wall. She walked over, tipped out the water into the long grass that had sprouted from the overflow and, walking back to the tree, began to fill the container with apricots.

That night when she re-entered The Sewing Room with *The World of Carrick's Cove* in her hand, she also carried the apricots. Kooka was glad to see them. He not only recognised them as fruit from his tree but he recognised the blue ice-cream container as well.

So they sat again in the pool of light, this time munching on the apricots. They both agreed they were delicious. Without being prompted, Kooka told The Blonde Maria how he'd had regular fruit from the tree over the years. The only exception, he said, was the summer after his wife, Mary, had died, when the tree didn't even flower, let alone produce any apricots.

'As if it was in mourning,' The Blonde Maria remarked, wiping juice from her chin.

Kooka just raised his eyebrows. 'She made a famous apricot jam, my Mary,' he said.

Having confirmed her suspicion and that she herself hadn't lost her marbles, The Blonde Maria was all of a sudden keen to get cracking. 'How about I read a little more of the book, Kooka?' she asked.

The old man smiled. 'Sounds like a fine idea, lassie, a fine idea.'

Once again Kooka settled himself into the blankets, as The Blonde Maria set the blue ice-cream container of apricots down on the wooden boards of the floor between them. She opened *The World of Carrick's Cove* on her lap.

Unlike on the previous night The Blonde Maria herself was now less absorbed by the novel and more interested in arriving at that moment when Kooka would raise his hand and announce that the reading should stop, that he might sleep for a little while. To lull him towards this mood, she tried to read the text as musically as she could.

This time, however, Kooka seemed perfectly content to listen at great length to the trials of the young boatbuilder of Carrick's Cove. Maria began to fear that in her keenness to lull Kooka to sleep, she was actually keeping him wide awake, that her 'beautiful story-voice' was not as natural and settled as on previous nights, and that she'd never get to test her theory.

Try as she might to slow her reading, to flatten its lilt, to immerse herself in its content, it seemed that Kooka was unperturbed and perfectly engaged. But then, just as the boy's sloop in the book was finally being caulked and painted and the people of the cove were readying themselves for its launch, Kooka announced, once again in a strong, wide-awake voice, that he wouldn't mind 'a bit of a spell'.

'Perhaps I'll kip for a bit, Maria. What do you reckon?'

'Sure, Kooka,' The Blonde Maria replied, 'if you're feeling tired. I'll sit here for a while if you like, in case you wake up in a bit and want to hear some more.'

'That's nice of you, love. Yes, I think I'll snooze for a bit.'

As on the previous night Kooka's left hand then reached out automatically and clicked on his little black transistor radio where it sat on the bedside table. He slipped down deeper into the bedclothes just as the radio news was finishing and a discussion about the history of the Australian film industry began. Maria leant down to the ice-cream container, got herself an apricot, and waited.

Out in the night, beyond the timber-scented darkness on the perimeter of the pool of light, she could no longer hear the Plinth bells from the rivermouth but rather the large branches of the two backyard pine trees brushing against the Sewing Room wall. She took a small bite from the apricot and listened as an erudite interviewee discussed the effects of tax deductibility on Australian creativity.

And then Kooka's dream took over.

'You can just bundle it all up, love, but you can't bundle me. Doesn't that tell you something? Take the charts and the cabinets and the files, the tapes and the teaspoons and tobacco pouches, and . . .'

A woman's voice. It was Mary, from the night before. Mary and John. Mary and Kooka. Mary's voice, Kooka's wife.

And now Kooka's voice as well, but so much younger, a young man in love.

'Oh, but look at this one, Mary. It's you, on the badge of the spoon. See, it says it – MARY DWYER MINAPRE HOSPITAL FUND . . .'

'It's not me, John.'

'What's that? Look, of course it's you.'

'No it's not, John. Am I not scattered to the winds?'

'Oh, Mary, don't say that.'

'The wind I'm on. You can't put my titties on the spoon, John. And our love . . . remember the eagle over the water . . . remember it gliding . . . our love, John . . . not a spoon.'

Maria herself had used Kooka's souvenir teaspoons many times since she'd arrived at the hotel. Kooka had in fact given her the WILLY COOPER BIGGEST BABY IN VICTORIA spoon to take upstairs to her room when she made such a great impression on him the day she first arrived. Now she began to join the dots as the transistor beside the bed crackled and cut away.

For a moment, though, there was silence, just the pines brushing the outside wall, before the voices recommenced.

'Remember how much putty we used, my dear John. But I've long forgiven you, love. I'll take the honey over the putty. Any day. I shouldn't have blamed you. She couldn't resist your charms.'

'But, Mary, I'm sticky with the putty. It's in my armpits now . . . I'm all stopped up with it, Mary . . .'

'You've got teaspoons in your ears, John . . . shire records for socks . . . what's your heart now, John, a recording?'

'But it's in my heart, Mary, all the putty, from the hard-ware, you've gone . . .'

'I'm not gone, John. That's why I took the apricots away . . .'

'To find love in the hollow tree.'

'We did that, John.'

'I grew fur, Mary . . . and then the fur grew on you and we lived in that hollow.'

'As one creature, dear John.'

Maria's mouth was open in awe. She looked down at the apricot in her hand. It was small and blushed. Ripe. Now it seemed like a magical thing, an out-of-the-ordinary thing, a part of heaven. And then the tranny glitched again. She heard the same watery sounds of the night before. And the list again, of the swimmer in the waves.

'Bronchitis Cure, The Best Test for the Chest . . . eighty barrels . . . wire the cooper from Corrievale for Tom String . . . mounts for the new ale mirror . . . fetch the grates . . . bring the flowers for the rooms off the dray . . .'

The swimmer dived again and in The Blonde Maria's heart the whole Sewing Room seemed to sunder deep into the ocean hum. In her mind she even saw the salty underwater grain. And then the swimmer rose and opened out with spray into the air and sky. She gasped, then let out a little squeal of joy.

The Blonde Maria watched Kooka intently now. His face was impassive on the pillow but once again there was move-ment behind his eyes.

She stared at the tranny. Just a small black rectangular box. How could it be so?

Then, with devastating predictability, came the roaring

sound of a burning building. And once again the screaming woman. FIRE! FIRE! NO I MUST SEE MY JOHNNY. OH GOD FIRE! SOMEONE PLEASE!

Maria had no idea who the woman was but looking over at Kooka now she could see his big brow knitting with concern. The screaming continued and then, as if by rote, there was the sound of horse's hooves and the voices of firemen. The fire was going out; the woman's voice had vanished.

In the pool of light Kooka's brow relaxed but now a single tear glittered as it slipped out of his dreaming eye. The voice of Mary came again: 'And I will love you, doubly for your old mum, for the love she sold to send you here, to the ocean . . . and I did, John . . . and I did . . .'

Kooka laughed. 'But it's overflowing now, Mary, and the blasted tap won't stop . . . it's better off in the grass, a love like that . . .'

'No container could hold it, John.'

'It's better off, Mary. Makes the grass grow.'

'No container, John, no cabinet, no pouch . . .'

'Mary, did you see the brolgas that Tom String bred?'

'I did. And all the feathers flying . . .'

Once again Kooka laughed in his dream but then he sniffed on the pillow, his body bunched up under the covers, and with an abrupt heave the old man turned over in the bed. The tranny glitched. And then, suddenly, Barry Humphries was talking about expatriate life in London in the 1960s.

Like a Dog on Heat

BECAUSE OF THE SUCCESSFUL PRECEDENTS WE'D SET WITH
Duchamp the Talking Urinal, with Veronica's frankincense fumigation, and with allowing community contributions
such as the screening of 'Nan's Towering Inferno' and Jim's
'The Dying Gardens of the Great Ocean Road' during Happy
Hour, we felt a duty among our committee to keep up the good
times and the vibrant flow of ideas. So, in the days following
my confrontation of Maria, and now that Kooka's bar game
about the mystery of the fire in the original Grand Hotel had
been superseded by his interesting new condition, we called a
committee meeting in The Horse Room where we agreed to
three brand new Grand Hotel competitions.

The first was to be a contest that would give character
names to our local winds, à la the Sirocco of the Mediterranean
and The Fremantle Doctor of Perth. This idea of Ash Bowen's

came from an awareness of how the devastation of the local Aboriginal people by white settlers had deprived us all of an authentic language with which to speak about the land we loved. As Ash pointed out at the meeting, the Wathaurong band in our area would surely have had names for all the various winds on the coast, but now those names were gone on the very winds they described. It therefore seemed not only worthwhile but also a good fun idea to hold a competition to come up with our own.

The second idea at that meeting was to begin what we would call our Tuesday Wellbeing Nights, where we would venture out into the town after stumps to creatively alter shire signage in the spirit of Dada and the freedom virus. This idea was the result of a collaboration between Veronica and Darren Traherne, both of whom were almost allergic to the excessive amounts of signage implemented by the shire, small tourism operators, and various state-government bodies in our area. On many occasions over the years, when he was returning from fishing the night tides, Darren himself had gone down on bended knee under the moonlight to dismantle newly erected signs he considered superfluous, only to see them replaced in the following days by the various powers that be. For a time Darren did this so regularly that he carried a hacksaw with extra blades and a shifting spanner in his fishing bag. In the end, however, he'd given up, such was the persistence of his more organised opponents. But now Veronica was suggesting a new approach. Rather than destroy the signs, we would merely use them as the raw material for public works of art. We would tag these noble civic contributions of the Grand Hotel clientele with an obscure signature – 'DTs', short for 'Dada Tourists' – and a prize would be awarded if anyone could create a work that was so effective and popular among the population that the shire refused to take it down.

The third competition suggested at the meeting was that we begin a Grand Hotel stoneskimming contest down among the Plinths near the rivermouth. This was Darren Traherne's idea alone, and it immediately aroused much excitement and enthusiasm from the group. I sensed in this unbridled enthusiasm a sudden yearning among the committee for some harmless fun. Joan Sutherland, for instance, was particularly keen, no doubt wanting to pretend the adulterous and licentious world he was now inhabiting was innocent and pure after all. Perhaps not surprisingly it was only Veronica, with her intense loyalty to Art with a capital A, and her relentless desire to subvert the marketing and development of the coast, who remained lukewarm about the stoneskimming idea.

In fact it was at this point, when it became obvious that her plan to refashion shire infrastructure was the least favourite of the three proposed competitions, that Veronica cracked it good and proper. For weeks now she'd been complaining to me about letting The Lazy Tenor stay in the pub, about the mainstream mediocrity of the nightly sets of The Barrels, and also about what she thought was my tendency to cater too much for what she liked to call 'the mob'. Veronica had always been ardent, driven, and hot-blooded, and didn't want to see her radical dream of a Dada hotel die a boring death. Calling me aside during the meeting and out onto the verandah, she began hectoring me in a frustrated and derisive voice. Eventually I held up my hand. I had enough on my plate and just wasn't in the mood.

So, promptly, and I must say with a touch of rich-kid snootiness, she threatened right there and then to have nothing more to do with the hotel. I was shocked, even despite her grievances, and only managed to placate her by saying we'd put the Wellbeing Nights at the top of the list. Grudgingly she accepted this olive branch but didn't look too convinced. Saying she wasn't going back into the meeting, she turned and stepped off the verandah to head back up the hill to her studio on the cliff. As I watched her go, I couldn't help but feel diminished in the eyes of an artist I truly admired.

I had to take a few deep breaths before re-entering the meeting. I felt caught. I knew exactly where Veronica was coming from but I also felt she was missing the point. The deepest of all the ironies that the Dada movement embodied was that they scoffed at any slavish adherence to Art with a capital A, or Politics with a capital P, while simultaneously being famous for a riotous display of both. Veronica seemed to have remembered all the Dada postures but this one, which was surely the solid *and* evershifting ground that gave Dada its incomparable cock-a-hoop freedom. As much as I was looking forward to participating in the Tuesday Wellbeing Nights, it would be impossibly boring of me now to just ignore the wishes and enthusiasms of the rest of those involved in the hotel in the name of either Art or Politics.

I went back into the meeting without breathing a word of her complaint – I just said she'd gone home because she wasn't feeling well – but when the possibility of a competition to name the local winds was brought up later that night in the bar it immediately captured everyone's imagination. Then, when the stoneskimming comp was mentioned, it wasn't long before the whole bar was getting quite carried away, even to the extent that someone joked that Mangowak could be the host of the first ever World Stoneskimming Championships! People sipped at their Dancing Brolgas and were seduced by the preposterous scale of such an idea, which was of course soon scotched by a brief scoot around the internet on the big Happy Hour screen, where we found a plethora of websites devoted not only to world stoneskimming championship events but also to the sophisticated physics of the art. Despite this blow to our hope that Mangowak had finally found its very own niche of global significance, everyone was full of praise for the hotel committee in coming up with such great ideas.

In the following days and weeks not a breath of wind coursed through our valley unnoticed and more and more people could be seen down on the beach practising their skimming techniques in readiness for the comp. It seemed pretty clear I'd made a promise to Veronica that I couldn't really keep.

It was as I lay in my loft later on the night of this meeting, trying to clear my mind of all my cares and worries by counting imaginary brolgas leaping over the fences on the riverflat, that I heard a resounding crash in the night as Big Joan Sutherland fell down off the drainpipe of the second storey of The Grand Hotel.

I rushed on some clothes and went out to find the big fella lying splayed across the yard like a truly unsuccessful dog on heat. Wincing in pain, he bleated to me that he had lost his hotel key. I didn't need to ask why he hadn't come and knocked on the barn door to borrow my key. Quite obviously he had gone home after stumps to check on Jen and the kids and then come back to rendezvous with The Blonde Maria.

When he had hit the ground, still clinging to the down-pipe, the crash he made was so loud it could well have been heard in the previous century. From the upstairs rooms of the hotel, however, there was absolutely no reaction. The windows were silent, inscrutably so, with no breeze to even flutter the curtains. At this stage we had a jetlagged university student from Rotterdam staying in Room Two, who perhaps under-standably was either too shy or too sleepy to peer down. But I had to wonder what particular cocktail of The Blonde Maria's affections was distracting the other rooms from noticing Joan's fall. Was she still sitting in the wicker chair beside Kooka, reading him to sleep from *The World of Carrick's Cove*, or was she at the other end of the hallway in The Lazy Tenor's room, her recently pleasured body sprawled across his naked frame as she tenderly whispered her plan for world musical domination into his ear?

Down on the ground Joan was very, very sore – in fact he hadn't moved a limb as yet. I knelt down beside him and asked if he was okay. He said he thought so but that his arm hurt. I asked him which arm and he simply said, 'My tap-arm.'

'Oh great,' I replied, with a thick lashing of sarcasm. 'That's all I need. A barman who can't pour drinks. Are you out of your mind?'

'Well, thanks for the sympathy, Noel.'

The dim starless night over the hotel yard was suddenly

lit up as Sergeant Greg Beer's police four-wheel drive pulled into the driveway. For a moment the ice-blue tinge of his high-beam headlights revealed more than just the Blossfeldt pattern of blackwood trees on my eastern boundary. I saw clearly and in a piercing instant that The Grand Hotel had in fact become much more than I'd bargained for, and more perhaps than I could adequately handle.

Greg Beer switched off his engine and headlights. He got out of his car and shut and locked his driver's door with a pneumatic squish and an electronic pop. He took a torch off his hip and shone it in our direction. 'Is everything alright here, Noel?' he said. 'I've had a report.'

'What kind of report?'

'Of a loud crash from your premises. What's happened to Mr Sutherland here?'

'Oh, he's just had a little accident,' I said. 'He misplaced his key and was attempting to find another way into the building.'

'And he fell?'

'Yes, he fell.'

Greg Beer stood right over us now and shone his halogen torchlight straight into Joan's face.

'Aw, shit. Turn that thing off would ya, Greg?' Joan complained. 'You tryin' to blind me or somethin'?'

Greg Beer clicked off his torch. Then he clicked it on again, this time pointing it at the wall of the hotel. As the light thoroughly frisked the building, he continued his investigation. 'Any broken bones?'

'Nah. Well, maybe my arm,' Joan replied.

'Can you get up? Can you walk?'

'I dunno.'

'Do you want to lay charges, Noel?'

'I'm sorry?' I said.

The policeman's torchlight scanned the upper storey of the hotel, obviously looking not just for signs of the accident but for anything at all incriminating he might find. I dreaded what he would see as the light moved from right to left towards The Blonde Maria's and The Lazy Tenor's rooms.

'Well this does qualify as a breaking-and-entering offence,' the sergeant said, without taking his eyes off the torch beam.

'Oh, come off it. Joan works here. He just lost his key that's all.'

'Well it's up to you, Noel. But there's been a lot of this kind of thing happening in Mangowak of late. Breaking and entering. I'm determined to stamp it out.'

'I see. Well that's very worrying. It's not like back when we were kids, eh, Greg?' I ventured.

'What do you mean by that, Noel?'

'There was never any break-ins back then was there?'

Greg Beer clicked off his torch again and swung around to face me. It was true, when we were growing up in Mangowak there weren't any robberies or vandalism at all, apart from the occasional celebratory Monday night sinking of a weekender's boat in the river. But that was just us kids on a bit of a lark. No, my comment was referring to the fact that Greg Beer's mother, Meryl, had been the one real exception to the rule. It wasn't that she was a kleptomaniac or anything, but from time to time she felt the overwhelming need to let herself into vacant beach-houses in the town, put her feet up on the couches and polish off the drinks cabinet. Those were the days before we had our own policeman in Mangowak, and if it wasn't for the sympathy and understanding extended to Meryl Beer and her kids by Sergeant Ted 'Prickly' Moses, the policeman in Minapre, she would have been put in the clink as a repeat offender and her son and daughter would have been placed in an orphanage. Even as it was, on a couple of occasions she had to sober up overnight in the Minapre lock-up, and Greg and his sister Lurline were given to the sisters in St Catherine's convent in the hills out the back of town.

Admittedly this was a low blow I'd delivered to the sergeant, but I felt it was justified. There was no criminal offence occurring here, just an everyday case of male sexual passion gone wrong. And surely the police didn't have to know about that.

As I stood up from kneeling beside Joan, who himself sat up for the first time since the fall and leant on the elbow of his unbroken left arm, Sergeant Greg Beer glared at us both with a thinly disguised loathing. He fixed his torch back into its position on his hip and straightened his uniform pullover.

'I'll leave you gentlemen to it then,' he said officiously, before striding back across the yard towards his car.

I called after him. 'But Sergeant. If Joan's arm is broken, someone will have to see to it. You couldn't drive him over to the Minapre Hospital to have it checked out could you?'

Despite the late hour this request was of course well within the bounds of what could be expected from a small town policeman. Knowing that Greg Beer was such a stickler for protocol, I couldn't see how he would refuse.

Amazingly, however, he did refuse, such was his fury at my reference to his mum's criminal habits of days gone by.

'You've got a car, Noel. You can drive him,' he said bluntly. 'But I . . .'

There were to be no 'buts'. I watched helplessly as Greg Beer hit the central-locking button on his key ring. The slotting sound of his car doors opening signalled his resolve. He got in behind the steering wheel. But just as he was about to start the car, something behind Joan and I seemed suddenly to distract his attention. With his hand poised on the key in his ignition, he stared up at the second storey of the hotel. By the light in the cabin of his car we saw his mouth drop open and his face go all slack.

As Joan nursed his arm on the ground at my feet, I turned around and looked up. There was now a light glowing from The Lazy Tenor's room. It was a weird glow, with what could only be described as a wasabi-coloured tinge to it. Subsequently I discovered the glow came as a result of The Blonde Maria draping her bra over the bald bedside lamp.

She stood at the window, surrounded by the wasabi glow, a wine glass in one hand and a cigarette in the other. The Blonde Maria. She was naked from the waist up, her full breasts on display to the evening. On her head was my father's favourite fishing beanie, pulled tight over her ears. She must've dug it out from the cupboard in The Lazy Tenor's room.

Looking up from the yard, the vision of her was unsettling, spectral. It could almost have been a ghost if it wasn't for the potent charge of her sexuality.

Just as quickly as she appeared, The Blonde Maria

disappeared from the window back into the room, leaving myself and the sergeant with the heady after-image of her glory in the wasabi light. After a few silent moments Greg Beer collected himself and started the car. Uncharacteristically forgetting to turn on his headlights, and without so much as a glance in my direction, he backed out under cover of the pine trees and drove away into the night.

I spent the hours until dawn in the Emergency Department of the Minapre Hospital, as Joan had his fractured tap-arm set and plastered. As he finally came out of the surgery room around 5.30 am, I could hear Minapre's famously steak-indulged kookaburras laughing in the trees all around the building.

Joan walked over with his arm in its fresh sling. I pulled a pen out of my coat pocket, held it high in the air, and said, 'May I?'

He grinned his old grin. 'I dunno, Noel. I don't think it's dry enough yet.'

But I was determined. I'd been planning it while I was waiting. I gently pulled back the cotton sling from the plaster-cast on his arm and began my inscription.

In blue biro I drew a heart with an arrow crossing through it diagonally. At the top of the arrow I wrote the name JOAN and at the bottom below the arrow point I wrote JEN. Then I brushed the mushy wet plaster off the tip of my pen, replaced it in my coat pocket, stood back and looked at him.

He inspected what I had written. Looking up at me sheepishly, he said, 'I do, Noel. I do love her.'

'Well stop trying to be Spiderman scaling buildings in the middle of the night and start showing it.'

'But, Noel, Maria . . . she's so . . .'

'Stop it!' I said, raising my voice. 'Don't you see? This is a warning. You've gotta cut it out.'

Joan frowned, then nodded his head towards the laughing kookaburras beyond the automatic doors. 'Let's get out of here,' he said.

Watching the Gannets

A S ALWAYS THAT MORNING THERE WERE THINGS I HAD
to do: cleaning, banking, ordering, etc., but all I really
felt like doing was diving into the ocean. What with the initial
excitement and then the various dramas in the hotel, I hadn't had
a swim for what seemed like weeks. So I put on a pair of swimming shorts in my barn, selected my favourite fiddleback staff
from the bundle in the corner near the big doors, and stepped
out from under the pine trees to head down to the waves.

As I walked across the flat and began the climb up to the
cliff above Horseshoe Cove, I was so bowed down with cares
and worries I could've had a butterfly saying prayers on my nose
and wouldn't have noticed. By the time I reached the top and
laid eyes on the water below, my tears fell like rain that had
been tangled up in my own personal bluestone-coloured cloud
for weeks.

The tears fell as I walked along the clifftop track towards Squeaky Beach. Before long my shirt was drenched from the familiar salty giant-sized droplets. It was becoming clear that to laugh properly, fully, you first of all had to know how to really cry. Well, you can see that in a child. What baby is born laughing after all? No, first we cry, then we laugh. But a child doesn't feel wooden, like I had when I left for the clefts and overhangs. And it's from that wooden unfeeling source, that terrifying place where nothing matters anymore, where you could quite easily hack off your own arm for kindling, that my new kind of laughter had been born. This was the laughter from the depths of the human well, the laughter of full surrender, of tragedy ripened rather than left unripe, the laughter that comes up in the bucket along with the pitch black of the darkness below.

In the midst of the hotel's shenanigans perhaps it was too easy to forget that the darkness was always there, slowly turning like a planet unto itself, just underneath the light, fuelling every bright joke and cackle. Well, the dramatic implications of recent events had certainly reminded me. Despite our self-assurances, our artistic platitudes and social certainties, we were all actually caught in our lives between reality on the one hand and fantasy on the other. Why else would a country boy with a beautiful wife who he loved, and two sons who he'd die for, put everything at risk for the sake of an exotic young bohemian who could take or leave him like a day at the races? And why would a beautiful young singer, with genuine artistic talent and a timeless gift for entertaining the troops, retreat into her shell, refuse to sing, and devote herself to a frankly dubious character to whom she was just another in a long line of notable conquests? Sure, Louis Daley had a miracle voice, but did he seem to care about it that much? Not from what I could tell. He sang in the mornings as habitually as he pulled on his pants, and he seemed to care much more about getting his pants off again, at the first available opportunity, than he did about a singing career that would make him a household name.

And just because I could see all this clearly, it didn't mean that I myself was immune. The irony for me, of course, was that amidst the mundane burdens, the surreal realisations and unforeseen complications of running the pub, The Lazy Tenor's singing was a deeply therapeutic way to start the day. Without fail it reassured me, despite Veronica's despair, that great beauty was still possible in this life, that we could still soar above the rucks of ugliness, even this late in the human story. That confidence alone, which I could rely upon for as long as The Lazy Tenor remained a lodger, was by itself almost worth all the anguish. So where was my own border between reality and fantasy? Frankly, I didn't know, and perhaps, after my charmed encounter with the brolga, the brolga that everyone assured me couldn't possibly exist, I didn't care to. All I knew was that The Lazy Tenor's singing was a privilege, and not only for the rich.

By the time I was approaching the track down to Squeaky Beach, my tears were satisfactorily spent and there was a spring in my step at the prospect of the swim. As I walked, I began to notice the little flowers in the undergrowth all around me: the wine-dark peas, the running postmans, the everlasting daisies and the fringe lilies. Before she died, Mum always liked to say that to notice the little flowers in the bush around Mangowak is to know your mind and heart are clear. They seemed to vanish, to disappear in the face of tension, or muddle-headedness, or madness, but of course they were always there, the little flowers, each in their own right season. It was only the looker who could go missing, Mum always told us; it was only the looker who would wander off into gloom and blindness. Not the little flowers.

I descended the Squeaky Beach steps and arrived on the sand to find no one else around. I stripped off and ran through the white breakers before plunging deep into the clear green water between the sets.

My instincts had been right. A walk and now a swim was doing me the world of good. I could feel my spirit shedding its burdens, my cells reawakening, the tawdry sexual life of the upstairs rooms of the hotel, and the worry over Veronica's dissatisfaction, being replaced by a purer saltwater sensation.

The swell was solid, with waves peeling off the reef at about three feet. I was surprised no one was out there surfing but didn't dwell on it. I took pleasure in the fact that for the moment it was all mine to enjoy.

For half an hour or so I bodysurfed, riding high with head and shoulders out above the tumbling white water. The massage of the surf relaxed my body, and afterwards I stood peacefully in the marbled slack between the waves, diving under each one as it came along.

I was sufficiently unwound now to allow everyday tasks to re-enter my mind. I dived and stroked in the underhum of the water and began to make a list of the things that needed ordering for The Grand.

A new delivery of The Dancing Brolga Ale from Rennie Vigata . . . ten one-kilo pats of butter from the Pollsmere farm at Gellibrand . . . two dozen seven-ounce glasses and one dozen five-ounce ponies from Stewart Cellars in Melbourne . . . three tonnes of white box from Mologa for the fire . . . two twenty-can boxes of Portuguese olive oil from Odysseus in Minapre . . . a new set of tablecloths, which Nan had told me were on sale at Dimmeys in Colac . . . a new back-up USB cable for the screen in the bar. Jim had also asked me to order bass guitar strings for Oscar on the hotel letterhead – apparently they cost the earth. What on earth the hotel was doing buying musical equipment for The Barrels was beyond me, but as I swam in the silky life-giving waters at Squeaky Beach I hardly cared.

Eventually I emerged from the ocean and sat, tingling all over, on the beach. Still no one was around; it was my lucky day. I lay back and let the warm sun dry me. Before long I had fallen fast asleep.

When I awoke groggily some time later, I sat up to see a woman I recognised at the far end of the beach. It was Jen Sutherland. She was sitting on a rock at the end of the cove, where the sand finishes and the tide begins to run in over the potholes of the reef just there.

I stood up quickly and put back on my clothes. I would have liked to leave her in peace and go my own way, but I felt paranoid about doing so. What if she suspected her husband's affair with The Blonde Maria and interpreted my departure from the beach as collusion, as if I was avoiding her? Fact was, I had colluded with Joan, even to the extent of agreeing to back him up with his bogus story of how he'd broken his arm. He'd told Jen he'd fallen off a ladder while trying to fix the hotel's outside light.

I decided I couldn't risk it. I liked Jen, I respected her good sense and kindness, and so, saying a quick farewell to my solitude, I strolled over towards the rock to dishonestly declare my innocence by saying hello.

Jen wasn't surprised to see me. She turned from her reverie and smiled sweetly. 'I saw you sleeping there, Noel. I didn't want to disturb you.'

She was naturally shy, so I knew this would have suited her. But now she moved over on the rock above the tide, to make room for me to sit down.

'Joan's at home with the kids, of course, because of his arm,' she said. 'I'm sure it's all a bit inconvenient for you, Noel, but it's a godsend for me. I can't remember the last time I sat by myself on the beach like this.'

'And now I've come along and ruined it,' I said.

'Oh no,' she laughed. 'I was just beginning to get bored.'

I didn't believe her; the dreamy looking woman I'd observed sitting on the rock as I woke up was far from bored.

We sat in silence watching the tide poking its way into all the igneous nooks and pots and crevices of the brown and jagged reef. I felt a little nervous; Jen had such a quiet dignity about her. Any dignity I had at that moment seemed a trifle compromised.

'I've always been superstitious about living on the coast,'

she said, breaking the silence. It was an unexpected remark from one usually so private.

'How come?'

'I dunno. There always seemed to be dickheads coming from this direction when I was growing up.'

I laughed, but actually I was taking note of the fact that it was the first time I'd ever heard Jen Sutherland swear. 'Dickhead' was just not one of her words. She was clearly feeling raw.

'But when I sit on a rock like this and get some time alone, I can understand what all the fuss is about.'

'Yeah, it's good,' I said.

'Back home I used to love crawling on my belly out onto the blackwood boughs above our river. To just be by myself there, at dusk, in all that peace and quiet. I even wrote a very bad poem about it once. "When Time Stands Still", it was called.'

She laughed a little at the memory. 'But this is different,' she said. 'This is like watching time passing.'

I nodded. We watched the water together.

Eventually I asked, 'How are the boys?'

Jen smiled. She raised her arm and pointed while answering, at a gannet plummeting into the water about a hundred metres out. 'Oh they're alright. Happy to have their dad home. Happy to write on his plaster.'

Again I laughed. She'd obviously seen what I had written in the hospital. The gannet bobbed on the water for a few seconds after its dive, then flew up into the air again. We both watched its path, hoping to see it dive again.

I said, 'You know years ago a guy Veronica and I went to

art school with turned his back on it all and went into advertising. A lot of people gave him shit about it, told him he was selling out and all that. Veronica was one of them. But I liked him and couldn't help feeling sorry that everyone was giving him such a rough time. So one day I rang him up to say I had an inspired idea and that he had to come down here to see me. When he arrived, I planned to bring him to the beach to watch the gannets dive. I was gonna explain that the only reason their heads didn't explode when they crashed into the water at over a hundred kilometres an hour was because they had little air sacs just under the skin of their brow to cushion the blow. I was gonna tell him that these were the world's first airbags. Then I was gonna suggest the ad. A beautiful luxury car snaking its way down the Great Ocean Road in dramatic winter weather. Out to sea behind the car the gannets are sheering down out of the sky, plummeting into the whitecaps. There's lush choral music in the background, the voice-over explains the connections. The car, complete with airbags and every other luxury feature, would be touched by the gannet's magic and included by implication in the beauty and wonder of the natural world. It was the perfect ad for a Volvo or Merc, and I knew it would get him off to a great start if he could get it to the right people.'

'Absolutely,' Jen said. 'It'd be a certainty.'

'Yeah. But what happened was when he got down here, and we walked down the beach and were sitting watching them dive, I just couldn't bring myself to do it, to give him the idea. It was embarrassing. We sat on the beach and I didn't say a word. It just felt wrong, to use the gannets like that. And he kept saying, "Come on, so what is it?" until I found myself trying to convince him of what Veronica and the others had been saying all along. That he shouldn't go into advertising. He got real cranky then, and fair enough too, but I was stuck, and I couldn't think of anything else to say.'

On cue the gannet hovered high in mid-air in front of us, tucked its wings back and dived again, straight down, an arrow into the water. Jen and I were in awe, of both the elegance of the bird and of its sheer power, and watched as it bobbed on the surface before taking off and flying away west towards the Two Pointer Rocks.

'Perhaps that's what Joan needed when he fell off the ladder the other night,' I joked. 'An airbag.'

'Might have saved a few hassles,' Jen laughed.

'Don't you worry about him, though, Jen,' I said. 'He'll be back at work soon. Do him good to have a spell at home anyway. And we're making enough to pay him while he's off.'

'Yeah. He told me that. That's nice, Noel.'

We fell silent again until out of the blue Jen started humming, and then her lips parted and she began to sing ever so quietly in a light airy voice. I didn't recognise the song but her voice seemed as clean as the clear cold water in front of us. Then, just as quickly as she started, she stopped again.

I didn't make any comment. I didn't want to embarrass her. So I said, 'Oh well, I better be off. Back to the madhouse.'

She turned to face me and smiled. 'Noel, it was nice to watch the gannets with you.'

I stepped down off the rock and laughed nervously, feeling guilty again in the face of her quiet grace. 'Yeah,' I said, 'you too, Jen. Anytime.'

A Black Velvet Session

I WALKED HOME WITH A GUILTY STEP, FEELING ROTTEN about what I knew and what I wasn't telling Jen. The brief rejuvenation I'd found by having a walk and a cry, and then a swim and a sleep on the beach, had already disappeared as I stepped along.

The air had turned thick and damp, as the southerly had brought in the sea mist and then died off to leave it just hanging there over the cliffs and the town. As I walked along Two Pointers Way, all the power poles were fizzing and crackling in the salty damp. If the mist stayed around till nightfall, all those poles would be sparking in the blackness, dotting the night with intermittent light, like crackers going off. When I was a kid and that happened, it was as if some kind of white man's magic had over-ruled the sky. Mum used to take me to the ocean window in The Sewing Room, pull back the curtain and point out the fizzing, crackling light coming and going all the way down the road. It was wonderful to see but it gave me an edgy feeling too: half scary, half as if a celebration had begun. It always added to the fun when Dad talked of how the salt-sparkle from the power poles was a 'death-trap'. 'Whole bloody town could catch fire,' he'd say, and inside I'd catch my breath at his gloomy forecast and imagine the town ablaze, and all because of the magic tottering power poles catching fire in the salt-mist.

By the time I got home, not only were my shorts wet from swimming but my shirt was still damp as well, from a mixture of the tears and walking in the mist-laden air. It was after lunch, a bit before two. The hotel would have to open in an hour and we were still a head barman short. I made straight for the barn and changed my clothes, and then hung the wet stuff up on the washing line down the side of the building. Eventually the mist would have to clear and they'd get dry.

I walked across the front of the hotel and entered through the double doors of the verandah. The Lazy Tenor was behind the bar fixing himself a drink. I must say it was starting to feel a little bit rich the way he and The Blonde Maria had taken to helping themselves to whatever food and drink they wanted, without lifting a finger to help with the running of the hotel.

As I walked in, The Lazy Tenor had a large glass beer jug, a bottle of champagne and two pint cans of Guinness out of the bar on the counter. He greeted me by popping the cork on the champagne bottle and knocking out the overhead light globe. 'Aw, shit. Sorry, Noel,' he said.

I said nothing and watched as he set the champagne bottle

down and opened one of the Guinness cans. Quickly he started pouring the contents into the beer jug with his left hand while he picked up the champagne bottle in his right and waited for the Guinness to settle. Placing the Guinness can aside, he then picked up a tablespoon he had ready on the bar, upturned it in his hand, and began pouring the champagne onto the back of the spoon, from where it spilt into the jug. The alcohol glittered and foamed, the Guinness remaining black and steady under the bubbles of the champagne, until slowly they fused. Rather expertly The Lazy Tenor managed to time the pouring so that the brew didn't overflow the jug. Before long it was brimming at the lip and, beaming from ear to ear with the sight of it, he set the champagne bottle aside.

'Maria said she'd never tasted a Black Velvet before,' he told me, before remembering to neck the remaining champagne in the bottle. 'So I had to do the honours. Nothing like it on a misty day like this. I mean, look at that!'

He held the jug up in the remaining natural light there was in the bar. He was right, it did look impressive. I hadn't laid eyes on a jug of Black Velvet for years, not since Father Leo Morris used to have one with his Saturday feed of couta, chips and coleslaw in the old Mangowak Hotel lounge. I was too young to ever get to taste one back then and now was keen to try. All of a sudden I felt like I could do with a good stiff drink.

'Do you mind?' I asked The Lazy Tenor, gesturing hopefully at the jug, and he replied, 'Go for your life.'

Perhaps inspired by my childhood memories, I ducked behind the counter and fossicked in the sideboard cupboard until I found the special Lalique champagne glasses that used to be my Aunty Rita's.

When I placed two of the Laliques on the bar, The Lazy Tenor was suitably impressed. 'Hey,' he said in his rich singer's timbre. 'Where did you get them?'

Aunty Rita's Laliques were beautiful. The stem between the bowl and the base of the glass was an art-deco figurine in opaque crystal – a naked female figure, a nymph no less.

The Lazy Tenor's lips puckered with amusement as he licked them with relish and poured the Black Velvet. In the pristine paper-thin glass of the Laliques the foaming matt-black concoction looked striking indeed. We each took up a glass and were giggling even before we'd tasted a drop. Such was the effect of Aunty Rita's Laliques. And then we wished each other good health and drank. And my word did it taste good.

The Lazy Tenor's interest in opera, of course, betrayed a high-mindedness that otherwise he kept well hidden. It had occurred to me that his bawdy tales from 'The Tradesman's Entrance' were set up to disguise the musical vocation he preferred to keep to himself. But perhaps relaxed now in the full knowledge that I'd not only heard but also appreciated his voice, he couldn't help but express his appreciation of the elegant craftsmanship of Aunty Rita's glasses.

'I feel like Tito fuckin' Gobbi, drinking from one of these!' was his ecstatic observation.

I'd heard him mention this name once before. 'Who is Tito Gobbi?' I dared ask.

The Lazy Tenor scoffed and stared at me with derision. But then he took another sip, raised the Lalique in the air again and said, 'Never mind. Tell me about these glasses.'

So I told him about Aunty Rita and her South Yarra parties and how we were the poor country cousins. And I told him also what I knew of René Lalique himself, whose biography was passed down to us in the paraphernalia that came with the glasses when Aunty Rita died. All I really remembered of it was that Lalique had been born in a tiny country town in France but at an early age the family had moved to a suburb of Paris. From that day on they had visited the country town on summer holidays, and young René had developed a deep affection for the river and the unspoiled natural world of his birthplace. When later he became famous for his art-nouveau glass design, it was the naturalism in his work, the filigree, the plant forms, the birds, that set him apart. And this was all due to his attachment to the nondescript little town where he was born. Beyond that and of course his fame, I couldn't really tell The Lazy Tenor much. Judging by his reaction, however, it seemed like it was enough.

'You see blokes like him were a dime a dozen in Europe back then,' he began enthusiastically, still holding his Lalique aloft. 'Work like this, the music, the architecture – yes, even the fuckin' glasses they drank from were fair dinkum.' Then he gave a bitter laugh. 'But growin' up in Blokey Hollow . . . mate, I might as well have grown up on the moon. It's like starting off the back-markers. You got Buckley's.'

Out of nowhere The Lazy Tenor had for the first time admitted to having thwarted ambitions. It was curious. Either the unique craftsmanship of Aunty Rita's Laliques had made a deep impression or The Blonde Maria had been getting in his ear about becoming a household name. The last thing I was gonna do was be nosey about it though. So I just stood at the bar and sipped the Black Velvet, and let him hold forth.

'But do you reckon this Lalique cunt was some kind of toff, just coz he made beautiful shit? I doubt it. You said he was from a small town too, hey? He was probably a terrible shagger, just like me. Thing is, people round here think you have to talk with a marble in your mouth to be artistic. So a bloke like me's gotta change, you know what I mean? You gotta change the way you talk, the way you walk, just coz God gave you a voice. Well where's the fuckin' logic in that? I've got the voice. That's all that matters, isn't it?'

He was getting het up now and gestured for me to drink up so he could pour me another one. I drained the glass and he poured from the jug. 'Isn't The Blonde Maria expecting you upstairs?' I asked.

He smiled. 'She'll keep,' he said. 'She's asleep anyway. The Black Velvet was gonna be a surprise. But what with these glasses you've pulled out of your arse, fact is, I can drink with you and cuddle the lady at the same time.'

We laughed, and toasted our good health again.

'Now where was I?' he said, with the velvety foam on his upper lip. 'That's right. Fuckin' hell, she's on at me upstairs about "getting my act together", as she calls it. "Well what would I wanna do that for?" I say. "Because you've got a gift," she says. "Yep, so why turn it into a punishment?" I say back.'

'How would it be a punishment,' I asked, 'to have a singing career?'

'Mate, have you ever been to the opera in this country?

It's a fuckin' joke. Half rate singers and fucknut tossers in the audience pretendin' they care. They wouldn't know Caruso from Perry Como half of 'em. I just couldn't tolerate it. All that grandstandin'. Back in Italy when the whole show started, it was an absolute shitfight. You had your toffs in the boxes and the riff-raff down below, and the toffs'd be pissin' and spittin' on the riff-raff from a great height, people'd be throwin' punches and fucking in the seats, and all while the opera was being performed. Now compare that to the Presbyterian shit they serve up in Melbourne. Fuck, if I'd been born in Venice in the fifteen hundreds I would have been a household name alright. You better believe it. But not now. Not here.'

'Well, you could go overseas,' I ventured.

The Lazy Tenor's jaw dropped. 'Don't you start,' he said. 'I thought we were having a pleasant drink. If I wanna be nagged at, I can just go back upstairs.'

'Sorry.'

'Yeah, well drink up, and tell me what you're gonna do now you've lost your head barman.'

I drained my glass and let The Lazy Tenor pour me another. But I was starting to feel peckish. So I went around behind the counter again and upturned a packet of peanuts into an imitation parquet bowl.

'Good idea,' said my drinking partner. 'That'll keep the orchestra in tune.'

With a bodysurf and two Black Velvets under my belt I was feeling unusually good now. The concoction was extraordinarily drinkable and as a result it occurred to me that The Lazy Tenor might have a way with alcohol as well as women and song. So I put it on him. Had he ever poured a beer behind a hotel bar?

'No,' he said. 'Matter of fact I haven't. But it can't be rocket science.'

I giggled, looking at the glassy nymph in my fingertips. 'Well why don't you fill in for Joan?'

'Me? Fill in for that galah?'

'Yeah. Why not? We could do with the help.'

'Yeah, yeah, but I'm writing a book here, mate. Don't you get it? And I'm paying you rent I might add.'

'Well, we can certainly waive that, come to some other arrangement.'

The Lazy Tenor drained his glass with a look of disgust. 'Didn't you hear what I said? *I'm writing a book here, mate.* Do you reckon I'd be holed up in this backwater for any other reason? If that mate of yours is silly enough to break his arm chasin' my skirt, then that's his problem. And yours I suppose.'

'Oh, well thanks for your kind consideration,' I said sarcastically.

The Lazy Tenor was outraged. 'What, are you havin' a go at me now? I'm a lodger here, mate. I pay my board and that's that. It's not my fault if you're one short. And anyway I'm in that fuckin' Horse Room every night entertaining your clientele with my literary efforts. You should be payin' me. Not hasslin' me to prop your whole fuckin' hotel up. Don't get me wrong, I like the joint and all that, but shit, Noel, you can't lay that on me. Nah. No way.'

As he poured another Black Velvet into my Lalique, I was feeling cheeky now. Oh dear: champagne and Guinness – what a combination. Those Black Velvets were dynamite. So I spoke up. And what I had to say worked like a cattle prod on a rooster. 'Well maybe it is your fault that we've lost our head barman. Yeah. You're entangled in all this whether you like it or not.'

The Lazy Tenor's brows lowered. His tongue flicked, licking the Black Velvet foam from his lip as quick as a skink darting off a bush track. All of a sudden he looked every bit of his six foot four inches standing there behind the bar. I wondered if I'd made a mistake.

'How do you mean?' he said sourly, with the stately monotone that often precedes violence.

'Well, you've stolen his girl. If it wasn't for you, he wouldn't have had to climb up the downpipe coz Maria would've thrown him the keys.'

The Lazy Tenor promptly burst into loud laughter. He hooted and guffawed, took a huge draught of Black Velvet and couldn't stop giggling. Eventually, through tears of red-faced mirth, he managed to get a word out.

'Fuck it's hard being me, Noel. I tell you it really is,' he said, wiping away the tears. 'She comes to my room one night, demands that I make love to her, which I do, and then she's hooked. And the *married man* she's been biding her time with previously goes crazy and starts climbing the walls, destroys a bit of the hotel plumbing and makes himself useless to his employer – and it's all my fault! I'm the villain. I tell ya, you should try it sometime, Noel, bein' me. You wouldn't last five minutes. It's not as easy as it looks ya know.'

He had a point. He had a few points actually. I paused, Lalique in hand, to wonder how on earth I came to be defending a man cheating on his wife while blaming a perfectly harmless bachelor who, as he said, paid his rent and made his bed. I felt as if I'd netted off a cove for a big run of whiting only to find when the fish came in that the net was riddled with huge flapping holes. Once again I felt hopelessly, scarily adrift. And increasingly drunk as well.

Before long The Lazy Tenor had made a fresh jug of Black Velvet and the stout and champagne were bubbling and foaming away again. Still chuckling at my accusations, he changed the subject. That was fine by me. We both knew he was right.

He wanted to tell me about Tito Gobbi, how he'd been a great Italian baritone, a star of La Scala and the Metropolitan Opera in New York City, and how he'd also once been King of Moomba in Melbourne. 'Imagine the poor bastard arriving out here in the late sixties,' said The Lazy Tenor with disgust. 'He wouldn't have known whether to take it seriously or not. King of fuckin' Moomba! What's that, hey? *Regio di Moomba che?* And all of Melbourne getting around with corks hangin' off their hats. Apart from those with marbles in their mouths of course. Can you imagine it? The great Tito Gobbi, partner of Callas! Fuck, it makes me wild just thinking about it.'

We talked and we drank – well, I did more listening than talking in actual fact – and unusually The Lazy Tenor spoke more about his interests than his conquests. Before long we were joined by a few passing travellers. It was well past three o'clock by then, the hotel was officially open, and whether he liked it or not The Lazy Tenor was on standby behind the bar.

I was outright pissed by this stage. The Lazy Tenor humoured me for a while by serving the three or four customers who wandered in, and he managed to do it very politely too, I might add. Then came a couple of the very ilk he seemed to hate the most: well heeled, but not exactly aristocratic, well mannered, but not exactly cultured, the kind of neatly dressed baby boomers who might these days be subscribers to the opera in town. But The Lazy Tenor handled them with aplomb. They walked up to the bar and asked if we had any Little Creatures Pale Ale from Fremantle in WA. 'Certainly,' he lied. 'We actually have it on tap, sir.' Well, you would've thought the bloke had won the lottery. He clapped his hands together, turned to his wife and said, 'Did you hear that? They've got Little Creatures on tap.' Then, turning back to The Lazy Tenor, he said, 'Can't drink any other beer these days. Nothing can touch Little Creatures.'

The Lazy Tenor nodded, smiled pleasantly, and began to pour two Dancing Brolgas from our brandless tap. As the couple waited, I sat quietly on my stool, wincing in anticipation.

The first beer he poured was absolutely perfect, with a nice half inch head. What a fluke! He placed it proudly on the bar mat and winked at me. The second one he had a bit more trouble with and probably poured a spare pot's worth down the drain before he got it looking reasonable. Luckily the couple weren't watching; they were busy raising their eyebrows at each other as they looked around at the contents of the room. It was like a bush bar but not quite – there were absurdist quotes on the walls for one thing, the ocean-facing windows were boarded up, and the air still smelt of frankincense, even months after Veronica's fumigation. I could see that a familiar confusion had replaced the initial curiosity in their eyes.

When their beers were ready, the affluently appointed couple sat on the pews of the big table. Temporarily bonded as we were, due to the magic of the Black Velvets, somehow The Lazy Tenor and I began effortlessly to feign an everyday conversation about a local grape grower who was hiring local lads with high-powered illegal slingshots to shoot the crows that were ruining his vines.

'Yairs,' The Lazy Tenor was saying, leaning iconically on the beer-tap with a mock-serious brow, 'the other day they stoned over three hundred crows between lunch and dusk.'

'Is that right?' I joined in.

'Yep. Left 'em in a pile down the northern end, by his pressin' shed there.'

'Geez, must've been a big pile. Three hundred crows you say?'

'Yep. Eight feet high it was. Handy with the ball bearin's, the young fellas.'

'Too right they are, Lou.'

Out of the corner of my eye I could see the couple quietly drinking their beers, with no recognition of the fact that it wasn't Little Creatures in the glass. They weren't talking, though. We had their undivided, if somewhat furtive, attention.

'Yairs, well anyway,' The Lazy Tenor went on, in a perfect rendition of the Blokey Hollow drawl he grew up among. 'Three hundred crows. What do ya reckon you do with 'em then, Noel, once they're dead?'

'Geez, I dunno, Lou. Too many to eat. I suppose you'd burn 'em.'

'Or bury 'em.'

'Yeah, or bury 'em.'

'Well they didn't have to worry about that problem anyway.'

'No?'

'Nah.'

The Lazy Tenor took a theatrical sip of his Black Velvet. His performance was faultless and his smile at the sight of René Lalique's nymph between his fingers merged seamlessly with the act. The couple, however, weren't daring to look our way from the pews, where they sat with their trusty pots of Little Creatures.

'Well, what did they do with the crows then?' I asked as Big Lou The Country Publican set down his drink.

'They did nothin',' was his reply.

'Well, what happened to the crows?'

'What do you reckon happened to 'em?'

'Geez, Lou, for the life of me I can't think what.'

'Aw, come on, Noel, how long have you lived around here?'

'Born and bred.'

'And you can't work out what happened to the crows?'

I scratched the crown of my head and thought about it. I noticed the wife steal a cautious glance my way in the silence.

'Well the only possibility, Lou, is that some other bastard got rid of 'em.'

Lou The Country Publican clicked his tongue in affirmation. 'Too bloody right they did, Noel. Jimbo reckons when they went back the next day to ping some more, the pile was gone. Feathers, heads, feet, guts, the lot. Goannas, mate.'

'You don't say.'

'Yep. Goannas. Ate 'em overnight. Three hundred crows.

Better than the council garbage truck. One minute the crows are in a pile, next minute nuffin'. Jimbo reckons it was awful to think about. But after they shot another couple of hundred that day he took his old man's video camera back that night to film the feast.'

'Fair dinkum? Geez, no flies on Jimbo.'

'Nah, you can say that again. Anyway, I've got it on DVD right here if you wanna watch it. It's grouse. Top qual too. We'll pop it on the big screen. Jimbo's old man's good with the video gear.'

'Shit yeah. I'll have a look.'

'Alrighty then.'

As if on cue the couple drained what was left of their phoney beers, stood up quickly, said thanks, and made for the door.

'Enjoy the Little Creatures?' The Lazy Tenor called after them.

'Yes, yes,' the man called back over his shoulder. 'My favourite. It's great you have it . . .' But then his pocket started clanging like an old wall-phone and with his wife he rushed outside through the sunroom to take the call.

The Publican and Her Slushy

As KOOKA HELD UP HIS HAND IN THE POOL OF LIGHT, The Blonde Maria closed the book on her lap and waited. The old man smiled sleepily at her, reached across to the bedside table and turned on the transistor.

At the tiny window high in the western wall beyond Kooka's bed she could see a single bogong moth batting its wings at the pool of light inside. She kept her eyes on the moth rather than on Kooka, for fear of having any kind of influence on what was about to happen.

They caught the tail end of an interview with a museum curator from the Riverina and then a Lee Kernaghan song took its place, 'She's My Ute'. Eventually the song went clunk, Kooka's bottom jaw relaxed into sleep and the tranny once again turned to static.

After many nights this had become the moment she waited

for, and she nodded confidently to herself, reassured by the fact that this was exactly how things had happened on the other nights. A few minutes later, without any sign that the static on the tranny or the moth at the high window were about to disappear, Maria began to get agitated. Then suddenly there was a harsh sound, like a gear being missed, the tranny spluttered, and the static was banished into the night. Once again there was silence and up in the glass of the tiny window the moth had flown away.

And then, after only a few seconds, there it was, the unmistakable sound of someone swimming in the ocean.

She sighed as she pissed. Maria imagined the water up at her neck like a frill of champagne lace, and silver clarity out on the horizon. But this time, before the swimming woman could even begin to make her lists or duck dive, a voice called. The cooee came from back on the beach. A man was trying to reach her over the ocean sounds. The cooee cut through the air: the 'coo' provided the stability, the 'ee' the open range. It was both distant and close, like a myth.

The swimmer must have felt some hold in the call because she didn't dive, as she had on previous nights. As the cooees went out across the spray, Maria heard the close sound of elastic-slap against skin as the swimmer adjusted her togs, and the breath of effort as she jumped up through a tumbling oncoming wave.

When the wave passed, the turbulent air calmed, there was a buckle in the wind, a long releasing hiss surrounded her and the cooee came clearer.

She turned now and called back. Presumably she waved.

'Tom String!' she cried.

Stepping back towards the beach, her knees rising high, her feet splashed down through the water with the double beat of a human heart. She said the name again but this time quietly to herself: *'Tom String.'* When her feet were slapping in only an inch or two of water on sand, she whispered, 'He and Paul have come to get the coal.'

The Blonde Maria was staring at Kooka's tranny, her mouth open in awe again at what she was hearing. As the woman trod up the beach towards the man called Tom String, she said, 'You've come to get the coal, Tom,' with her feet now almost silent on the flat tide-slickened sand.

'Yes, missus. My apologies for upsetting your bath. You looked like a real jollytail out there. I dunno where you get the nerve.'

'Oh, that's alright, Tom. It's a mystery to me why the likes of you resist it.'

Tom String chuckled. His voice had a slow softness about it, almost as if it had grown a fur. 'Well I tried it once as it happens. As a sapling on Deal Island with my da. Thing was I got a thrashin' to within an inch of me life. For not knowing my place and thinkin' I was a fish. You could say I was put off it for good. But as I recall it wasn't my cup of tea anyhow. I was windy the whole time I was out there.'

'Well, Tom, I'm sure the thrashing didn't help,' the woman said. 'And do I look like a fish to you? How did Paul travel with the dray?'

'Oh he played up. Been in a good paddock for too long. Tell me, missus, can a horse become an alcoholic? We've gotta stop letting him thorough out the dregs. He's not meant for a slushy, after all. He's a palomino for goodness' sake!'

The woman laughed happily at Tom String's jesting. Well, at least one thing was cleared up: Tom's companion Paul was a horse. In the background Maria could hear the tinkle of a harness.

'Yairs, I got him up the hill on the Boatbuilder's alright,' continued Tom String. 'But cranky? On the level ground across to here you should have seen the fuss. I'm sure he's got a headache. Then, comin' down the track to the beach here, he was just plain obstinate. Can't wait to see him goin' back uphill with the coal.'

'But it's light isn't it?'

'Yairs, the coal is. But the dray's not.'

The woman laughed again. The two were obviously fond of each other, on better terms at least than Tom String and Paul.

Tom String groaned. 'And don't go talking to him like a man, Mrs Sweeney. He'll be ordering whiskey next.'

'Well I've had worse customers in my hotel than poor old Paul.'

'To be sure. But that's no reason. Now I suppose I better be getting on with this reef here.'

'I suppose you know best. What's say I linger with Paul and hitch a ride back with you on the dray when you're done? I could help you load and unload.'

'Aw, there's no need for that, missus. As you said, this stuff's nice and light. You duck back into the water if you want. You're welcome for a ride anyhow.'

'Thank you, Tom String.'

'Yairs, missus. And no chattin' up Paul here while I'm working.'

When Maria first heard the voice and then the mention of the coal, she was none the wiser, but when Tom String actually called her name it was plain.

Mrs Sweeney, he'd said. Maria's head began to swim. Like everyone else in the hotel she knew the name. Joan Sweeney ran The Grand Hotel for thirteen years till it mysteriously burnt to a crisp sometime in the late 1890s. That was how Joan Sutherland had got his nickname. And now here she was, Joan Sweeney, trying hard not to be too nice to the palomino as Tom String chipped away at the reef with a mattock.

It was a hard sound to listen to – the metal on the rock sent shivers down Maria's spine – and under the bedclothes in the pool of light even Kooka was stirring. She bit her lip, hoping he wouldn't wake.

Thankfully the mattock now began to hit softer rock, presumably the coal. It was a lot easier to listen to, more like the sound of an axe on soft wood, and Kooka settled down again among the sheets. He no longer looked so pale either; now there was a freckly blush in his cheeks, as if he, like Joan Sweeney's offsider, was being warmed by the action.

Gradually the ocean once again stole into the foreground, as Joan Sweeney left off chatting to Paul and made her way back over the sand and into the water. This time she did duck dive, threading her way through the subaquatic hum, breast-stroking beneath the waves, before emerging back into the hiss of pure oxygen. But there were no lists, not like on previous nights, no chicory, no rum, no rushlights or pickled onions, and Maria wondered if that was because Tom String was on the beach. There was no mention of barrels either, no two gross of buttons. Instead she just breathed deep and satisfied sounding breaths, sniffed the salt back into her nostrils and occasionally blew it out again with a honk like a swan.

By the time Joan Sweeney had finished her second swim, Maria's throat was dry. She didn't dare budge to go and get a drink, and was kicking herself that she hadn't brought something into the room with her – a glass of The Dancing Brolga perhaps, or a bottle of Laphroaig.

Now Joan Sweeney was repeating her walk back along the beach to Tom String. The tinkle of Paul's harness could be heard but no longer the mattock chipping the reef. Presumably Tom had a drayful.

'That's a good load,' she said, as another sound, of the coal thudding and rolling into the timber dray, could be heard.

'Any more and the drunk'll strike,' Tom String replied between hefting. 'Do they have a union for alcoholic horses, Mrs Sweeney?'

'I'm sure I don't know, Tom, but I doubt it. There's no union for swimming publicans after all.'

Tom String half laughed, half hefted now, causing himself to snort, as if he was the horse in question. 'Nor for overweight slushies like myself.'

'Oh I wouldn't know about that. But I don't like to hear you call yourself a slushy, Tom. Where would The Grand be without you? Where would I be?'

Tom String scoffed. 'Oh you'd be fine, missus. There's plenty of other fellas about who can pour a drink.'

'Oh yes? And plenty of others who can brew a beer as good as you? And punt the barrels back and forth between the hotel and your camp upstream? And smithy for the nags of the clientele? Polish the fish cutlery, the bone-tweezers, the crab scoops? Remove the brawlers? Boil the eggs for the bar? And all with a lady for a boss, a widow? No, no, Tom, in my experience a slushy is a down-and-out who you feel sorry for, some old swaggie who needs a few bob, some fella with the DTs who you haven't the heart to throw on the tip. Or a boy for that matter, who can run the glasses and plates for a loose bob. Now that's a fact, Tom String. I know your mum was native born and I'm from the city, but I'm speaking from experience and you should know better than to call yourself such a thing.'

For a moment the chips of coal ceased thudding into the cart. A gull squawked nearby. There was a tapping sound on fabric as if Tom String was searching in his pockets for a jocular reply.

But then there was a rich knocking sound of wood on wood: his pipe on the edge of the coal-cart. And he said, 'Phew, missus. There's no need to get so het up about it. I was only having a lend.'

'Yes, well nevertheless . . . it's an important trait . . . for a man to know what he is worth.'

'That it is, Mrs Sweeney. And for a horse.'

Now there was silence again – if you could call it that, with the ocean so close – and eventually the sound of a match being struck. Then the crackle and pucker of a pipe being sucked.

'It always buggers me,' Tom String said, 'the way those

gannets dive out there like that. You'd think their heads would explode as they hit the water.'

'You would, Tom String. I suppose God made the world though.'

'Do you think so, Mrs Sweeney? Nah. Tough birds. Hungry birds. It's amazin' what you'll do to get a feed.'

'I suppose they've worked out how. Do you not think there's a god, Tom?'

'Do you, missus?'

'Sometimes, on days like this. When it's fine enough to swim.'

'Well, as you know, I'm no swimmer.'

'Nor was your father?'

'No, Mrs Sweeney, I don't believe he was. Always said there was nothin' but your own nous. He believed the world gone wrong, you see. Since the devil got into it.'

'The devil?'

'Man. Mankind.'

'And what was it like before that?'

'He said it was like early autumn on the northeast side of King Island. Calm weather and plenty of seals.'

'But no one to sell the skins to, Tom.'

Tom String paused to suck at his pipe. 'I suppose you've got a point there, missus. No mistakin' your husband was a lawyer, eh?'

'Well, I didn't get my ability to reason from him.'

'No? Where did it come from then?'

'Same place as those gannets I suppose.'

Tom String chuckled again; it seemed he couldn't resist

a joke. 'Yairs, well, there are some at the hotel who call you a tough bird.'

Joan Sweeney laughed too now. 'Oh, Paul,' she exclaimed, talking to the horse, 'no wonder you get cranky with him.'

Maria was on the edge of her seat, feeling both the pleasure and the strain. She couldn't help but keep expecting the tranny to glitch or for Kooka's sleep to roll over into some other blank style of restfulness, but it didn't. This time it stayed constant and clear. Now Tom String and Joan Sweeney were getting up on the cart to ride back to The Grand.

'Ho, thee! Up there, Pauly!'

Tom String had no plaited whip but a wattle-switch whose leaves could be heard rustling in the air before he brought it down on the flank of the horse. As the cart moved up off the beach and onto the beach track, the timber wheels and joints knocked and jostled, and the iron parts rattled with the uneven ground. 'He'll be right when we get him past this shoulder, round the hook and up through the elbow there,' said Tom String in an anxious voice. 'Ho, thee, Paul, my friend. Up, up!'

'Right you are, Tom,' Joan Sweeney replied.

The cart jostled on, with Paul snorting, his shod feet clinking on what sounded like shelly rather than stony ground. The coal in the back could be heard too, shifting about lightly as first one wheel of the cart then the other rose and fell on the rooty camber. Occasionally, too, the ratcheting sound of a wattlebird would pierce all this with harshness.

Apart from Tom String's geeing of the horse, neither he nor Joan Sweeney spoke for some time now, presumably until the difficulties of the track had been negotiated. Either that or they were absorbed enough by their progress to sit silently on the dray in the sunshine, as Paul did the work. But when eventually the publican did speak, it was to point out a burrowing echidna that had stopped Paul in his tracks.

Tom String had put the sudden halt down to his horse's pure contrariness and had begun to curse. 'You can't prop here and leave us hangin' off the hillside! C'mon, horse, it's not just me and the coal you're haulin'. Think of your good friend, Mrs Sweeney, damn you!'

Then Joan Sweeney had called out, 'It's a hedgehog, Tom, in the middle of the track. That's what's stopped him.'

Sure enough the next thing was Tom String jumping down off the cart and shoo-shooing the echidna. He knew Paul wasn't budging and he grew increasingly frustrated, caught as he was between the stubborn self-preserving instincts of two animals. Eventually he asked Joan Sweeney to pass him down the mattock from the cart. 'Nothing that a bump on the scone won't fix,' he said.

In The Sewing Room Maria was alarmed, but quickly there was a dull thump, a crunch, and then a bosky slither-sound in sandy soil, as Tom String pushed the dead echidna to the side of the track. By the gristly noise of it he gutted the creature right on the spot and then picked it up, no doubt tentatively, and placed it with the coal in the back of the dray. He laid the mattock in its toolbox, hauled himself back into position with a grunt, and once again geed the horse. With the echidna out of his line the tinkle of Paul's harness resumed, as did the wooden music of the dray.

When they reached the top of their climb, the effort in

Paul's nostrils grew easy, and he was even congratulated by Tom String. 'There's a boy, Pauly, we're back on top of the world now, old son.'

'Yes, and thanks to you we've got a hedgehog to boil tonight,' Joan Sweeney chimed in. 'Good work, Pauly.'

'Now don't get too excited, missus,' said Tom String. 'One won't go far in the 'otel. Unless you're Jesus Christ.'

'Mmm, that's right. It's a delicacy, Tom. I'd nearly eat one all by myself. If we see another one heading back, let's get it.'

'Rightio, missus. And look out for some pigface would ya, to cut the fat.'

The level ground now reduced the sound of the dray, and the tread of the palomino's hooves was duller in the dirt. Tom String had mentioned the Boatbuilder's Track previously, and naturally Maria took it to be what these days we call Boatbuilder's Road. So now she pictured the dray heading across the long ridge to where the Boatbuilder's eventually descends steeply down onto the riverflat.

As they jigged along more easily, Joan Sweeney discussed hotel matters with her right-hand man while he pursed away again at his pipe.

'Mr Arvo suggested he might stay another week,' she said matter-of-factly. 'Said he approves of the fare and there's no point leaving the sea in fine weather.'

'Exotic lodgers eh, Mrs Sweeney?' replied Tom String, his voice suddenly a little surly. 'Well, a few extra coins I suppose. Mind you he's got the top room. But make sure he pays in pounds and shillin's. Not books like last time. Come to think of it, what do they use for money in the Baltic?'

'I asked him, Tom. It's markkas where he's from. But he's not out here for the gold. And he only left the books last time because I suggested it – for the hotel shelf. A bit of reading matter for weary travellers. Don't you worry, he'll have the right stuff.'

'Oh well, you know best. But don't get me wrong, missus. I don't mind Mr Arvo.'

'Turn it up, Tom String, that's not what I heard.'

'How do you mean, missus?'

'I heard you told him to stop singing the other night.'

'Aw, that was only because he was making the beer go flat.'

Joan Sweeney scoffed in amusement.

'No, but in all seriousness, missus, a few of the boys were concentratin' hard on Bertie Bolitho's round of poker. Didn't want any blood spilt. Not from the old Balt. Plus, his music's from a different country to mine. Must say, though, he was quite accommodatin' when I put it to 'im.'

'I bet he was. A man of your size.'

'Well, you know me, missus. I don't throw me weight around unless it's warranted.'

'That's true, Tom. But Mr Arvo doesn't know that.'

For a moment then the tranny glitched, Maria gave a start in the wicker chair, and Kooka adjusted himself in the bedclothes. Her thirst was raging as she watched him hunch up his shoulders and chap his lips together, before turning off his side and away from where he'd been facing the tranny, to lie flat on his back right in front of her. The tranny spluttered, as if mis-receiving short wave, once again she bit her lip, not able to bear the thought that she'd lose contact, and then, as a gust of night wind fluttered the curtains in the inland window beyond the pool of light, the transmission cleared. Kooka chapped his lips together one last time, and the sound of the rollicking cart, with its load of black Bass Strait coal and a gutted echidna, disappeared from the room.

Naming the Winds

IT WAS AROUND TEN O'CLOCK THAT NIGHT, AFTER MY Black Velvet session with The Lazy Tenor, when The Blonde Maria made an unexpected but brief visit downstairs. She burst frantically into the bar, started fossicking madly around in the spirits store for booze, before dashing straight back out again with a bottle of Yarra Valley Marsala in her fist. Of course by that stage I was too drunk to take any notice and she was too desperate to get back upstairs to Kooka to mention a word of what was happening up there to me.

Earlier on The Lazy Tenor hadn't hung around after we'd polished off the Black Velvets. He said it was all too much, he was having too much fun. He left me alone in the bar, with more end-of-the-day customers rolling in. It was hopeless; even then I was too far gone to run the Happy Hour, and dinnertime was fast approaching. Veronica was rostered to handle the food,

Darren would be in at some point, but they'd need a hand, and frankly I didn't feel up to it.

But I kept drinking – something was willing me on. I poured a few Dancing Brolgas for the punters in the bar, gingerly handwashed Aunty Rita's Laliques in the sink and realised I hadn't refreshed the loop in Duchamp. We still had an old bush verse in there from the day before. It had been Nan Burns's choice. She'd dug it out of a book in her fire tower. We couldn't get Kooka to read it – he was snoring his head off at the time – so we'd had an impromptu lucky dip in the bar to see who'd do the honours. Joan and Jen's youngest, Dougie, was the name we pulled out of the hat. He was up for it, keen to be involved, so it was his clear as crystal eight-year-old voice that went onto the loop. Given his vintage it was inevitable his performance had a whiff of hip-hop about it.

Though the rich lie soft, yet we sleep well
On our bed of the fragrant leaves;
And we're better than those who in mansions dwell
In this – that we fear no thieves.

Dougie was chuffed with his contribution. He'd hovered outside the toilet door all the previous evening, listening for himself on the loop and also for the comments at the pissoir. Before he went home that night, he told me his brother Dylan had renamed him DJ Dunny, and Joan, who with his broken arm and hangdog heart needed cheering up, apparently thought this was every bit as funny as Dougie did.

I decided, conveniently for me, that given how much

Dougie had enjoyed his debut on Duchamp it would be okay to leave his contribution there for another night. That, at least, was one responsibility I didn't have to deal with. And then just as I was pouring myself a glass of the Finnish wine I'd been serving up to Kooka at lunchtimes, and consoling myself that I'd been working too hard, too hard in fact to find time for a swim or to get drunk, and that today was the day to do both, Jen Sutherland walked into the bar and declared herself available as her husband's replacement.

'There's only one condition,' she said. 'I want Frankie with me behind the bar. A kindred spirit to talk to, you know.'

Perhaps if I'd been sober I would've argued the point – not about the canary, but about her as a barmaid – but in my velveteen state I immediately grew fond of the idea. For a start the Sutherlands would be getting a double income – a thought that appealed. I've always liked the idea of money going to a good home. And if I was perfectly honest with myself, I had to admit that I also liked the idea of having Jen around the place all the time. I watched her slip around behind the bar and pick up a dishrag, all the time pretending that she hadn't noticed I was drunk, and I thought she looked about as good as a woman could in jeans and a freshly ironed Miller shirt. And then Darren walked in and between them they started organising things for Happy Hour. They went straight into action. It was seamless. The Grand Hotel was fast becoming a well run pub as well as an emotionally dysfunctional off-the-wall folly. Satisfied, I dug out a longneck of Coopers Stout from the coolroom and made straight for The Horse Room to continue my session.

With the barman problem fixed for the time being, and none of us any the wiser about what was going on up in The Sewing Room, we could continue our usual routines and events. Jen performed more than adequately that first night, and there were a lot of wry jokes about Joan never getting his job back. She seemed to take it all in her stride, so much so that she left me sprawled over the pool table in The Horse Room at stumps, snoring my head off. Perhaps on Darren's advice she didn't bother to wake me but instead just tucked a cushion between my head and the hard edges of the corner pocket, placed a blanket over me and locked up on her own.

The next morning, of course, I felt terrible about this but had no time to dwell on it because it was not only banking day but also the day we'd set aside for our Naming the Winds garden party. As I opened my eyes on the dust motes of The Horse Room, I realised we hadn't even sorted through the entries.

My head felt as leaden and spiky as a late summer haybale, but I levered myself up off the pool table and went and had a shower upstairs. The hot jet of tangy Mangowak water soothed me as it hit my skin. Then, just as I started to feel normal enough to attempt an in-the-shower version of 'Flame Trees' by Cold Chisel, I heard someone else singing through the walls. Of course it was The Lazy Tenor and his morning aria.

I turned off the water and slowly dried myself to this exceptional accompaniment. He was right next door in his room. The song was so close I fancied I could hear The Blonde Maria gasping with pleasure as he sang, but I'm sure my hung-over mind was playing tricks on me. Still, the aria was worth a gasp or two, and when it finally came to an end I was almost tempted to drop my towel and applaud.

Skipping breakfast, but for a can of Coke, or 'Choke' as we call it around these parts, due to its ability to help start a hungover early-morning engine, I drove around the winding road of the coast to Minapre to do the banking. I had the windows wound up in Kooka's Brumby but still the cold southerly found its way into the cabin to keep me alert. The Wake-Up Wind, I ventured aloud as I drove, thinking of the contest scheduled for later that day. Or maybe Hair of the Dog.

By eleven o'clock I was back in Mangowak with hamburger stains on my shirt, fully fed and with the banking all done, ready for the specially convened Naming the Winds luncheon scheduled for 12.30 pm in the beer garden behind the hedge. Yes, we were opening uncharacteristically early and had thirty-two bookings for the lunch. I had no doubt others would turn up unannounced as well, given that it was a Friday.

In the bar Oscar, Nan and Ash Bowen were cooking up a storm, while out in the beer garden Jen was setting tablecloths and placing flowers on all the tables, and putting our best fish cutlery down as well. With the tea tree hedge in bloom and morning coastal cloud clearing from the sky overhead, every-thing looked set for a royal afternoon.

We'd had a Naming the Winds box and an information sheet in the bar for over a month, explaining the rules and purpose of the competition. Of course if you dangle something as contested and provocative as theories on the local weather in front of the locals as they drink every night, you're gonna get a genuine discussion. I'd heard a lot of anecdotes and ideas over the preceding couple of weeks, and a lot of potential names for all directions of the compass, as well as for the often more conspicuous gradations in between.

Travellers passing through had also put their two bob's worth in, and in fact it was our Dutch guest from Room Two who had unwittingly kickstarted the whole idea. One night he was telling a few of us in the bar how he grew up in a little farming town just out of Rotterdam called Skee. Apparently in Skee there were two distinctive local winds. One was an icy breeze that sprang out of a nearby lake, even in the middle of summer. He said that no matter the temperature of the air, as the wind rolled from the north towards the lake, by the time it got to the other side of it and reached Skee it was freezing, as if the lake itself was acting like some kind of Coolgardie Safe. He said the locals in Skee called this wind the *Ousburg Opspringen*, or Ousburg Shiver in English, after the Ousburg lake.

From the other side of Skee came another distinctive wind, he said. This south wind was like a distant northern cousin to the Sirocco. In the imagination of the residents of Skee this wind blew its way over farming country from way down south, accruing heat from the baking summer lands as it did so. He told us they called this one The Coughing Wind, due to the hoarse staccato sounds it made in the crisp drying wheat crops all about them. I remember thinking it curious that the people of Skee imagined the character of the two winds as being determined not by currents in the air or meteorological concentrations in the sky but rather always by the land itself. That part of Europe isn't called The Low Countries for nothing, I suppose.

There'd been an old Greek fella in the bar as our Rotterdam

lodger was describing the winds of Skee. He was an occasional drinker in the hotel and this night had been fishing unsuccessfully for salmon on the beach in the flood-tide. Now he was sitting on a low stool near the fire, still wearing his scaly and surf-sodden mittens and thigh-boots. He'd lived in an outer suburb of Geelong for the last thirty years, but that didn't stop him beginning to speak about the winds with all the authority of blind Homer himself.

He sneered derisively at the Dutch lodger and his town of Skee for only having two noteworthy winds. 'It's because you're atheists,' he said belligerently. 'You always were in Holland. Only gods can explain the winds.'

I got up quickly from where I'd been eating my dinner at the big table and ducked around behind the bar to fetch the fisherman a Metaxa on the house.

'Where I'm from,' he went on, as he accepted the drink from me without batting an eyelid, 'we have Aeolus, and that's that. He keeps all the winds, all their different moods, in a bag by his side. It'd be a bloody pathetic bag if he only had two winds in it, eh?'

Our guest from Rotterdam smiled ironically, having already made up his mind with characteristic northern European rationality that the Greek fisherman was both bonkers and very entertaining company as well.

'And did they ever tell you by your silly little lake that a wind can impregnate a horse?' the fisherman went on, between smoking his cigarette, sipping the Metaxa and spitting in the hearth. 'Of course they didn't. The fastest horses are always fathered by Boreas, the north wind.'

Despite the growing bemusement of the drinkers in the bar, the lesson continued unabated like this for a good half an hour. The fisherman from Geelong's initial look of scorn for the pathetic two winds of Skee transformed into something quite possessed as he told us that even to this day he always had to contend with Aeolus and his winds in his quest for the perfect fish.

'Tonight for instance,' he spat, 'what was that shitty *harpy-iai* that came in from the east after the sun? Then it got dark, the line went limp and sparks started flying into the air, all the way down the dunes. What was that if it wasn't a pest sent on behalf of Zeus? I packed up straightaway when I saw it. Next thing I came in here for the warmth of the fire. And find this wanker holding his own among midgets. Bah.'

He hunched his shoulders and moved closer to the fire, turning his broad back on the rest of us. Before long everyone was listening to Joe Conebush the electrician as he explained how an easterly was the most salt-laced of our local winds and that the salt in the air fizzed and crackled on the hot metal pans of the power poles on the roadside, causing the 'sparks of Zeus' that the Greek bloke was talking about. 'It's like throwing salt onto a hot frypan,' Joe explained. 'It crackles, fizzes. It's the same in the easterly.'

The fisherman appeared not to even notice this explanation as he stared at the fire and no doubt the dancing horses within. But then, after observing everyone spend the rest of the night debating the vagaries and temperaments of our local winds around the fire, and prompted by the discussion to wonder what the local band of the Wathaurong had called them, on his walk home from the pub Ash Bowen had his brainwave. Before long his idea of officially naming the local winds was being discussed and heartily approved of in the conducive atmosphere by the fire in the bar.

Nan had been wanting to stage a special luncheon in the pub for weeks, ostensibly to support some local winegrowers out near her farm who'd been having a rough trot trying to compete with the big corporate wineries moving into the area. This was the perfect excuse.

THE GRAND HOTEL CORDIALLY INVITES YOU

TO THE **NAMING OF THE WINDS** GARDEN PARTY

TO BE HELD ON THE HEDGE LAWN

ON 26 NOVEMBER AT 12.30 PM.

In our first venture into the highly controversial waters of junk mail we popped this invitation into everyone's post-office box the very next day and had thirty-two takers in no time; and in the weeks leading up to the actual event we had so many ideas for wind-names dropped into the box in the bar that we had to empty it out three times before the big day arrived.

Unfortunately for the evolution of our very late in the day local dialects, a veritable cyclone took over the garden party, laying waste to everything before it. But this wasn't as synchronous or apt as it sounds, for the cyclone was not one of a meteorological nature but rather of a kind far more disastrous for those concerned. Yes, it was Cyclone Joan, an unrequited hailstorm of the heart.

The Garden Party Brawl

IT WAS AROUND ONE O'CLOCK, THE TABLES WERE ALL resplendent in the spring sun, and Mary and Kooka's heirloom fish cutlery, including bone-tweezers and crab scoops, was shining like it hadn't for years. The dusty pink of late flowering ficifolias was arranged along with pelargoniums and banksia fronds in crystal vases on the white cotton tablecloths of every round table. As the guests arrived and the tables were filling up, a group of galahs perched on the powerline just on the other side of the hedge. Usually when they propped right there, they faced in the direction of the dunes, but this time they were looking our way, as if they had come to catch the show from front row seats. Mistakenly I took it for a good omen.

There were five tables of eight spread out across the lawn behind the hedge and in no time at all they were almost full. At the head table, where the proposed names of the winds would be read out from the box that had been in the bar for the previous six weeks, sat myself, Veronica, Ash Bowen and his wife, Vita, Darren Traherne and his sister, Barbara, with two chairs empty, waiting for The Blonde Maria and The Lazy Tenor to come downstairs and join us. When I'd got back from the banking in Minapre, I'd knocked on both of their doors to make sure they were coming to the party. I'd found The Lazy Tenor sitting at his window desk with the curtains drawn, reading the newspaper cartoons in his underwear. He said as far as he was concerned, the party sounded like a good excuse to get back on the Black Velvets.

Once again I noticed beyond the open cartoons on his desk that the lid of his laptop was firmly shut, and I don't think I was mistaken that a thick film of dust, salt, and eucalypt pollen had begun to gather in the debossed logo on the lid. The Lazy Tenor said that although he was keen, he couldn't speak for The Blonde Maria and that I'd find her in The Sewing Room with Kooka, whom she'd taken to giving a daily foot massage in his bed. 'The naughty old cunt,' The Lazy Tenor said as he stood up in his jocks without a hint of self-consciousness to show me to the door. 'I betcha he gets his jollies from that.' I laughed dubiously, said seeya, and walked up the hallway towards The Sewing Room.

I found The Blonde Maria washing Kooka's feet in olive and peppermint oils. The old fella was propped up on three pillows, with his corny old toes poking out from under the sheets at the bottom. He looked like he'd just won Tattslotto and proceeded to tell me that at his age a life in bed beat an upright life hands down.

'Well, that's of course if you've got the right attendants,' I said.

Kooka laughed and wholeheartedly agreed. 'She's an angel, Noel. She sits with me at night, reads to me from marvellous books, and then carries on like this in the mornings. God bless her.'

The Blonde Maria looked up at me smiling. I reminded her about the party that arvo and that The Lazy Tenor had said he'd come down for it. Maria told me she'd be there, with bells on. Purely out of courtesy I then invited Kooka to the party as well but unsurprisingly he said he'd pass. 'Oh, the afternoons up here in this room are not to be missed, Noel,' he said. 'The sun filters through the pines, hits the floorboards like honey. I'm gettin' quite used to tranquillity like that.' He nodded in Maria's direction. 'With Maria's help of course.'

I said goodbye and was about to make for the door. 'One thing before you go, Noel,' Kooka said. 'When it comes to wind, there's only ever been one nickname that I remember from round here: The Leveller. That's what Ron McCoy used to call the first day of the northerly – when the wind swings around offshore and takes the tops off the waves. Three or four tides later the sea's flat as glass – without fail. As you remember, old Ron never did talk much but when he did you tended to listen. The Leveller. Why don't ya throw that one into the mix?'

I thanked him for the tip and quietly left the room.

Nan Burns and Jen had agreed to pour the drinks and serve the menu, which read as follows:

SMOKED-TROUT FETTUCCINE
made with officially provenanced fish plucked
from a late Shoalhaven River canvas by Arthur Boyd.

STOLEN MINAPRE CRAYFISH
served with an Aeolian salad of riverflat spinach,
Timboon parmesan, estuary beans, fallen nectarines,
fresh mirth, and other local bluster.

PROVENÇAL APPLE CRUMBLE
made with Aix-en-Provence apples supplied by the
Cezanne estate from 'Still Life with Compotier'.

Just after one o'clock Joan Sutherland arrived unexpectedly with his plaster in a tea-towel sling, declaring that as the kids had gone to stay with their cousins in Bendigo he thought he could at least lend a hand with clearing tables and the like. Nan and Jen, of course, were happy to see him, and the big fella with the broken wing looked jovial, almost as if he was relieved to be back in the pub.

But I was worried. If, as they had promised, The Lazy Tenor and The Blonde Maria were coming to the party, how would Joan cope with what would be their first official public appearance as a couple?

Well, I didn't have to wait long to find out. As the local wines were poured in the sunshine and we at the head table were readying ourselves to begin the official proceedings, a resounding crash was heard from inside the bar. All heads turned, but before anyone could get up to see if everything was alright who should come waltzing out the verandah doors, arm in arm and dressed to the hilt for the gala occasion, but The Lazy Tenor and The Blonde Maria.

A collective gasp rose from the tables on the lawn. Mangowak hadn't seen such a glamorous pair for many a long year, if ever. He was dressed in an emerald-green velvet suit with black cloth buttons, a jet-black shirt, a vermilion silk tie and cornflower-blue cufflinks. His hair was oiled and swept back from his brow expertly, the oil darkening his bright-red hair to a rich ochre colour; his jaw was clean-shaven and on his feet were a pair of blue suede slip-on shoes that harmonised with the cufflinks. It was the genius of Blokey Hollow, the golden-voiced Lazy Tenor, in a display of style and colour we'd never seen from him before.

Next to him The Blonde Maria's hair was piled high in a spiralling Spanish braid. Her dress was a close-fitting turquoise crêpe with fine silver threads through it. From her ears hung two miniature brass bells that tinkled as she sashayed from the verandah doors down to the lawn, her hips swaying, her legs poured into lace stockings the identical colour of The Lazy Tenor's vermilion tie. She smiled radiantly, her eyes glittering like diamonds, obviously relishing the surprise of their entrance. What was most striking about her appearance, however, was not the peachy clarity of her complexion, nor the pale Irish creaminess of her long neck or the glinting shots of silver in her dress, but rather the unavoidable rich russet mark she proudly wore on the bunched-up flesh of her left bosom. Yes, with the blood-stippled texture that only freshness can supply, The Blonde Maria's outstanding fashion accoutrement for the Naming the Winds garden party was a lovebite, obviously administered by her beau only minutes before descending the Grand Hotel staircase. This hiccy seemed still to be pulsing with blood-red passion and not only attracted everyone's immediate attention but also no doubt explained the cacophonous crash from the kitchen just before the resplendent couple had emerged onto the lawn. At the sight of it I knew instinctively that we were in trouble and, abandoning my post at the official table, dashed back inside to investigate.

Behind the counter in the bar the Shoalhaven trout, once so painstakingly reproduced by one of our country's great artists, and then so lovingly prepared and cooked into a Sémillon, dill and cream sauce by Nan and Jen, was now scattered in fibrous lumpen dollops all over the checked lino floor. The large cast iron pot in which the fish had been simmering had been knocked off the stove and lay clattered into a corner. I could see by the look on everyone's faces in the kitchen that this had been no accident. A sudden and familiar flash of colour raced across my vision, and for a moment all I saw were the front-row galahs flying from the powerlines in a burst of pink and grey.

Our good omen gone, Jen was gesticulating at Joan, wanting to know what the hell he was up to. Nan, meanwhile, was staring at me with a sober expression, having immediately deduced the reasons for the tumult.

'Oh well,' I said, reverting to levity for no other reason than to avoid my own guilt in front of Jen, 'that's the first course over.'

I don't think anyone heard me. Joan was standing stiff as a board in the corner by the sink, with the haunted blinkered expression of a nightmare-ridden child, as Jen demanded an explanation. Whether or not she had already twigged, it was hard to say, but for the time being at least she was feigning innocence and giving her love-addled husband the compassionate good grace to explain himself.

But Joan was tight-lipped, his face aflame with pent-up emotion. And nothing that Jen could say would move him. It was brutal to watch; he had a mad stare in his eye, a look simultaneously cold and hot, distant and close. Jen eventually threw her hands up into the air in exasperation. She turned and looked at me for clues. And once again, in a critical moment of cowardice, I looked away from her gaze.

Then Nan burst into action. 'Well don't just stand there like a mad bastard, Joan. Get the hell out of here and let us clean up the mess you've made.'

When Nan Burns was riled, there were few who would brook an argument with her. Joan Sutherland was definitely not up to the task. Nursing his broken tap-arm with his other hand, he stepped through the remains of the dish on the floor, rounded the bar and stood glaring out the verandah doors at the crowd outside. We could hear the hubbub rising as the local wines were sipped on the lawn: Pinot Gris, Rosé, Grenache, Merlot Petit Verdot – everyone no doubt presuming that things had been taken in hand back inside.

But things had not been taken in hand, and what happened in that next fateful hour constituted my greatest failure in my brief tenure as a publican. What was it that Joan had said, on that starry night as he lay floating on his back in the river? That he should be allowed to fall in love, not only as an innocent youth but as a fully grown man. That belief and the magnetic sexuality of The Blonde Maria were causing this. Joan Sutherland was in exile, after all, and now was flailing in a zone of new temptations. For his whole life the lush blackwood-bordered dairy pastures on the Barroworn had shaped him, given him air and pride and purpose, but now he had been dislocated, his passions disorientated, and all the held-back anguish of his hereditary loss was unstitching his life at the seams.

What could I have done? How could I have diverted the disaster? I'm not quite sure, but what I am sure of is this: at the crucial moment – the 'psychological moment', as our old footy coach Barry Anguilla used to call it – I decided selfishly that the proceedings of the Naming the Winds garden party were too important to interrupt and chose to pretend that the air could be cleared as easily as Arthur Boyd's trout on the floor.

On the surface what happened next could be directly attributable to that Saturday forty-five years previously, when my bachelor-girl Aunt Rita, in the prime of her social glory, called a Silver Top taxi to her flat in South Yarra to take her into the Georges department store in Collins Street, Melbourne, to lay-by the set of René Lalique champagne glasses that had caught her eye during her lunch hour the day before. Little did she know as the Holden EH taxi lumbered over Princes Bridge and past St Paul's Cathedral that all those years later the Lalique glasses she was about to buy would cause a hardworking dairy farmer with a heart as big as the Southern Ocean to crumple into a blubbering leviathan mess and be given up for insane.

The Lazy Tenor and The Blonde Maria arrived at their

chairs at the head table to find a crisp jug of Black Velvet waiting for them. This was my doing. Caught up in the excitement of the occasion and happy that they had agreed to attend, I had painstakingly poured the jug twenty minutes before they had made their grand, and lovebitten, entrance. On either side of the jug of Black Velvet I had specially placed one of Aunt Rita's Lalique glasses, in the vain and ridiculous hope that with such flattering and high calibre encouragement we may have been able to persuade an inebriated Lazy Tenor to adorn the gala event behind the flowering tea tree hedge with a famous aria in his golden voice. In my inebriated state the previous evening I had lain prostrate over the Horse Room pool table dreaming of just such an event. With at least a handful of wind-names established and everyone well fed and well sluiced, I had pictured my fork tapping a glass, the crowd's happiness falling silent, and The Lazy Tenor rising to ensure the day would take pride of place in the brief but momentous history of the reawakened Grand Hotel.

As it happened, The Lazy Tenor did rise, to his full stature, after pouring himself and The Blonde Maria a glass each of the Black Velvet. But not to sing; instead to gloat. At the same time as Joan Sutherland had rounded the bar and was glaring through the verandah doors, The Lazy Tenor, inspired by the naked nymph resting between his fingers, stood to raise a longwinded and boorish toast to the 'magnificence of the female body and in particular to the current beneficiary of my vast physical prowess, The Blonde Maria'.

If it was the eternal motif of pure sexual envy that propelled Joan Sutherland's destiny forward, it was at least to lay a blow for sincerity and humility against the conceit of this unabashed nemesis. Forgetting even to open my papa's handcrafted verandah screen doors, he simply burst straight through them, just as The Lazy Tenor was raising the Lalique to the sky. He leapt down from the hardwood planks of the verandah, skittled two of the tables on landing, and lunged at the maker of the toast.

The Lazy Tenor, his slickened hair glistening under the galah-less sky, was so enraptured by the sound of his own voice that he was caught by surprise. Joan was able to enclose that throat of vainglory and golden song in a massive Otway grip. Then, with natural propulsion, these two huge men tumbled onto and then straight over the head table, bringing the fish cutlery, the jug of Black Velvet, Ash and Vita Bowen, Veronica, Darren and Barbara Traherne, and of course Aunty Rita's Laliques crashing to the ground.

No wonder the galahs on the powerline had got out of there. Birds are not this planet's auguries for no reason. If they had've stayed, however, they would've witnessed in broad daylight the first genuine all-in brawl in Mangowak since a travelling car-fridge salesman had accused Big Martin Elliot of watering the beer down in the Mangowak Hotel on Remembrance Day, 1979.

That was a long time ago, when fist fights in hotels were as common as brains and bacon. Which made it even more surprising to see the almost genetic relish with which that whole sartorially dressed garden party in The Grand Hotel took to the brawl. Was it race memory, or just the held-in frustrations of our era of bloodless bureaucracies and litigation?

Joan Sutherland's ample frame was sprawled on top of a

struggling and furious Lazy Tenor. In a cartoon you would've seen steam coming from both their ears. The Blonde Maria, of course, was aghast at what was happening, but before she could dive onto the back of Joan Sutherland and pummel him with her sharp Dookie fists The Lazy Tenor managed to upturn the big dairy farmer and with scant regard for his already broken arm thrust him into the bindi-infested kikuyu lawn. Joan, however, still had the singer by the throat, and The Lazy Tenor's face was now the colour of the canned tomato juice my father used to drink on that very lawn every breakfast time on summer weekends. Perhaps alarmed by this, and disappointed no doubt that his Dancing Brolga Ale had been spilt all down the front of his heirloom pinstripe Hersch's suit, Darren Traherne, as stout as a keg and well toned from abalone-diving, launched himself at the pair on the grass like a bowling ball at a set of pins.

The three of them splayed across the kikuyu, Joan and The Lazy Tenor momentarily separating before scrambling back towards each other on their hands and knees with Darren throwing wild punches in between them. One of these punches managed to catch Vita Bowen on the back of the head as she was picking herself up off the ground, having toppled over with the table. I'm quite sure, having grown up with three elder brothers, that Vita would've been familiar with the burning sensation of an old fashioned clip over the ear but her husband, Ash, who was of course well known in the town for his balanced outlook on all local issues and also for his calm advocation of yoga and non-violence, had never before witnessed his wife take a hit. It was too much for him, and his deep devotion to Vita, mother of his children and light of his life, surfaced in a most surprising hail of expletives and abuse before he ripped off his rimless glasses and threw himself grimacing into the fray.

Vita Bowen simply shrieked at the sight of it. You could make a strong case to say she was tougher than Ash, who at five foot nine inches and weighing in at sixty-five kilograms was of a delicate constitution. So, fearing her husband snapping sheer in half like a twig, Vita stepped sideways into the action, bending at the hips like an expert wrestler before tackling The Lazy Tenor around his emerald-suited waist.

Well, the sight of a woman getting involved was what the climate-change experts would have called the 'tipping point' of the brawl. All those who had been standing aghast at the other tables, shouting and screaming at Joan and The Lazy Tenor to STOP IT PLEASE STOP IT were now torn from the passive horror of spectating and galvanised in their direction. First Simon Karinis from Minapre, a well-known 'basher' in his days at Minapre High before becoming a respected ice-cream shop owner, stripped off his jacket to jump in. Then the party of Boat Creek lifesavers on Table Three did the same, their blond zinc-creamed heads, tanned legs and arms and bright Lycra surfwear adding a riot of bronze and iridescence to the spectacle. In no time whatsoever at least fifteen of the garden party guests were in the fight, blood was spattering the pelargoniums on one side and the flowering tea tree of the hedge on the other, spittle was flying, and curses were threading the air. The Blonde Maria was screaming in distress, as were at least a handful of other non-participants, while the remaining onlookers either barracked with a long-forgotten aptitude or furiously prodded their mobile phones to pass on the dramatic news to the rest of the town.

I stood untouched, as if in the eye of the storm, wondering how on earth things had come to this. All I'd ever wanted from this hotel was to express myself freely, to give everyone the chance to do likewise, and sure, to lance a few wounds in the process, but this was ridiculous! I watched on as if immune to the pain. We may all have been sage at times, calm like Ash Bowen, honest like Nan Burns, inspired like Veronica Khouri, and dignified like Jen, but who among us did not have a walled-in knot of personal frustrations, of forgotten animal instincts that just wanted to shout out HELLO!, to scream, and to strike out in anguish at whatever was nearest at hand? Well, the scene in front of me was proof of it, and in that brief moment of stillness I felt no shame or despair at the gnashing, clawing mob in my midst but rather a mild and quite airy humour, as if some rightful catharsis was all that had occurred.

Much sartorial finery was ripped and torn in that brawl on the Grand Hotel lawn, although miraculously no one was too badly hurt. There were cuts and scratches, of course, torn fingernails, gashes that later required a few stitches, and even clumps of hair lying about among the bindies; but expensive suits and dresses, flash jewellery and hi-tech watches and phones and the like were ruined beyond repair. As often happens with all-in brawls, the mob eventually evolved into one organism, one grappling lump of fifteen or so bodies wobbling around the yard like a giant jellyfish. Eventually the jellyfish began to divide itself again into duelling pairs and threesomes: Givva Way boxing on with Darren Traherne; Jamie Niall from Boat

Creek cramming Simon Karinis's head into the tea tree hedge as if he was stuffing a sleeping-bag back into its outer skin; Ash and Vita Bowen, teaming up now to fight the one-armed Joan Sutherland, who in the chaos of the donnybrook had lost his tea-towel sling and was waving his graffitied plaster-cast about like a lethal weapon. Meanwhile The Lazy Tenor was sprawled on the kikuyu, with a quartet of Boat Creek lifesavers pounding into him as if their lives depended on it. Our reluctant household name gnashed his teeth and struck back at them with both his vitriolic inlander's tongue and his slip-on blue suede shoes.

Eventually, and ironically I suppose, it was the weather that brought an end to the garden party brawl. As the fists and feet were flying, the day had been darkening in more ways than one. Clouds had been massing in the southwest. As Ash and Vita finally wrestled Big Joan to the ground and he began to unclench his rage and loosen instead into a crumpled, sobbing mess, the wind picked up out of the east, as if to remind us of the very reason for the gathering.

It began to blow hard, in snapping, chilling gusts. One by one the fighters registered the drop in temperature and also the sound of Joan's heartrending sobs where he lay under Ash and Vita on the lawn. The punches slowed, the headlocks loosened, Jamie Niall allowed Simon Karinis to rest unmolested in the hedge, Givva Way started looking around for some alcoholic refreshment, and Ash Bowen began whispering a soothing mantra into Joan's ear. The gnarly wind from the east, the only wind that ever managed to pry into the garden space between the hotel and its south facing hedge, began one by one to pick up the strewn paper entries for the Naming the Winds competition, which had been scattered when the head table fell, and send them fluttering, first into the air around us, then gradually lifting them higher and higher until the sky above us was momentarily blotted with the unread lexicon of our local winds, the ideas scattering like the ashes of a great personage on one of the very winds we had failed to call by name.

I feel certain that as we all looked skyward, to the soundtrack of the dairy farmer's lovebitten, land-torn grief, every one of us at the party had a strong sense of our great and eternal human idiocy. We stood among blood-splattered flowers and smashed antique glassware, watching as the unread names, turned up at the edges by the wind, sailed off like paper boats towards our river, towards Boat Creek, Turtle Head, and the hills beyond. The paper boats sailed away from us like a lost communal knowledge we weren't equipped to know. The afternoon had been overtaken by demons, and not for the first time we had feet of clay in our own locale.

As Joan continued to sob and Ash to whisper his Sanskrit mantra, others began to giggle and then to outright laugh at the scene as they finally took a look about them. Before long it was a strange type of music that laced the air in the wake of the wind-name flotilla, a music born half from primal grief and half from hopeless failure, a music of concussive sobs, consoling cadences, and surrendering mirth. The laughter was the humble outlook of little Mangowak caught in the signature human tune of loss and pain. And of course Ash's mantra, whispered close in poor Joan's ear but audible to all, was, as always, a yearning for the very gods that flew away from us in disgust upon the air.

It was at that moment, and only then, that I first had an

inkling of The Grand Hotel as a truly magical place, a hotel where profound and confronting telepathies were somehow possible, a hotel born from the very human music I was now listening to. But before I could indulge any further in such thoughts, I caught Jen Sutherland out the corner of my eye, watching from the verandah, with the silent tears of love's eternal tragedy running down her cheeks. I knew then that for her the penny had dropped long ago. All I'd been through out in the clefts and overhangs, and all my fumbling attempts at coping since, was old knowledge to Jen. And now, as her husband lost his mind on the lawn in front of us, she had had enough. She'd known all along what he was up to, that was clear to me now, but she also knew what it had meant to him to leave the cows behind and come to town. She had given him what my mother would've called 'a period of grace', and his participation in the Grand Hotel shenanigans was all part of that grace. It seemed that now, however, the grace was over.

A brief moment of indecision crossed her eyes as she turned to watch her husband losing his mind on the lawn. For a split second she contemplated if she could be bothered walking across to comfort him in this his most stricken and undignified moment. But then there was a flicker in her eyes as her love for him reasserted itself, and, wiping back the tears, she moved off the verandah and over to his side.

Poor Joan lay drooling, bleeding, and babbling like a madman. His talk had finally unhooked itself from what was going on around him and he muttered phrases broken and incomprehensible. Jen nursed his head in her lap and spoke to him in what was obviously their own intimate language. She half warbled and half sang in their own wedded dialect in an attempt to calm him down. For a while it seemed to work; his mutterings lessened, his breathing slowed. But then he suddenly sat bolt upright, nearly knocking her over and, pointing at the cloudy afternoon sky, began to name the constellations of the night sky, as if it was midnight. He raved, listing stars and planets, marvelling at the Pleiades one minute then trying to get a due south bearing from the Two Pointers the next. It was as if his eyes had glassed over and he was looking at another world, a world turned upside-down. And then he started calling out: 'There's the brolga! See the brolga dancing! Up there in the Milky Way!'

Before long everyone began to notice what was happening to the man we were all so fond of. The mood behind the hedge grew solemn. People stood back and watched while licking their wounds. Simon Karinis stepped forward with a glass of water for Joan only to trip over an upturned chair and send the water flying. Nan called out gruffly for everyone to just stand back and give Jen and Joan some space.

'Even better,' I said, flabbergasted by what was coming out of Joan's mouth, 'why don't you all just piss off home now and leave us to get Joan sorted out. I think it's safe to say the party's over.'

Half an hour later, with Jen and Joan still sitting among the aftermath of the brawl on the lawn, as Darren, Veronica, Nan and I sat on the pews back in the bar discussing what to do, Sergeant Greg Beer turned up with a young constable in tow. He said he'd been notified of a public disturbance at The Grand Hotel and had come to investigate. Apparently there'd been a fight, he said, and began to crane his neck towards the strewn chaos out behind the hedge, where occasionally we could hear Joan calling out at a falling star. The sergeant then proceeded to make a little speech, chiefly for the new constable's benefit no doubt, about how Mangowak had a proud tradition of public restraint and good behaviour, how it had become in the town's best interests to market itself as a 'charming and community-minded coastal village', and how any interruption to that proud tradition of public order would not only have consequences in the law but could also damage us all economically.

'I can see that there has been some kind of ruckus here today, Noel,' the sergeant continued. 'The garden out there looks like it's been hit by a bomb. And who's that I can hear out there? No one drunk and disorderly I hope.'

'No, no, Sergeant,' I said, mustering an energetic voice. 'It's all just been a bit of fun. And that's Jen and Joan Sutherland out there, getting a bit of time alone from the kids.'

'Well, do you mind if myself and the constable take a look, Noel?'

'No, not at all.'

Well, what else could I do? As we waited for the policemen to inspect the scene, Darren poured us all a Dancing Brolga, which given Joan's cries on the lawn seemed now to contain some weird sort of portent. We discussed what the police would find in low voices and even began to amuse ourselves at the thought of Greg Beer picking his way through the broken glass.

'Ah yes, the "charming community of Mangowak", now there's a toast,' whispered Nan, raising her pot.

We all clinked glasses and had a sip. I prayed that Jen

would be able to control Joan while the coppas were out there. The only way that Greg Beer could lay anything on us would be if Joan suddenly flew into a rage again.

Eventually Greg Beer and the constable re-appeared with notebooks in hand and stern expressions. Greg Beer's bloodless lips pursed, his grey eyes narrowed, and he asked me if I'd step outside into the backyard for a chat. I drained the remainder of my beer and joined him.

We stood beside his police four-wheel drive where he had parked it under the driveway pines. 'It's quite obvious, Noel, that a sizeable fracas has taken place in this establishment today. That was the information I received earlier by phone and has only been confirmed by what I have now seen with my own eyes. We both know that I have arrived too late to make any arrests, but this matter is nevertheless of great concern. To be frank I have long considered this hotel of yours a blot on the good character of this town. The establishment is your responsibility and I deplore the way you are exploiting the community's need for a licensed meeting place for your own personal benefit. It's too easy, Noel, isn't it? But who's to take responsibility for this breakdown in the family unit occurring right here in our midst? Who's to blame for the distress of good people such as the Sutherlands, who are sitting out there in your garden in a terrible state? You and I both know what fine upstanding country people they are. And now look at them. Do you feel any responsibility for that, Noel? No, I doubt it. But as far as I am concerned, as both a police officer and a citizen of this town, you are *directly* responsible. And I'm hereby putting you on notice. I'll be watching this place, Noel, and if you give me even the slightest reason to close it down, rest assured I will.'

And with that he nodded to the young constable and the two of them got into the car and drove away.

I

II

A Gentle and Magical Aftermath

WHEN I LOOK BACK AT MY YEARS GROWING UP HERE IN Mangowak, I don't think I could say I was an unusual child – I did all the fishing, swimming, watching telly and playing footy that other boys did – but I did perhaps have an unusually strong sense of vocation at quite an early age. One weekend when I was about twelve years old, I remember attempting to arrange the pictures I enjoyed finding in the gumleaves on my wanderings through the bush. I had collected a cereal box full of them, and emptying them out onto the floor of the sunroom I began annotating each leaf on cardboard labels my mother had lent me from her kitchen drawer. I described the leaf-pictures with titles and also recorded the date and the spot in which I found them. To my surprise, however, by the time the leaves had been in the cereal box for not much longer than a month or two, the beautiful acidic greens and sunburnt reds, and the scribbly discolourations and lines that created the figures within the leaf-face, had faded and changed decidedly. The life, and it seemed the art, had begun to leach out of them.

This got me thinking. Would the pictures on the leaves fade as quickly if they had never been removed from the spot where they had fallen in the bush? Or, exposed to the air and light where they fell, would the images fade, or at least change, even more quickly than they had in the cereal box? All of a sudden this seemed a most important question, and I decided to see if I could find out the answer, if for no other reason than to make sure I hadn't begun to destroy the very thing I had lovingly noticed in the first place.

On a Sunday morning I went back out into the bush and tied little bits of string to new picture-leaves I found, attaching the strings at the other end to a fencewire or a branch, or some other thing that would be suitable as a stay. And then, the following Saturday, I went back out to the leaves to check what had happened. To my surprise I found the leaves completely transformed, to the extent that not only had the images vanished but also the whole palette of each leaf had become unrecognisable in only a week's worth of weather and light. Green had become russet, russet had become pale gold, pale gold had become a kind of oaten white. Totally disenchanted, but reassured in my task of collecting the leaves for annotating and safekeeping, I went home thinking of new storage techniques, convinced that I was to the pictures in the leaves as a curator is to the objects in a museum. Without the impulse to preserve, the beauty of the natural world would simply waste away all around us.

It took me ages – well, it actually took me until I was

sixteen – to find the deeper lesson in the beauty of the leaves I had collected. My elder brothers had all moved out of home by this time and thus I was in line to take up residence in the much treasured barn, where of course I still reside to this day. Gathering all my stuff together from my bedroom in the house, in order to carry it out to the barn, I came upon the old cereal box of gumleaves from years ago. Opening it up, I gently tipped out the contents onto my bedroom chair and began to sort through them.

As I flicked through the leaves, I was invaded by a mounting sense of what I could only describe as shame. One by one I checked the script on the cardboard labels against the leaves they had once described. And time and again, without fail, I was left with an empty sense of nothing but my own imagination. Stuffed away in the forgotten box, the leaves had of course lost all their vibrancy, all their imagery, and were, without exception, drab, brittle and grey. And yet, on the labels, written in my immature hand of four years previous, were wondrous titles like 'Reef in the Sky', 'The Flight of the Eagle', and 'The Singing Leaf'.

In one instant I realised what it was that I treasured so much about seeing the pictures in the leaves. It was not just the images I had been enjoying but each image's special span of existence, each picture's fragile time in the light, and in each brief and imaginary moment it was the air itself that was the painter.

This was happenstance – 'accident and chance' my mum would call it – but to me it was a lot more. By the vanishing of the images in the cereal box, I understood instantly that the world itself was a kind of artist, that time was a kind of music, and that it was a misunderstanding of nature, in short a sin, to stuff that music away in some old forgotten box. That was like throwing a blanket over beauty, like silencing music, silencing time, which in the end was the same as silencing life. I swore to myself, right there on the very day that I moved into the barn, in the kind of moral swoon readily available to a dreamy and excitable sixteen-year-old, that I would endeavour never to silence the world's music again. Instead, I swore, I would treasure the pictures in the leaves as I noticed them, and leave them where they lay. I would treat them as my teachers of time, colour and the universe, and I would spend my life trying to make pictures that no museum curator's blanket could be thrown over.

Well, I'd be the last person to suggest that I've succeeded in such pure ambitions, but in The Grand Hotel at least, I've had a taste of what I understood so deeply back when I was sixteen.

In those days following the brawl, The Lazy Tenor and The Blonde Maria were often seen out walking when normally they would have been holed up in their rooms. The Lazy Tenor's neck had three deep gouges in it from where Joan's Otway claws had grappled him, and he'd been persuaded by Maria that swimming in the ocean would help them heal more quickly. It struck me again, as I occasionally sighted them walking the clifftops or lying beside the Siren's rockpool, what a handsome couple they were. The Christmas holiday tourist season was fast approaching but for the time being the two of them could lounge about the quiet spring shoreline like a pair of millionaires.

The Lazy Tenor held no grudges from the fight; in fact he'd laughed the whole thing off when he re-emerged from his room later that same night to continue recording the exploits from 'The Tradesman's Entrance' in The Horse Room. The wounds on his neck were his only concern, and whether or not they would affect his morning arias. As it happened, that was the main purpose of their walks to the beach.

When he'd begun to sing his aria on the morning after the brawl, the expansion of his vocal muscles had reopened the fresh wounds. According to Maria he sang on despite the pain and with blood trickling from his neck, across his collarbones and down his naked chest. She told me this with the telltale wide eyes of devotion you see on people who claim to have witnessed some kind of religious miracle at Lourdes or some other sacred site. I understood straightaway how appealing the trickling blood would have been to Maria, a true marriage of sacrifice and song, and I listened every morning for any difference in The Lazy Tenor's actual tone. But I couldn't detect any extra profundity or artistry, or indeed any divine atmosphere around the arias. Of course, as far as I was concerned, his voice could not possibly have improved from what I had already heard, but Maria begged to differ.

The very person I needed to keep an eye on things and to make sure we didn't make ourselves vulnerable to the prying gaze of Sergeant Greg Beer was the person whose madness had kickstarted our new problems: Joan Sutherland. It was Joan, after all, who had averted the disaster when Greg Beer came to inspect the smoke alarms. But now that he was sick at home, and Jen was required to nurse him, once again I felt as if I had to do the work of three men. I decided not to complicate matters by employing a replacement bartender but rather to redouble my own efforts and to keep a closer eye on the goings on of the hotel. All the clientele, bar the passing trade, knew the police were waiting to pounce, and it was heartening to observe everyone on their best behaviour in those next few days – still enjoying themselves, of course, but with no inclination to cause another stir.

I actually have fond memories of the lovely rhythm we settled into during those fateful days, beginning each morning with The Lazy Tenor's bloodletting aria. I'd have a quiet breakfast with whoever came down to the bar before taking something up to Kooka. Then I'd make my way over to the river and swim like a merman on the seaward end of the indoor creek while listening to the Plinth bells ringing down at the rivermouth. After lunch we'd ready ourselves to open and after 3 pm we were of course in full swing right until stumps.

Such was my weariness after mopping and tidying beyond closing that come one o'clock I often couldn't get to sleep in the barn. Those early December nights were quiet and warm, and it was pleasant just to sit up in my loft with a cigarette and a sketchbook, and unwind. There would be no more wild parties in The Blonde Maria's room, no more frankincense fumigations in the bar down below, not while Greg Beer was watching. The ironic thing, however, was that right under his nose, and right under mine for that matter, the most radical events to ever take place in The Grand Hotel were unfolding on those quiet, seemingly innocuous evenings in the wake of the brawl.

Every night, after making love with The Lazy Tenor,

The Blonde Maria had been treading her path through the willows and ducks in the hallway to read aloud to Kooka from the novels in the bookcase in her room. By early December, a week after the garden party brawl, they were re-reading *The World of Carrick's Cove*, after making their way through *The Country of the Pointed Firs* and nearly all the novels of Esther May Protheroe. But of course it wasn't the novels that were drawing The Blonde Maria to Kooka's bedside every night but rather the electronic telepathies being transmitted through his little black transistor.

Initially Maria would listen, as if in a pact of good faith, to the old man's dreams, and in the morning, by asking him apparently unimportant questions while massaging his feet, she would patch together a version of what was taking place in them, of who was who and what referred to what. At first, of course, she'd had no idea who the woman was screaming in the fire, just as she'd had no idea who the woman was swimming in the waves with her lists. But then one night Kooka burst into wakefulness in the middle of the fire-woman's screams. Or at least Maria thought he'd awoken. He sat up straight in the bed, his eyes even opened and looked wildly all about the room, but he was still locked inside the dream. And then, in tandem with the tranny on the bedside table, Kooka spoke – in fact he yelled – calling MOTHER MOTHER I'M HERE OUT HERE! THROUGH THE DOORWAY! IT'S JOHNNY MOTHER! I CAUGHT THE TRAIN! And before Maria could lean over to quieten the poor old man, he slumped back into the bed again, closed his eyes and lay there quietly as the horses' hooves came clattering down the street and the firemen appeared.

The Blonde Maria sat dead still. She wondered if anyone else in the hotel had heard Kooka's cry. She waited. As usual The Barrels were still playing downstairs; she could hear the dull thud of Oscar's bass through the floorboards. But no unusual movements. And no one coming up the stairs.

The tranny glitched again and went silent. And then on came Mary and John, and an everyday conversation about Mary's brother Vin, who was a trainee-priest in the seminary at Manly and wanted to come home for Christmas.

At that moment, however, Maria cared about nothing but the fire. It had been Kooka's mother who was screaming all along. And the 'Johnny' was him. Of course she knew nothing of Kooka's history – she had no idea his mother was a Tivoli dancer who became a prostitute in St Kilda and had sent him to her Conebush cousins in Mangowak to give him a future. But now at least she knew something about the fire.

The following evening, when she entered The Sewing Room with *The World of Carrick's Cove* in her hand, she managed to broach the subject by referring to the book. 'You know, Kooka,' she said gently, 'I feel sorry for this poor boy in Carrick's Cove. He's got such a hopeless father. Every time he's starting to get somewhere with his boat, the old man ruins it for him. It would be hard to have a parent like that.'

'I reckon so,' Kooka said.

'What about your parents, Kooka?' she went on. 'How did you get along with them? Were they a help or a hindrance?'

Kooka pursed his lips and looked towards the seaward wall. 'Well,' he said, after a pause, 'I never knew my father, but my mother was no hindrance at all.'

'Well, I'm happy to hear it.'

'In fact,' Kooka went on, 'some might say that it was the other way around.'

'How do you mean?'

'Yairs, well, she was an entertainer, my mum. A little like you, Maria. But they were hard days, and having a bub around as a single mum didn't really suit her talents.'

'What kind of entertainer was she, Kooka? A singer?'

'No, love, she was a dancer. At the Tivoli up in Melbourne. And she sent me to her cousins down here, the Conebushes, for a better chance in life.'

'Can I ask you a personal question, Kooka?' Maria said.

'Go ahead.'

'Did she die in a fire?'

Kooka's eyes narrowed and he sat up a little in bed. 'Well, how on earth would you know that, young lady? Has Noely been gasbagging to you?'

The Blonde Maria winced. 'No,' she said. 'But some nights when I'm sitting by your bed, well, you have dreams. It's like you talk in your sleep or something.'

'Is that so?'

'Yeah, and . . . there's often something about a fire.'

Kooka smiled at The Blonde Maria. 'Yes, well, Mum died in a fire alright. When I was just a kid. But I got my dancing shoes from her. And I got my lovely Mary by dint of dancing. At the 1949 Minapre Debutantes' Ball.'

The Blonde Maria's face broadened into a grin. 'I never knew you were a dancer, Kooka.'

'Oh, too right I was. Mary and I. I got the talent from my

mum. But as for Mary's talent, well, it was a gift from God I suppose.'

He licked his lips in satisfaction at the thought. 'You know, Maria, it's a long time since anyone's been close enough to listen in on my dreams. Not since Mary died. I like the thought of it.' Then he pointed at the book. 'But let's get back to that boy and his boat now. I'm keen to see how he gets on.'

For fear of disturbing the old man's sleep, she had wept silent tears then as night after night he revisited the St Kilda brothel fire that had killed his mother, thereby proving her love and foresight in sending him to Mangowak to live with her cousins the Conebushes. She had also wept silently, though this time for joy, when by constant dreaming reassurance his beloved Mary had proven to Kooka that yes it was her who had stopped the apricot tree from bearing fruit that first year after she died. By convincing him of this from beyond the grave, she had healed him of the great anguish he'd felt over the vanishing act of her death, and, as a consequence, of the fanatical interest in history that had taken over his life when she died. Or so at first it appeared.

Maria had listened in wonder as both Kooka's burning mother and Mary slowly, ever so slowly, disappeared from his nightly broadcasts altogether.

For a time what remained seemed only the random associative assemblages of an old man's reconciled mind. There were scenes with present day figures such as Darren Traherne or Nan Burns going out on ferreting trips with Ron McCoy and old Fred Ayling, or other people long dead. There was one long broadcast, which kept Maria up till dawn, where a dead body had been found adorned with forest flowers on the end of the Minapre Pier. The police were called to the scene only to find not a human being but a dead sea elephant ringed with the flowers.

For Maria these evenings were too weird and magical to communicate, until it became evident that the other mysterious recurring figure she had not been able to explain, the swimming woman with the lists, turned out to be Joan Sweeney, the publican of the original Grand Hotel.

It was very late one night, around 2 am, three weeks after Greg Beer's threat. I was drawing up in my loft, with a glass of the Finland wine, when I heard the hotel door open and close and footsteps coming across the yard. Naturally I was curious about who it was but the drawing I was working on – of poor Joan Sutherland curled up in foetal position within a giant Lalique glass – was so absorbing that I didn't bother to open the timber shutter of the old open-air window in the loft to look out.

I continued the picture with one ear cocked, noticing that the footsteps did not continue along the crunch of the driveway and out onto the road as I expected but instead had crossed straight over the yard, padding softly, before coming to a standstill next to my barn.

Now I looked up from the picture of Joan in the Lalique and waited. Silence. Until the anxious call of a plover, way out on the riverflat.

Then I heard my name called tentatively in the night. 'Noel. Are you up there, Noel?'

I put the drawing aside, came down the ironbark ladder,

and a few minutes later was sitting quietly downstairs in the barn, sharing my wine with Maria.

The sweet taste of the Baltic liquor on her lips must have fortified her against the unlikely nature of what she was about to tell me. After the usual enquiries about the chaos of bush refuse and ocean flotsam and jetsam scattered everywhere around my barn, she began to relate the amazing tale she'd gingerly crossed the night yard to tell.

As I listened without a word to Maria describing what had been happening with Kooka and the tranny beside his bed, I could see that she felt she was gambling on her relationship with me by recounting it. Would I believe her? Would I suspect she was having a lend of me? Would I write her off as finally and categorically mad, like Joan Sutherland seeing constellations in the daylight?

She needn't have worried. As she told me in great detail about Kooka's mother and the fire, about Mary and the apricots, and how these scenes would repeat themselves over and over through the little tranny until gradually they faded away to be replaced by more typical, if fanciful things, it was clear that not even in her most unhinged state could Maria have possibly concocted the scenario she was expecting me to believe. The final proof for me, however, was when she made a particular point of describing what Mary's voice was like as she spoke with Kooka in the broadcasts. The voice Maria described was inimitably Mary, with the exact characteristics I remember so fondly from my childhood. Mary Dwyer was well brought up, in a country-town sort of way, with her father being Dr Bernard Feast's liberal-minded medical predecessor in Minapre; and so, as Maria described, Mary spoke not with a plum as such but with well-educated vowels tempered and textured by her more practical country life. As Maria said, you would not have described Mary's accent as in any way 'tough' but there was a matter-of-factness about the way she spoke that precluded her being described as merely upper crust. But more importantly, Maria described to a tee the occasional speech impediment Mary had, a little difficulty with pronouncing the letter 'r' when it occurred in the middle of a word. I remember clearly as a child that lovely Mary often said 'Chwistmas' for 'Christmas', and my brothers and I used to make the usual jokes about such a thing among ourselves. As Maria told me, the word 'apricot' often, but not always, brought out this impediment in Mary's speech, so that when Maria sat in The Sewing Room listening night after night to their love affair from beyond the grave she found the voice of Kooka's wife unmistakable and distinctive. She said she couldn't count the amount of times she'd heard Mary say 'apwicot' for 'apricot', but almost as if it was a hangover from when she was a little girl, because she didn't always pronounce the word that way.

Finally then, once she could see that I was at least halfway open to what she had to say, and that I wasn't writing her off as a lunatic, Maria told me about the other dream that Kooka had been having, the dream of the swimming woman and the lists, the dream that after many nights was the only one that kept recurring, until finally the swimming woman had emerged from the ocean to reveal herself as Joan Sweeney and make the trip back towards the hotel with the half Aboriginal fella called Tom String and the dray of coal.

For the life of me now I could hardly believe what I was being told. It was one thing for Kooka to dream about people from his past but quite another entirely for him to be conjuring up the long-ago history of the town. But, as Maria rambled on, excitedly describing Tom String and his dray, and how he'd gathered the coal from the ocean reefs and how he killed and gutted the echidna, and also as she recounted the contents of the lists Joan Sweeney would recite as she swam in the waves, the most intense feeling of déjà vu rose up within me. I felt as if I was about to burst into tears.

The surge of emotion was both overwhelming and mysterious. I had to excuse myself and go outside into the yard for a piss. The stars were out, and as I looked up at the three studs in Orion's Belt the urge to cry passed, only to be replaced by an acute sensation inside my head, which I can only describe as my mind butting up against something, like a goat butts a fence when there's blackberries on the other side. I shivered, a little freaked out, and then was distracted by the sound of Maria slopping more of the Finland wine into our glasses back in the barn. I zipped up, deciding I needed another drink to calm me down, and went back inside.

We talked for another couple of hours, and before she left Maria and I excitedly agreed that I should join her in The Sewing Room after stumps the following evening, both to satisfy my own curiosity and to see whether or not she wasn't just imagining it all. I slept like a top once she'd gone, and dreamt not of Joan Sweeney, nor of Tom String and the drayload of coal, but of a long-legged angel descending into my unfinished drawing. It was Jen Sutherland, all feathery and elongated, flying over the reeds and nobby clubrushes of the riverflat, with closed eyelids pushed back by the breeze and with her husband's curled-up body sleeping blissfully in the grip of her talons. Together they flew with a loping wingbeat westward towards the Otway hills. I knew where they were headed, off over Snook Bay and the forest to the quiet lap-lap of the Barroworn River on the Sutherland dairy farm property. I watched them go in the dream and wished them well, happily assured that my good friend Joan was safe now in the loving claws of his bird.

Gravity Feed

THE NEXT DAY WAS A DAY LIKE ANY OTHER IN THE HOTEL – we had a new delivery of beer from Rennie Vigata, a new guest arrive, a new loop in Duchamp (perhaps chastened by Veronica's frustrations, I chose for this one a tone-poem recording Kurt Schwitters had made in England before he died a Dada legend at the ripe old age of seventy-six), and as usual we opened right on the dot of three. But for me, of course, it was a day with an extra dimension, as I wandered from task to task with a swarm of fluttering butterflies in my stomach at the thought of what I might be privy to later that evening.

I saw hide nor hair of The Blonde Maria all day. When I took Kooka up his breakfast in the morning, he said she'd obviously needed a good sleep-in because she hadn't appeared to give him his morning foot massage. I half fibbed to Kooka, saying yes, The Blonde Maria and I had been up late in my barn drinking the Finland wine. At the mention of this wine his eyes brightened and he asked me if he could have a 'drop of that beautiful Baltic nectar' with his sausages and eggs for breakfast. Laughing, I went downstairs to fetch him a bottle, and by the time I collected his dirty dishes at one o'clock the old bugger had drunk almost all of it. I told him he had an iron gut but he just laughed and said he felt like 'waxing lyrical'. I said, 'How do you mean, Kooka?' and he started going on about how he'd never been happier since he'd given up the history-bug and taken to the Sewing Room bed.

'That wouldn't by any chance have anything to do with the bottle of wine you've had for breakfast?' I joked.

Kooka arranged his lips into a perfect O shape, his bright eyes shone and he released a hoarse and play-acting breath. 'No, Noel,' he said emphatically. 'You know yourself the grog's just oiling the machine. Sometimes we just need an extra drop or two for the old contraption to run smoothly.'

I smiled and leant over to take the bottle off Kooka's bedside table, feigning the stern cast of a Lutheran missionary as I did so. Beside the bottle was his black transistor radio and I couldn't help but stare at it. In the dappled morning light of The Sewing Room I couldn't imagine how that ordinary little box with its station dial and its two AAA batteries tucked away inside, seemingly so inanimate and ordinary, could perform the task that The Blonde Maria had assured me it did. I looked at it as if for some sign that it was special, that it wasn't just a run-of-the-mill tranny, but found none. Gathering up Kooka's plate and cup, I told him I was rapt he was so happy in The

Sewing Room and that Mum would be too, and if he liked he was welcome to stay until he met his maker.

'You're a good boy, Noel,' he replied, 'and you run a good pub. But there's no need to get maudlin about things.'

He winked at me and with a knowing smile turned on his side to face the light filtering through the pines outside the inland window. He reached over and clicked on the tranny, pulled up his blankets, and began to hum along with the French hurdy-gurdy tune that started coming out of the magic box.

I turned for the door, full of questions, and left him to it.

Happy Hour that night was a risky affair, as it was Craig Wilson from Breheny Creek's turn to show his wares on the big screen. Craig was rhythm guitarist in The Barrels and had been quietly pestering us all to give him a spot for weeks. He reckoned he and his girlfriend, Angela, had put a little pearler together, but when we actually got to see it that night, well, with Sergeant Greg Beer watching the place like a fish-hawk, the content of the film made us all a little nervous.

Craig Wilson runs a cafe in Minapre but when he first showed up in Mangowak a few years ago it was to work for one of our local estate agents, Colin Batty, up at Batty Real Estate. Craig soon learnt he was a bit sensitive for the often brutal cut and thrust of selling people's homes, though not before it had cost him his marriage and, temporarily at least, his peace of mind. These days he lives a much happier life with his new girl-friend, Angela, in their cedar house on the front row at Breheny Creek. As well as running his popular cafe and playing in the band, he surfs a bit, mucks around online and takes off for long stints in the Top End every winter. He told me with a grin that his humble little Happy Hour creation was called 'Gravity Feed' and that he'd gone to a lot of trouble and expense with a new Red One camera and digital-editing software to get it right.

As it flickered onto the screen, 'Gravity Feed' immediately drew the attention of the Happy Hour crowd, most of whom, like me, had been primed for the occasion by Craig and Angela for weeks. The film began innocently enough, with a nice series of shots of home watertanks on the first sloping ridge of houses at Breheny Creek. Craig and Ange live at the bottom of this ridge, right near the main road and the dunes, and slowly, as one by one the camera switched from watertank to watertank in the back and front yards of the weekenders' houses on the ridge, an old fashioned alarm clock pasted into the top right-hand corner of the screen showed the minutes and hours of a normal day on the coast ticking by. Time passed and the camera went from old watertank to new watertank, from hooped iron tanks wedged into silver scrub on the upslopes of old holiday blocks to modern plastic tanks positioned snugly under elevated Murcuttish weekenders. Eventually the daylight began slowly to leach out of the picture until finally, as the hands of the alarm clock showed nine o'clock, the alarm began to ring, the sun disappeared beyond the western hills, and nightfall with its canopy of stars began.

This long sequence of ordinary watertanks captured in the passing light was shot in the style of the opening credits to a spy thriller, complete with a foreboding soundtrack and typewritten dossier-style text that appeared letter by letter on the screen along with each and every different tank. As the text appeared, the soundtrack was overlaid with the clicking sound of the typewriter, which gave us the address of the property the watertank belonged to, the occupation of its owners, and the approximate amount of days and nights those owners had spent in their beach-house the previous year. For instance, the rusty twin tanks we saw as the clock showed twelve noon were apparently from 'SALT WINDS, WALLABY STREET, BREHENY CREEK . . . DEMOGRAPHER . . . FLORIST . . . 22/365 . . .', whereas the brand new charcoal-black watertanks shown at 4 pm were from 'AMALFI, CORREA AVENUE, BREHENY CREEK . . . QUEEN'S COUNSEL . . . GALLERY OWNER . . . 12/365'.

As night fell and the faux alarm clock began to ring with a *Looney Tunes* style clangety-clang, the increasingly enigmatic sequence of watertanks was exchanged for wobbly *verité* style footage of Craig and Ange hauling large rings of industrial rubber hose out of their fibro garage. With collar-microphones on they chatted to each other in good spirits – Craig had obviously had to hand over the cameraman and lighting duties to others for these shots, as the action continually went in and out of focus, as well as in and out of the single high-powered lamp they were using to light the scenes.

The technical difficulties didn't matter so much at this stage, however – at least not to the audience in the Grand Hotel bar, as everyone stood sipping their Dancing Brolgas and craning their necks to find out what the hell Craig and Ange were up to in 'Gravity Feed'.

Well, the title must surely have given it away to some, but those who didn't twig didn't have to wait long. The next stage of the film was the juicy bit. It showed Angela, po-faced with a torch, strategically placing the end of the large industrial hose into their own two concrete watertanks. Next we saw Craig and Ange trudging under cover of the night, unwinding the big hose as they went back up the ridge along sheoak and wattle lined shortcuts, before attaching the other end of the hose to one of the weekenders' watertanks they'd filmed during the day. One by one, in scenes which by their lack of continuity were obviously shot on a succession of midweek evenings, Craig and Ange part-drained each and every one of the weekenders' watertanks, running the stolen rainwater down the slope of the first Breheny Creek ridge and straight into their own supply nestled in beside the boobiallas back next to their house.

There was a cheery chorus of hoots and boos as everyone in the bar finally cottoned on to what they were watching. Craig and Angela were stealing water. It all felt very illicit, almost like watching a snuff movie. Because neither the hose nor the tanks were transparent, no one could be absolutely sure whether Craig and Ange had actually drained the water or not, but one thing was for sure: they demonstrated how easy it would've been to do exactly that if anyone was ever inclined to in a drought.

The final shots of the film would have been in bad taste were it not for the soundtrack switching ridiculously to the theme from the old British comedy *The Benny Hill Show* as Craig and Ange enjoyed long showers and champagne and crayfish spas together in their home with its big waterviews over Snook Bay.

I for one was relieved when the Happy Hour drew to a close and the twelve minutes of 'Gravity Feed' was shown for the third and final time. Reading my mind, Darren leant over as he continued pouring Dancing Brolgas for the happy crowd. 'If the good Sergeant Beer gets wind of that one, Noel, he's not gonna like it.'

I nodded, frowning, although given it wasn't me or any of the hotel staff who'd made the film I couldn't see how we could get in trouble for it. Even so, it was true enough that we knew without a doubt now that Greg Beer wanted to shut us down; we'd forever kick ourselves if we were stupid enough to hand him an easy excuse.

The rest of the evening sailed by with music from The Barrels and a queue of zipping-up patrons emerging from their encounter with Duchamp with quizzical looks on their faces. The Lazy Tenor held court with the Grundig in The Horse Room, and Donny 'Shark Bait' Johnston from Minapre won the pool comp. This caused a great stir, as Nan had been the champion for the last six weeks in a row after Donny had made a few cracks about women not being able to play pool. To fiery Nan, of course, this was like laying down some kind of gauntlet, and over the next few weeks she concentrated hard, hell-bent on rubbing Donny's nose in it. Well, she'd succeeded alright, and Donny had copped a lot of stick as a result. He'd taken it all pretty good-humouredly. A lot of his macho bluster was just that: bluster – or, to be more precise, like a lot of fishermen in their prime Donny loved nothing better than laying out the bait and then winding a few people up with it. He'd certainly hooked Nan this time, but after a few weeks of champion status she decided to relax and let Donny reassume the crown. Or that was how she described her loss anyway.

But I was distracted the whole night, and even the roar

from The Horse Room when Donny Johnston'd potted the black didn't really make an impression. All I could think about was going upstairs later on to sit by Kooka's bed with The Blonde Maria. So at 11 pm, when the crowd in the hotel began to dwindle, I decided to shut up shop, knowing that in The Sewing Room Maria would already be sitting in the wicker chair reading to the old-timer in the pool of light.

'Time, please!' was my tried-and-true cry as I went from room to room and out onto the verandah, gathering up glasses and moving people on. Luckily for me they were a tame bunch that night and even the mob in The Horse Room celebrating the pool-comp final made no real objections. Of course The Lazy Tenor glared at me as he leant over to switch off the Grundig, but I was used to that, and less than half an hour after first calling 'Time' the pub was empty but for Darren, Veronica and myself wiping down the benches and bar, loading and unloading the dishwasher, counting the takings and making notes of which stock needed topping up and which liquor suppliers needed calling. We were experts at all that by now and did it with a glass of port each and a platter of Bennett's wallaby salami – a combination that I had at first been dubious about (I would have preferred cashews) until Darren insisted and made it our ritual every night as we cleaned up.

Nan had hung around and was full of beans, wanting to sit down at the pews, kick on with the port and salami and chat about the fact that she had let Donny win the pool comp. She thought it was hilarious how excited he'd got – she was nothing if not a fiercely proud loser – but of course I had other fish to fry and so kept yawning big mock-yawns and saying how tired I was until she got the message and followed Darren and Veronica out into the warm early summer night.

By the time I got to the top of the stairs twenty minutes later, after ducking out to my barn to slip the night's cash takings into the shoebox, the watery light of the old fashioned hallway globes and the willows of the wallpaper made for an almost Oriental river scene, if it weren't for the very local looking black ducks and platypi still swimming about in the carpet.

I stood for a few moments with my hand still on the banister-knob, wondering what on earth was going to ensue when I entered The Sewing Room. Finally, I shrugged my shoulders and made my way along the hall, before gently turning the metal handle of the Sewing Room door and slipping inside.

After the watery light in the hallway the cavernous Sewing Room was gloomy and dim, full of dark recesses, with the smell of twill and drill, corduroy, the unpacked archive, and hand-sawn, unsealed wood. That was of course but for the pool of light where Maria sat on the wicker chair beside old Kooka in the bed.

She was reading from George Santayana, a writer whom my mother used to mention from time to time because he was the fella who had first come up with the phrase 'Those who cannot remember the past are condemned to repeat it'. As kids that strange name 'George Santayana' became syn-onymous with some kind of irritating know-all. The only time Mum would trot out the famous line was when we had done something repeatedly wrong and she was cross at us about it. 'Santayaaaana' – the second-last vowel stretched with twanging teenage sarcasm – became the family nickname for someone who'd made the same mistake twice. I'd never read the actual writing of this man whose name had become a family joke and so found myself unexpectedly interested and amused as I pulled up a bentwood chair as Maria read from Mum's weighty hardback version of *The Last Puritan*.

Neither Kooka nor The Blonde Maria even seemed to notice my interloping on their nightly ritual. As I sat down, Maria may have ever so briefly paused in her reading to acknowledge that I'd come, and Kooka may have opened his eyes just for a moment where he was lying back on his pillows listening, but they said nothing, obviously too absorbed in the story and too deeply immersed in its atmosphere and that of The Sewing Room to speak.

Maria just continued reading, from the book of my mum's old mate George *Santayaaaana*.

Before long the novel's hero had travelled from Boston to Europe to further his education, but I couldn't get my eyes off the transistor beside Kooka's bed. As the hero met with his future love outside a church in a small town called Iffley in England, Kooka seemed to nestle more comfortably down into the bedclothes. Then, as the suitor was told by the vicar that he might have had what it took for some type of spiritual calling, Kooka's hand went up from where it was cradling at his chest and he gestured for Maria to stop.

Maria completed the sentence, closed the book, and all was silent. Then she leant across from the wicker chair and switched on the transistor. She adjusted the volume and settled back in her seat.

Kooka turned on his side to face the transistor by the bed.

Now I watched his brow knit ever so slightly, as a man on the radio talked about refurbishing an old 1920s house in Darwin. The house was one of only a few in the town to have survived the famous Cyclone Tracy of 1974. The man had discovered it abandoned and overgrown while visiting Darwin from Canberra on holiday. He fell in love with the place and decided to see if he could buy it. That had been ten years ago and he'd been lovingly restoring it ever since.

As the enthusiastic man spoke on the radio, Maria and I dared not look at each other for fear of disturbing the process. So far so good. Kooka was looking decidedly relaxed; he already seemed to be sleeping among the blankets. My presence in the room had not bothered him one bit. But would it bother the little black transistor? That was the question.

As the man waxed lyrical about how the ingenious old Darwin houses were the forerunners of new environmental design, the tranny suddenly glitched and his voice was cut off. For a moment or two we were subjected to just pure static before, just as suddenly, the static ceased and a new set of sounds emerged.

Immediately, through the shifting sounds of the load of coal, wood knocking on wood, the buckle of the wheels, and the tinkling of a horse's harness, I recognised what Maria had already described to me. It was Joan Sweeney and Tom String, taking the ocean coal back to The Grand Hotel on the dray.

Meeting Mr Arvo

I LEANT FORWARD IN MY CHAIR. WITHIN ONLY A FEW seconds of our listening to Tom String and Joan Sweeney jigging along in the dray, they came to a resounding halt. Tom String started cursing. They were at the top of the Boatbuilder's Track. To this day Boatbuilder's Road, as we call it, remains dangerously steep, so much so that my sister-in-law recently used it as a training ground for her trekking holiday in Nepal. It seemed, however, that the palomino of history had other ideas. He was digging his feet in.

'Oh blow you, you two-faced mule,' Tom String was calling. 'You've done it before. What's the rub?'

'It's obviously the full dray behind him,' said a reasoning Joan Sweeney. 'He's scared it'll come down on top of him.'

'Pah. I've had him bring a load of ironbark down this hill. I tell you he's got a bloody headache – from those dregs you let him in on.'

'Well, maybe you're right,' laughed Joan Sweeney. 'What about we give him a hair of the dog?'

This time Tom String snorted like a horse. 'You're a fine one, missus. That's quite enough of the lighter side, thank you very much.'

'No, Tom, I'm serious,' she replied, but still with a humorous tone. 'You'd do the same for a man who couldn't work for a hangover.'

Tom String blew an exasperated breath. 'How many times do I have to tell you, missus? This ain't a man, it's a horse. Let's start treatin' him as such.'

And with that came the rustling sound of the wattle-switch, before it rapped down on the hide of poor Paul. Tom String hit the horse three times in succession, with cries of 'Ho, thee!' before giving up in disgust.

The horse snorted, then chewed its cud. The harness tinkled as Paul shifted his feet where he stood, looking headfirst down the precarious Boatbuilder's hill.

For a time there was silence, a stymie. Then Joan Sweeney said, 'Here, Tom, at least let's try it. You don't seem to have any other bright ideas.'

'I am not feedin' this horse from my cask of grog in broad daylight. It's what your dead husband would call "half caste behaviour", Mrs Sweeney.'

'Yes, but the point is all bets are off, Tom. The hotel must open for lunch and it's getting on. I demand we try it.'

Tom String sighed. 'Very well then, missus.'

The sound of his feet landing on the ground as he hopped

off the cart preceded a rummaging in the toolbox before the telltale sound of a cork squeaking from a bottle was heard. Then the liquid glug of beer being poured into a metal container.

'Would the good lady like to do the honours?' said Tom String, with sarcasm in his voice.

'Certainly,' said Joan Sweeney, before she too hopped down off the cart. 'Thank you, Tom,' she said, as he handed her the beer. 'Now, Pauly, all your Christmases have come at once, old boy. You take it from me, I'm a publican, I know. This'll fix you up.'

As the horse slurped the beer out of its container, Maria and I looked at each other for the first time. Both of us were smiling.

Before long the beer had been drunk and the palomino's tongue could be heard scouring the empty metal. Then he neighed, quite distinctly asking for more.

'A top up? Most certainly, sir,' said Joan Sweeney. 'Tom, a top up of your Native Companion Ale for this gentleman, please.'

I could only imagine the look on Tom String's face as he rolled his eyes before pouring more beer from his travelling cask into the horse's cup. Once again Paul slurped it up. Then, if I am not mistaken, he farted. Either that or it was Tom String, expressing his disgust. I think it was the horse, however, because Joan Sweeney said, 'Hear that, Tom? The sweet sound of satisfaction. That's music to the mine hostess's ears.'

The cork was then squeaked back into the cask, the cask returned to its place beside the mattock and other tools, and the two passengers, Tom String and Joan Sweeney, resumed their positions in the dray.

After a few moments the swish of the wattle was heard

again but no resounding thwack on the hide was needed. It was enough this time that the wattle had been raised. The horse and cart set off, ever so gingerly negotiating the steep downslope of the Boatbuilder's hill.

A shiver went up my spine when finally they made it to the bottom, rounded the left-hand corner and Paul broke into a trot along the Dray Road, heading seawards on the riverflat. Surely they weren't far from the hotel now, and for the life of me I tried to picture the scene. For a start there would be no houses, and not as many trees because of the stock. There would be no Ocean Road either; where the Dray Road terminated at the hotel corner there would have only been a sandy bridle track running away westways along the shoreline. Before too long I was smelling wild freesias by the roadside, seeing trout jumping in the riverbend, watching wedgies sailing in the thermals high above, with freshwater springs every mile or so and the whole air of the place tangy and pure. I was reminded of the Reconstructed Inlet picture we had on the wall of the bar downstairs, except that now the picture had come to life, there was a cart in a trot, and from the Dray Road the original Grand Hotel would soon come into view.

And then, blazing across my vision, to the right of the melodic cart, I saw the brolga pairs dotting the riverflat. The grass was green and lush, and they pranced, frisked, bowing, jumping suddenly into the air, browsing the ground with their bright crimson heads, in the same stable blue weather in which Joan Sweeney had enjoyed her swim.

'Woah there, Pauly,' Tom String cried as the dray reached the riverbend. Then he called out, 'That's no place to read, Mr

Arvo. That pontoon was built for loading and unloading my barrels.'

'Don't you mind him,' called Joan Sweeney. 'He doesn't even know his own horse.'

'Mrs Sweeney, Tom String – a fine day,' called the man on the riverbend pontoon politely, in a European accent.

'Yairs. A top day for workin'. Readin's for the rain,' Tom String called back, continuing his jest.

There was no reply from Mr Arvo.

'That's right, Mr Arvo, you just ignore him. His horse does,' Joan Sweeney joked.

Tom String geed the palomino lightly, manoeuvring the dray off the clip-clop of the road and onto the softer grass of the riverbank proper, closer to the pontoon.

'What would they say back in your country, Mr Arvo, about a lady publican who feeds good grog to the horses?' he asked, as Paul's hooves settled on the grass of the bank.

Mr Arvo's reply was light and good humoured. 'My apologies, Tom, you cannot corner me to say a cross word of Mrs Sweeney. I'm sure my room is the best in the whole colony, let alone in The Grand Hotel.'

At this Tom String burst into howls of sardonic laughter. His palm could be heard slapping his big thigh where he sat on the cart. The laughter was so forceful that by rights it should have scared the horse, but there was no movement from Paul, not even a shift of feet. 'That's a good one, Mr Arvo! The best in the colony you say. And how long have you been 'ere?'

'I first arrived in '75.'

'Why, that's over a couple of decades ago now. You been

sleepin' in hollow logs all that time? No one's ever mentioned The Windsor to you, in Melbourne, not even in passin'?'

'Oh, I've heard of The Windsor, Tom. I imagine it's very fine. But far too noisy for me.'

'Noisy you say?'

'Yes,' Joan Sweeney chimed in. 'Like you, Tom String. Noisy. At this rate Mr Arvo will be moving on sooner than he'd wish.'

'Aw, that'd be a shame,' said Tom String. 'I'd like to hear more of his imaginin's. The Grand Hotel the finest in the colony! What other secrets can be found in that book you're readin', Mr Arvo?'

The Balt laughed a little defensively. Then Joan Sweeney asked, 'Will you be wanting lunch today, Mr Arvo?'

'No, Mrs Sweeney. Your cook, Mrs Lynch, made me a sandwich for my walk.'

'And I s'pose if you get peckish you can always catch a fish,' said Tom String, laughing still, mainly to himself.

'Or pick some of the blackberries further along the bank,' Joan Sweeney cut in.

'Yes, all that, yes,' said Mr Arvo. 'No, but for now I think the sandwich will be plenty. Perhaps I'll take a berry or two when it's time to leave.'

'Well, Bertie Bolitho'll be grateful if you do. They're the bane of his life those berries,' said Tom String.

'Anyhow then. Cheerio, Mr Arvo,' said Joan Sweeney. 'We must get this coal unloaded and open doors. You never know who's to show up at The Grand on a fine day at this time of year.'

Tom String clicked his tongue and geed his Pauly to move. The horse let out a deeply resistant groan. 'Ho, thee!' Tom String cried, and swished the wattle through the air.

Groaning again, Paul reluctantly moved off. The planks and hasps of the dray began their knocking sounds. The harness tinkled as they covered the uneven ground of the riverbank back to the road.

'You see, missus, what you've done now?' Tom String said, as the wheels levelled out and Paul began to huff and snort. 'You've spoilt him. He thinks it's time for a nap. Ho, thee! Yea get up, you moke!' the jesting slushy cried, and the half boozed palomino lumbered into a heavy trot.

As the cart trotted off on the dirt of the Dray Road, Kooka switched position in the bed, this time rolling over onto his right side to face the ocean window of The Sewing Room, away from the bedside table and the tranny. Now we could no longer see his face clearly, just in profile, and like the palomino after it had drunk the two cups of beer at the top of the Boatbuilder's hill, Kooka now began to fart like a trooper. The tranny glitched, we lost the sound of horse's hooves and the jingling harness, and then, after a brief gap of nothingness, The Sewing Room was filled with pure static.

In the absence of the dream the white noise came as a shock but as we sat there, unable to move, hoping the broadcast would recommence, it gradually began to sound just like the ocean. I grimaced, thinking how cruel it would be if just as they were approaching The Grand Hotel Kooka's dream was broken.

But broken it was. The ocean static lasted for only a few seconds before a man's voice could be heard talking about the plight of the homeless in Australian cities. I'll never forget those first words he spoke as Maria and I were ripped away from the dream. '*It is a common misconception among the population that only the unemployed are homeless. It is becoming increasingly common for people with jobs to sleep on the streets as well.*'

The word 'abrupt' does not adequately describe the transition from listening to Tom String and Joan Sweeney on the dray, to an ordinary man's voice on night-time radio. The Blonde Maria and I sat in a common stupor of silence for the entire duration of the interview about 'the new homeless'. When it finished, we were treated to the theme music for the four o'clock radio news.

The Easy Glory of Her Smile

EVEN AFTER THE FOUR O'CLOCK NEWS HAD STARTED, I hadn't wanted to leave Kooka's bedside, thinking that somehow the dreams might find frequency again. Eventually, after half an hour of excited whispering in the pool of light, Maria convinced me that the pattern of Kooka's sleep could be relied upon. Every night he would dream soon after she finished reading the book, but when the dream was over there would be nothing more – just news reports, film reviews, talkback and comedy re-runs.

So gently we tiptoed out of the room and spent the hour or so until light down in the bar. At last I could quench my thirst. To do so I chose a cup of black Lady Grey tea laced with Black Bush. We both lit cigarettes and by candlelight helped each other join the dots.

I couldn't contain my excitement – at times I was literally

shivering with it – but I was also disappointed that the broadcast had been cut short before the cart got to the hotel. Maria said there was no guarantee that we would progress any further the following night; in fact she suggested it was a distinct possibility that Kooka may simply revert back to Joan Sweeney swimming in the ocean with her lists. I disagreed with her on this; I felt in my bones that by some miracle Kooka was dreaming us towards an explanation for why the old Grand Hotel had burnt down. As far as I was concerned, my vision of the valley full of brolgas proved it.

In hindsight I think my head was full of greedy thoughts as we sat there in the early hours. I should have been satisfied and amazed with what I'd just experienced rather than immediately hankering for more. But, unwise and immature as I am, I wanted more. I wanted everything I could get of these uncanny nightly broadcasts, which by their very occurrence seemed to prove to me that with The Grand Hotel my own life was finally on exactly the right track.

At first light Maria said she would try to get some sleep, so I sat alone on the pews at the big table in the bar. I could no sooner sleep than sing like The Lazy Tenor. My stomach was swarming with local butterflies and my mind retracing again and again the contents of the night. For a start it was intriguing to me that Tom String seemed so familiar. I had never heard his name, nor had Kooka ever mentioned Joan Sweeney having such an offsider. He had always described Joan Sweeney as a phenomenally capable woman who ran the pub with charm and an iron fist, but single-handedly. Now I was wondering what had happened to Tom String, and as I wondered I realised I could simply ask Kooka about him later in the day, or, better still, when I took the old fella up his breakfast.

I looked at the cuckoo clock above the catfish skeleton on the wall. It showed 6.45 am. I would wait until 7.30 and then fix Kooka an omelette. Oregano, tarragon, rosemary and mushroom, sea salt from Horseshoe Cove and fresh Otway pepper: a Grand Hotel special, just as he liked it. Then, suddenly exhausted, I rested my forehead on the hardwood of the big table and closed my eyes. And before you could say 'yellow-bellied water-rat', I had fallen fast asleep.

When I awoke, it was 8.25 and I recalled that it was Saturday – the day we'd set aside for our stoneskimming comp down near the Plinths. After the night I'd had, stoneskimming was the last thing I felt like doing but there was no getting around it. There were a dozen or so people who were really looking forward to the event, and I had agreed to be there on behalf of the hotel. The comp was set to kick off at 10 am and then finish with a barbecue in the afternoon. But first I had to talk to Kooka.

I found him sitting up in bed watching a welcome swallow flit about The Sewing Room. The poor bird was in a panic, and Kooka asked me if I'd open both the inland and ocean windows so it could find its way back outside.

After flinging the windows open onto the new morning, I placed the tray with Kooka's omelette, toast and tea onto his lap and sat down in the wicker chair beside the bed. 'Sleep well?' I asked innocently.

'Bloody oath. Like a twit,' he said. 'It was only the swallow that woke me up.'

'Is that right?'

'Yairs. It was sittin' right here on the bedside table when I opened my eyes. Just starin' at me. Buggered if I know how it got in.'

We both looked up to where the swallow was flying back and forth now along the room's knotty unpainted rafters.

'You'd think it would smell the air and just head straight out now the windows are open,' Kooka said.

'I suppose it will eventually,' I replied. 'Doesn't look real happy in here.'

'No it doesn't. Unlike yours truly,' said Kooka, as he began to tuck into the omelette with relish.

I let Kooka eat his breakfast in peace for a while until I couldn't wait any longer. 'I've got a question for ya, Kooka. About the old Grand Hotel.'

'The old Grand?' he said perfectly innocently. 'Now that was a wild joint. They used to dance like brolgas in that old hotel.'

My eyes widened. 'Is that right?' I said.

'Well, by all accounts, Noely, it'd make your Grand look like the Women's Temperance Union! No offence of course.'

'None taken, Kooka. They were different times I suppose.'

'Yes, that's right. Mind you, even back then the old Grand had a bit of a reputation.'

'How do you mean?'

'Oh well, I think Joan Sweeney was an enlightened woman. She ran a clean house, kept a nice table, but she also knew what keeps a man in the sticks sane. I mean there's no point feeding 'em grog on the one hand and tryin' to convert 'em on the other.'

'What? Was she religious?'

Kooka looked up from the plate. 'Joan Sweeney? No, I wouldn't reckon. But she was of a strong mind. She had deep beliefs.'

'What kind of beliefs?'

'Well it's hard for me to say I suppose. I mean I'm only going on what I've got in the archive, just a scrap of info here and part of an old letter there, but I'd say she was, well, a modern thinker.'

'In what way, Kooka?'

'Well, for a start she believed she was definitely the equal of any fella. I can recall a part of a letter one of her offsiders wrote, where he said that "if it wasn't for the easy glory of her smile, most coves'd think she was a toff. She has that natural dignity which no money can provide."'

I loved the way Kooka quoted from the letter, and wondered straightaway if it was Tom String who wrote it.

'Mind you, Noel, she wasn't short of a quid,' Kooka said.

'No? Where did her money come from?'

'Well she was a widow. Her husband was a barrister, part of the old squattocracy.'

'I see. And who was this offsider whose letter you've read?'

'Oh he was a fella called String. Thomas String.'

'Mmm, and what was his story?'

'Oh well, the story goes she picked him up off the roadside on her way to open the hotel.'

'What, was he a swaggie or something?'

Kooka rested his fork against the plate and with his eyes followed the swallow's flight as he thought about this. 'Not exactly,' he said. 'Lots of people camped out in those days, under the stars or in a cave or in the scrub by the roadside. People were on the move. It didn't mean you were homeless.'

'So he just came with her right there and then and helped her run the hotel?'

'Yairs, something like that. He was like a general hand. But most importantly he brewed the beer for her. In a camp upstream. He didn't live in the hotel you see. Perhaps because he was half black, I dunno. But he was a great help. She couldn't have done it without him. No matter how strong she was.'

'Too right.'

'Yep, and he stayed for the duration from what I could make out. Now you could never get a swaggie to do that. Not with the call of the road.'

'The call of the road,' I repeated.

'Yairs. They'd feel all cooped up before too long. Like our friend the swallow here.'

I tilted my head back again to watch the panicky little creature scooting and whizzing around the rafters of the room. Even with my mum's tall broom he was too high up in The Sewing Room to help brush him towards the window.

'But anyway, that's enough of all the old stuff,' Kooka said. 'As you know, I'm done with it. If I do nothing else, Noel, I'm gonna spend the rest of my life right smack bang in the here and now. I've only realised recently what a privilege it is to have lived this long.'

'Well why don't you get up out of bed and go and take a look around?' I joked. 'There's not much of the twenty-first century happening up here.'

Kooka shook his head with a kind smile. 'Oh yes there is, son,' he said. 'I've got the tranny, the newspaper in the morning, and besides, I'm happy up here on my own. I'm like Joan Sweeney. I'm thinkin' modern thoughts. That's of course unless you're thinkin' of throwin' me out.'

I scoffed. 'Yeah right, Kooka. As if. The Grand Hotel is at your service, kind sir.'

The old man took his last bite of omelette and beamed at me. 'You're a good boy, Noel,' he said. 'Well brought up.'

'Yeah, well some wouldn't agree,' I sniggered, thinking of Greg Beer. 'One last thing, Kooka. Whatever happened to that Thomas String you mentioned? Joan Sweeney's offsider?'

Kooka raised an exasperated time-blotched hand and blew air through his lips like the horse from his dream. 'Get on with ya,' he cried. 'That's all in the long ago. You've got your own Grand Hotel, Noel, and a damn good one it is. The old one burnt down remember, and no matter how hard you look you won't see old Tom String for the smoke.'

I stood up from the wicker chair, not wanting to push the subject any further. Kooka ran his index finger across the buttery remains of the omelette and toast on the plate and then nodded for me to take the tray. 'I suppose Maria will be in soon,' he said, 'for my massage.'

'It's alright for some,' I replied, motioning for him to finish his cup of tea so I could collect it with the tray. He slurped it up noisily, and I headed for the door.

The Inaugural Mangowak Stoneskimming Championship

DOWN ON THE BEACH AT 10 AM THE BELLS ON THE Plinths were ringing intermittently in the light breeze. Neat piles of flatstones had been gathered and placed along the shore of the estuary, and Givva Way and his son, Alex, had already set up the registration table on the sand by the beach steps leading down from the outdoor swimmers' shower. Young Alex Way was by all accounts a demon skimmer and hot favourite for the event after spending the last few months taking long daily walks along the beach on his doctor's advice. His recovery from the mishap on the indoor creek swing-rope was going well and the whole town was much relieved. His progress was largely because of his new found love of stoneskimming, which he'd discovered on his walks and which he could freely indulge on account of his health. It was an unusual obsession

336

for a teenager, especially one with the larrikin streak he had before the accident on the river had twisted his spine. When he had got wind of our upcoming contest, his competitive juices had begun to flow and what had been merely a fun way to while away the walks his doctor had ordered had become a flared ambition.

His father Givva was right behind him in all this and his mother thought that yes it was at least a less dangerous sport than football or surfing, not to mention hanging catastrophic bombs off the polypropylene swing-rope into the roofed-in river. So as the hour approached and they waited for the other competitors on the sand, Givva was behaving like any other obsessive sporting parent, constantly whispering motivational gems into Alex's ear, and reminding him of all the hard work he'd put in during the course of his rehabilitation. Eventually, when a few kids of Alex's own age turned up to watch the event, Givva reluctantly left his son to socialise and came across to talk to me.

'We've been here since seven, Noel. Gettin' the stones ready and that, working out the throw-point. It's lookin' good eh?'

'Yep, Givva. Certainly is.'

'Alex is primed. He's gonna leave 'em for dead you know. The other day he skimmed it twenty-one times.'

'Geez. That's gonna be hard to beat.'

'I'd reckon. But he gets toey you know, in front of people and that. His technique falls apart, he stresses out and then his back starts playin' up. That's the worry.'

'Oh I'm sure he'll be fine, Givva,' I said, trying to placate the nervous father. 'And anyway, it's just a bit of fun. A nice way to brighten up the morning.'

'No, no, Noel. This means a helluva lot to Alex. He's been through hell, mate. And winning here, well, you never know, it could lead to something. Who knows? He could get to travel overseas and compete, with his compo money and that.'

Rather than suggest to Givva that there might be more productive ways to spend the hundred and twenty thousand dollars they'd been told to expect as a result of the accident, I hailed Jen and Joan Sutherland, who to my surprise were stepping off the beach stairs and down onto the sand with their two boys. Extricating myself from Givva, I made my way over and said hello.

It would be an understatement to say that big Joan was looking much more himself than the last time I'd seen him. His free arm was placed around his wife's waist in a relaxed and affectionate manner, and we had a pleasant and entirely normal chat. The kids seemed happy too. I got the impression that, between them all, they'd managed to turn a corner and that things were looking up again for the Sutherlands.

By about 10.30 there were twenty people gathered on the beach, half of whom were competitors. Givva had taken it upon himself to write the official rules of the event and also to ask Raelene Press from the Brinbeal shire to adjudicate as a non-partisan judge. Raelene lived back up the coast at Devon Beach and because she knew none of the competitors in the event Givva was sure she'd remain impartial.

After I asked for a bit of shoosh from the assembled throng, Raelene Press stood by the registration table and read out the rules. Unfortunately it was hard to hear some of what she said because of the sporadic clanging of the bells on the Plinths, but the general gist was that each competitor would get three throws in each round and at the end of ten rounds the winners of the various categories would be announced. The judges were to be myself, Raelene, and Tommy Collins from The Barrels, who as it happened had prepared a new version of the REM classic 'Nightswimming' for the occasion, renaming it 'Stoneskimming'. After Raelene had battled to read out the rules over the clanging bells, there was a timely lull in the southerly in which Tommy performed his composition on acoustic guitar. It went down a treat among the FM-radio lovers and then everyone took up their positions and the inaugural Mangowak Stoneskimming Championship commenced.

The throw-point was marked by an orange banner attached to a blue pole that was stuck into the sand on the eastern side of the estuary, where Givva and Alex had lined up the flatstones. The three judges were placed strategically to cover the throw: Raelene at the throw-point, Tommy on the western shore some fifty metres across the brown water and myself on the sand at the southern edge, to get a side-on perspective. For fairness' sake the participants were to throw in alphabetical order, and Dave Buckley was first cab off the rank.

Dave is not only a master waterman who's lived by the ocean all his life, he is also the local transcendental meditation teacher. Because of these qualities I had reasonably assumed that he would have the experience, the poise and the mental strength required to focus on an ephemeral, almost non-existent point in the water and successfully skim a beach stone. How wrong I was.

After a few prolonged callisthenic stretches and a protracted gaze into the distance, Dave stepped up to the pole with his three stones and let the first one fly. Rather than skimming as he'd hoped, it simply plopped into the water and sank without a trace.

Of course everyone thought this was a great joke, and Dave himself could see the funny side. 'Great start, Dave,' called Joan Sutherland from where he was standing with his family beside me on the sand. Most of the crowd laughed at this dry crack out of pure relief, happy as they were to see Big Joan had his humour back.

Dave Buckley's next throw wasn't much better than his first, and it was odd to see this second stone disappear under the water without so much as a skiffle. We were all so used to Dave being in control when it came to water-sports that to watch him fail was now a little embarrassing. When his third throw did nothing more than skip once and then slam into the limestone of the southernmost Plinth, the crowd went silent. Dave raised his hands in the air in frustration before quickly recovering his trademark equanimity and standing aside for the next competitor. Beside me young Dylan Sutherland remarked to his mother that Dave Buckley's attempt was 'totally gay'.

The next competitor was Nan Burns; she'd decided to ham it up. She straightaway bent into a low crouch beside the blue pole, adopted a mean, peering expression and then let fly. Off went the stone, skimming once, twice, three times on the water before disappearing below the surface. The small crowd cheered and Nan remarked, 'Well, at least now we've got a leader.'

Nan's second throw was again delivered with the theatrics: the low crouch, the squinting of the eyes. Because everyone was well acquainted with Nan's at times uncompromising temper, it made us all happy to see her playing the ham. We all felt the same sense of reprieve that hovers around a sleeping bull. This second throw went one better than her first, skipping four times across the water before it sank. We watched as a quartet of perfect circles radiated out across the water from where the stone had skimmed. All three of us judges called the word 'Four!' into the air, which made it easy for the shire official to certify that indeed four was the official result of the throw.

For her third throw Nan seemed to suddenly discover some real ambition. After weighing the flatstone carefully in her right hand, she threw off her slapstick approach and gazed meaningfully at the water. This time she didn't crouch, rather she merely dropped her right shoulder into an advantageous position, turned side-on to the water and with an experienced flick of the wrist hurled the stone. It hit the water perfectly, too perfectly in fact. On contact the stone seemed to gather momentum rather than lose it. It gained velocity as well and the whole crowd watched as it whanged into the air before crashing into the Plinth without ever touching the water again. A cloud of blonde dust rose from the Plinth and as if in acknowledgement the bell clanged loudly.

'Whoops,' said Nan at her duffer of a throw and stepped back from the throw-point.

Next up was Tyson Conebush, Joe's twenty-four-year-old son. Tyson's a huge tree of a kid who's famous locally for his prodigious hitting on the golf course. I played with him and his dad once and couldn't believe my eyes when Tyson, who was only sixteen at the time, whacked the ball into outer space off the first tee. But three hours later, when we'd finally made it to the ninth hole, I'd realised why despite his power off the tee the Conebush family trophy cabinet back in the garage at Breheny Creek remained full only of lifesaving certificates and the silverware from his mother's netball triumphs. To put it succinctly, Tyson could hit a golf ball anywhere but on the fairway.

As he collected the three stones ascribed to him and stepped up to the blue pole, Raelene Press raised her hand for him to pause before his throw. 'Could all competitors please be careful not to throw in the direction of the Year of the Maritime Plinths. They are shire property and as works of public art must be protected.'

She should never have said it – not with our local version of Long John Daly about to step up to the plate. On the sidelines I groaned, knowing that even though Tyson hadn't thrown a stone yet, the die of his stoneskimming destiny had been cast. With intense seriousness he bent into a similar crouch to the one Nan had adopted in jest. He paused and then unleashed his projectile out over the water.

And out over the water it certainly went! At no stage did it even look like skimming on the surface of the estuary. Instead it sailed like a bullet through the air, some two metres above the patiently waiting water. On the far shore Tommy Collins surrendered his responsibilities and ducked for cover. He needn't have bothered. Halfway across the water Tyson Conebush's exocet flatstone sundered once again into the southernmost Plinth, causing a sizeable wedge of the sculpture to plop into the water like the shard of a melting polar ice cap.

A hush came over the crowd. Young Dylan Sutherland said quietly to his brother, 'Anyone'd think they're aiming for it.' Back near the throw-point I could see Givva and Alex Way rolling their eyes.

Before Raelene Press could stop him, Tyson the Tree cast off again, this time with a better result. The stone hit the water at the perfect angle and at a ferocious speed. Once, twice, three times it skimmed, but it hadn't near finished. When it finally ran out of puff and sank slowly to the bottom of the estuary, I had counted a grand total of fifteen skims. It was incredible. On the far shore Tommy Collins excitedly shouted 'FIFTEEN' as well, and we waited for Raelene Press to concur.

She wasn't forthcoming. 'Well? How many?' Tyson eagerly asked her. Raelene's face was set, her lips shut. Slowly she reached into the pocket of her Brinbeal shire polar fleece jacket and pulled out her phone. Holding one hand up to placate the crowd, she methodically thumbed in a number.

'What, are you calling the third umpire?' Joan Sutherland called cheekily across the water.

'She is the third umpire,' a frustrated Givva Way called back in response.

Raelene Press's call was answered at the other end, and as she spoke she began to wander away from the throw-point and back towards the beach steps. I knew immediately what she was discussing: it wasn't how many times Tyson Conebush's extraordinary second throw had skimmed across the water but rather the damage his first throw had done to the Plinth.

Raelene Press remained in deep discussion for a good ten minutes, by which time the crowd was getting decidedly edgy. I was regretting allowing a shire official to be involved in what should have just been a bit of Grand Hotel fun, but with Greg Beer watching for the slightest slip-up I'd figured we'd run this event by the book. Now it looked like we were on the verge of trouble anyway.

With the phone at her ear Raelene started looking down the body of the estuary, to where the other two untouched Plinths were standing with their bells momentarily idle. She began pointing and then shaking her head, and I could tell she was discussing the possibilities with someone back at the shire head office of changing the throw-point. That was a waste of time. Choosing our site had in the end been very straightforward because neither the positioning of the three Plinths on the water or the protected sedge and marshland further back behind the dunes had allowed for us to do it anywhere else. We had to be on the sandy shore for the throw so we didn't cop a fine for trampling native species, and the arrangement of the two Plinths further back in the water meant that throwing alongside the single Plinth at the southern end was the only option.

Eventually Raelene Press looked back towards the waiting crowd and began to nod and frown as she wound up her call. It seemed that together with head office she had reached a difficult conclusion. I dreaded to hear what it was.

As she clapped her phone shut and replaced it in her pocket, she walked back to where Tyson Conebush was now skulling a Gatorade at the throw-point.

'So, what's the verdict?' asked Givva Way, in an already disgusted tone. Perhaps he too had an inkling of what was to come.

'Unfortunately,' Raelene Press called out for everyone to hear, 'I am going to have to call off the contest. It seems that due to the risk of further damage to the Year of the Maritime Plinths there is no suitable site here in Mangowak to run the event. Unless of course everyone is prepared to hold the event on the ocean itself. But we would have to wait for a day a little stiller than this. As you can see, it's pretty choppy out there.'

Givva Way exploded. 'You're fuckin' joking aren't ya?' he shouted at Raelene Press, sensing his son's global sporting career being jeopardised because of the risk of damage to public art.

'There's no need to swear, sir,' Raelene Press replied. 'But no, I am not joking. We just cannot risk further damage to the Plinths.'

'But my Alex is a dead-eye,' Givva said. 'He won't hit the stupid fuckin' things. He'll throw exactly where he intends to. That's what he's been practising for.'

Raelene Press was conciliatory. 'I'm sure you are right. But unfortunately, as we have seen, not all the competitors are likely to be that well practised.'

'What? So you punish my poor son, who's already broken his back because of you bastards at the shire, just because Tyson here's a loose cannon? That's not fair.'

'Hey, watch your mouth, Givva,' Tyson Conebush said, from beside the blue pole. 'I just skimmed that stone fifteen times. Alex'd be battlin' to beat that.'

Givva Way's jaw dropped. 'For your information, young fella, only last week Alex skimmed one twenty-one times in far from perfect conditions.'

'Yeah, but that wasn't under pressure. With a crowd and that. Not like mine.'

Unwittingly with this comment Tyson Conebush had touched on the doubts that Givva had earlier expressed to me about his son not holding up to the strains of competition. I decided it was time I left my judging post and went across before the animosity escalated. Givva was fuming, things were about to get out of control. Fresh from the garden party brawl the last thing I wanted was a repeat performance.

Arriving at the throw-point just in time, I stood between Tyson Conebush and Givva Way as they began to hurl threats and abuse at each other. And, glancing hurriedly up onto the brow of bearded heath above the beach, I thought I caught a glimpse of a blue police uniform standing behind the railing of the lookout. But just as quickly it was gone.

I heard the words coming out of my mouth before I could stop them. 'I think the lady's right, you guys. We can't ruin the Plinths. It just wouldn't be good. So calm down, calm down. We'll reschedule all this for a nice offshore day on the ocean, and sort out who's the champ. So just calm down.'

Givva Way looked at me with a shocked expression. I could tell he thought that right then and there I was a traitor, a turncoat, that I'd crossed over to the dark side.

'And look,' I said. 'Come back to The Grand and I'll put on a lunch. On the house. For all stoneskimmers. And spectators.'

But Tyson Conebush was having none of it. 'Nah,' he said.

'I want an official judging of that throw of mine. Two of youse said it was a fifteen and I want this lady here to confirm it.'

'Aw forget it would ya, Tyson?' I said. 'The contest's been postponed, because of the Plinths.'

'Well in that case I reckon I'm the champion,' he said.

'You bloody well are not,' Givva Way shot out. 'Your first throw was a fresh-air shot and your second hasn't even been properly judged. That means if there's any kind of temporary champion it's Nan. With a throw of four skims.'

'I would agree with that,' said Raelene Press, 'with the proviso that it's only a provisional measure, until another time and place can be arranged.'

Hearing all this, Nan Burns had broken into a huge grin over by the registration desk. She raised both fists into the air in mock-triumph and began jumping up and down on the balls of her feet like a victorious boxer. The mood in the crowd changed on seeing this and they began to cheer her victory. Before long Joan Sutherland and his sons were calling 'Speech, speech'. Thankfully what had looked like a potentially violent situation had been avoided. Everyone agreed to pack up and retire back to the hotel to celebrate with Nan.

The Lazy Tenor and The Blonde Maria had not graced us with their presence down at the stoneskimming comp, which was a source of some relief when I'd first seen the Sutherlands coming happily down the steps to the beach. Now, of course, with everyone adjourning back to the hotel, I was worried that another conflict was at hand. Despite how well Joan looked, there was no way the derangement that had surfaced in him at the garden party could have been entirely cured so soon. Does love fly from the nest of the heart so quickly? I don't think so. And nor does the brindled moulting bird of sexual jealousy. So as we wandered away from the shore of the inlet, with the tell-tale bells of the Plinths ringing in our ears, I was much relieved when the big dairyman with the broken wing came over to say goodbye.

'I'm off to Minapre, Noely, to have the plaster removed,' Joan told me, as Jen waved from where she and the boys were getting into the car by the road.

'Is that right?' I replied happily. 'And everything else is okay then is it?'

'Oh yeah, well as can be expected, given the muck-ups and that.'

'Jen seems okay?'

'Oh no, she's had a rough trot, there's no doubting that. But shit, Noel, a man's not a saint is he? Well, not this one anyway.'

'So what, are you coming back to work?'

'To tell you the truth I dunno. Still thinkin'. About whether I can handle it. But I know you've got a lot on your plate so I won't think for long. I'll let you know real soon.'

'You know if it's a question of you or Maria, I'd have to choose you every time. The Grand needs you, Joan. She's not even singing anymore, you know.'

'Yeah, well thanks, Noel. I appreciate it. I'll see ya.'

As I walked back with the rest of the stragglers from the stoneskimming comp, across the kikuyu and pigface flats on our way to the hotel, I noticed five swallows sitting like quavers and crotchets on the musical-stave powerlines running alongside the main road. I knew that what I'd said to Joan about valuing him over Maria was no longer strictly true. Not now that she'd let me in on Kooka and the broadcasts from his tranny. I was working the hours of three men without Joan behind the bar, but the truth was I could put up with that if I was able to visit the old Grand with Kooka and the magic tranny every night. But all that was dependent on Maria. I resolved as I walked home that if the old Grand Hotel was to somehow come alive once again in The Sewing Room that night, I'd ring Joan Sutherland the next morning and tell him he was welcome to a few more weeks of paid leave. No ifs or ands or buts. One should never say no to a miracle after all.

The Local Spree

*T*HE COUNTRY MAY BE DRY IN MOST PARTS BUT IN OUR *world it's as wet and marshy as Ireland for months – so rather than supply beer for the thirst of hot dwellers, here we supply the liquid, i.e. alcohol, so as to be in good harmony with our green surroundings. As a matter of fact we do also supply peanuts, not to soak up the effects of the liquor you understand – hard-boiled eggs from our hotel chooks, which are at all times available on the bar, are more than adequate for that purpose – but rather to be in league with the salt-laden air as it wafts in billows up our coastal valley.*

The cold southerly had been brewing during the stoneskimming competition and now had simply snapped like a twig. Both The Blonde Maria and I were wrapped up in blankets as we sat beside Kooka's bed in The Sewing Room later that night. The old man himself was lying under two doonas and a brightly coloured rug, and with his brow and beak poking out from under these heavy covers he reminded me of an aged kookaburra being nursed with cotton wool in a shoebox.

We had been treated to the sound of the surf again, and the swimming publican, and for a moment after my initial excitement I had feared that the dream would indeed just be a repeat of the night before. But I needn't have worried. The ocean hiss took over from the radio's brief transitional static, the waves tumbled and churned, Joan Sweeney sighed and gasped with release and exhilaration but there were no calls from Tom String back on shore. There were none of the lists that Maria had mentioned either. Instead the swimming publican seemed to be composing a letter.

To suggest, by hearsay, as you do, that the ground outside my establishment is commonly 'strewn with broken bottles, glasses, peanut shells, crayfish heads' and that my licence is being 'improvised upon' to include the activities of a 'brothel of the wilds' is, in short, stupendous.

My concern, it is true, is for the satisfaction of my patrons, whether they be loyal, irregular, local or itinerant, in each case in need of an inn. Nevertheless I maintain an always clean, ruly and law-abiding premises, so as to dignify both my own labour and the necessity of recreation hardworking men require in this the littoral bush. These men strive, not to conquer the implacable red heat of the inland but rather to eke out stability of produce amidst the daily fluctuations of these southwest skies. Far from fraternising with imported purveyors of prostitution from the Bass Strait Islands, the lives of my patrons, without exception, are indebted to honesty, goodwill and self-sacrifice. Indeed many of them, both in their employment as fishermen and in their cast of fine feeling, are nothing if not reminiscent of the Galileans of the Gospels. Even those stockmen who rely on The Grand Hotel for our smithy and as a traveller's rest often inspire in me feelings of admiration for the arduous and lonely nature of the labours they have undertaken.

They battle on God's earth and amidst his elements, and the little I can do for them I shall. But at no time as the licence-holder of this hotel have I been so presumptuous as to provide latitude from the law. In twelve years of marriage to my deceased husband I saw its worth to a colonial society time and again, and I watched him uphold it in his profession as one would watch a shepherd with his sheep.

Consequently, the intended visitation under your instructions of the sergeant from Ballaarat holds no fear for me. On the contrary I consider the expense of his journey to be a waste of government money, which in these straitened times could in all likelihood be better spent. Nevertheless, upon his arrival he shall be treated no differently from any other weary traveller who arrives at my door. His horse shall be watered, he himself shall have a bed should there be one vacant, and every effort will be made to ensure his comfort in regard to victuals. I am sure that after a brief stay he shall depart The

*Grand Hotel wondering why it was he received the orders
he did. And on his journey home he may well reflect how far
the southwestern region of the state of Victoria has progressed
since the lawless days among the pirates, sealers and whalers
earlier in the century.*

She composed this letter out loud among the waves, but all in
a tone of mock-seriousness, and with satisfied laughter between
the sentences. Then she dived and we heard the underhum of
the ocean Maria had described to me previously. The room
went quiet but for this drone and her breathing, and I imagined
Joan Sweeney, with arms out wide and legs kicking like a frog,
swimming underwater now her letter was complete.

But what was the letter all about? And who were these
Bass Strait prostitutes, and who had made the accusations? She
emerged from the water and the hum disappeared in the daylight. Once again the sound of the ocean was open, swish and
effervescent. Joan Sweeney didn't say any more but her mirth
could be sensed, even at a distance of over a hundred years. She
was having a lend of somebody – no, not just anybody, she was
playing funny buggers with the powers that be.

This woman whom Kooka had only ever met in his archives
had not surprisingly pricked his interest, to the extent that after
unburdening himself of the ghosts of his mother and his wife,
he was now dreaming purely of her. There was such bold
charisma in the tone of her letter that beside me Maria was
smiling her head off, her enjoyment lingering still in the wake
of it. I began to smile too, and to nod involuntarily, and to
watch Kooka closely. His face was impassive; there was no

outward sign of the world inside his head, no evidence of Joan Sweeney still swimming in the waves. He was just an old man of the bird family *Halcyonidae*, wrapped up in two doonas and a crocheted rug, in a sudden snap chill on the twenty-first-century coast.

I should have been tired from the lack of sleep the night before, not to mention the disappointment of the stoneskimming competition and the forty-six counter meals that resulted. But I felt not one hint of fatigue and leant forward again on the edge of my seat as now the transistor seemed suddenly to switch channels. Gradually through a flux of static we heard the unmistakable sound of a cork being pulled from a bottle and then Tom String saying the words, 'Your port, Mr Arvo. Port in a storm I might say.'

'Thank you, Tom. You wouldn't want to be out in it.'

'No fear. The Grand's a racket of a roof to be sure but it beats a drenching.'

It was true; we could hear now the sound of rain pouring on the roof of the old hotel.

'Do you always bring the goats in from a shower?' Mr Arvo was asking Tom String.

'Yairs we do, but seldom here into the bar. It's only the stables are full with the girls' horses. And a little later of course they'll be full with the girls. Mrs Sweeney's a practical woman.'

'Oh yes. So the girls don't work upstairs?'

'Oh no. Not with the sound of it, Mr Arvo – can you imagine? No, not down the hallway from your room – now there's a condition you'd want laid down.'

'I see. Well the girls and the goats don't seem to mind each other's company, all huddled there by the fire.'

'Yairs well, it's blazing, eh? "Ash that burns", that's our tree around here, and our little joke.'

From further along the bar Joan Sweeney's voice was now heard, calling to the female customers: 'Jadey, Rose, Cumquat May, would you care for another drink with your food there? Cook says it's nearly done.'

'Aye, and it ain't goat!' Tom String chimed in.

'That's enough out of you, Tom String. You be ready with the brush and shovel now. And top up Mr Arvo's port. You'll give my hotel a tight reputation.'

There were sniggers from the girls beside the fire and the clicking sounds of the goats' hooves on the hearth.

'Anyway, girls, what'll it be?' Joan Sweeney called. 'Underground mutton or pork fed on bread and peaches? Or hedgehog, known as porcupine in your parts I believe?'

'Ooh, the bread and peaches pork for me thank you, Mrs Sweeney,' came a young female voice from the fire. 'Sounds lovely.'

'And you, Jadey?' the dutiful publican asked. 'Don't be shy now.'

'I'll have the same, missus, thank you,' said a quiet voice with an Irish lilt.

'And Cumquat May? What would you like for your tea?'

'Porcupine thank you, missus,' Cumquat May replied, in a voice a little harder than the rest, and more mature. 'And a plonk with that thank you. One for each of us please.'

'Yes, well, you'll be needing your strength when the

boys roll in. If they ever make it through this rain, that is.'

'What about the bearded jokers?' said Tom String, from where he was topping up Mr Arvo's port. 'Don't they get a plonk?'

'What was that, Tom?' Joan Sweeney replied. 'I couldn't hear you for the rain.'

'The goats, Mrs Sweeney. Don't they get some mulled plonk to sip by the fire?'

Joan Sweeney laughed, a high laugh, as if Tom String was an incorrigible child. 'I'll just ignore that bait shall I, Tom String? And if you'd kindly take down Mr Arvo's dinner order, I'd be much obliged.'

The cork was squeaked back into the port bottle and Tom String asked Mr Arvo what he would have. Mr Arvo seemed to consider the menu for a moment before asking, 'Tell me, Tom, what exactly is underground mutton?'

'Rabbit, Mr Arvo. Shot with me own parrot gun.'

'I see. Mmm. No quail tonight?'

'You always have to ask, don't ya? But no, sir. Me pointer's havin' pups. When you were last here, it was autumn, the quail were like mice on the ground. If you're still here at the end of summer, we'll see what we can do. That's if Candle ever recovers from childbirth.'

'Candle?'

'Yairs. Me pointer.'

'Oh, I see. Well, in that case I'll have the pork.'

'Good choice, Mr Arvo. A hotel's pigs are happy pigs. What with all the throw-outs. And doubly so here at The Grand, with all the fruit back up in the valley. If peaches were pounds, they'd rename this joint El Dorado.'

'Well it's to my liking anyway, Tom,' Mr Arvo replied.

'To mine as well, Mr Arvo,' said Tom String. 'And working for the good lady beats crackin' stones for a living.'

Gradually now the rain on the old Grand Hotel roof seemed to be lessening, but as it did we heard a few heavy drops falling on our own. The flashing of the roof above The Sewing Room pinged as the first drops hit and before long there had been some kind of downpour exchange: the roof of Joan Sweeney's Grand had gone quiet while my own was now thrumming away.

Back in the old Grand, in burst *the boys* they'd been waiting for and, as Tom String remarked, they'd timed their run. They were just in the nick of time for tea.

The new noisy influx into the bar seemed to amuse the girls but disturb the goats, who could now be heard anxiously pitter-pattering in circles on the stone floor and occasionally bleating as well.

'Now look what you done, you brutes. There was us girls and the goats having a nice quiet yarn by Mrs Sweeney's fire and you had to go and ruin it. Come here, you Heides all. Come and settle again.'

It was the comely voice of Rose, who had been the first of the three whores to order her meal.

'Oh bejaysus! We're not gonna get the fleas tonight are we, Bait?' exclaimed one of the men who had burst into the bar. 'I'm just over gettin' drenched. The last thing I need are a goat's old nits as well.'

'I dunno about nits, but would you have a look at those

tits?' replied his companion called Bait. 'And I don't mean on the goat.'

The men started laughing but Joan Sweeney cracked down hard. 'That's quite enough of such guff from you fellows. Any more and you're out on your ear. If Cumquat May, Jadey and Rose have been kind enough to make the journey, you'll behave, do you hear?'

'Well, as a matter of fact, missus, I am a bit hard of hearing. What was that you said?' asked another one of the men, in a sincere and humble tone.

'You tell Ding, Bait Belcher. He's genuine. You tell him I'll have no more dirty talk in my hotel. I'm not used to it and I don't like it. And if he doesn't believe me, he can try wrestling with Tom.'

'Good evening, you fellas,' cried Tom String cheerily across the bar. 'And g'day to you too, Ding Dong,' he called out with extra relish.

'Tom String,' they all replied at once, with the man called Ding Dong's voice louder and reedier than the rest.

'Now you're just in time for tea, boys,' said Joan Sweeney matter-of-factly. 'I'd appreciate it if you'd order now so we can get this show on the road.'

With no further discussion the four men each ordered underground mutton but for Ding Dong, who ordered a serving of the hedgehog, perhaps on account of not hearing the menu properly. They then ordered their drinks as well, their Native Companion Ales, which was the beer Tom String brewed in his upstream camp. As they took their first long draughts and smacked their lips with satisfaction, I found myself hankering to know what a Native Companion tasted like, and more particularly to know how it compared with our Dancing Brolgas.

The Grand Hotel goats now seemed to have settled again with the girls by the hearth and for the time being, at least, the men and women kept to separate areas of the bar. Tom String was pouring the drinks and Joan Sweeney had taken a stool next to Mr Arvo, where together they were chatting pleasantly as they enjoyed their meals. Beside me now Maria had opened her eyes and was grinning from ear to ear from the fun of it all.

'Yes, they had threatened to send a sergeant from Ballaarat. By all accounts he'd made his name as a young man cleaning up the diggings back in the early sixties,' Joan Sweeney was saying to Mr Arvo between mouthfuls of a rather chewy boiled echidna. 'Hard to believe, isn't it? Unfortunately the old fella couldn't make the ride. He's well over sixty by all accounts. But yes, perhaps that was due also in part to my letter.'

'And what, may I ask, Mrs Sweeney, would you have done if the sergeant had made the ride?' said Mr Arvo.

'Well to be perfectly frank, Mr Arvo, I'm not sure. My scouts on the route would've given me notice. But you see, that is not the issue here. The issue is that Victoria as defined by the borders is a large colony – you know yourself it's as big as England – and the great majority of it is unknown to the powers back in Melbourne where I grew up. They have no idea of the requirements of a hotel in a small outpost such as ours and no experience of the way we are living. And yet they tut-tut and stroke their beards, while we are carrying on with the business. But really, the aspersions they were casting on The Grand were factually incorrect and, practically speaking, quite irrelevant. I wrote the letter not to avert the sergeant's visit but to educate the administrator!'

'Well I must admit it has been an education for myself lodging here.'

'Indeed. You obviously approve, Mr Arvo?'

'Oh yes, yes. That's why I came back. Not only for the peace in the valley but also for the, how shall I say . . . *civilisation* of your hotel, Mrs Sweeney. Even in Australia now, the difference between man and beast is growing.'

'I don't follow you, Mr Arvo.'

'Well you see, Mrs Sweeney, I believe not in the lion lying down with the lamb, which of course is an impossibility, but rather that mankind and the animals are in fact kindred, rather than enemies. That they are not so different, you see.'

'Yes?'

'Yes, and here we are chatting pleasantly, sharing your hotel bar with goats.'

'And prostitutes,' laughed Joan Sweeney.

'Indeed. And prostitutes. And also, I may add, beautiful flowers.'

'Aah yes, my flowers.'

'I counted eight vases.'

'That's right, Mr Arvo. All collected and cut by myself in the hereabouts. Very kind of you to count the vases.'

'Yes, but that of course doesn't include those in the parlour, or the upstairs hallway and rooms. There are three in my room alone, Mrs Sweeney.'

'And also three in my own, Mr Arvo. But now you've mentioned it, the flowers are a case in point.'

'How so, Mrs Sweeney?'

'Well then, do you see many roses among my vases, or Calla lilies, carnations, lupins or marigolds?'

'No, no, hardly at all. There is a rose in each of my bedroom vases, obviously from your beds down by the well, but surrounded by so much other colour. And no lupins, or marigolds or lilies, no.'

'There, you see. Half the flowers I use in this hotel I don't even know the names of myself! But at the same time I know these flowers as well as the contents of my bulk spirits order. I gather them in the valley or up on the ridge or along the dunes where another pair of eyes might not even notice them. The orchids, the hues of the heath, the "tassel flowers" – well, that's what I call them – that grow among the wiregrasses where the stock have never browsed. But an important personage from Melbourne wouldn't know the half of it, wouldn't even know that some of these flowers that fill my vases exist! It's a different country out here, Mr Arvo. And this is the point. There are different colours in the hotel vases, different shapes too, and it's the same with the clientele. Take little Ding Dong over there. He'll take Rosie tonight. You'll hear him crying out from the stables, even with your window shut. And if there weren't a Rosie, he'd be crying out a different tune. A man's heart needs the occasional shelter. And out here it's my duty to supply it – otherwise the men are in drought, no matter the rain. Yet the powers that be feel quite within their rights to tell me how to run my hotel. Pah. It's a different country.'

There was a brief silence after this speech of Joan Sweeney's. Then through the tranny Mr Arvo asked the very question

I'd been thinking myself. 'What about the girls though, Mrs Sweeney? How are they benefiting, if you don't mind me asking?'

'Not at all, Mr Arvo,' came the publican's reply. 'I may love to pick flowers but I also run a profitable business which is at the same time a community service. Look at it like this. A man's lust is as old as the world itself. And wherever there is desire, there is also money. So by rights this earth we're holed up in is just one almighty Grand Hotel. There you have it. But contrary to the information the inspectors in Melbourne received, these girls are not harpies from the Bass Strait Islands. All three of them are from Ballaarat, the same as the doddering sergeant who couldn't make the ride. Cumquat May there is half Chinese and third generation in the trade. Rose is the illegitimate child of a prominent politician from New South Wales, no names mentioned, and as such cannot stake her claim for fear of a tragic accident involving the broken axle of a jinker. And Jadey, the shy one, was saved from pure destitution by Cumquat May only last week, and is trialling a new path. This way she at least can hear the rain on the roof rather than standing out in it catching her death. So that's how I see it, Mr Arvo. And if, as you say, there is a fine line between man and beast, then who am I to deny it?'

'Mmm, quite right. Mind you, if I myself had a daughter and I found . . .'

'Mr Arvo, if I may interrupt. To have a daughter is not a notion, not a hypothesis or idea, but a firm reality for those who are so destined. But often, in the case of sons as well, that reality is too great to bear. Some daughters are farmed out to nuns, some are left with a rug and a prayer of hope on an

Emerald Hill porch, others quite simply perish; some sons are lucky enough to be billeted out with relatives in further regions for farm work. I could go on but you take my point. These girls here are no worse off in many ways than the men over there who are right now deciding which ones they fancy. Do you think those coves wouldn't like a well-mannered slip to come home to at night? Of course they would. But in my experience, Mr Arvo, if I may be brutally honest with you, were it not for Cumquat May, Jadey and Rose being here tonight, Bait and Jimmy, Ding Dong and Ted over there would be eyeing off the goats. Quite seriously.'

The Blonde Maria swung my way on the wicker chair, with a wide-eyed expression as if to say, 'Did you hear what she just said?' Her movement in the room after a long period of captivated stillness must have registered upon Kooka, because suddenly he groaned and chapped his lips together before rolling over to lie flat on his back. We were on tenterhooks, hoping that he wouldn't wake up, and thankfully he didn't. The tranny gave out only a brief glitch as he readjusted himself under the heavy bedclothes and then delivered us safely back into the hospitable arms of Joan Sweeney's hotel.

It seemed that Joan and Mr Arvo had polished off their meals by now, as the sound of their plates and cutlery being cleared away by Tom String could be heard.

'And how was that hedgehog, missus?' the all-rounder asked, only to be told by his boss that it could've done with more pigface.

'Bit fatty was it?' he replied. 'Still, killing it meant we could get the coal home on the cart.'

'That's true, Tom,' Joan Sweeney replied. 'But the fact remains we should have stopped for more pigface.'

'Maybe, missus. But Mr Arvo distracted us, didn't he, with his chat at the riverbend?'

'Right you are,' exclaimed Joan Sweeney, quickly turning Tom's criticism into a lighthearted moment. 'The fatty hedgehog was all Mr Arvo's fault. I'd like to know how you're going to make it up to me, sir, aside from distracting me with subjects I am passionate about, to take my mind off the food you've spoiled.'

Mr Arvo chuckled happily without quite having the wit to continue the joke. 'Well all I can say is that the pork was the best ever. Absolutely first class,' he said.

'Peachy, you might say,' called Tom String dryly over his shoulder, as he rattled through what sounded like swinging saloon doors, presumably ferrying the dirty dishes back through the bar to the kitchen.

Now it seemed a conversation was beginning between the boys at the bar and the three girls from Ballarat who sat by the fire with the goats. This was initiated by Bait Belcher, who was now finding the goats to come in handy. Venturing away from the bar towards the girls, his rough twang was quiet and conciliatory as he spoke. 'So youse're keen on goats are ya, ladies?'

'Not really,' Cumquat May shot back with authority. 'Well, not as keen as some,' and then she cackled, and Jadey and Rose giggled beside her.

Bait Belcher, however, seemed to take no offence – either because he didn't twig as to what Cumquat May was referring to, or because he was in no way ashamed of his apparently near-famous history with goats. 'Poor dumb creatures,' was all he said, and it wasn't entirely clear whether he was referring to the goats or Cumquat May, Jadey and Rose. Nevertheless the ice had been broken. 'If you let us pull up a pew or two, me and the other coves here could tell you a thing or two about goats. Very entertainin' stories too.'

'Please yourself, Bait Belcher,' Cumquat May said, with the unmistakable tone of someone who had undertaken this exact process before, and with the very same gentlemen.

Bait Belcher called back to his mates at the bar. 'Here, Jimmy, Ted, pull up a pew and be kind to the girls. They're sick of yarnin' to the willow-munchers. And get Ding to bring over some jugs. Mrs Sweeney! Three jugs of the Native Companion Ale if you will. Ding'll bring 'em over to the mantle.'

'Certainly, Bait Belcher,' Mrs Sweeney replied and, excusing herself from Mr Arvo, got up to pour the drinks.

Tom String re-emerged from the kitchen right then and told Joan Sweeney how well the coal was burning in the stove. 'If anythin', it's glowin' too fast. Just as well we got that load on the cart today.'

'Yes,' Joan Sweeney replied, 'I could tell by the rag over the new girl's nose that it was putting out. She's never been here before, Tom. Make her welcome would you, and help Ding take over these drinks?'

'Too right, missus.'

By the sound of it Tom String and Ding arranged the jugs and the glasses between them and carried them across the room to the mantle, where they could be heard setting them down. 'You're first up, lassie,' Tom String said to Jadey, the Grand

Hotel virgin. 'Will ya look at the head on that one, eh? No one can say Tom String doesn't know how to pour his own ale. Got a line on it straight as the blue horizon. And it's got your name on it too, lassie!'

'Thank Tom for the beer, Jadey,' Cumquat May instructed.

The girl's voice was muffled, obviously by the rag over her nose, but a faint 'Thank you, Tom' was heard over the rain that was still falling, ever so lightly, on the Sewing Room roof.

'I'm sorry for the stink of the coal there, lassie,' Tom String said then. 'Thing is, we don't even notice anymore. And you won't after a couple of my beers, will she, Cumquat May?'

'I dare say not,' Cumquat May agreed.

'Nah, and you'll have no rag up your nose when we get you out to the stables,' said the man called Ted, in a Scottish brogue. 'But you'll have somethin' else up ya out there. Too bloody right ya will, yer fresh'n.'

There was a sudden commotion after this remark; the goats' hooves could be heard clicking again on the stones. And then the fella called Ted was bleating like a goat himself. 'Aw, Tom,' he winced. 'Aw, bugger off. Blimey, I meant nothin' by it. Och! Let go o' me would ya, ya big black oaf? I was only havin' a bit of a lark with the whores!'

Tom String however was firm. 'Nup, Ted. You're barred. Out you go into the wet, ya jummy you. Mrs Sweeney's set her rules for the seasonal entertainment. You knew that. She'll look after us all, but only to a point. Now get out o' here and go swim with the river rats!'

And with that the Scotsman Ted was thrown out into the night and the door was slammed behind him.

'By jingo!' cried Ding. 'I never seen a shirt collar used like a jug handle before! Hey, Tom String, you *poured* him out into the night.'

'Too bloody right I did, Ding. And I'll do the same to you if you act up. Now let's get on with this spree, hey, and you fellas make these inlanders welcome. Especially young Jadey there. Drink up, lassie. And don't mind Ted. There's a reason he lives in a hut made of old kero tins. He's a deadset river rat.'

Once again the goats could be heard resettling in front of the crackling mountain-ash logs of the fire. The rest of the first jug of Native Companion Ale was poured, and before long the room had well and truly tempered and was full of quiet conversation.

'He's an invaluable asset that Tom String,' Mr Arvo was saying to Joan Sweeney, who had joined him again at the end of the bar.

'Particularly on a night such as this,' the publican replied. 'We only do it once a season – it's too long a trip for the girls and all – but there's always bound to be some trouble. Often enough it's with Ted. Or some blow-in who can't believe his luck.'

'Yes, I can imagine. I suppose if a working man stumbled in here off a boat or a wagon and struck such potential comfort, he'd become quite excitable.'

Joan Sweeney laughed. 'You're not wrong there, Mr Arvo. Tom's an asset right then and there, make no mistake.'

The gang-gangish sound of squeaking cork was heard again and Joan Sweeney offered Mr Arvo another port, this time on the house.

'That's very kind,' said Mr Arvo. 'Now, Mrs Sweeney, about your flowers. I was wondering if I may be able to help you with them.'

'With the flowers?' replied Joan Sweeney. 'Oh never mind that, Mr Arvo. I enjoy collecting them. It's that and swimming which keeps me sane around here.'

'No, no, Mrs Sweeney, I didn't mean you'd need help with the collecting. More with the naming.'

'The naming?'

'Yes. You were saying just before that you don't know half the names of the flowers you pick for your vases.'

'That's right.'

'Well, you see, it's there where I might be able to help.'

'How so, Mr Arvo?'

'It's a long story, Mrs Sweeney, but in essence, before I left Finland, I had trained for a time as a botanist. As a very young man, you understand.'

'How interesting,' said Joan Sweeney.

'Yes, well I never did complete my studies – my true vocation was to travel the wide world and it's that which I pursued. But, after spending four or five unsuccessful years in the dregs of the diggings, on Bendigo, Ballaarat and Blackwood, a man told me one day that the Baron von Mueller was in need of botanical fieldworkers in Melbourne – to assist with the collection at the Botanical Gardens there, you understand.'

'I do, Mr Arvo, I do.'

'So you see, Mrs Sweeney, I found employment with von Mueller and thankfully got off the parsimonious diggings. As it turns out, the very week that I left I received news that my father had died back in Finland. Being an only child, I had inherited the whole of his estate. I was no longer in need of an income. But my interest was now aroused by the opportunity to work alongside the baron, so I went to enquire about the post. I met von Mueller in his cottage and we got on well, for he too had an interest in travel as well as plants. In short, Mrs Sweeney, I was appointed as his assistant-in-the-field and spent the next four years neglecting the duties of my inheritance back in Finland and ranging across Victoria instead, predominantly in the mountainous areas, collecting and classifying native species on his and the governor's behalf. As such there was for a brief time even a small herb named in my honour by the baron, for I had collected this hitherto undiscovered plant in quite precipitous circumstances on the upper reaches of the Yarra near Warburton.'

'Oh, Mr Arvo, I had no idea. We knew you were a man of music, and like my late husband you always have your nose in a book, but really, a botanist. And working with von Mueller! Tell me, what was the name of the herb in your honour?'

'It is a native wild mint, Mrs Sweeney. Von Mueller named it *Mentha Longifolia variation Nuortila*, or in English simply the Nuortila mint, after me, Arvo Nuortila. I must say, to have such an honour even for so brief a time was the final persuasion I needed to settle permanently here. Of course I had to return to Finland to tie up my affairs, but as soon as I could I returned to Victoria, where I am destined now to stay. After all there are no fir trees back in Finland named after me. My family have all passed on. And I was never made so welcome in America. So here I am.'

'Here you are indeed, Mr Arvo,' said Joan Sweeney, obviously impressed.

'But the point of all this, Mrs Sweeney, is not the Nuortila mint as such, but the fact that I may be able to assist you with the naming of the flowers you love so much.'

'Yes, yes, I see, Mr Arvo. But really, I should be calling you Mr Nuortila, shouldn't I?'

'No, Mrs Sweeney. Mr Arvo is my name here at The Grand Hotel and I like it just fine.'

'But now I know the Nuortila name is famous, it doesn't seem right.'

Mr Arvo began to laugh, in a satisfied kind of way. 'Oh no, the only famous name around here is Sweeney, and you well know that. Your courage and hospitality is famous from here to the Glenelg River. And please, now let me return some of your favours and help you with the flowers. Perhaps I could accompany you when you're out collecting one day?'

'Mr Arvo,' said Joan Sweeney, in an ironic tone, 'are you asking me to join you on a picnic?'

Once again the Balt laughed with relish, as he fervently denied any connotations that might be construed from his request. But Joan Sweeney was quite obviously in charge of the situation, and now she set his mind to rest. 'Mr Arvo, don't perturb yourself. Of course I'd be honoured if you'd come collecting in the bush with me sometime soon. And I'd be more than curious to know the flowers' official names. It's a very kind offer.'

In full swing Mr Arvo began naming the flowers right away. 'Well, for a start, Mrs Sweeney,' he said, 'the "tassel flowers", as you call them, in the vase there by the quart of boiled eggs on the bar, they are known botanically as *Thysanotus tuberosus*. In common speech, the fringe lily.'

'The fringe lily,' Joan Sweeney repeated to herself. 'My old tassel flowers, eh? They're lilies. Who would've thought? It makes me wonder what constitutes a lily. Thank you for that, Mr Arvo. I look forward to learning more.'

Tom String could be heard muttering to himself behind the bar now and demonstratively clattering among the dishes. Joan Sweeney called across to him from where she was sitting with Mr Arvo. 'Tom, you'd never believe it but Mr Arvo here had a plant named after him by the Baron von Mueller!'

'The Baron von who?' replied Tom String, gruffly.

'Von Mueller, Tom. The German. The famous botanist.'

'You don't say, missus. So, Mr Arvo, you're a big knob are ya?'

'No, no, Tom, don't be like that,' said Joan Sweeney. 'He's offered to come collecting with me and tell me what the names of these flowers we fill the pub with are. You see, Mr Arvo's a botanist himself.'

'No, no, Mrs Sweeney,' interrupted Mr Arvo. 'As I said, I didn't take my degree in botany, I took it in —'

'Oh don't fret yourself,' said Joan Sweeney, cutting him off. 'You worked for von Mueller and you've had a mint bush named in your honour. That's good enough for us. Isn't it, Tom?'

'Whatever you say, missus.'

'Yes. See, Mr Arvo, we're an understanding lot here. And as I was saying earlier tonight, we value experience of life in The Grand Hotel over university educations any day of the week.

Tom, this is exciting. What was it called again, Mr Arvo? The mint, that is?'

'The Nuortila mint. But it's no –'

Joan Sweeney interrupted him again. 'I think this calls for a toast, Tom, don't you? It's not every day The Grand has a lodger like this. Talk about hiding your light under a bushel! Let's rustle up that leftover champagne from the anniversary dinner and have a Black Velvet to celebrate. Make enough for the girls too. And the lads over there. I know Ding Dong's partial to a nobbler. Well don't just stand there making a racket, Tom String. Set to, old chap. We're going to toast the Nuortila mint. With the man himself, our very own Mr Arvo Nuortila.'

Joan Sweeney's obvious excitement with Mr Arvo's tale of the Nuortila mint was surprising in one seemingly so level-headed – at least it was to myself and Maria as we sat glued to the transistor in The Sewing Room. Tom String grunted unceremoniously as she hurried him along to fix the Black Velvets for the toast. He was nothing if not dutiful and soon the sound of wooden latches could be heard clicking and unclicking behind the bar followed by the sibilant double-cascading sound of stout and champagne being poured into a jug.

I was enthralled by absolutely everything we'd heard since Kooka had fallen asleep, but now I was especially happy to listen as the gang in the old Grand Hotel toasted Mr Arvo's Nuortila mint with the very Black Velvets we had enjoyed so recently ourselves down below in our own bar.

As Bait Belcher, Jimmy and Ding Dong raised the free celebratory drinks to their lips, along with the three whores from Ballarat, it seemed the ice had been broken and that everyone was getting along famously. Everyone except Tom String that is. As his annoyed clattering recommenced behind the bar, Arvo Nuortila began to sing in a rich and formal baritone.

> *The sun still shines, even though you're gone*
> *The wind still rhymes, even though you're gone*
> *The birds still sing, even though you're gone*
> *And nest for the spring, even though you're gone*

Mr Arvo's song was accomplished and strong but at the sound of it Tom's racket seemed to increase even further. In a short voice Joan Sweeney quickly told him to shoosh.

It wasn't long before the shuffle of dancing could be heard on the old hotel floor. Even young Jadey was giggling, with the rag removed from her nose, and amidst all the fun the occasional bleating of the goats, who were still ensconced by the fire, could almost have been mistaken for bestial laughter. Whatever the case the spree in the pub was now well underway, so much so that all the activity ruffled Kooka's feathers somewhat. His face started to twitch and he let out a jovial 'Hoy!' before turning over to face the blaring tranny, which at that precise moment lost its contact with the dream.

Pure static returned to The Sewing Room and we let out a disappointed sigh. For a few moments we waited in hope, but we knew the rub. And when soon after the tranny glitched again and the prime minister's voice could be heard discussing his government's new policy on carbon emissions, we knew the fun was over.

People Are Stupid

WHEN I AWOKE IN THE LOFT OF MY BARN THE NEXT morning, after another measly two hours of sleep, it was to my phone ringing at the bottom of the ladder. Checking the clock radio, I found it was barely 7 am. I hadn't had a call that early since my father used to ring me from the main house to make sure I got up for work on my holidays from art school. He absolutely hated the thought of having a layabout for a son.

My head was pounding from the lack of sleep, and my stomach was queasy too as I stumbled down the old ironbark ladder. I was in such a state of fatigue I had no choice other than to take my time – I'd gone arse over tit down the ladder once before and had nearly skewered myself on a drying fox skeleton in the process. Rushing my descent has never been worth the risk.

Whoever was on the other end of the line was persistent,

so much so that by the time I picked up the receiver I was convinced my old dad had come back to life. I wasn't prepared to rule anything out after what had been going on in The Sewing Room. Such was my surprise, then, when I heard not my dad's voice but a very gruff and muffled, 'Is that you, Noel?' coming down the line.

'It is,' I replied. 'And who have I the pleasure of talking to at this, shall we say, unprofessional hour?'

'Don't shit me, Noel,' the gruff voice now said, and the penny dropped. It was the aggressive tone with the bonafide hint of violence that did the trick. It was Rennie Vigata from out in the Poorool hills.

'Rennie. Sorry, mate, I didn't recognise you. You don't normally call. How can I help?'

There was a silence on the other end of the phone, a silence so long I thought the line had been gnawed at by a possum, but finally, just as I was about to hang up, Rennie said, 'Noel, I was wondering if you'd come out here for a visit.'

'What's up, Rennie? You normally leave the hospitality stuff to me.'

Once again there was silence, but this time I knew to wait. 'Don't shit me, Noel,' he said again, and this time with even more of an edge to his already scary voice. 'I'll see you out here in a couple of hours, okay.'

He hung up, without even giving me a chance to answer. I could've been giving the eulogy at a close friend's funeral that day for all he knew. 'Shit,' I said aloud, standing bed-haired at the bottom of the ladder in my T-shirt. 'That's all I need.'

By nine o'clock, however, I was dutifully backing out

under the pine trees in Kooka's Brumby, with a can of Choke wedged between the handbrake and the seat. The sun was out and after the night I'd had sunglasses were just not enough protection against the glare. I felt each bump as the Brumby rumbled along, eventually swinging inland from the sealed onto the unsealed Dray Road. All the while I was wondering what the hell it was that'd got up Rennie's nose so much that it required a visit.

Rennie Vigata's place is deeply hidden in the hills, in a depression between the two Poorool saddles that back onto the old Victree Pine plantation. You wouldn't know it's there until you actually arrive on the spot and begin to notice the elaborate security set-up, which was installed by his friends in the Melbourne underground when he was sent into exile. No one around our parts knows exactly why Rennie had to go live out there, and you can bet your bottom dollar no one's been game to ask. But when you do finally arrive on the fenceline of his property, you can be mistaken for thinking he's running a kangaroo farm. And that's not because there's mobs of kanga-roos hanging around – it's pretty much all wallaby country out there anyway – it's because his fences are so high that not even a Big Red from out Broken Hill way could jump over them. Added to that there are cameras and spotlights posted every fifty metres or so and at least three teeth-baring Alsatians just hankering to eat both you and your tyres as you drive up to the gate.

All in all it's pretty welcoming, which made me even more curious as to why on earth he'd invited me out there. Back when we'd decided upon his Dancing Brolga Ale as our

Recommended Loosener, I'd suggested a visit to discuss the fine detail, but Rennie wasn't keen. He said at the time that he had to come into town anyway, but I got the distinct impression that his place was off limits to your average punter like myself. God knows what went on out there behind the high-wires, with just him, his girlfriend, Lee, and the dogs. One thing was for sure though: Rennie Vigata wasn't using the seclusion out at Poorool to run an ashram.

I pulled up at the gate, got out of the car and stretched my limbs. Only a few months ago I'd decided to live with a new lightness in my step and to let my imagination run free, and now I was spending my nights listening to an old man's dreams being broadcast over a tranny and my mornings visiting my one and only bulk beer supplier, who just happened to live in what resembled the local concentration camp. It was one of those situations where if you stepped outside yourself and looked in, you might go absolutely bonkers. Whatever happened, I wondered, to my quiet simple life drawing the world I knew and loved?

Through a black speaker hidden among gumleaves to the left of the gun-metal high gates I heard Rennie's voice talking to me from somewhere inside the property. 'G'day, Noel,' he growled. 'When the gates open, take your car up the driveway and park it in the red shed that says "Wood". You'll see my beast in the shed next to it. I'll meet ya there.'

Rennie hung up and sure enough the heavy gates slowly opened inwards onto the property, revealing an innocuous driveway, at the end of which was a two-storey hippy-ish looking timber house with a red Colorbond roof, the kind that was all the rage during the government compensation schemes after the 1983 bushfires. Somehow I'd expected Rennie to have built his own place out there, or to have had it built for him by his gangland philanthropists, but it appeared that once you'd got past the grizzly perimeter of his property, Rennie Vigata and Lee lived on a small Poorool farm just like any other.

I followed his instructions and drove the Brumby up the drive, wondering where the snarling Alsatians had disappeared to. I spotted the red shed, which had a large and very productive looking vegetable patch to one side of it. On the other side of it was Rennie's black vehicle.

Coming down a short path running through a kitchen garden from the house to the vegie patch were Rennie and Lee, dressed in symmetrical blue and black, followed by a white toy poodle and a tortoiseshell cat. They were smiling and waving hello as if I'd just arrived for Christmas. It was all very odd.

I parked the Brumby in the shed. As I got out, the cat was the first to greet me, with a nuzzle against my ankles and a coquettish *meeow*. Rennie and Lee and the poodle followed, and their mood was uncharacteristically bright.

'Welcome to our little patch of paradise, Noel,' Lee said, extending her long arm and smiling.

'Yeah,' said Rennie in his gravelly voice, shaking my hand after Lee. 'Sorry about the short notice, Noel, but I'm glad you could make it.'

Bemused by all the good cheer, I went straight into my usual polite mode, with plenty of 'no worries' and a couple of 'it was good to get out for a drive' type lines. We made our way with the cat and the poodle back up the path through the kitchen garden and entered the house through a screen door under a bull nose awning.

'I'm cooking us all some breakfast,' Lee said, rounding an island kitchen bench in the far left-hand corner of a big living room. Despite the fact I'd cooked myself some greasy bacon on toast before I'd left the hotel, I didn't refuse. I wasn't at all sure my sleep-deprived tummy could handle anything more to eat, but I just couldn't disappoint Lee, whose enthusiasm was that of a woman who rarely, if ever, had visitors to cook for. 'Great,' I said. 'I could do with a bit of a pep-up.'

As the sausages, eggs and bacon fried, and the Poorool field mushrooms were tossed with herbs in a separate pot by Lee, Rennie poured me a strong espresso from a retro Gaggia coffee machine on the bench and bade me sit down on one of two immaculate red leather chesterfield couches that were the centrepiece of the room. He started to chitchat in a way I'd never heard him do before. He talked about a recent burn-off the DSE had done a few miles south of where we sat, and I told him I'd seen the smoke from way back down in the valley. He talked about the bits and pieces of carpentry he was doing around the house and about his 'fog-fed sheep', which he had managed to get an organic classification for and was butchering himself in an old limestone signal-house that stood on the cleared spur of his pasture below the house. He had a vacuum-packing machine, he said, and he'd give me some of the lamb before I left, to trial in the hotel. That got him on to talking about self-sufficiency, and by the time Lee called 'Ready or not', in a sweet angelic voice from the kitchen, he was properly bashing my ear about peak oil.

'I've teed up with this fella over near Beech Forest. He's got a tourist cafe he runs just near that treetop walk. He reckons I can have all the vegie oil he normally chucks, for nix. Shit, he reckons there's so many people goin' through there these days that I'll have more than enough to run the van. You just boil it up – you don't even have to mix it with ethanol if you don't want – and I've got the old digger-arm on the bobcat here to make a pit to store the drums. So pretty soon fuel won't be cheap for me, Noel, it'll be free! I'll be able to drive flatchat right through the fuckin' apocalypse.'

We sat at the dining table talking as Lee brought the plates over, piled high with pork sausages, crispy bacon, toast, mush-rooms, and even a little steamed spinach. There was HP Sauce, tomato sauce, apple sauce, French mustard, English mustard, kelp chutney, Woody's Junction tomato relish, Worcestershire sauce and a selection of home-made jams, marmalades and jellies arranged on the table, all unopened, as if they'd been waiting for my visit.

I said nothing but graciously accepted Rennie's offer of another espresso from the shining chrome coffee machine. And then we all tucked in.

When they'd last been to the hotel for anything other than a delivery of Dancing Brolga kegs, Rennie and Lee had danced all night in a tight clinch to The Blonde Maria and The Connotations. They'd seemed about as dangerous and hot as a couple could get. No one dared to bump into them on the dance floor and at the time I imagined them out there at Poorool, deep in the fog, locked in that very same clinch for months on end. But now, sitting down with them over breakfast, in their sunny down-home living room, they could almost have been mistaken for a couple running a B&B. That's of course if it wasn't for Rennie's unshaven jaw and the scary glint of his coal-black eyes.

Eventually the pleasant chat died off and we ate in silence for a time, with Rennie grinding his jaw noisily to my left and occasionally spitting out bacon rind onto his plate. Lee didn't seem to notice this; she was obviously used to it. There was not a word from either of them about the hotel, not even a 'how's it all going?'.

I broke the uncomfortable silence by venturing, 'Nice snags. And beautifully cooked, Lee. You don't need a job do ya?'

Rennie looked up urgently from his plate and for a brief moment Lee watched him closely. Then she laughed it off. 'Oh, Noel, can you imagine having to drive over those potholes down to Mangowak every day of the week? Nah. Last time we ate at your pub the food was spectacular.'

'Thanks, Lee. But seriously, I wasn't sure if I was hungry until you put this down in front of me.'

'We have a cooked breakfast every morning up here in winter and right through into spring,' Rennie said. 'Warms you up. It's brass-monkey weather up here most of the year.'

'Yeah. So I gather.'

Breakfast was finished off with a third straight espresso from the Gaggia, an Amaretti biscuit each but no further clue as to the reason for my visit. Instead, the little tortoiseshell cat was re-acquainting herself with me under the table and finally got up the gumption to jump onto my lap. 'Marilyn, you naughty little starlet,' Lee said, as she began clearing away the plates.

'She's no starlet, baby, she's a slut,' Rennie said, smiling and sucking breakfast dregs from his teeth. And then, 'C'mon, Noel, I'll show you the brewery.'

We walked out a door at the opposite end of the room to which we came in and now I was struck by the secluded beauty of the property. With no security fences, cameras or dogs on this side of the house all you could see for miles beyond Rennie and Lee's sloping paddocks were the tree-clad hills. Even in the clear sunshine the hills retained their fuzzy lines as they rolled away into the west, one after another, going higher and higher off into the Otways where finally they took on a Himalayan, almost mystic cast.

Off to our right and below were the impressive spur and signal-hut where Rennie told me he slaughtered his sheep. And a couple of hundred metres or so to our left was the eastern fenceline of the property, beyond which it was all national park to the sea. Lower down the slope of this fenceline I could see another shed, not an old bush-pole and tin job like where the cars were parked but a recently assembled olive-green kit-shed, quite large in area, nestled with its back edge up against the national park trees. Rennie pointed to it and nodded. I gathered that's where we were headed.

As we approached from the high side of the shed, I could see a tall stack of wooden warehouse pallets and the bobcat Rennie had mentioned over breakfast, with a forklift attachment on it. Although he had never delivered his kegs to me on pallets, I thought nothing of this detail and was keen to head inside the shed and inspect his set-up. But when we arrived at the door, Rennie paused rather than heading inside. Again I was too timid to enquire as to what was going on. After all a man could meet his maker on a remote outlaw property like that, and no one would be any the wiser.

Now Rennie stared into the mid distance, back up the slope and past the house, and then dug into the front pocket of his jeans and produced a packet of chewing gum. 'Want one?' he asked bluntly. Of course I accepted his kind offer.

'Now, Noel, you're not gonna like what you see in here but I'm showin' you for your own good, okay?'

I gulped, as quietly as I could. 'Okay,' I replied. 'Whatever you reckon, Rennie.'

'It's just that that cunt Greg Beer's been sniffin' around – well, he's been doin' more than sniffin' around actually – and you and me, well, we're both gonna be affected by this.'

'How do you mean?'

He muttered something under his breath that I couldn't make out and then turned and opened the shed door.

For a moment I was confused, as Rennie flicked on the light in the shed. I'd expected to see a brewery set-up, with steel vats, bags of barley, hops, yeast, troughs, hoses, kegs, but instead all I was looking at was a concrete floor covered in pallets full of slab-boxes with the brand XXXX on their sides. Of course XXXX is the traditional beer in the state of Queensland, named in the colony's early days when the Queenslanders apparently couldn't spell 'beer', but what the hell was Rennie Vigata doing with a shed full of it in the foggy Poorool hills?

And then I twigged, in one blinding cataclysmic flash, to the whole disastrous arrangement.

There must have been sixty slab-boxes on each pallet in the shed, and I reckon there were at least a hundred pallets in there, stacked on top of one another. What I was looking at was not a soulful locavore microbrewery but a black-market XXXX warehouse. My jaw hit the floor as the full significance hit me. I turned to Rennie, who was staring at the pallets, chewing aggressively on his sugar-free gum. I said nothing, waiting for him to start the conversation. He wasn't forthcoming. So eventually I said, 'I gather that's not Dancing Brolga Ale there in those boxes.'

Rennie set his jaw, lowered his dark forehead and shook his head solemnly. He started to explain.

It seemed that I'd been taken for a ride, and not just a short ride round the block but back and forth and up and down the east coast of Australia from Victoria to Queensland, and time and time again over the course of the last few months. Rennie confessed that he had never ever brewed one single drop of The Dancing Brolga Ale that the clientele of The Grand Hotel loved so much. The closest he'd come was watching Lee design a phoney logo for it on her computer back in the house. Rennie had suspected that the existence of the logo would put everyone off the trail, and he'd been right. The power of branding had triumphed over the so-called discerning alcoholic palettes of the whole of Mangowak.

That lovely colourful etching of the brolga in full prance, which Rennie now told me Lee had pinched off the internet, and the Dancing Brolga slogan, 'Dance your way to the bottom

of the glass', which they'd also nicked off some poor anony-
mous bush-poet's website, were a stroke of devious genius. The
supposed purity of the marketing had allowed Rennie to take
up an opportunity put to him by an old mate, a fellow crook up
in Brisbane. Apparently this bloke had found a source of more
cheap XXXX than you could poke a stick at. The irony was that
due to the boutique beer market and the modern drinker's pen-
chant for cloudy chemical-free pale ales such as Little Creatures
and Coopers Green, there'd been less of a demand for the old
fashioned XXXX in the last couple of years. The XXXX brewery had begun production of a few different recipes in order
to stay in touch with contemporary tastes but had a little too
much of their old staple XXXX in the warehouse as a result.
Their solution, and very enlightened it was of them too, was to
donate a whole surplus warehouse full of the stuff to various
fundraising charities, and in so doing placate a lot of humour-
less do-gooders left over from the maniacal Temperance Guild
days of the colonies' early years. They shipped this mountain of
old-school XXXX, palette by charitable palette, to an off-site
pre-fab on the edge of Brisbane, where the grateful and surprised recipients of the company's visionary largesse were to
pick it up.

The thing was, Rennie's no doubt omniscient mate got
wind that there was an unwanted lake of beer in a lonely thistle-
bordered warehouse on the edge of Brissy and he decided he
could do everyone a favour by finding it a good home. His only
problem, or so he reckoned, was that the 'good home' needed
to be somewhere well and truly out of Queensland. The first
person he contacted was Rennie. He knew Rennie and Lee had

recently been sent into the Poorool fog to chill out for a while but all he wanted was a lead, the name of someone who could handle it, someone who could get the beer offshore or squirrel it away somewhere lucrative down south. There was a large amount of money to be made, and he didn't want to muck it up by making a false move in a hurry.

Well, as Rennie told me in the shed, the very day after he'd received the call from Queensland someone told Lee down in Minapre about the new Grand Hotel's search for the Recommended Loosener. The light bulb went off in Rennie's head and straightaway he drove the black beast out to the supermarket in Colac and bought himself a few slabs of XXXX. Then Lee designed the logo, they siphoned the contents of the XXXX slabs into two sleek looking Schaefer kegs and entered the entirely fictional Dancing Brolga Ale in our tasting competition.

Well, this was embarrassing. As Rennie unravelled the story for me, I went from pale-faced stupefaction to crimson-faced fury and finally to blushing pink like a virgin. There we had sat, back in the new Grand Hotel dreamtime – myself, Darren, Nan Burns, my brother Jim, Ash Bowen and Joan Sutherland – sipping the very best handcrafted beers Australia has to offer, carrying on with our 'expert' opinions, searching quite puritanically for the beer that most resembled the pick-me-up qualities of a fast running Otway brook. And what did we come up with, after we tasted exquisite coriander and ginger beer from third generation brewers in Gippsland, delicious pale ales from Benedictine monks in Western Australia, highly potent and effortlessly drinkable ales and stouts from the eastern Tasmanian riviera, and clear refreshing lagers from Broome and the Top End? Yep, you guessed it. We awarded the semi-lucrative prize as The Grand Hotel Recommended Loosener to a mass-produced chemical-laden XXXX whose key ingredient was the grain of salt you had to take it with.

And not only did we approve of this bullshit furphy beer then, we'd been approving of it ever since. Talk about a bunch of romantics! Each week when Rennie and Lee would roll up in the black beast full of Schaefer kegs with the stylish aubergine rubber rings on their tops and bottoms, my mouth would salivate at the prospect. And I wasn't alone. The thought of yet another great week in The Grand Hotel drinking beer brewed from the creeks up in the hills behind us was a life-affirming prospect. If anyone had ever cast aspersions on the quality of The Dancing Brolga Ale, either I or Joan Sutherland would've banned them for life. But we never did hear anyone complain. Instead we heard the whole gamut of alcoholic accolades, from traditional Aussie 'you beaut's and 'top drop's to twenty-first-century mumblings about the enigmatic pleasures of *umami* and *terroir*. It had gone on for months, night after night, and now I stood with Rennie, despondent and humiliated in the kit-shed source of the sham.

Or should I say 'scam'? Coz that's what Rennie had pulled off here, and all at my expense. He had made literally tens of thousands of dollars out of me and my pub. The audacity of it was breathtaking.

Spying a stool beside a workbench on the far side of the shed, where thirty or so of those now pretentious looking Schaefer kegs stood waiting to be filled with XXXX, I said to Rennie, 'Mate, I think I need to sit down.' He just nodded gravely and watched as I crossed the concrete floor.

I sat on the stool, leant my elbows on the bench and rested my cheek against the palm of my left hand. I was sitting in the exact same position as the figure in the famous Cezanne painting 'Boy in a Red Waistcoat', except unlike that boy there was no hint of a smile on my lips, only a bewildered gaze. And anyway I'm sad to say that this was no time for art, even despite the fact that Rennie had been so creative. I felt like a fool and I was one. After my redeeming vision of the brolga in the old camp in the bush, I simply hadn't been able to resist a beer by that name. It had all seemed preordained. And now I wanted nothing more than to shut my eyes and for the world to go away: people, beer, paintings, ocean, the lot.

Rennie walked over and feebly, for him, offered me another chewy. This time I refused. I never wanted to accept anything from this hairy-headed gangster ever again. The chewy was probably made from the bone marrow of dead racehorses for all I knew. No, first things first. I had a few questions for him, especially now that I was sitting down and could cope with the potential shock of his answers.

For a start I asked him if he'd ever, at any point in his entire life, had a mother. Automatically his underworld brows lowered at this insult but I could tell he wasn't gonna whack me. I wouldn't have cared if he did. He could've whacked me and whacked me, like a kookaburra whacks a field mouse over a gum bough. At that moment I quite fancied the idea of becoming human pulp.

'So what's this about Greg Beer then?' I asked him next.

'Have you been busted or what? Why have you dragged me out here? Surely not just to finally ruin my faith in humanity?'

Rennie chuckled, through what sounded like a wad of phlegm at the back of his throat. 'People are stupid, Noel. What else can I say? But this Greg Beer bloke . . . he's not a person at all. He's like a fuckin' wolf.'

'How do you mean?'

'He waited, Noel. He waited and he watched. You mad bastards at that pub of yours must've really upset him. That's all I can put it down to. And then finally, by last night, he'd put the whole paperless trail together, from here to my mate's holding shed on a farm in northern New South Wales.'

'What? Did he show up here?'

'No, no, nothin' that obvious. He started at the other end first. If one more drop of beer leaves my mate's shed for my joint, he's gonna nab him good and proper. But that's not really what he wants to do, is it, Noel?'

I groaned, realising what Rennie was implying.

'No,' he went on. 'He doesn't even really care about me either. I might be big fry for some, but not for that dickhead. No, we're talkin' about something personal here, a grudge, a very old and festering wound. He wouldn't know the first thing about taking on the likes of me anyway. I'm just collateral here. It's just you he wants, Noel. And it's you he's gonna get.'

'You know what, Rennie?'

'What?'

'Greg Beer might be a cunt but you're a cunt too.'

'Watch your mouth, Noel.'

'Nah. Why should I? What are ya gonna do? Drown me in a watertank? Butcher me like a lamb down in the signal-house on your spur there? Nuh, I haven't been fed on fog like your dumb sheep, Rennie. I'm even dumber. I've been fed on bullshit. Your bullshit. And now I'm up to my ears in it. He's gonna bust my Grand Hotel wide open, close it down for trading in black-market grog. You and your type might be used to the strip-search every time you go back into the clink but I'm certainly not. Do you hear me, Rennie? Do you realise what you've done?'

Rennie Vigata placed his hands on his hips and snorted in contempt. 'People are stupid, Noel,' he repeated. 'What more can I say?'

'Obviously nothing much,' I replied scornfully. 'Do you think I don't know that? Don't you think that's one of the reasons my hotel is the way it is?'

'Well then catch up, dickhead. Come into the here and now. I never brought you out here to confess my sins, mate. I can tell you I'm well beyond needing to cleanse my soul. I brought you out here coz I like you. And more to the point, so does Lee. So I'm giving you the scoop. That prick's gonna turn up at your pub any minute and blow your talking pissoir and all that other crazy shit away. Do you hear?'

'Yeah, I hear, Rennie. But if you and Lee like me so much, how come you've been selling me bodgy grog all this time?'

Rennie's swarthy face creased into a smile. 'Well everyone enjoyed it didn't they?'

'That's beside the point!' I yelled.

'Is it? You bought it at a fair price, sold it on for a profit, everyone but Greg Beer had a whale of a time, so who cares? People are stupid.'

'Will you stop saying that!'

'Well they are.'

I groaned again. 'Oh, Jesus,' I said despairingly, looking over at the hundreds of XXXX logos repeating on the pallets in front of me.

'Anyway, Noel,' Rennie said, 'the point is you've got an option.'

'Oh yeah? What, on a time-share in Siberia? You specialise in out-of-the-way places don't you, Rennie?'

'Will you stop that cheap shit for a second and listen. I'm serious,' he said, also raising his voice.

'So am I.'

'Okay, fuck ya then!' Rennie shouted, his temper exploding. 'I've got a semi rollin' in here tonight to get rid of all this shit, so I'll be sweet. And because you and I worked on a handshake – coz that's the way you wanted it, if you remember – they won't pin anythin' on me. But you, well, you'll be rooted. You've got this Queensland shit in your pipes and all they'll have to do is take it off to be tested. And no one around here's game enough to give evidence you got it from me. So it'll be your rap. You won't even be able to plead ignorance, you stupid cunt.'

'Oh yeah? Well what if I call the cops in Colac and tell them to come up here tonight to intercept the semi?'

Rennie smiled. 'You wouldn't do that,' he said, in a voice as flat as a basalt plain.

'Why not?'

'Because it would be pointless, that's why not. Do you

think the Colac police don't know who I am, Noel? How do you think I got the permits to have all the security lights on my fences? This is all national park round here and my track's lit up like Bourke Street every night. How do ya think that's possible? Do you think it was a clerical error or something, mate?'

'No, I suppose not,' I said, dejected.

Basically what Rennie was trying to tell me, in his traditionally charming manner, was that the police force was on his side but not on mine. And incredibly enough, it appeared to be true. Either way he was gonna get away with feeding The Grand Hotel hot liquor, so now he was extending an olive branch and offering me protection.

I felt a telltale bead of sweat trickling down my spine. Suddenly this was getting heavy. 'Okay, I'm listening,' I said.

Like all the great ideas in the history of Western culture what Rennie Vigata proposed to me over the next few minutes was quite beautiful in its simplicity. Greg Beer would get a call that same afternoon notifying him of his long wished-for promotion to senior sergeant. He'd be posted to Sydney to take up his new job and a 'friendly' policeman would be appointed as his replacement. If Greg Beer refused the position, his ambitious little career in the police force would be ruined. What was he going to choose, ruining The Grand Hotel over the advancement of his career? Not likely – not Greg Beer. Then, once he was single-handedly sorting out traffic and graffiti problems in the harbour city, Rennie and I would continue our little arrangement until we'd emptied the shed we were sitting in of its contents. Rennie wouldn't take any more deliveries from up north and in the meantime I could settle on a new supplier – maybe that South Australian convent beer that The Dancing Brolga Ale had pipped at the post. Rennie'd turn his full attention to his fog-fed lambs and The Grand Hotel could continue on as if nothing had ever happened beyond an unforeseen change of beer in the tap.

'So what do ya reckon?' Rennie asked, jawing vigorously on his chewy now that he'd laid out his master plan. 'I don't have to do this for you, you know.'

'No, I know that,' I said solemnly. 'And I can't quite work out exactly why you're bothering.'

'Well, put it this way, Noel – it's because I can. A bloke doesn't agree to take the pill and come live out here in the fog like I have without being able to ask important people for a few favours.'

'I see.'

'So?'

'There's no way.'

'What do you mean?'

'There's no way I can do it.'

'You're kidding!'

'Nup.'

'Why not?'

'Because it's not my scene.'

Rennie blew out hard through his nose and stamped a Cuban heel on the concrete floor. 'What do you mean it's not your scene? It is your scene, it's gotta be now, and that's what I'm tellin' ya.'

'You can stamp your foot all you like, mate, but I'm not gonna do it,' I said defiantly.

'Why the fuck not?' he shouted. 'You just agreed people are stupid, the world's fucked up. So what are you? Pure as the driven snow or somethin'?'

I sat up straight on the stool. From Rennie's passionate reaction I was beginning to sense that there was one other thing, one important ingredient in all this that he wasn't telling me. And something, call it an artist's intuition if you like, was telling me exactly what it was.

Feeling quite careless and confident now, I opened my arms out wide. 'What are you getting so upset about it for?' I asked. 'You'll be alright. You'll get away scot-free. And I'll look after myself, thanks very much.'

Now it was Rennie's turn to groan. 'Yeah right,' he said. 'And I'll be out here in the fog doing exactly the same if you don't agree to what I'm askin' you.'

'What the fuck is that supposed to mean?'

'Well put it this way, Noel – it's not much fun for a beautiful young girl like Lee to live holed up out here with no friends but a poodle, a cat, and a pack of Alsatians trained by the police dog unit.'

Aha, my little hunch had been right. Somehow or other Rennie was on his last chance with Lee and I was caught in the sandwich.

'Yeah, that's right,' he said, seeing the realisation of the situation in my eyes. 'She didn't want to have a bar of this XXXX shit. The deal was she'd come out here with me and live behind the gates just so long as we made it wholesome. She's a fuckin' hippy at heart, Noel. She wanted the vegie patch, the organic farming, and I agreed to do it her way. Well I wasn't gonna

394

come out here on me own, mate. Besides, I love her, she's hot.'

He went on, relaxing his grip on the chewy, 'Anyway, when the first truck of beer arrived one night she went properly ballistic. She'd tricked up the logo for the slab we entered in your competition but as far as she was concerned that was just a bit of a lark. I hadn't told her what was behind it of course, what was happening up north. I couldn't. I thought I'd just deal with the problem when it arose, as usual. That's my way. And I couldn't refuse the grog, mate. Not once you blokes down at The Grand had decided to put it on tap as The Dancing Brolga. It was too neat. You were a perfect front. And to tell you the truth, it was pretty amusing as well. We'd go down there to listen to the band some nights and everyone'd be carrying on about the beer. I'd be pissing myself on the way home in the beast, but Lee was dark. Real dark. She kept threatening to leave. She said I'd broken the deal we had and, "If that sweet bloke Noel gets in trouble for this, you won't see me for dust, Rennie Vigata." So now you can see what I'm on about. I don't give a fuck about you, Noel, but I give a fuck about Lee. If she left me, I'd top myself, I reckon. Couldn't live out here on me own. So anyway, that's what I'm so fuckin' upset about, mate. And that's why she's made me fill you in on what's goin' on. She won't hear of my solution to the problem without you goin' along with it. That's why you've got to agree to my plan.'

I wasn't sure whether Rennie was threatening me with that last comment or not, but I knew one thing for certain – I was decidedly uncomfortable about suddenly being the third person in the bed with him and Lee. It felt very cramped. My body temperature was rising rapidly. My skin was beginning to crawl. I wanted out, and *pronto*.

'Look, let me think about it for a while would you, Rennie?' I said, almost gasping for air. 'All this has come right out of the blue.'

'Nah, mate. There's no time. I told ya, the mail's come through only last night. I rang you first thing. The fuckin' sergeant's likely to roll up and bust you tonight unless we do something about it.'

I sighed, running my hand through my hair. The pressure was too much. It was beginning to hit home that if I got busted and Lee left Rennie, then I could be in far deeper shit than losing my hotel. This Vigata character standing there glaring at me in the shed was a murderer; I was sure of it.

'Look, mate,' I said, 'I just can't decide right here on the spot, in this fuckin' shed. I need to breathe. What's say I think about it on the way home in the Brumby and I call you as soon as I get there? It only takes thirty minutes or so. Sound fair?'

Rennie stroked his unshaven chin with his fingers and started hammering his chewy again. He was dubious. 'Alright then,' he said eventually. 'But you make sure you ring me as soon as you get there. Do you hear?'

'Yep. It's a deal. Now for pity's sake can we get out of this bloody shed. I need some air.'

The Valley of Vision

THE DRIVE HOME, ONCE I'D NERVOUSLY SAID GOODBYE AND accepted Lee's kind gift of a jar of blackberry jam, was like no other I've experienced. I've driven the tracks and roads out in those hills countless times but never in such a state of terror and bewilderment.

I drove flat out from Rennie's gun-metal gates until I got off the Poorool saddles and back onto the Dray Road. What kind of cruel twist of destiny was it that had landed me in this situation? I had to wonder. If I said no to Rennie, there was no telling what he might do, but if I said yes then the whole concept of my hotel would be rendered a fraud. I'd be standing there poker-faced behind the bar while the rest of my friends were innocently drinking XXXX and thinking it was The Dancing Brolga Ale. And by the look of how many full pallets there were in Rennie's storage shed, that situation would last for quite a while. What's more, although Greg Beer was a prude and a terrible wowser, I had no interest in becoming the puppet-master at the crossroads of his life. Frankly I didn't want that much influence over anyone's life. Live and let live: that was my motto. All I really wanted was to sit on the old lichened ironstones out the back of the Bootleg Creek and paint some blue air, have a bit of ham and tabouli for lunch and see if I could get the atmos just right.

I really couldn't see how any of it was any fault of my own, except that my seeing the play-acting brolga in the bush had made me susceptible. So, was it just my imagination that had got me into all this trouble? Was it pure sentiment? Well, hardly. I'd also been bloody stupid enough to take on a bloke who needed to live behind high security out at Poorool as my beer supplier. Sure he was local, no matter how recent, and so was the grog – or so we thought – but in the end it was just dumb. And the fact that his relationship with Lee had come to have anything to do with me was debilitating. I felt like a bream who's just been swimming along minding his own business in the river until suddenly *whack*, he's got a shiny steel hook in his mouth, and someone's pulling him towards the surface of the water. If he tries to swim the other way, he's gonna rip his own face apart, but if he just lets it all happen pretty soon he's gonna be drowning in oxygen. Yeah, that's how I felt as I bumped along in the Brumby on my way back to town.

I cursed Rennie, Greg Beer, even Lee. And in the end I cursed my own hopeful visions. I could've cried. Right there on the Dray Road, I could've cried a whole pondful of tears, but I didn't. Instead I laughed. I laughed as hard as any kookaburra but maniacally, tearing along the tree-lined road in Kooka's bespoke Brumby, with the windows down and the wind whistling wildly.

The animals hiding in the roadside trees must have watched stunned as I sped by. By the shallow dam at Termite Junction a man and his young son sitting with yabby-strings in the water nearly got cleaned up as I tore around the bend. They scattered like dotterels at a skiffle-board, only narrowly escaping disaster. By the time I passed the Birdsong Quarry and got up onto Mexico Bend, my laughter was finally stalling into a pathetic series of chuckles.

I came round the fox-coloured bend and saw my home valley laid out in front of me – the green flats, the ridges on either side, the golden headland, the dune hummock, the eel of a river winding seaward to the mouth. It looked so lovely in the gentle December sunshine that immediately I was touched and my laughter disappeared. For the umpteenth time I realised that the perfect scale and beauty of this little valley was my deepest luck, my brightest joy, my most profound inspiration. Its gentle figurative truth had always been the measure by which I compared myself and my actions.

And so it came to me, clean as a fish, what I should do. I pulled over to the side of the road and switched off the engine.

The madness was over. The day went still. I began to cry. I wept long and silent. My tears were the size of dewdrops and they tasted like the sea.

The Mangowak Ode

As soon as I got home, I went straight to the barn and made two phone calls. Firstly I called Rennie but found that the call was diverted and that Lee answered instead. That flummoxed me. I asked her if I could speak to Rennie but she said he was down in the signal-hut doing a spot of butchering. She said he'd taken his mobile with him, but occasionally he lost reception out there on the spur – that must've been why the call was diverted back to the house. I said okay and then rummaged madly around in my mind for what message to leave. I didn't want to give anything away to Lee but I was buggered if I was gonna ring that bastard's farm ever again. I mean, how cocky was he? Telling me to call as soon as I got home and then pissing off to that signal-hut knowing there was a chance his phone would lose reception! He obviously thought there was no way a little wimp like me was gonna say no to his threats. Either that or he was already so enraged by my obstinacy that he had to let off a bit of steam by cleavering a few more innocent lambs.

Eventually I told Lee to tell Rennie that the Beer, with a capital B, was staying put in Mangowak. Not knowing if she knew the exact details of Rennie's plan, I asked her if she wouldn't mind writing the message down word for word, complete with the 'capital B' part. I said it was a little joke of mine and that Rennie would find it funny. I told her he'd probably piss himself laughing, in fact.

Lee was cheery, and her voice over the phone sounded not so much sexy as just plain young. Without the tight jeans and the mascara, you could've mistaken her for some Facebook-addicted gopi girl. Now I understood what Rennie was up against: it wasn't me who was 'pure as the driven snow', as he had put it; it was Lee. And something in him, in some deep, almost forgotten, uncriminalised part of himself, needed that. Desperately. Otherwise his own life was irredeemable and, as he had said, he might just take to himself with his own cleaver down in the fog-shrouded, blood-spattered signal-hut. Having delivered the message, my only chance was that he'd do that to himself before he'd bother doing it to yours truly.

Lee wrote down the message and thanked me; she said Rennie could do with a laugh. I said bye and accepted her offer to come out and visit them again soon. She was keen, she was befriending me – what could I say? She'd find out the real picture soon enough.

The next call I made was to Joan Sutherland. Once again the phone rang and rang before diverting to another line.

Joan, Jen and the kids were on their way back from mass at St Catherine's Convent, and I'd got him on his mobile. 'I want you back at work,' I told him. 'I haven't slept for days and it's all too much.'

There was a pause on the other end of the line, just the sound of the Sutherland twin-cab whooshing down the road. 'Yeah. But, Noel, I dunno if . . .'

'Aw come on, Joan,' I interrupted. 'You've been off for weeks. Just forget her would ya? You're a happily married man. And if you don't get back into the cot with Jen, I bloody well will!'

'Sorry, Noel, what was that? I think we just lost reception there for a tick.'

In the barn I looked into the rafters and thanked the Lord. Until that very moment I'd had no idea I even felt that way about Joan's wife.

I took a deep breath. It seemed the whole grand edifice of so-called reality was unravelling right before my eyes. 'I said you don't have to worry about Maria. She hasn't been downstairs once since the garden party. You won't even clap eyes on her. And plus, it's time you just got over it, mate. I need you.'

The voice on the other end of the line was nervous but chastened now. I was appealing to his better instincts, more precisely to his old fashioned country loyalty. 'Okay, Noely, when do you want me?'

'Today,' I said. 'Before the doors open.'

Now I could hear Joan running it all by Jen in the passenger seat. Then he said, 'Alright, mate, I'll be there.' At which point the reception dropped out for good.

I put down the phone and decided to take a shower. I

stripped out of my sweat and tear stained clothes and under the hot jet of the barn shower found myself thinking of Kooka and his tranny full of magic. Now that The Grand Hotel was under siege from all sides, how could I possibly take it seriously? Surely someone was having a lend. But how? And then again, if things were going to come apart at the seams all I wanted was one more chance, at least one more night, with those dream broadcasts, with that magic. Unlike the rest of us Kooka had sloughed off his worldly skin of cares and worries. His tormented mother and his beautiful wife were now no more or less than ministering angels of the distant heavens. He had become a pure vessel for us, a giver, a mystery solver, a transmitter of the place. In a world so clogged with carnage and doubt and stupidity, this was as rare as gold. And I, being inextricably me, desperately wanted more of it.

Eventually getting out of the shower, I put my purple dress shirt on, with its embroidered chest and collar and its starched cuffs with the crimson cloth cufflinks still in them. This was the shirt I always wore for special occasions – for weddings, baptisms, special birthdays, exhibition openings, boat launchings and the like – and I could think of no more special occasion than the last hurrah of The Grand Hotel.

After dressing, I stepped out of the big double doors, steeled myself, and began to cross the yard. There was work to do, glasses to wash, soft drinks to top up, a menu to organise. In short there was a hotel to run, perhaps for the very last time. The whole thing, upstairs and down, may well have been a fraud, but I resolved that if nothing else I would make this send-off a fair-dinkum hoot.

When I got into the bar, I found Veronica already in there, swabbing the benches and cleaning the glass of the fridge-doors, but with sliced discs of cucumber stuck all over her face. It was an old trick of her Lebanese grandmother's, she said, to keep the complexion fresh, but it reminded me immediately of the surreal masks worn by our Dada heroes on stage back in Zurich at the Cabaret Voltaire. 'It's right up there with Hugo Ball's Piano-Hat,' I told her, smiling.

'Oh leave me alone would you?' she said. 'We've gotta get this done, and if you make me laugh all the cucumber will fall off.'

'Okay, then. I'll be back down to help as soon as I've fixed up Duchamp.'

'Good,' she said. 'Coz I've got a bone to pick with you, Noel.'

I left her to it and went out through the sunroom to orga-nise the day's pissoir recording. As I went, I looked to my left out the louvre windows, half anticipating the sight of Greg Beer's police four-wheel drive rolling up to break the dream. Although the worn grass of the driveway under the pines was empty, the very thought of the sergeant took the spring out of my step. I grimaced, then caught my reflection in the glass. I looked younger than I felt. Taking courage from this, I pushed my chest out like a riverflat kangaroo and kept on going.

Glancing into The Horse Room on my way to the stairs, I spied the old Grundig on the long bench where The Lazy Tenor had left it the night before. I went in to pick it up to take it upstairs to record Kooka for the day's Duchamp, but before I did that I rewound it a little and pressed 'play'. Amidst the clinking of glasses, burping, the sound of Frankie trilling in his cage and the clicking of pool balls on the table, there was The Lazy Tenor's sonorous voice, clear and strong: 'So anyway, as soon as I got in the sedan beside her my mate hit the button on the hoist and up we went. In more ways than one, I might add.'

I hadn't realised The Lazy Tenor had begun to repeat the same stories. He'd been at the hotel so long he had run out of material – that one about him and the chemist girl up on the garage hoist was one of the first instalments of 'The Tradesman's Entrance' we'd ever been treated to. It wasn't funny the first time, let alone having to hear it again. I fast-forwarded straight past it and as soon as the green and red EQ meters went still pushed 'stop', picked up the Grundig, and continued on up the stairs.

When I got to the top, the wide hallway seemed dusty and dry, the ducks still and flat in the weave of the carpet. How depressing! Ridiculously I scuffed at the floor with the bottom of my shoe, attempting to bring the creek back to life. And then I heard voices from behind the door of The Lazy Tenor's room. He and Maria were having a blue. I froze on the spot, with the nauseous feeling I always get when overhearing an argument. Their voices were harsh, his violent and booming, hers sarcastic and shrill. Quickly I stepped out from the staircase and hurried on down the hall.

I found Kooka sitting up in bed, happy as a velvet crab in a February rockpool. The dappled light from the pines outside the window was brocading his crocheted lap and legs. Seeing the Grundig under my arm, he rubbed his hands together and said, 'That time is it, Noel?'

I put on a brave face, no doubt assisted by the relief of being back in congenial company. 'It certainly is, Kooka. I've got a little ripper for you today. It's a poem actually, by a woman from a long time ago.'

Before I had a chance to take the poem from my pocket, however, Kooka put one of his big square-fingered tradesman's hands up and shook his head. 'No, young man,' he said. 'I've been your happy parrot for long enough. Now it's my turn to have a go.'

'What do you mean, Kooka?' I asked.

'Well, I've spruiked all that stuff for you over the last few months and now I've taken the time up here on me Pat Malone to have a go at my own piece for the pissoir. It's a poem too, first one I ever wrote.'

Kooka squirrelled around under the bedclothes for a bit until he produced a scrappy piece of paper that looked like it had been torn out of an old invoice book. Waving it proudly in the air, he said, 'Now hit the red button on the old Grundig, Noel, and give us a bit of shoosh, would you?'

I placed the Grundig beside the tranny on the bedside table, hit 'record' and walked away from the bed and over to the inland window.

The old fella cleared his throat, paused, then announced, in a resonant voice chocked with gravitas, the title of the poem. 'The Mangowak Ode,' he intoned, with his trademark warble, 'by Young John Nugent.'

Looking out the window at the pines, I raised an eyebrow and smiled. What followed became the very last tape-loop we played through Duchamp the Talking Pissoir.

I don't remember the wild streets of St Kilda
I can only speak from the time I was made new
But I understand no happiness can exist
without a mother
So now the bloody fire's gone out, dear Mum,
I want to thank you.
Because life is full of fires like that
And only some are lucky to find love before they burn
When I waltzed down on the beach at the rivermouth
with Mary
There was sea-breezy music in our every step and turn
The way you held me, Mary
The way you let me be myself forever more
Well there was no greater way of loving a bloke
During our long happy life here on the shore.
Speaking of which, now that you've gone
I think it's high time I let you know
The magpies are still singin' of a morning
And the river's still on the go
And every daybreak when I hear those birds
And I look out, either north or south, from my bed
I know the place we love still loves us back
And that I'll see you when I'm dead.
Yes indeed. See ya then my dear.

I waited by the window until I was absolutely certain Kooka had finished. It was safe to say he was no Lord Tennyson but I was very moved regardless. I turned around to find him staring in my direction, eager for a reaction.

'Geez, Kooka,' I said. 'I don't know what to say.'

'You liked it, Noel?' he asked, his bird-face creasing with pleasure.

'I did,' I told him, walking back towards his bedside to press 'stop' on the Grundig.

The old man exhaled with pleasure. 'Yairs, well I don't rightly know what came over me. Never written a poem before. I've always been one for hard facts. But I just woke up this morning with the sky all rosy out over the ocean and the words in my head – the lot. All I had to do was write it down, like a flippin' secretary taking dictation.'

'What a shame,' I joked. 'You can't take any credit for it then.'

Kooka snorted loudly. 'You're a bloody card, son, you really are. I'm past carin' about stuff like that.'

As I picked up the Grundig to take the poem downstairs, I touched Kooka lightly on the shoulder. 'It's a real beauty, old fella. Everyone's gonna love it. You might even have to come down yourself for a piss.'

He shook his head. 'No, no, there'll be no need for that, son. Maria'll empty my pan before she starts out on our novel later on.'

With my heart replenished, I stepped out of The Sewing Room into the hallway to find that once again the creek had come to life. The black ducks swam jauntily along beside me as I headed for the stairs, and this time from The Lazy Tenor's room there was not a sound.

Radios Don't Broadcast Dreams

BY THE TIME I HAD INSTALLED THE LOOP, IT WAS CLOSE to three o'clock and from the bar I could hear Joan Sutherland's big laughter as he, Jen and their two boys had arrived to help prepare for the night ahead. Of course his laughter was due to Veronica's cucumber mask, and as I walked into the bar Jen was painstakingly helping Veronica to take it off. I could see Jen biting her lip as slowly she unpeeled each disc, trying to keep herself from giggling. Veronica, however, was unamused. Seeing me walk in, she said, 'So are you ready for our little chat now, Noel?'

'G'day, Noel,' Joan Sutherland said, cutting in. And then nodding over towards Veronica near the bar sink, he said, 'Glad to see the ol' Grand is still full of surprises.'

Once all the cucumber had been removed from Veronica's face, the Sutherlands set about opening the pub while Veronica and I stepped out onto the verandah and down into the beer garden so she could tell me what was on her mind. We sat on the coloured gymkhana wheels and Veronica's face was so serious that I wondered for a brief moment whether somehow she had found out about the XXXX fiasco.

'Noel, I was talking with Givva Way up at the shop this morning and he reckons you're starting to get beaten down by the powers that be at the shire. He reckons you've started to sell out.'

I made a slow blink and put on a droll face, out of pure exasperation. 'Well, if Givva Way says it,' I said, 'then it must be true.'

As usual Veronica had no ear for sarcasm and continued with her Maoist-style show-trial of my moral and political worth. 'He said that yesterday you collaborated with the shire to have the stoneskimming comp shut down.'

'Yes,' I said. 'Thereby denying his son the chance for inter-national glory *and* denying Givva the chance to waste young Alex's compo money on some ridiculous stoneskimming tour overseas.'

Veronica's lips pursed. 'Yes, well there's selfish motivation in all our actions, Noel, but the point is you've started collabo-rating with the enemy.'

'The enemy? That's a bit strong, Ronnie. All I did was avoid a blue so as not to give Sergeant Beer another reason to shut us down.'

'Aha!' she said. 'So Givva was right. You *compromised*.'

'No, you're wrong,' I said angrily. 'What I did was make sure the future of the hotel wasn't compromised. That's what I did.'

'So are you saying now that any type of behaviour that draws the attention of the police to the pub is off limits? Is that what this means?'

'No, not at all. Just about anything we do at the moment draws the attention of the police anyway. Opening the hotel doors draws their attention. Greg Beer's hell-bent. You can take it from me.'

'Okay, then. So it's about time we started those Grand Hotel Wellbeing Nights we'd planned.'

Veronica was testing me now, seeing how much truth there was in what Givva had told her at the shop. 'Wellbeing' was a word that a lot of us had nailed early on as being a classic example of the Brinbeal shire's corporate muzak. According to their signage and marketing statements, everywhere you turned in our part of the world you came face to face with your own rude health.

The fact that the term had been handed to them on a heavily invoiced platter by a consultant from Melbourne, who in their language had only ever been an *excursionist* in the shire – i.e. *'a visitor who doesn't stay the night'* – and who had driven down from the city when the shire was rebadging itself a few years ago, was never mentioned. Presumably the consultant drove onto the coast road, registered the unnerving sense of space and the tart astringent air, and quickly scanned his bullet lists for the appropriate term: *wellbeing*. In actual fact the consultant was probably feeling something other than wellbeing at the time. Perhaps he was feeling a little *anxious*, a touch *agoraphobic*, a trifle *rushed*, maybe even a little bit *panicky*, but knew himself well enough to understand that these types of edgy feelings usually *translated financially*. When he arrived in Minapre, he would've rustled up a quick laptop precis of his proposal over a strong macchiato and once inside the meeting all the gurus around the board table would've nodded in agreement. The deal, and the language, would have been locked in, as if purposely to irritate those spirits of the past and present whose souls, unlike that of the consultant, will have to dwell in this shire for all eternity.

Early on, when Veronica and I had discussed what we would get up to on the weekly Wellbeing Nights, she'd been full of brilliant ideas. Since then, in her studio up on the cliff, she'd been busily making preparations. For instance, with the shire's neurotic addiction to gardening machinery, they made sure these days that no blade of grass in any public space ever grew higher than ten centimetres. So Veronica had been patiently making what she called 'Mocking Grass', which was basically hundreds of unruly looking wire and paper blades of grass stitched onto sheets of green shadecloth that could be pinned into the soil on top of the shaven shire nature strips and verges. She had a vision of one morning waking up in Mangowak to see her wild Mocking Grass in all the prominent manicured spots. The point would be made and the 'wellbeing' of everyone in the town would be restored by having a bloody good laugh about it.

Our other ideas ranged quite widely, from a large sign at the entrance of the town depicting an oversized Robert Crumb-style rooster declaring war on insomniac weekenders from the city, to our own mock-heritage plaques that we would erect at night on popular tourist walks. These plaques would say things such as Otway Creeks Are Currently Streaming Live or Can Wallabies Buy Real Estate? or The Only Locals Are the Trees. And not only would the humorous effect of our weekly escapades enhance the wellbeing of anyone who came across them (apart from bleary-eyed weekenders and shire officials, of course, and members of the temperance guilds and straight-out wowsers) but they would also stimulate our own wellbeing as perpetrators of the creations. Simply by going out under starlight, we would be lancing old wounds, healing old sores, cathartically curing long-held frustrations. For brief hilarious moments we would achieve a deep understanding of the term wellbeing. And no one would be any the worse off for us doing so.

The sad thing of course was that now, as Veronica raised the possibility of finally getting the Wellbeing Nights up and running, I knew that our whole audacious experiment, The Grand Hotel no less, was doomed. But I couldn't tell her – partly because I didn't know precisely when Greg Beer was going to pounce and also because I knew exactly how the hot-blooded Veronica would react. She'd head straight out to Poorool to confront Rennie Vigata and could get herself killed in the process. Plus I couldn't see the point of ruining everyone's final hours of enjoyment as the hotel descended to its close. So, as if rising to the challenge in her shining brown eyes, I agreed wholeheartedly with getting the Wellbeing Nights up and running – thereby quietening the Givva Way inspired murmurs that I'd sold out – even though I knew very well that it would all now never happen. Sheer delight instantly appeared on her cucumber-shiny face and she hugged me tightly there on the gymkhana wheels and told me how it was all gonna be great fun. 'Yep,' I said, 'I'm looking forward to it too, Ronnie. The Mocking Grass alone will make the whole thing a blast.'

We could hear voices inside the bar now, as the first drinkers started arriving. It was with a sad but invisible stomach-knowledge of foreboding, and a bright and illusory mine host smile, that I walked up the verandah steps and into the bar to greet the patrons.

The crowd grew quickly, and as with Kooka's 'Mangowak Ode' it was almost as if everyone intuited the significance of the day. Craig Wilson, whose 'Gravity Feed' film had been an entertaining contribution to Happy Hour, now approached me from across the room with the idea of us running a Grand Hotel short-film festival. With a frosty glass of 'Dancing Brolga Ale' in his hand he confessed how dubious he had been about my unconventional establishment at first, but now he wanted to show his appreciation of all the good times, to put something back into it. What did I think about the idea of a festival, he asked.

I put an affectionate hand on the shoulder of the ex-real-estate agent and smiled. I liked Craig, but somehow he had missed the point. How could you have a festival in The Grand Hotel when The Grand Hotel was a festival in itself? Once again feeling a mixture of guilt and wistfulness, I told him I thought a film festival was a great idea. He beamed back at me happily and began to knock around a few possibilities. I listened patiently until making the excuse that Joan looked like he needed a bit of a help behind the bar. I left Craig to it.

In actual fact Big Joan was handling things fine behind

the bar, and apart from an occasional twitch of his shoulder and a few darting glances towards the doorway into the sunroom, one could've been mistaken for thinking he'd never clapped eyes on The Blonde Maria or that he'd ever needed to take time off work.

An hour or so later, however, when Happy Hour was bubbling along and the crowd in the bar was spilling out onto the verandah and the beer garden, The Blonde Maria did appear, dishevelled, half dressed, distraught, in the sunroom doorway, and gave Joan the shock of his life. I watched as he stepped back from the tap and valiantly tried to hold himself together. As if on cue Darren Traherne dropped the big mulloway he'd been scaling on the bench and moved seamlessly into Joan's position, pouring Dancing Brolgas for the thirsty customers who were ordering them thick and fast, almost as if they were going out of fashion.

The Blonde Maria didn't even notice that Big Joan was in the pub. She looked wildly around the room, with her hair in a mess, wearing only a lilac bodice with a frilly lace edge and a pair of jeans. Eventually her eyes rested on me where I was standing under the catfish skeleton on the wall, talking to Ash Bowen and Dave Buckley.

She pushed her way through the crowd. 'Noel, he's gone nuts!' she cried out to me as she approached. 'I'm scared.'

'Who's gone nuts?' I said, throwing a glance over to the bar where Joan was nodding calmly while Jen spoke intently into his face.

'That fucking big red-haired bastard, that's who. Louis. The Lazy Tenor.'

'The Lazy Tenor. Why? What's wrong with him?'

'He thinks you and I are having an affair.'

I rolled my eyes. That must've been what they were arguing about when I went up to record the loop with Kooka earlier on.

'He's crazed,' she went on. 'He reckons you and me are out in your barn fucking all night when we're in The Sewing Room listening to Kooka.'

I groaned with dread, as the logic behind The Lazy Tenor's suspicions became clear. It was true that for the last two nights we'd been up till nearly dawn together, but even so The Lazy Tenor's reaction was a bit weird, given that he always gave the impression that as far as women went, The Blonde Maria included, he could take 'em or leave 'em.

'Yeah, well now he wants to kill me, or you, or somebody,' Maria said. 'He's so upset he didn't even sing his aria this morning. Didn't you notice?'

'I was out.'

'Well he didn't – for the first time ever. He was too busy bawling like a baby and then smashing up the room. I don't know what to do, Noel. He's so out of control I'm thinking maybe we should ring the cops.'

Maria, of course, didn't know how preposterous this suggestion was. 'No, no, no,' I said quickly. 'We can't do that. Maybe you should go out for a while, go for a walk or some-thing. Or even better just stay down here with us all night until he calms down.'

Maria looked down at what she was wearing, as if to sug-gest that she wasn't quite dressed for socialising.

'Don't worry about that,' I said. 'You look fine – you always do. But listen, just stay out of Joan Sutherland's way, okay? Otherwise you'll have to handle the problem upstairs yourself.'

The Blonde Maria looked over at Joan behind the bar, who now had his back to the room, washing the dishes. Jen, however, was looking straight at Maria and as their eyes met she had an all-knowing look.

'I don't think that woman likes me,' Maria said, with a hint of the little-girl voice she had adopted during her St Thérèse of Lisieux phase.

Ash Bowen started laughing. 'Oh really, Maria, whatever makes you think that?' he said.

Maria let Ash's comment fly right over her head and promptly asked me if I'd go behind the bar and fix her a drink.

'Okay,' I drawled, a little dubiously. 'What'll it be?'

The Blonde Maria broke into a beautiful glittery smile. 'Well how about one of those ones that Joan Sweeney and the whores were drinking last night? You know, the Black Velvets.'

Ash Bowen and Dave Buckley looked at me, both with querulous grins. I waved my hand at them and said quickly, 'Don't worry. It's a long story,' before making a beeline for the bar to fix us all the drinks.

As I poured the Guinness and champagne into a jug behind the bar, I asked Joan quietly if he was alright.

'Yeah, I'm fine,' he said, with his head bent low over the sink. 'But did she have to come down half dressed?'

When the Black Velvet had settled magnificently in its jug, I took it over to where Maria, Ash and Dave had planted themselves on the pews at the big communal table. Meanwhile Oscar had sighted Maria and wandered over to see if he could convince her to get up again and sing with the band. She hadn't been seen in the bar during the evening for weeks, and Oscar, on behalf of The Barrels, was super-keen.

Maria, however, wasn't having a bar of it. She was more interested in talking to Ash and Dave. They were quizzing her about who this Joan Sweeney was she had mentioned earlier, and who the hell the whores were she'd also mentioned. For a while Maria just played dumb and pretended that they must have been hearing things.

'That's right,' I chimed in with support. 'I don't know what the two of you are on about. You're obviously a bit distracted by Maria's casual attire. Despite the fact that you're spiritually enlightened.'

'No, no,' Dave Buckley said emphatically. 'As comely as you do look tonight, Maria, I distinctly heard you refer to the Black Velvets here as something that was drunk last night by "Joan Sweeney and the whores".'

'Joan Sweeney and the Whores,' repeated Givva Way, as he was passing the table on his way to the bar. 'Good band name that. What do ya reckon, Maria?'

The Blonde Maria smiled up at Givva with Black Velvet foam on her upper lip.

'Seriously, though,' Oscar said, taking his bass plectrum out of his big white teeth. 'Wasn't Joan Sweeney the name of the publican of the original Grand Hotel? The one that Kooka was always on about? The one Big Joan got his nickname from?'

'Of course!' cried Ash Bowen and Dave Buckley in unison.

'Yeah. But, Dave, who are the whores?' asked Oscar. And

then, with a mischievous young grin, 'Or should I say *where* are the whores?'

'Well, you're the muso, Ossie,' said Ash Bowen. 'You tell us.'

After everyone had had a chuckle at this, Dave Buckley, sporting a very fetching Black Velvet moustache himself now, said determinedly, 'Come on, you two. Why were you referring to Joan Sweeney and whores? And what happened last night?'

'Aw, get over it would you, Dave?' I said. 'Surely a spiritual fella like you has something better to meditate on.'

As Oscar wandered off to get ready to go on stage, The Blonde Maria drained the last dregs of her pot glass of Black Velvet and poured herself another. I could see a familiar little rose in her cheeks now. The alcohol was relaxing her, no doubt helping her to forget about the belligerent bloke from Blokey Hollow upstairs.

'Wow, this is a very nice drop, isn't it?' she said. 'You've been hiding this one under a bushel, Noely.'

'Not really,' I said. 'If you hadn't been holed up with your pet project upstairs for the last few weeks, you might have discovered it earlier.'

She smiled meekly. 'You might be right,' she said. And then, with the Black Velvet coursing happily through her veins, she pushed out her breasts proudly and said, 'Well anyway, here's to Mr Arvo Nuortila's mint. Hey? What do you reckon, Noely?'

I couldn't help but laugh. This girl had always had a loose tongue and a playful sense of humour when she got on the grog. It felt nice to have her back in the bar.

'Okay,' I said, raising my glass to deliberately bait Ash and Dave. 'Here's to the Nuortila mint.'

The two of us clinked our glasses, drinking long and deep as Ash and Dave looked on none the wiser. Maria gave a cute wink in my direction. She was beginning to look radiant.

'Well, folks,' I said, 'I've got some tables to clear. I'll leave you with the Black Velvets. You know where the bar is if you fancy some more. I'll let Maria field any more questions you might have about the Nuortila mint, Joan Sweeney or the whores. I'll guarantee you won't get any satisfactory answers though.'

By the time The Barrels took to the stage, everyone was getting well and truly sloshed. It was the biggest crowd we'd had in the pub for a few weeks, and I was sure Greg Beer was gonna show up to shut it all down at any tick of the clock.

People kept coming up to me to comment on 'The Mangowak Ode', and it seemed the more pissed they were the more they liked it. Nan Burns told me she went in expecting another laugh and came out with a tear in her eye. Only Givva Way had any objections to the poem on the loop. He told me in a slurry voice that he'd come to rely on The Grand Hotel to cheer him up, not to drag him down. 'Nah, this joint is losing the plot, Noel. You especially. And as for this band . . . well, they're alright, I suppose, but not a patch on some we used to get comin' through town. Did I ever tell you about the time I smoked bucket bongs with Brod Smith and The Dingoes? Geez, it was unreal, just when they were at their . . .'

I waved my hand in the pissed house-painter's face, not even bothering with the niceties. 'Shut the fuck up would ya, Givva? Or I'll show you the door.'

Givva's jaw dropped in appalled vindication. It was as if he'd caught a ten-kilo fish on a ten-pound line. 'Oh, so that's it now is it? The great pub that never kicks anyone out is barring its most loyal customers! You've lost it, Noel, you've crossed over to the dark side.'

'Yeah, whatever you reckon, Givva,' I said, shouldering past him to make my way out to the sunroom.

Now I needed some fresh air. As ridiculous as he was, Givva had got under my collar. Maybe he was right, I thought, stepping outside into the crisp night of the backyard. Maybe the responsibilities of running the pub had changed me – all the bookwork, the restocking and ordering, having to be social every day of your life. I'd had a lot of help but still the brunt of the place was mine. It even occurred to me that maybe it wouldn't be so bad if the whole thing was shut down. Otherwise it was bound to end up going straight. It was a strange fact after all that I had *collaborated*, as Veronica had put it, with Raelene Press to shut the stoneskimming down. I mean, who cares if the Plinths were being wrecked? If that had've happened back when we opened the hotel, we all would have been throwing twice as hard, me included. Maybe The Grand Hotel was just like any other institution that starts to calcify as it does what has to be done to survive over time. Of course that was the thing about the Dada greats – they did it in a blaze then got out quickly. They were elemental, a passing storm. You never saw Tristan Tzara or Hugo Ball doing Dada Classic Hits Tours down through the decades of the twentieth century. And definitely not my hero Arthur Cravan!

Standing in the driveway now with a head full of such

thoughts, I figured I needed a stroll. I walked out the back, under the pines and onto the Dray Road. There was no one about, either north or south, looking up and down the road. It seemed the whole of Mangowak, but for the sick, the pious, and Sergeant Greg Beer, was in The Grand Hotel. At that moment a cheer went up inside the hotel, and as it did I raised my hand to the night sky as if in a gesture of farewell. A weight seemed to lift from my shoulders. I had surrendered. As far as I was concerned, my time as an unlikely publican was over. All that was left now was to enjoy what was left of the night.

The cheer I'd heard outside on the road was for The Blonde Maria, who with the help of a few more Black Velvets had finally agreed to get back up on stage and resume her career with The Connotations. By the time I walked back into the bar, the joint was absolutely rocking as she strutted her stuff in what suddenly seemed like the ultimate Blonde Maria sex-kitten costume.

The Connotations played a blistering reunion set – 'Stinging Snake Blues', 'Comb Your Kitty Cat', 'You Got to Give Me Some of It', 'Keep On Eatin'', 'The Best Jockey in Town', finishing off with the Shirley Bassey classic 'Diamonds Are Forever'. For this one my brother Jim pulled out his sun-stained old trumpet and played the horn solo under the melody. Maria let her singing kick and soar above the horn. Her voice seemed to have new maturity; she was sounding better than ever. She must've learnt a thing or two by spending all those weeks upstairs devoting herself to The Lazy Tenor's prodigious gift. But now, as she belted out the middle eight of 'Diamonds Are Forever', with her whole heart and body behind the song, she was letting us know she'd been betrayed by that gift and was kissing it goodbye forever.

When the song finished, the crowd in the bar went wild. Maria raised both hands in the air before taking a deep bow. Everyone could feel that she had just got something major off her chest. Big Joan behind the bar was clapping, with a broad smile, no doubt happy that she'd just publicly dispensed with The Lazy Tenor. And like the rest of us he couldn't help but be delighted to have her back on stage with the band.

Of course The Lazy Tenor himself was nowhere to be seen, not even in The Horse Room, which remained empty throughout that last night, as everyone was drawn in by the magnetic atmosphere of the bar. By ten o'clock a few people started to wander off home, so I cut to the chase and declared all drinks on the house. Darren and Nan both came up to me independently and asked if I'd gone stark raving mad, and I said that yeah, maybe I had, but that it had been a bumper crowd with a magnificent thirst and we'd already taken a small fortune.

'And besides,' I said, 'we're celebrating Mr Arvo and the Nuortila mint. Haven't you heard?'

They both looked at me as if I'd just confirmed their suspicions about my sanity and wandered off in separate directions to keep clearing tables.

When the cuckoo clock above the catfish opened its tiny doors to strike ten thirty, we were half an hour past our Sunday night licence. It was as if I was laying out obvious bait for Greg Beer, daring him to come and shut down the fun. Little Dougie, the youngest of the two Sutherland boys, had got up on a stool behind the bar and taken over from his dad behind the tap. He'd been well brought up – for an eight-year-old he was pouring a pretty damn fine illegal beer. Next to him his mum and dad were busy pouring the Black Velvets, Jen on the champagne side of each jug and Joan on the Guinness side. By this stage I was getting stuck into it myself and remained unaware of the whisper going around the bar concerning The Blonde Maria's drunken confessions about what had been taking place in The Sewing Room every night.

Before long Ash Bowen and Dave Buckley had cornered me over near the fireplace and demanded I tell them it was all lies. That put me in a dilemma. On the one hand I didn't want to say anything because I knew their curiosity could potentially threaten whatever dream Kooka had in store for us that night, but on the other hand, given that I'd just surrendered out on the road to the night sky, it seemed as if this wider awakening to Kooka's magic tranny was simply written above. In the end, and in the true spirit of Dada, I decided to deny nothing.

Ash and Dave were incredulous and derisive, saying it couldn't possibly be true. I laughed and proceeded to tell them what I knew about the visual capabilities of goldfish. 'There's stuff all around us here that we can't see,' I said. 'But meanwhile the humble goldfish can. It sees well beyond us, right into the ultraviolet spectrum. So who knows the things that are swirling about if we'd only open our hearts and minds. For supposedly spiritual men you two are pretty damn materialistic when it comes down to it.'

By eleven o'clock there were only a dozen or so of us left in the room, and Kooka's dreams were all that anyone was discussing. Now I was afraid that with Maria still down in the bar with us it was getting too late and that Kooka may well have already fallen asleep upstairs. At the very least he'd be wondering what was going on. So I called everyone, the two Sutherland kids included, over to the pews at the communal table, and Maria and I began officially to fill them in.

First we told them about Kooka's mother, about his wife, Mary, and how initially the dreams broadcast through the tranny were about them. Now that they'd all sampled 'The Mangowak Ode' on Duchamp countless times, this was at least half familiar information. Then we talked about Joan Sweeney and her publican's lists in the waves and then about Tom String, the ride in the cart with the reef-coal, and Mr Arvo, before clearing up the mystery of the Nuortila mint. We talked about the whores of the previous night, about Cumquat May, Jadey and Rose, and how Joan Sweeney had a way of telling the authorities what they wanted to hear and then continuing with what she thought was best regardless. We even told them about Ted the Scotsman being kicked out of the hotel for talking disrespectfully to the whores, and also about Bait Belcher and Ding Dong.

By the end of our descriptions, it was clear to almost everyone that we couldn't have made it all up. Certainly it was hard to believe but no one was point-blank sceptical anymore except for Givva Way, my brother Jim, and young Dylan Sutherland. Givva was a perpetual naysayer and perhaps his fetish for the stories of days gone by just couldn't cope with this ultimate double-barrel hit. Jim was not quite as dismissive but was convinced that his little brother was busy pulling one god-almighty hoax; whereas Dylan was very matter of fact, as eleven-year-olds can be, saying straight out that the whole thing was impossible because 'radios don't broadcast dreams'.

A Never Ending Echo

GATHERING UP OUR DRINKS, AND A FEW EXTRA BOTTLES of wine, there was no alternative now but for us all to climb the stairs and wait till Maria's bedside reading lulled Kooka into sleep. Then, one by one, everyone could ever so quietly tiptoe into the room and sit down on the floor around the walls outside the bedside pool of light so that if Kooka woke up he wouldn't see them. Any doubts I had about this invasion en masse of Kooka's dreaming space were dismissed by the overwhelming destiny of the moment. I felt sure that the tranny broadcasts had gone beyond the privacy of an old man's retrospecting heart. Surely now this was a history we all had a share in.

There was only one difficult matter I wanted to clear up first, and that was Givva Way. Well, he wasn't called Givva Way for nothing. I felt sure that if Givva was allowed into The

Sewing Room to listen to the dreams, he was bound to find a way to ruin everything. Either he'd drop a glass or trip over or even shout out some contrary piece of nonsense from where he was sitting against the wall. He might even just take it upon himself to wake Kooka up and protect him from the eavesdroppers. Either way he would, as he always did, find a way to put his foot in it, and we couldn't run the risk.

Taking him aside as everyone went off to have a final leak before what could be a long night, I told him I didn't want him upstairs with the rest of us. Naturally enough, he was outraged. After pleading with me for a while but getting nowhere, he threatened to stand outside in the backyard and throw stones at the Sewing Room window. 'That'll sure wake him up,' he said triumphantly.

He had me stymied. It seemed the lesser risk now was to let him come. But I made him swear, on the ghost of all the great bands that had played in Mangowak in the 1970s, that he wouldn't act up. He agreed, solemnly, then smiling like a winner went off through the sunroom for a last piss on Duchamp.

We assembled at the bottom of the staircase like a select group of novitiates waiting to be inducted into a sacred form of knowledge. I suppose the only difference between us and a group of novitiates was that we were all, except for Dylan and Dougie and their mother, pretty bloody drunk. I noticed that Joan was keeping himself way back and away from The Blonde Maria, who already had one foot on the stairs and was about to lead us up. I also noticed that Oscar had produced an iPod out of his pocket to which he was busily fixing a little black microphone. I placed my palm over the light from the iPod screen and said, 'No, Ossie. I don't think that'd be wise.'

Oscar looked surprised for a moment but then nodded his head sagaciously, saying, 'Oh, of course, Uncle Noely, sorry. It might affect the reception.'

As quietly as fourteen people in various states of inebriation could, we began to climb the hotel stairs, with The Blonde Maria up front and myself right behind her. On the erstwhile ironbark my grandfather had used to build the staircase all those years ago the twenty-eight feet of our drunken party played all kinds of creaking bung notes as we ascended.

When we reached the top, it was quiet on the creek, with just a light breeze rustling in the wallpaper willows. For a moment we all paused, milling about near the banister rail, partly no doubt to prepare ourselves for what was to come and partly because of the mercurial watery light of the old hallway globes.

From The Lazy Tenor's room there wasn't a sound as one by one we stepped gingerly out among the carpet ducks and platypi. I went first, with Maria, Ash Bowen and Oscar just beside me, Oscar still with his bass plectrum between his teeth. Nan Burns followed, with Jen, Big Joan and the two boys. My brother Jim, Darren Traherne and Dave Buckley came next, with Veronica and Givva Way following. As I looked back over my shoulder, I saw Darren thrusting his nose in the air, as if sniffing for fish swimming past on the current downstream. And behind him Givva Way was peering with concern down at his shoes, as if they were being ruined by the imaginary waters of our very own indoor creek.

Before the hotel had begun, none of them could ever have expected to have seen what they'd seen, heard what they'd heard, and been exposed to so many unlikely experiences. The pleasures had been immense, the surprises had been incessant, and now this unwitting education was having the desired effect. A hush came over the crowd as we approached the Sewing Room door, and I sensed that even the doubters were thinking again. No one said a word. I was sure they understood now, perhaps for the first time, that anything was possible in The Grand Hotel.

It was an exciting moment, with us all full of anticipation, but it was always in the back of my mind that Greg Beer might turn up when we least expected it. As we arrived at the door, Maria carefully clicked the waggly old doorknob and the two of us went inside, leaving the others to wait, just as we'd planned. We stepped into The Sewing Room to find Kooka in high spirits, though a little miffed that we were both so late.

'By the sound of it it's been a big night down there,' the old fella said. 'I was beginning to think you'd forgotten all about me.'

Maria sat down in the wicker chair and opened the book on her lap. Kooka for the moment couldn't keep his eyes off her cleavage. Not only was her lilac undergarment very low-cut but it was also made of a lightly elasticised silk so that her nipples were pert and prominent. I saw the old man swallow hard with pleasure as she began to read George Santayana from where we'd left off the previous night.

Since there was nothing doing and the flat shore was not very
interesting, Oliver had stretched himself, with his hands
behind his head, on a bench that partly surrounded what
in a small yacht would have been the cockpit and in a great
ship the quarter deck. In the Black Swan *it was something*
betwixt and between: a part of the after-deck, between the
Poop and the cabin skylight, over which, when they were in
port, an awning could be spread, and even a rug with some
wicker chairs and a table; for this boat was no racing toy, but
a floating bungalow, yet not meant to lie half hidden under
the willow branches of some inland back-water; rather to sail
sturdily from sea to sea, and be a home for the hermit at the
ends of the earth.

As Maria read, Kooka closed his eyes so as not to be distracted
by her dishevelled beauty. As a consequence it wasn't at all long
before he raised his hand for the nightly instalment to finish. It
was late after all; the old fella was obviously very tired.

Of course we were very thankful for this, not only because
of the others waiting at the Sewing Room door but also
because, in her now-drunken state, Maria was having great
trouble reading without slurring the words. As she gratefully
closed the pages of George Santayana, I slowly leant across her
to the bedside table and switched the tranny on.

Three commentators were discussing the long-forgotten
sketchbooks of the Australian artist Jean Gullyside. Two of
them were gushing about her position in the 'outsider art' and
'brute art' movements while the other one was dismissing the
Gullyside sketchbooks as 'purely psychiatric'. Now this was the

first discussion I'd heard on the radio for months that interested me, but I couldn't believe the timing. I was suddenly caught between not wanting Kooka to fall asleep and send the tranny into static and, of course, wanting him to very much.

For better or worse, however, I could see Kooka showing the telltale signs of sleepiness where he lay under the crocheted rug. Our plan was that when (or if, as we still couldn't be absolutely sure that the broadcasts would continue) the static began, we would use it as sound cover to let everyone quietly file into the room. We just had to bank on the fact that the static would last long enough for this to be achieved.

As I say, I was torn, as on the tranny the two commentators went deeper and deeper into their appreciation of Jean Gullyside's work, the sceptical third commentator out in the cold. Eventually, as the discussion turned to the possibility of staging an exhibition called *Scrawl*, devoted purely to Australian works done in coloured pencil, old Kooka finally crossed over and the tranny spluttered before going completely silent.

Maria and I looked at each other, concerned. All we could hear were the frogs in the night, and beyond that the hiss and occasional crash of the ocean down at the rivermouth. There were no Plinth bells, and looking up to the tiny window high in the western wall it was blank, with no bogong moth trying to get in to the light, just bare cold glass and the unpainted sheoak sill.

We sat frozen in our chairs and waited to see what would happen. On the pillow Kooka's closed eyes had narrowed his brow into a furrow. It was a look of concentration, even though he was asleep, as if the dreaming kookaburra on the branch had once again spotted his prey. Eventually his face relaxed into a deep pleasured smile as someone out in the hallway bumped lightly against the door. At that very moment the tranny burst back into life; well, into the raucous half life of oceanic static anyway.

Carefully I got off my chair and tiptoed to the door. This was the moment we'd all been waiting for. Turning the knob, I found my friends just as I'd left them, waiting patiently and attentively, proving that it doesn't always take a bucket of cold water to sober people up. Between them they had drunk a lot of Dancing Brolgas and a lot of Black Velvets that night, but no one had the giggles and no one was throwing up. It was only The Blonde Maria back on the wicker chair next to Kooka's bed who was showing signs of being a little worse for wear.

First Nan then Darren stepped up and quietly entered the room. Under directions they stuck close to the eastern wall, well away from the pool of light, before rounding the northeast corner and lowering themselves to sit on the floor under the inland window. Carefully then Joan Sutherland and his dairy family came in, Dylan and Dougie obviously enraptured by the late-night adventure; I winked at them all as they stepped past me in the doorway. They turned right along the eastern wall in the same direction as Nan and Darren. Finally came Ash and Dave, Jim, Oscar, Givva and Veronica, again under my directions. These six entered the open Sewing Room door and headed the other way, to the left along the eastern wall, towards the ocean window where the lump of Kooka's boxed-up archive sat inert and shadowy in the dark. I watched as the silhouettes of Ash and Dave crossed in front of the ocean window before they sat down with their backs against the boxes of the archive. Jim and Oscar followed them and sat under the window while Givva and Veronica sat on either side of the southeastern corner of the room.

Thankfully the static continued as I gently closed the door on the creek and made my way back to my chair. Kooka's sleep had not been disturbed and the knot of pleasure on his face seemed if anything to have deepened since I had got up to let everyone in.

Minutes passed. Still the static reigned, and I feared it would be the two Sutherland boys sitting with their parents on the wall behind me and to my right who would grow impatient first. They were only kids after all.

I needn't have worried. What followed next most definitely kept their interest. As the shape of Kooka's mouth opened into a perfect O, the static ceased on the tranny, to be replaced by the solitary pleasure of Tom String.

He was obviously out in the bush because the first sounds we heard were the ratcheting and sawing of nearby wattlebirds in the trees. Then the charismatic song of a dusky woodswallow and the flow of a river nearby. And then Tom String's voice, in a tone Maria and I had not heard before, groaning with pleasure. We could hear a bright rhythmic sound too, of liquid and skin squelching, and it became clear that we were listening to him masturbating.

Immediately I was wondering what everyone in the darkness against the walls was making of it, and in particular I could sense Jen Sutherland's disapproval that her boys were in the room. Tom String's groans became more fervent, until they turned from just sounds of sexual pleasure into words of pure devotion. 'Aw, missus . . . they're like raspberries . . . so pink and right. Can I juice them, here, in my teeth, like this? . . . oh yes . . . and feel here, put your lovely lady's hand on big Tom String . . . oh yairs . . . oh, my sweet missus . . . Joan . . . and slip 'em off . . . oh missus, that's right . . . look at that . . . it's you, oh . . . how do ya do? . . . let me . . . touch . . . oh . . . oh . . . your arse, your lilywhite arse . . . oh yes, and there it is . . . oh, like silk, like a silk purse . . . can you feel that? . . . oh yairs . . . the full . . . yes it's good . . . and you . . . you're good . . . I love . . . oh . . . Joan . . . aw . . . 'ere . . . oh . . . oh, missus! . . . missus! oh, *fark*, *fark*, oh *faark*, aw . . . yairs . . . I love . . . oaaah.'

With a huge exhalation Tom String arrived at his destination and his voice descended into a soft vulnerable whimpering. His ecstasy stilled. In front of us Kooka hadn't moved but the O shape of his mouth had closed and the look of intense pleasure had exchanged itself for the usual impervious peace of a sleeping face.

Maria looked over at me, her eyes bright with surprise, as if to say, 'We weren't expecting that!'

She was right; we weren't. The half Aboriginal ex-stonecracker's love for a barrister's widow was a love played out alone, and it ended in a sound almost like sobbing. My heart couldn't help but go out to him.

In the deep stillness after Tom String's whimpering finally ceased, a crow called from somewhere out in the day, a slow lazy *raark* that echoed in the air, followed by another *raark*, and eventually, after almost a minute of silence, another. Then, from below where Tom sat, came a sound I'd heard before. It was unmistakable: the rough bark of the brolga – first once; then twice; and then it made a fibrillating kind of clucking sound. I shivered, realising in a flash where Tom String was: on the ironstone rise above his upstream brewer's camp, where months ago I had found myself laughing for joy at the wondrous dancing brolga. But before I had a chance to dwell on the implications of this, other human voices began to be heard, and the light tinkling of metal. Then a bell, yes, unmistakably a bicycle bell.

In the Grass-Tree Glade

IT WAS A MAN'S VOICE, AND A WOMAN'S, AND AS THE FOCUS of Kooka's dream left Tom String on the ironstone rise it became clear that it was the voices of Mr Arvo and Joan Sweeney we were hearing, as they were preparing to set off from the hotel for their picnic.

'I hope you approve of corned silverside, Mr Arvo,' Joan Sweeney was saying, 'because that's what was left over and I've used it for the sandwiches. We've got fruit as well, of course – apples and peaches – and Tom String smoked an eel. Plus I took down two boiled eggs from the jar in the hotel bar and some peanuts. And I brought two bottles of Native Companion Ale, which I thought we could share.'

'Oh that's all very kind of you, Mrs Sweeney, but I didn't think you drank alcohol?'

'I don't. Not as far as the hotel is concerned. It's challenging enough being a publican out here without getting slipshod on the grog. It's the number one rule for the lady hostess: don't drink with the clientele. You'll get yourself into all sorts of trouble.'

'I see.'

'Yes, but today you're not so much clientele, Mr Arvo, as my guide to the bush. So I thought a glass of Tom String's beer might be nice.'

'Well I'm honoured, Mrs Sweeney.'

'Don't be. I can assure you my motives are selfish.'

With their picnic basket strapped atop the back wheel of Mr Arvo's bicycle, the publican and the musical botanist pedalled off from The Grand Hotel. Joan Sweeney was the navigator and on her instructions they headed inland across the riverflat on the Dray Road.

From behind me, on the wall to my left, it was Veronica who gasped audibly at this first mention of a local landmark that still exists to this day. Of course I could well understand her excitement but raised my hand above my head in the pool of light to remind her not to make any noise. The last thing we wanted now was for Kooka to be awoken.

As Joan Sweeney and Arvo Nuortila headed along the bumpy Dray Road, we could hear the spokes and guards of their bicycles rattling, as well as the cascading chirrup of wagtails and the chuckles of honeyeaters in the bushes as they passed. It wasn't long before they had found their way, on a track Joan Sweeney called 'The Blackboys', into the hush of the trees. Then, riding into an open sounding glade, they stopped their bicycles and Mr Arvo explained that the plants by which the track had got its name (and which these days we call grass-trees) were actually called *Xanthorrhoea*. 'With an X,' he told her.

'*Xanthorrhoea*,' Joan Sweeney replied happily. 'What an unfortunate name. It rhymes with diarrhoea.'

It was an inauspicious beginning to their botanical lesson but both of them were nevertheless amused. Mr Arvo laughed and said, 'I didn't invent these names, Mrs Sweeney, I only learnt them.'

'Mmm,' Joan Sweeney replied, a little unconvinced. 'Well anyway, shall we leave the bicycles here and take a stroll? I'm sure there are more pleasant names for the flowers all about.'

Resting their bicycles in the grass-tree glade, their footfalls became audible as they ranged off into the bush.

'What you call "palm" is actually "bracken",' Mr Arvo was saying, for the benefit of his host. 'I've seen the way you so cleverly set your flowers in the vases among it. It is also known by its Latin name, *Pteridium*.'

'I see,' said Joan Sweeney, with a hint of embarrassment in her voice. 'I suppose the resemblance is why I called it "palm". No one else does around the hotel. But you see it always reminds me of Egypt.'

'Have you been to Egypt?' Mr Arvo asked, surprised.

'Oh no,' Joan Sweeney replied. 'But my husband promised to take me there, just before he died.'

'You must miss him,' Mr Arvo ventured.

'My husband? Oh no, Mr Arvo. We didn't get on. Though I still have his suits in camphor and pepper in the bottom drawers of my bedroom dresser.'

Perhaps deeming it wise to change the subject, Mr Arvo said, 'Do you see the tiny pale crimson spray there? Underneath the acacia?'

'Yes, of course,' said Joan Sweeney. 'It's the Cheery Bell.'

'The Cheery Bell,' Mr Arvo repeated mildly. 'Well here's a case in point. That, Mrs Sweeney, is your state's floral emblem.'

'The Cheery Bell?' Joan Sweeney exclaimed, delighted. 'Victoria's floral emblem?'

'Yes indeed. Although I'm sorry to inform you that no one else would know it by your charming name.'

Joan Sweeney laughed. '*Touché*, Mr Arvo. But alright then, go on. Tell me what my husband's friends in Government House call the poor little darlings.'

'The flower is known by the name of *Epacris*, Mrs Sweeney. Or in pure Linnaean Latin, *Epacris impressa*. Not to be confused with the similar looking Spanish heath, which is also known by its Latin name as *Erica lusitanica*, or the Erica heath.'

'Erica heath,' Joan Sweeney replied, once again delighted by this outdoors education. 'Well, that's a lovely name for a woman. And I knew an Erica once. She was just a tot. The newborn child of a friend of mine.'

'And was she named after the flower?' Mr Arvo enquired.

'Well, if she was, no one informed me,' Joan Sweeney replied, with a youthful giggle.

They wandered through the undergrowth chatting like this for at least half an hour, in which time Mr Arvo corrected Joan Sweeney's names for many other flowers. These included *Comesperma volubile*, *Imperata cylindrica*, *Acacia verticulata* and *Kennedia prostrata*. The last of them, the small pea-flower she called The Burnt Tongue, because of its tongue-shaped leaf and its burnt looking russet tone, was called *Canaliculata*. Joan Sweeney burst into more girlish laughter at this and would only explain why after much cajoling by her guide. 'Say it slowly, syllable by syllable, Mr Arvo,' she instructed. 'Can-a-lic-u-lata? See? It's very rude.'

Mr Arvo, worldly and confident by temperament, was audibly titillated by Joan Sweeney's pun. 'Oh my dear, you are right,' he said. 'They didn't mention that back in the Baron von Mueller's herbarium!'

'I bet they didn't,' Joan Sweeney replied.

Later on, when they'd made their way back to the grass-tree glade and had spread their picnic rug and laid out their food, Joan Sweeney asked Mr Arvo what it was like to have a herb named after him.

Chewing very deliberately on the silverside sandwich, the Balt thought for a moment before saying, 'Well, I suppose it was quite a feather in my cap for a time. But only for a time.'

'Why?' asked Joan Sweeney. 'Why only for a time?'

'Well, as I was trying to tell you the other night in the hotel, the Nuortila mint only actually existed for a short period of time.'

'What do you mean, Mr Arvo? Has it become extinct?'

'No, no, no,' he laughed. 'No, nothing like that! Unfortunately what happened was I fell out with von Mueller over my praise of Mr Guilfoyle's approach as the superintendent of the Botanical Gardens in Melbourne. Mr Guilfoyle has done a superb job as superintendent but at the time of his appointment Baron von Mueller was most upset at being replaced.'

'I see. And you are a supporter of Mr Guilfoyle's?'

'Oh, it's not so much a case of taking sides, for I am a great admirer of the baron. It was just that . . . well, yes . . . I felt, like others did, that the Melbourne gardens had benefited from a fresh approach. In his time as superintendent the baron's model was Kew in London, which as a repository for plants from all over the known world is splendid. But what Mr Guilfoyle has achieved in his new landscape in Melbourne, the way that he, with the engineer Catani, has adapted the river to suit his purposes, and the new picturesque roll of the ground, has brought so much happiness to so many.'

'So are you telling me, Mr Arvo, that the great Baron von Mueller was petty enough to hold a grudge? And to strip you of the honour of having the native mint named after you?'

'Yes, Mrs Sweeney, I suppose I am. The Nuortila mint is now simply known as the Warburton mint, after the place where it was found. Curious isn't it?'

'Curious!' Joan Sweeney cried. 'That's putting it favourably, Mr Arvo. But upon reflection I can't say I'm really that surprised. The authorities, Mr Arvo, otherwise known as "men of importance", from my experience are rarely to be trusted. Their supposed discernment and loyalty must always be taken with a grain of salt.'

'Ah,' said Mr Arvo, *'cum grano salis?'*

'I beg your pardon?'

'Cum grano salis. "With a grain of salt". One of my favourite of the Latin maxims.'

The familiar clink of heavy glass could now be heard as Joan Sweeney produced the bottles of Native Companion Ale from the picnic basket and proposed a defiant toast. There was no slosh, however, of the beer being poured, only the squeaking of two corks and then the glassy tink of the toast. Mr Arvo and Joan Sweeney were obviously drinking straight from the bottlenecks as they celebrated the afterlife of the Nuortila mint.

Their lips came away as they finished their initial swig. They both gasped with breathless satisfaction at the impressive carbonation of Tom String's beer.

'It's odd to see a lady such as you drink from the bottle,' Mr Arvo remarked.

There was a brief pause, in which Joan Sweeney could be heard taking another swig. Incredibly she then burped deeply, apologised lightly, and said with an unmistakably flirtatious air, 'Well, even ladies can be bold in the bush.'

It was now Mr Arvo's turn to take another gulp of the Native Companion, which he did in what seemed like an awful hurry. He was either embarrassed by Joan Sweeney's teasing remark or just plain excited.

'It's true what I say about the powers that be, Mr Arvo,' Joan Sweeney went on. 'I lived with one of those men for the twelve years of my married life. I watched him free cold criminals at the bar and put innocent men in jail. I watched him amass a sizeable fortune with his land claims out in the west here while having Tom String's countrymen shot, or poisoned by the arsenic in the damper. Of course when my husband died, I inherited that fortune. And the blood that was staining it. Only recently I wrote a letter to the authorities rebutting their disapproval of the way I am running The Grand Hotel. Nearly every word I wrote them was a lie designed to intimidate, in my husband's name – the respected Sweeney name. But did you know, Mr Arvo, that the Sweeney name is most famous back in Ireland for the proud warrior who long ago, having thrown the supposedly holy book of the occupying powers into a lake, was turned into a bird and condemned to eke out an existence in the treetops of the wild west coast?'

'No, I did not know that, Mrs Sweeney.'

'Well that's how I see my life as a widow, and the burden of the Sweeney name.'

Mr Arvo, buoyed up by the obvious passion of his hostess, and the beer, proposed another toast. 'Well, here's to you then, Mrs Sweeney. You are a remarkably singular woman indeed. And now I learn that you are also, according to Irish tradition, quite literally the bird in the bush.'

Joan Sweeney, however, wasn't quite finished. She took a brief slug of the beer and said, 'Oh yes, and that's why I run my hotel as I do. I make sure the men around here have what they need to make them happy and I care little for the so-called *consequences*. The Grand Hotel's been great while it's lasted.'

'Yes indeed, Joan, if I may call you that. But why talk as if its days are numbered?'

'They are, Mr Arvo, they are. As are all our days. I don't for one minute expect the hotel inspectors to be dissuaded by my letter to them. This has been quite a protracted correspondence. I'm expecting them to arrive any day now to close us down.'

'But didn't you say that the appointed sergeant from Ballaarat wasn't well enough to make the ride?'

'I did, Mr Arvo. But that old cripple won't be the end of it. There were some in Port Phillip aghast when I left Melbourne to come out here to run The Grand. Eminent friends of my husband's who were appalled to see his money spent like that. They had always tolerated me in society, while he was alive, but almost entirely for his sake. And I suppose because I was his charming, attractive – and much younger, I might add – wife. I was naive at first. But now that he's dead and I've declared my intentions, there'll be no more special favours for this bird in the bush!'

'From the picture you paint, it sounds as if it's been an achievement to have run The Grand Hotel for this long.'

'Oh I'd like to think so, Arvo. Thirteen years out here is not to be sneezed at.'

'Indeed!'

'But I have enjoyed every minute of it, in a way that those eminences back in Melbourne would never even begin to understand. To slip out of the corsets of town and swim freely in the waves of Mangowak has been my joy. My most excellent freedom.'

A lone magpie started warbling in the trees around the glade. The voices paused, presumably to hear the song.

Eventually Arvo Nuortila sighed deeply. 'I understand that freedom, Joan. I really do,' he said, with increased fervour. 'Unlike yours my fortune is not bloodstained, and yes I have briefly had a mint named after me, but the spiritual wealth I've found in my freedom in this country has been my greatest boon. I caught a glimpse of that freedom on my first visit here and I came back to do nothing other than be fully alive! To study life, to examine it in the river and on the shore, to fish for my food, to read the great works and to sing my songs in clean air. Unlike you I have never married, but I have had my disappointments in love. It is inevitable I suppose. But I am gratefully alone now, thankfully alone, in that I come and go as I choose. One can never know when one shall be called from this life to the next.'

'That is true, Arvo,' Joan Sweeney replied, obviously moved by this speech of Arvo Nuortila's. 'And you put it so eloquently.'

Once again they both enjoyed a refreshing swig on their bottles, and Joan Sweeney made Mr Arvo take a slice of the expertly smoked eel. As he chewed, he murmured in satisfaction, and when he'd swallowed he began to speak of the river. Around the walls of The Sewing Room not a sound was to be heard, as Arvo Nuortila wooed Mrs Joan Sweeney. 'I know you like your blue ocean best, Joan, but I prefer the river. Perhaps it's my Finnish melancholia, I don't know, but I enjoy nothing more than to sit in the late afternoon, listen to the folding of the water onto the bank, watch the white thistledowns sail along in the air, just above the surface, with the light catching in them, making them glow, as they go with the current and the wind, towards your sea.'

The silence of The Sewing Room was joined now by the silence at the picnic. In the pool of light Kooka looked so still and peaceful he could almost have been mistaken for having died a happy death.

We heard then not Tom String's brolga but a kookaburra, testing the echo of silence in a branch beside the grass-tree glade. Its call came like a divine ascending scale, climbing rung by humorous rung, and when it reached the top note it paused, before descending down in slower steps, back to earth as if from heaven.

'May I take your hand?' Joan Sweeney said to Arvo Nuortila on the picnic rug.

There was no answer.

Silence reigned, nothing at all, until finally we heard the lightest of sounds, the kissing of lips, so light and rhythmic that it could almost have been mistaken for a simple tapping of the breeze.

Then there was laughter, as the lips came away.

'May I get you a drink, sir?' said the publican, picking up a bottle of the beer Tom String had carefully and lovingly brewed for her. By Arvo Nuortila's gasping and gulping, it seemed that Joan Sweeney was holding the bottle up to his tingling lips for him to drink.

He swallowed and swallowed. Then he returned the favour for Joan Sweeney.

The gentlest of breezes was getting up now; you could hear it threading the wattles and crisping the fronds of the grass-trees in the glade. And also among it came the shimmying of fabric, of clothes, as trousers were unbuttoned and a blouse was lifted. The kissing now became percussive, aggressive, as Joan Sweeney and Arvo Nuortila clutched at each other, went seeking one another out on the picnic rug. Cutlery and plates were swept aside in a clatter and the publican cried, 'Arvo, oh, Arvo, please . . . Arvo . . .'

Cicadas now began to sound in the background. The bush was suddenly loud. But no brolga. Joan Sweeney tore at the Balt, whose breath was too heavy to carry a single needless word. She, on the other hand, kept saying his name, breathlessly over and over, and then she said, 'Oh, please . . . Arvo . . . knock me off . . . fuck me here.'

Mr Arvo began to grunt, and kissed her and groaned, and after a time she said, 'Oh, yes, here now . . . like a . . . oh . . . oh my God,' and before long she was screaming gutturally and Arvo Nuortila was climaxing in shattered groans after her.

When their breathing calmed, they lay for a long time on the rug, with the cicadas switching off and on in the background. They nibbled at the smoked eel and blithely swigged at the Native Companion. Very little was said but there was a good deal of nuzzling. Then, just before they rose to take their leave, as the cicadas began to rise again all around them, Joan Sweeney whispered, but brightly, 'You were my river, Arvo, your glowing thistledown coming into me.'

Arvo Nuortila chuckled, before replying with amusement in his voice, 'Then you were my ocean, Joan Sweeney.'

The Night Is a Different Country

As the two lovers rose from their picnic rug, the listeners sitting on the floor around the walls of The Sewing Room, under cover of the plates, bottles and cutlery being packed away, began briefly to loosen their limbs. In the bed Kooka also loosened his, stretching his toes out and upwards under the heavy blankets and the crocheted rug. I froze in my seat, thinking these were the movements of a man about to wake, but I was wrong. His feet and toes relaxed again, but he turned from his back onto his side so that now he was facing the tranny.

I looked across at Maria, who was staring straight at the old man, smiling her head off. But I wasn't so happy. This was a story that had taken a long time to tell – over a hundred years in fact – but it had begun for me with the dancing brolga in Tom String's upstream camp only a matter of months ago. I sensed now, this time by the absence of the brolga's rough bark, that something was amiss. But was there anything I could do? Surely not. What we'd become privy to had already happened hadn't it, way back in time? It was a tune already scored. There was no way we could influence things after the fact. I felt suddenly inert, trapped, powerless to intervene in events that were affecting my own life greatly.

I took a quick glance over my right shoulder, where in the dim light by the wall I could see Dougie Sutherland sound asleep with his head in his mother's lap. Big Joan was sitting beside them, with his arm around the shoulder of Dylan. Joan had his eyes closed and his face tilted upwards, intently listening to the picnic being put away.

Joan Sweeney and Arvo Nuortila eventually climbed back onto their bicycles, kissing briefly before saying goodbye to the grass-tree glade and heading back along the track they called The Blackboys. They pedalled slowly and without talking through the bush, which must have been darkening, as not only the cicadas could be heard but also the early hoot of a mopoke owl.

'Now here's the Dray Road, Arvo,' Joan Sweeney said at last, after what must have been at least a twenty-minute ride on The Blackboys. 'I was beginning to think we weren't going to find it.'

'Yes, it is darker now,' Mr Arvo said, 'quite difficult to see. But it was never going to vanish in our midst now, was it?'

'No, I suppose not,' Joan Sweeney replied. 'Although at times the night is a different country.'

Arvo Nuortila laughed lightly. 'Oh yes, there is that,' he replied.

'But now,' Joan Sweeney said, 'before we turn onto it, please one last kiss. You know of course that what has happened must remain in the glade.'

'Oh yes. But also in my heart.'

'And mine.'

They kissed, leaning aslant on their bicycles. It sounded awkward.

'You do know, Mrs Sweeney,' Mr Arvo said, 'that there are many more little flowers out in the bush here we could name.'

'Oh yes, Mr Arvo. There must be hundreds. Thank the Lord for Sundays.'

'Indeed, Mrs Sweeney. Thank the Lord for Sundays.'

They pedalled off again, turning onto the Dray Road, still high on the ironbark ridge but heading back for the riverflat and The Grand Hotel. You could feel, by the sound of the bicycles, that they still pedalled slowly, no doubt reluctant, despite the dark, for their romantic day to be over.

'It's a pleasant ride back, with this gentle north wind behind us,' Mr Arvo remarked at one point.

Joan Sweeney must have simply smiled in agreement, for there was no audible reply.

In my mind I followed the course of the road, as it curls to the east before falling out of the ironbarks and into the valley. The bicycles clattered as they made the descent and then quietened as they reached the bottom, where once again the road turns to head for the sea.

'There's the Southern Cross,' Mr Arvo said, 'up there over the ocean. See the Two Pointers . . .'

His voice trailed off. Once again Joan Sweeney made no reply.

But then gradually, out of the night, we began to hear another voice, from a long way off. At first I thought it was the usual panicky sound of the riverflat plovers, but as it came closer and clearer we could hear it was calling and shouting as well.

'Who's that?' Joan Sweeney said immediately, alarmed. 'Mr Arvo, can you hear that voice?'

'I can. And listen, a horse . . . there's someone coming.'

Soon there were galloping hooves and we began to make out the words the distressed voice was calling. In the pool of light Kooka's face also took on a look of distress, as the voice called, 'Missus Sweeney! Missus Sweee-ney! Coo-ee! Mista Arvo! Coo-ee!'

'Oh Lordy me, it's Ding Dong!' Joan Sweeney cried. 'Something's happened. Here he comes now.'

Ding Dong's horse rode up in a welter of blowing nostrils and thudding hooves.

'Oh, Mrs Sweeney!' he cried in his parroty pitch, as he came to them. 'It's Tom String, the flippin' bitzer! He's gone and euchred the 'otel!'

'He's what? What are you saying, Ding?' Joan Sweeney shouted with alarm.

'Tom String! I told him *what*!'

'What?' Joan Sweeney repeated. 'For pity's sake what, Ding?'

The horse was still snorting and restless on the sandy road as Ding cried, 'He's stoked the oven so high with that

Heatherbrae coal! He's stoked and stoked it. Cursin' and carryin' on. Till it exploded! BOOM, Mrs Sweeney, BOOM! He's sheared the kitchen. The wart's burning The Grand down! Look, missus, can't you hear?'

'Oh God preserve us,' Mr Arvo said. 'Look, Joan, he's right. Can you see the glow?'

Without replying, Joan Sweeney took off on her bicycle. The horse was reared about by Ding Dong and galloped off and past her. Mr Arvo set off panting, at top speed as well.

The Sewing Room filled with a natural foreboding and tension. Behind me bodies moved and shifted about in the dark, and Veronica kept gasping. Meanwhile, in the pool of light Kooka was becoming restless in the bed, his face frowning and his head leaning away from the bedside table and then back again, as if the tranny or the lamp were distressing him.

Joan Sweeney rode her bicycle hell for leather through the night, with Ding Dong on the horse out front and Mr Arvo right behind her. Soon enough she started exclaiming and swearing, as the hotel came into view. 'No!' she called, still riding. 'Oh no! Oh, it's on *fire*!'

Only a bit further along she threw down her bicycle amidst the crackling of flames. Distressed horses were neighing, poultry shrieking, and Ding Dong coughing and spluttering just up ahead of her. And then Kooka himself started to cough and breathe heavily in the bed in front of me. For a moment I thought I too wanted to cough, but I managed to suppress the urge. But over near the boxes of the archive Ash Bowen couldn't help it. He coughed not once but twice, then made a harsh throat-clearing sound that seemed to echo in the room like the fire of the dream. And then, just after Ash's cough, Kooka started to moan and whimper, and behind me Dougie Sutherland woke up in his mother's lap and said, 'Mummy, I smell smoke.'

I looked across at Maria. She was no longer smiling. Then Kooka started to call out from his sleep, 'Out! Get out! Get out of the hotel! There's smoke, oh, everyone . . . Out, *out*!'

Ash Bowen stood straight up over near the archive and said loudly, 'He's right! There is smoke. The kid's right!'

At the opposite end of the room Nan and Darren both got up from under the window, and Nan said, 'There is, Noel. Can't you smell it? That's fucking smoke alright.'

We heard a huge crash from somewhere else in the hotel. I stood bolt upright from my chair, turned and rushed for the door. I opened it and a wave of hot air took me by surprise as I fell clean over, backwards into the room. Behind me Maria screamed and Dougie started to cry. And Kooka was shouting now, 'GET OUT! IS THERE ANYONE UPSTAIRS? GET OUT OF THE HOTEL!'

Suddenly everyone was on their feet and rushing over to where I was getting to my feet in the doorway. I remember Joan Sutherland standing there, peering down the hallway. 'Jesus, Noel,' he said, in almost a tone of quiet surprise, 'I reckon the downstairs of the bloody pub's on fire.'

I got up coughing, as smoke started to filter up through the top of the staircase. We could see, as we looked through the doorway for a final few seconds, that it was beginning to billow up from below. The air was turning gradually bluish, spectral. There was no possibility of us escaping down the stairs.

'Darren,' I yelled, 'open that window! I can jump out onto the pine tree!'

As a kid I had made the leap countless times from the Sewing Room window onto the thick branch of the pine-tree canopy. I'd never done it as an adult though. Would the branch hold my weight?

They were chaotic moments as my mind groped wildly amidst the noise for a way out. Kooka was still shouting and Maria was singing out in full voice, 'Oh God! It's Louis! Louis has set the hotel on fire!'

Jen Sutherland was trying to comfort her youngest son while the older Dylan was standing bravely by his father's side.

In a flash of inspiration I realised he was the solution. I mightn't be able to jump out onto the pine tree but Dylan could. He was light enough, perhaps even lighter than I used to be when I did it all the time. It was a lot to ask but what choice did we have? I could show him how it was done, and if he could manage it he could then climb down out of the tree, get my telescopic ladder from behind the barn and bring it over to the window, and we could all climb out.

It was hard to explain, amidst the increasing smoke and noise and the awful urgency, but I brought the boy and his father over to the window and quickly told him what I reckoned. Young Dylan and Joan listened carefully, and then the boy looked up frightened into his father's eyes. Joan asked him straight out, 'Do you think you can do what your Uncle Noely used to do?'

The boy nodded yes, without hesitation.

'Okay, then, quickly,' Joan said, and I helped his eldest son climb out onto the sill. He had to crouch there like a frog and then leap across four feet of gaping air to the branch, which he then had to koala-tackle with both his arms and his knees as well.

Now, as Dylan got into position on the sill, I could see the fear in his eyes and I dared not glance over at his mother where she was comforting his younger brother by the wall.

'Okay, Dylan, are you ready?' I asked, with the upper half of my body leaning out into the air with him. Only the two of us could see the yard below as it was lit up in arhythmic flickers of orange light, the downstairs storey burning. It was a terrifying sight.

'Alright. On the count of three,' I said. 'And remember, just focus your eyes on the spot where you want to land and then grip it tight when you get there. It'll definitely hold you.'

'Okay, Uncle Noel,' he said, with a mixture of determination and apprehension.

For a moment all the noise seemed to cease as I called, 'One . . . two . . . *three!*'

The boy sprang off the sill like a pobblebonk frog and for a split second was spreadeagled in the air of glowing theatrical light. His father gripped my shoulder as Dylan seemed to hover there, in a suspension of destiny, his gangly arms and legs splayed out as if from the dangers of not one but two hotels burning, until, with history finally satisfied and assenting to the future, he came crashing down onto the branch and clung on for dear life. The huge old craquelured pine branch, of the very tree first planted beside Joan Sweeney's hotel, the tree that still stood in the days of her successor, bounced gently, like a blade of grass hit by a raindrop, before it settled back into position.

Dylan had done just as I had told him, gripping the branch with both his arms and his knees. The room sighed, and then everyone called out encouragement in chorus. On my left Givva Way said quietly, 'The kid's a legend.' And then the chaos of the fire and the sound of shifting timber below resumed.

Now I was leaning out the inland window again, calling out instructions to Dylan as he shimmied his way backwards into the body of the tree. He knew what he was doing now. He'd probably climbed a million trees out on the Barroworn, which was just as well, as the loudest crashing sound yet – part bass rumble, part clashing steel – rang out from the bottom storey as he clambered down.

When he'd made it back on the branch to nearly the trunk of the tree, Dylan gripped the thick old tugboat rope hanging there and slipped himself down to the ground. Briefly he squinted at the hot glow coming from the downstairs of the building before turning and running like a hare across the yard towards the barn. He disappeared behind it at the far end of the block. The gang of us clustered around the window saw him re-appear, grappling with the big aluminium ladder. At first he tried to carry it above the ground but then cut to the chase and just dragged it bumping along behind him.

As he drew close to the side of the burning building, I realised the danger would be possible explosions of heat and flying debris from the sunroom below. There was nothing we could do but pray that he'd be lucky.

With an almighty effort in the scalding air Dylan extended the telescopic ladder out to its full height and then heaved it up against the side of the building. As I reached out to my left and dragged the high end of it into position, Joan screamed for Dylan to get away from the building as Jim assembled everyone back in the room in the order in which they would come down. First Jen, who would wait a few rungs down the ladder for her terrified youngest son to come behind her, then Veronica, Maria, Nan, Givva, Ash, Darren, Oscar, Jim, and then Joan and I would together help move Kooka. In all the drama of Dylan jumping out the window, everyone had forgotten about the old fella, who had now woken up and was watching the goings on silently from his bed.

As Jen Sutherland stepped out onto the ladder to escape the burning hotel, the brave boy at the bottom stood grimacing in the heat while holding the ladder steady. Joan leant out of the window and screamed at him to get back, assuring him that his mum would be alright, that we'd hold the ladder secure from above. Dylan nodded thankfully and darted away from the building, where he stood watching from halfway back towards the barn.

Jen and Dougie were slow to come down but eventually they made it and ran over to hug their Dylan. From there everyone moved quickly and in an orderly fashion, except for Maria, who was bawling and crying out that the fire was all her fault. Eventually Nan slapped her clean across the cheek and without saying another word The Blonde Maria descended.

By the time everyone but Joan, myself and my brother Jim were safely down, the smoke in The Sewing Room was becoming almost too thick to breathe in. The lights had gone out, visibility was non-existent, and we could hear out in the direction of the hallway that the upstairs storey was now catching alight as well. Jim stubbornly refused to get down before he'd checked on Kooka, who had almost disappeared in a Prussian blue fug now in the centre of the room. Squinting and gasping, with our shirts up over our mouths and noses, the three of us rushed in the direction of the bed to help the old man. With our faces flushed from the anxiety and the heat, we called his name. When we got to him, we could barely see but could feel the lumps of his heavily blanketed body in the bed. When we called his name, there was no reply.

'Stand back!' shouted Joan through the smoke, and Jim and I did as we were told. Through the nightmarish light I dimly saw big Joan Sutherland lift Kooka's form out of the bed and throw him over his shoulder. Then he staggered in the direction of the window.

Jim and I followed, and as we did I heard sirens from somewhere in the night. Joan screamed for Jim to take Kooka and then the big dairy farmer stepped through the window onto the ladder and demanded him back. Old Kooka, all eighty-two years of him, winnowed away as his body was by time and life, was passed to Joan through the window. He managed to wrap his recently mended arm around Kooka's waist and carry him down the ladder to safety.

The flashing light of the CFA fire truck pulled into the driveway as first Jim, then I, followed Joan and Kooka down the ladder. We hit the ground running, and as we reached the others right down near the barn at the back of the yard the upper storey of the hotel shifted then collapsed in one almighty and resounding finale of timber, sparks and flying cinders. The scalding whoosh that came after this nearly knocked us all to the ground.

We watched as the CFA guys turned on their hoses to put out the fire. The ambulance from Minapre also arrived out on the Dray Road. Veronica ran quickly to greet them and to tell them about Kooka, who was now lying in Nan's arms, unconscious on the grass. The ambos rushed in with a stretcher and went straight to work trying to revive him. Unsuccessful, they placed him on the stretcher and hurried him to the ambulance, where they could work on him out of the flying sparks and billowing heat. One of them went around checking that everyone else was okay, which seemed to be the case. A couple of bottles of water were passed among us and we stood in a ragged arrangement on the grass and watched the hotel burn.

—

It was just before dawn when Sergeant Greg Beer and an offsider walked onto the scene. By this time we were all sitting down on the grass in a tight group, with blankets around our shoulders, passing around two bottles of cold champagne, which, along with a bottle of lemonade for the two Sutherland boys, were the only drinks I could find when I went looking in the barn. Even in our state of shock we had already managed to raise two toasts to the bravery of Joan and Jen's eldest son.

The sergeant stood with his constable watching the smouldering heap that was both my family home and the grandest of hotels. He began talking and the constable, like a secretary, started taking notes. One of the CFA guys, who was still hosing the rubble, seeing the two policemen standing there, called out, 'What kept you guys?'

Neither Sergeant Beer nor his constable answered. Instead they went on with what they were doing, completely ignoring the question.

Eventually, after wandering around what remained of the fire, I heard the sergeant ask the CFA officer in charge if there had been any casualties. He told Greg Beer that an elderly man had been rushed to Minapre Hospital suffering from smoke inhalation and that one of the lodgers in the hotel had not been accounted for.

'Very well then,' said the sergeant, turning to his offsider. 'Constable, we'll need to cordon off the area.'

The constable went off under the pines and out the drive-way to get the police tape.

Greg Beer thanked the fireman and then walked back across the yard to where we were sitting drinking the champagne and the lemonade. 'Is everyone okay here?' he asked officiously.

'Yep. We're all okay,' Ash Bowen told him.

'Well, it mightn't be the time right now but you all under-stand I will have to interview you about this. It's rather early to say, but the CFA opinion seems to be that the fire was lit intentionally.'

'Yeah, whatever . . .' Darren Traherne replied, taking a swig from the champagne.

Greg Beer stood alone in front of us, looking tight and uncomfortable.

For a brief minute I tossed up whether I could be bothered

saying anything to him but in the end I just decided what the heck.

'Oh, Sergeant,' I said, in a matter-of-fact voice.

He turned and replied sternly, 'Yes, Noel?'

'I was just thinking. I'd offer you a drink but the champagne's running low, and of course the kids need the lemonade. Oh yeah, and we're clean out of XXXX.'

The sergeant narrowed his eyes into a look that could kill. Then he stormed off in the direction of his car.

'What was all that about?' asked Darren, sitting next to me. 'We've never even stocked XXXX.'

I shook my head slowly from side to side, as the morning's first magpie began to sing from the top of the barn roof behind us. 'Believe me,' I said, draping an arm around the shoulder of my friend, 'you really don't want to know.'

Afterword in Autumn

AFTER A HOT AND BARREN SUMMER THE AUTUMN after the hotel burnt down was downright classical in its proliferation of mushrooms, chestnuts, yabbies, whiting and black duck. Not to mention rain. As if the hotel fire still needed dousing, the rain fell in roof-thrumming bucketloads, in looping pitter-pats and wild staccato bursts, and all as if in sympathy with the ashes. Right down the coast the creeks were swollen, their brown mouths brimming to the edge of the white waves, as if they were about to give birth to something. I wore my Rainbird coat and wandered about the riverflat deliriously, throwing a line in here, sliding fingers under the chocolate gills of field mushrooms there, at a loose end but nevertheless ecstatic at the mercurial nature of the light.

Kooka was in the recently rebuilt Minapre Hospital, in the old people's wing, not so much as a patient but as a permanent resident. He'd recovered fully from the smoke inhalation and, according to the doctors, there was absolutely nothing else physically wrong with him. He'd only decided to stay put in the residential wing because now that there was no longer a house or a hotel for him to live in, he couldn't be bothered organising anything else.

Through the curtains of rain filing into the bay from the southwest, you couldn't even see Minapre from Mangowak during those days; it was as if the old glamour cove had receded to an entirely separate and more western universe. Kooka was over there – we knew that – and occasionally we'd brave the bends and visit him, but because of the weather Minapre may as well have ascended into its own rather heavenly idea of itself, taking Kooka along with it, away from our own lowly and worrybeaten world.

One day in early April, in a rare clear-skied moment, I decided to take him round a feed from his old home patch. The last time I'd visited, he'd been complaining about the food, and I knew there was a flash new kitchen down the hall from his room. I figured he might well be up to catering for himself if he had the right ingredients.

So I drove around the road in the shining break, entered the town and parked on the slope between the hospital and the sea.

Upstairs I was ushered by a young male nurse onto the hospital's new verandah, where Kooka was sitting solo in a floppy lady's hat, taking in the sun.

We said hello, and he seemed glad enough to see me, though a bit weary. I handed over the bag of food, explaining my idea that he might like to cook himself a meal, and described the contents: yabbies already cooked and peeled, chestnuts already scored, freshly picked mushrooms, Otway pepper, plus my own garlic and herbs. He said he was more than grateful.

We sat on silver slatted seats, comfortable but for the coldness of the metal. We looked back east over the tops of the bluegums and across Snook Bay to Mangowak. In silence. I couldn't help but wonder, after all that had happened, what was in Kooka's head nowadays.

'I've been watching the box, Noel,' he said to me eventually, closing his eyes and letting the sun warm his face. 'In the common room, just on the other side of the glass there.'

'Oh yeah, Kooka?' I replied. 'Anything decent on?'

'Nah, not really. It's just the bloody weather's been like it has. I keep eyein' off this perch out here but can never get out to it. So yairs, I've been watchin' the box.'

'Well, it's bloody nice out here today,' I said.

'Mmm. Too right.'

'You know, Kooka, I'd have you at my place don't you? It's just that all I've got left is the barn.'

He waved a hand dismissively. 'Nah, don't worry about it, kid. Nan's offered me a room at hers too, but I don't want it. You know I could rebuild if I chose. Get out the nailbag. But nah, that's all in the past.'

'Fair enough. But how do you go with the others up here, Kooka? There's a few in worse nick than you. Especially in the top paddock.'

Kooka smiled and shook his head, as if I was a bit of a dill. 'What are you talkin' about, Noely? They're no trouble. It's just a halfway house, my boy. We're all in it together. And we'll all be checkin' out soon enough.'

I frowned at this but he laughed. 'It's no bloody hotel, Noel. More like the holding cell they put you in after a big night. Speaking of which, did they ever catch up with the big fella? You know, the singer Maria was keen on?'

'Nah, they never did, Kooka. But we're all still waiting for his book to appear. We're hoping it might explain a few things. Maria's doin' well though. She's back in Melbourne, but come July she's touring Europe with her new band.'

'Tourin' Europe? You don't say?'

'Yeah, Europe. They're supportin' some big acts too. She'll blow 'em away no doubt.'

'No doubt,' Kooka agreed. 'The girl's a one-off. You know she came and saw me here, when I was still on the oxygen mask?'

'Is that right?'

'Yairs. I was a bit rusty to tell ya the truth, Noel. High as a balloon actually, from all that pure air.'

'Sounds alright,' I chuckled.

'Yairs, I suppose it was. But I couldn't make hide nor hair outa what she was sayin'. She was tellin' me the strangest stuff, about the fire an' that, and I reckon I was mishearing her anyway. Poor girl, she must've thought I was a looney.'

'Well, she knows you're not now. I've filled her in about how well you're doing.'

Kooka nodded. 'Yairs, well that's good then. Send her my best won't you?'

'I will.'

We sat in silence again, looking out across the water. We could see the Mangowak lighthouse, standing tall, far in the distance.

'Yairs, so anyway, Noel, I've been watching the box.'

'So you said, Kooka.'

'You know I met my Mary here don't you? Her old man was the doctor at this hospital. He ran the joint. They lived in the big house across the road.'

'Yeah, you've told me that.'

'Yairs, well, I was a nobody then. Son of a dead St Kilda prostitute. Reckoned I had no chance. Thought Mary was a Minapre snob.'

'But she wasn't was she, Kooka?'

'Nah, no fear. Not Mary. Had a definite touch of class though. A definite touch of class.'

'No question.'

'So anyway, Noel. Did I tell you I've been watching the box?'

'You did, Kooka. Nothing decent on, eh?'

'Nup, not really. Bit of sport. Mass on Sundays. But nah.'

Behind us in the common room a group of patients and nurses had come in to get ready for an exercise class. They began moving the furniture about and then the sun went behind a cloud. Kooka winced and I helped him up to go inside.

Briefly we went to the kitchen to put his food in the cupboard and then I saw him down the hallway to his room. He plonked himself in the chair by the corner window, which looked out not on Snook Bay but on an internal courtyard. It was pleasant enough but it wasn't the sea and you couldn't see the lighthouse.

Kooka picked up the remote and turned on the television. We sat together in virtual silence then, for perhaps two hours, watching daytime television from America. Early on I protested, but he waved me down, said it was fine, told me to relax. When they came around to get him for his lunch, I reminded him about the food I'd brought, but again he waved me down. Said he might have it for tea.

By the time I was back in the car and rounding the high cliffs at Turtle Head, the rain was belting down. I swished down onto the flat at Bonafide View, took a left at Breheny Creek, and drove the back way home through the bush.

When I got to my driveway, my tears had already dried. And as I got out of the car, I heard a sound and noticed a movement in the ditches near the road. The ditches were full with the rain and now I recognised the sound. The time had come, the local eels were up and about, making their way towards the river and then out to sea for their big migration. Kooka had had a long and wonderful life and now the cycle was beginning all over again. I walked back out towards the road along the driveway, and came out from under the pines and into the rain.

Author's Note

This is the third, and, for the time being at least, the final of my books set in the imaginary Mangowak. It seems an appropriate occasion therefore to thank all the various bits of god around me, and in particular the angels who have in their own invaluable ways ministered to this long and often tempestuous process.

First, Alistair Stewart, poet of geological depth and glittering humour, a dear friend and grand guide. TonTon Hanna for her inner sight, her deep loyalty and uncompromising faith in the bluewater dream. My mother, Patricia, and my brothers, Bill, Peter and Tim, for their great example, their love, and their natural understanding of the often contrary and confronting life of the creative artist. Chris Grierson for his enthusiastic solidarity and great commitment to Australian literature. Michael Epis and Lawrence Mooney for their generosity, nous and wit. Lindon Crossland for her astute considerations, her trust, and her love of moonlight. John O'Brien at Random House for getting it all the way along, even back in the wild days of Barroworn. Robert Ashton and Jane Grant for the lunchtime debates, the bush nectar and fine friendship. Christos at Lorne Fisheries and Petros at Barwon Booksellers, for making it their own way and nourishing my body and mind. My publisher, Nikki Christer, to whose integrity and judgement I owe so much. Hilary McPhee for noticing me as a fledgling by the river. And lastly, but mostly, my delicate avocet, mother of our two beautiful boys, Sian Marlow.